PRAISE FOR CAROLYN BROWN

The Daydream Cabin

"I absolutely loved this novel. With moments of laughter and tears, I could not stop reading and imagining the beautiful changes that were taking place within each character's heart! Author Carolyn Brown's novels always give me a feeling of hope!"

—Goodreads reader review

Miss Janie's Girls

"[A] heartfelt tale of familial love and self-acceptance."

—*Publishers Weekly*

"Heartfelt moments and family drama collide in this saga about sisters."

—*Woman's World*

The Banty House

"Brown throws together a colorful cast of characters to excellent effect and maximum charm in this small-town contemporary romance . . . This first-rate romance will delight readers young and old."

—*Publishers Weekly*

The Family Journal

HOLT MEDALLION FINALIST

"Reading a Carolyn Brown book is like coming home again."
— *Harlequin Junkie* (top pick)

The Empty Nesters

"A delightful journey of hope and healing."
— *Woman's World*

"The story is full of emotion . . . and the joy of friendship and family. Carolyn Brown is known for her strong, loving characters, and this book is full of them."
— *Harlequin Junkie*

"Carolyn Brown takes us back to small-town Texas with a story about women, friendships, love, loss, and hope for the future."
— *Storeybook Reviews*

"Ms. Brown has fast become one of my favorite authors!"
— *Romance Junkies*

The Perfect Dress

"Fans of Brown will swoon for this sweet contemporary, which skillfully pairs a shy small-town bridal shop owner and a softhearted car dealership owner . . . The expected but welcomed happily ever after for all involved will make readers of all ages sigh with satisfaction."

—*Publishers Weekly*

"Carolyn Brown writes the best comfort-for-the-soul, heartwarming stories, and she never disappoints . . . You won't go wrong with *The Perfect Dress!*"

—*Harlequin Junkie*

The Magnolia Inn

"The author does a first-rate job of depicting the devastating stages of grief, provides a simple but appealing plot with a sympathetic hero and heroine and a cast of lovable supporting characters, and wraps it all up with a happily ever after to cheer for."

—*Publishers Weekly*

"*The Magnolia Inn* by Carolyn Brown is a feel-good story about friendship, fighting your demons, and finding love, and maybe, just a little bit of magic."

—*Harlequin Junkie*

"Chock-full of Carolyn Brown's signature country charm, *The Magnolia Inn* is a sweet and heartwarming story of two people trying to make the most of their lives, even when they have no idea what exactly is at stake."

—*Fresh Fiction*

Small Town Rumors

"Carolyn Brown is a master at writing warm, complex characters who find their way into your heart."

—*Harlequin Junkie*

The Sometimes Sisters

"Carolyn Brown continues her streak of winning, heartfelt novels with *The Sometimes Sisters*, a story of estranged sisters and frustrated romance."

—All About Romance

"This is an amazing feel-good story that will make you wish you were a part of this amazing family."

—*Harlequin Junkie* (top pick)

The Strawberry Hearts Diner

"Sweet and satisfying romance from the queen of Texas romance."

—Fresh Fiction

"A heartwarming cast of characters brings laughter and tears to the mix, and readers will find themselves rooting for more than one romance on the menu. From the first page to the last, Brown perfectly captures the mood as well as the atmosphere and creates a charming story that appeals to a wide range of readers."

—RT Book Reviews

The Barefoot Summer

"Prolific romance author Brown shows she can also write women's fiction in this charming story, which uses humor and vivid characters to show the value of building an unconventional chosen family."

—*Publishers Weekly*

"This story takes you and carries you along for a wonderful ride full of laughter, tears, and three amazing HEAs. I feel like these characters are not just people in a book, but they are truly family and I feel so invested in their journey. Another amazing HIT for Carolyn Brown."

—*Harlequin Junkie* (top pick)

The Lullaby Sky

"I really loved and enjoyed this story. Definitely a good comfort read, when you're in a reading funk or just don't know what to read. The secondary characters bring much love and laughter into this book; your cheeks will definitely hurt from smiling so hard while reading. Carolyn is one of my most favorite authors. I know without a doubt that no matter what book of hers I read, I can just get lost in it and know it will be a good story. Better than the last. Can't wait to read more from her."

—*The Bookworm's Obsession*

The Lilac Bouquet

"Brown pulls readers along for an enjoyable ride. It's impossible not to be touched by Brown's protagonists, particularly Seth, and a cast of strong supporting characters underpins the charming tale."

—*Publishers Weekly*

"If a reader is looking for a book more geared toward family and long-held secrets, this would be a good fit."

—RT Book Reviews

"Carolyn Brown absolutely blew me away with this epically beautiful story. I cried, I giggled, I sobbed, and I guffawed; this book had it all. I've come to expect great things from this author and she more than lived up to anything I could have hoped for. Emmy Jo Massey and her great-granny Tandy are absolute masterpieces not because they are perfect but because they are perfectly painted. They are so alive, so full of flaws and spunk and determination. I cannot recommend this book highly enough."

—Night Owl Romance (5 stars and top pick)

The Wedding Pearls

"*The Wedding Pearls* by Carolyn Brown is an amazing story about family, life, love, and finding out who you are and where you came from. This book is a lot like *The Golden Girls* meets *Thelma and Louise*."

—*Harlequin Junkie*

The Yellow Rose Beauty Shop

"*The Yellow Rose Beauty Shop* was hilarious, and so much fun to read. But sweet romances, strong female friendships, and family bonds make this more than just a humorous read."

—*The Reader's Den*

Long, Hot Texas Summer

"This is one of those lighthearted, feel-good, make-me-happy kind of stories. But, at the same time, the essence of this story is family and love with a big ole dose of laughter and country living thrown in the mix. This is the first installment in what promises to be another fascinating series from Brown. Find a comfortable chair, sit back, and relax because once you start reading *Long, Hot Texas Summer* you won't be able to put it down. This is a super fun and sassy romance."

—*Thoughts in Progress*

Daisies in the Canyon

"I just loved the symbolism in *Daisies in the Canyon*. As I mentioned before, Carolyn Brown has a way with character development with few if any contemporaries. I am sure there are more stories to tell in this series. Brown just touched the surface first with *Long, Hot Texas Summer* and now continuing on with *Daisies in the Canyon*."

—Fresh Fiction

the
Bluebonnet
Battle

the
Bluebonnet
Battle

CAROLYN
BROWN

Published by Montlake, Seattle

www.apub.com

Amazon, the Amazon logo, and Montlake are trademarks of Amazon.com, Inc., or its affiliates.

ISBN-13: 9781542035583
ISBN-10: 1542035589

Cover design by Leah Jacobs-Gordon

Printed in the United States of America

This one is for
Theodore and Nora Fierman.
They picked the lemons for Aunt Liddy's pies
and sent them to me all the way from California!

Chapter One

Aunt Liddy, this is Clovis. Bridget and I are on the way to the hospital right now. Do you know the news? Wanda Massey lives a couple of doors down from me and Bridget, and we walked down there to see if we could help out, but they were already loading her into the hearse to take her straight to the funeral home."

"Well, if that don't beat all," Liddy said. "She wasn't much more than fifty years old. Are we still on for lunch in the cafeteria?"

"Yes. Bridget says to tell you that we'll talk about it more then. She's on the phone with her dad right now," Clovis said.

It didn't matter which of the three churches in town a person attended; when there was a death, Liddy Latham usually got *the call* before the body was even put on a gurney and taken to the only funeral home in town. The family would plan the funeral, but Liddy could coordinate a family dinner with her eyes closed, and she always brought one of her famous lemon pies to the event.

The story around Bonnet was that the Taylors, Liddy's grandparents, had squatted in a pasture right about where one of the two traffic lights on Main Street was now located and bought up acres and acres of land. They had built a church by the time Harry Davis's grandparents arrived, and that's when the feud started. Harry's grandparents wanted to buy some of the Taylors' land to build a saloon, and the Taylors were a religious family. For three generations and more than a hundred years now, the struggle over property had been an issue between the two families.

Liddy was born in Bonnet and had gotten married right after she graduated from high school. Her claim to fame was that she and her brother, Paul Taylor, still owned most of the stores on Main Street, as well as acreage to the east of Bonnet—and that she made the best lemon pies in the universe. Her kitchen walls were covered with framed ribbons she had won every year at the county fair. Only Liddy and Jesus—with whom she was sure her great-grandmother had shared when she got to heaven—now had the recipes for her lemon meringue and lemon chess pies, and she was bound by a solemn oath to share the recipes with a relative when she was nigh unto death.

As she drove to the hospital where she volunteered until noon on Tuesdays, she was thinking that she hadn't had to make a pie in weeks. She pushed the button to call her younger brother, Paul, and laid the phone on the bench seat of her hot-pink 1965 Caddy.

"Hey, did you hear that Wanda Massey passed this morning?" she asked when he answered after the third ring.

"Yes, I did. Bridget just called. She told me that Wanda worked yesterday right up until closing and even went home and fried chicken for supper last night. When her husband tried to wake her this morning, she was already gone."

"I didn't even know she was sick," Liddy said. "I reckon the funeral will be Thursday or Friday."

"Did she go to our church?" Paul asked.

"On Easter and Christmas, but I expect that don't matter now. Everyone has a family and needs a dinner served to them after the services. That's part of getting closure," Liddy said. "I'll find out this afternoon the exact time of the funeral and get the dinner planned. I wonder what happened. She's only about fifty. Poor old Harry will be lost. Wanda has kept the office for him since she finished high school."

"That's the truth," Paul said. "Has Ruth Ann made it to the hospital yet? She reminded me this morning that she'll be volunteering with you and then y'all have lunch with the kids in the cafeteria."

"That's right." Liddy saw her sister-in-law's SUV pass her. She didn't usually talk and drive, but that morning she had a phone pressed to her left ear. "No one will ever do the job as good as Wanda does . . . or maybe I should say *did* at this point. I saw her in the office yesterday when I walked down to the drugstore to get some medicine and she looked perfectly fine."

"Bridget said Wanda's husband told her that Wanda had an aneurysm for a while and kept it a secret," Paul said.

Liddy nosed her car into a parking spot in front of the hospital and turned off the engine. Before she could open the door, Ruth Ann had gotten out of her car and waved. "Ruth Ann just parked, so I'd better get on to the hospital. See you tonight."

"I'll be there. Think you might make an extra lemon chess pie?" Paul asked.

"You've always been able to sweet-talk me into anything." Liddy laughed. "I've got a pot of beans going in the slow cooker. I'll fry some potatoes and make a pan of corn bread, and yes, I'll make a lemon pie."

"I love that you're twenty years older than me and you spoiled me from the time I was born." Paul chuckled. "See you at supper."

Ruth Ann tucked a strand of red hair behind her ear. "Did you hear about Wanda just up and dying in her sleep? Hits home pretty hard since she's my age. We graduated from high school the same year, even though we were in two different states." Ruth Ann had been in Texas for thirty years and yet still had a soft Louisiana accent.

"What I can't believe is that she kept a secret in Bonnet, Texas." Liddy shook her head in disbelief. "If she hadn't passed away, she would deserve a trophy for doing that, or maybe we should have thought about making her the very first Bluebonnet Queen of the festival. Keeping anything private in this town is quite a thing."

"Amen," Ruth Ann agreed as they walked across the lobby toward the hospital's small gift store, where the two of them volunteered half a day on Tuesday. Her phone rang and she stopped and answered it while Liddy unlocked the door and turned on the lights to the store. "You've got to be kiddin' me." Her normally deep voice shot up to almost a squeal. "Yes, I'll tell her. We're going to have a busy weekend."

"Tell me what?" Liddy asked.

"That was Paul telling me that Jack Dawson has died, too." Her green eyes filled with tears.

Liddy hurried over to her and wrapped her up in a hug. "I'm so sorry. I know you and Paul were good friends with Harry, Jack, and Barbara."

Ruth Ann took a few deep breaths and then stepped back. "Paul said he'll go see Barbara and take some food during his lunch break, and don't worry, Harry's not that kind of guy."

"He might not be, but his sister, Matilda, will be out for blood," Liddy said. "You know how bad that woman hates me. Honey, do you want to go on out to Jack's place and be there to help? I can run this gift shop by myself. But I got to admit, I'm worried. We own the building the real estate office is in. What if Barbara's or Wanda's families sue us?"

"No, I'm sure all their daughters are there to help with things," Ruth Ann said, "but I would like to help you with the dinner. And Matilda's all hot air, so don't give her suing us another thought."

"I hope so." Liddy picked up her volunteer vest and slipped it over her head. "What happened to Jack?"

"Paul said that he had a heart attack, and they rushed him out here to the hospital, but he was gone before they got here."

"Two in one weekend and both of them work for Harry Davis at the real estate office." Liddy frowned. "Neither of them was even retirement age. Poor old Harry. Even though our families never got along, I liked him better than the rest of those Davis scoundrels. I wonder what he'll do. He's been talking about retiring. Maybe he'll just close up the office and quit. He can't do all that work without some help."

"If he's smart, he'll stay away from that office. There could be something in that place that's killing people off," Ruth Ann suggested.

"Don't even think such a thing. Three dinners in one weekend would be almost impossible," Liddy said.

Ruth Ann laid a hand over her heart. "Oh. My. God!"

"Sweet Jesus!" Liddy gasped. "Should I call Bridget or Clovis?"

"No, I just realized that Matilda will be coming for the funerals. What if she decides to stay in Bonnet?" Ruth Ann's words tumbled out.

Liddy clamped a hand over her mouth, then said, "Good Lord! I hadn't thought of her staying in Bonnet more than a few days."

"This is going to be a mess." Ruth Ann sighed.

"Mama." Bridget burst through the door and crossed the room to hug her mother. "I just heard about Jack. I'm so, so sorry. I have to get back to the ER pretty quick. We've got a waiting room full of folks, but I just had to be sure you were all right."

"I'm sad, but I'll be fine." Ruth Ann pulled a tissue from the box on the counter and dabbed her eyes. "We'll see you at lunch, *chère*."

"Okay, then, but if you need me, just call . . ." Bridget turned around and gave Liddy a hug. "That goes for you, too, Aunt Liddy."

Liddy hugged her back and said, "Thank you, darlin'." Bridget hurried out of the gift shop and disappeared down a long hallway. She was the image of her mother—redhaired and with mossy green eyes. Ruth Ann had blessed both of her daughters, Bridget and Amelia, with her Irish genes—and her temper.

"What are we going to do about all this?" Ruth Ann asked.

"We're not going to borrow trouble until we know there's trouble to be had," Liddy said. "And if Matilda comes in with both guns loaded, then I guess we load ours and finally have a shoot-out on Main Street."

"Y'all should have sold that damn building to Harry years ago," Ruth Ann grumbled.

"There's nothing wrong with anything in that building, and we don't sell land or property. The good Lord only made so much, and we don't give up any of what we own," Liddy argued, "and besides, I wouldn't sell Matilda a cup of water if she was on fire. Paul is a lawyer. If she thinks she's got a leg to stand on . . ."

Ruth Ann's cell phone rang, and she fished it out of the pocket of her jeans. "We were just talking about that very thing," she said.

"Put it on speaker," Liddy whispered.

"Now you're on speaker with me and your sister," Ruth Ann said. "There's no one else in the gift shop."

"I called Harry," Paul said, "and we've agreed that it would be best for him to stay out of the office for a few days. We're going to pay to have it inspected from top to bottom to be sure there's nothing in there that could have caused either one of Wanda's or Jack's problems."

"I wouldn't put it past Matilda to try to bring a lawsuit against us, so hire licensed inspectors," Liddy said.

"I already thought of that," Paul said, "and I've got Bridget working on a list of who we can get to do all the inspections. We'll batten down the hatches and get ready for Tornado Matilda to arrive tomorrow. Harry says that she and Nick will be here before suppertime."

Liddy sucked in a lungful of air and let it out in a whoosh. "I was hoping that Matilda would never come back to Bonnet."

"Me too," Ruth Ann and Paul said at the same time.

"Take me off speaker, darlin'," Paul said.

"Have to anyway, we've got a customer. Ethel just came into the shop." Ruth Ann listened a minute, ended the call, and turned to face Ethel and Liddy. "Well, it is the Ides of March today, and you know what that means."

"Beware! That's what it means, because bad things are coming," Liddy said.

"Or in our case," Ethel said with a nod, "they're already here with two deaths in Bonnet in one day. I was visiting my neighbor in the hospital when I heard. I remembered that you and Ruth Ann volunteer here on Tuesdays, so I popped down to tell you that I'll be glad to help with both dinners."

Liddy was glad to see her. There had been three of them in their clique—Clara, Liddy, and Ethel—but Clara had passed a few years ago. They'd made quite the trio in their day. Clara was the tall redhead, Ethel the average-height blonde, and Liddy the short brunette. Nowadays, both Liddy and Ethel had gray hair and were growing wrinkles like wildflowers in the spring.

"Thank you. Ruth Ann and I will start making phone calls this afternoon, but you know how much folks love your potato salad, so is it all right if I put you down for that?" Liddy managed a smile.

"Sure thing." Ethel nodded. "I suppose Matilda will be coming to town."

"Just the mention of that woman's name gives me hives," Liddy said.

"Don't let her know that, or she'll make your life miserable," Ethel said as she left the shop.

"She's right," Ruth Ann said, "and we'll probably only have to deal with her at the two funerals."

"Oh, I won't." Liddy sighed. "I just hope she comes for the funerals and then goes back to Sweetwater. I hadn't thought about today being the Ides of March, but it seems appropriate with two deaths and Matilda coming to town."

Ruth Ann grabbed a dustrag, sprayed it with a little lemony-smelling stuff that the hospital provided, and started cleaning. "You know I've got a Cajun grandmother, so I'm more than a little superstitious, so I'm going to be really careful. I might even call Granny Dee and see if she can figure out a spell for me to put on Matilda to soften her up."

Liddy shivered. "Honey, not even God is powerful enough to have a spell that will soften up that woman."

Ruth Ann chuckled. "How long has it been since the last funeral in town?"

Liddy pursed her lips and drew down her brows. "Must be a month now. Rural Johnston died just about Valentine's Day," she answered.

"Do you think maybe folks have missed your lemon pies so much that they poisoned the water or maybe put something in the coffee machine at the real estate office?"

"Surely not!" Liddy laughed so hard that she got the hiccups. "Dammit! Look what you caused."

Ruth Ann rounded the end of the counter and hugged her. "I'm not even sorry. We both needed a good laugh."

"When you get to be seventy, and when you know Matilda is coming to town, nothing will be funny, but darlin' girl, I could use one of those magic spells. Tell your Granny Dee to send me a bill if there's a charge." Liddy grabbed a tissue from the counter and wiped her eyes.

"You either got to laugh about it or you'll worry yourself crazy," Ruth Ann told her and then gave her another brief hug. "Two people passing away today makes me realize that I need to tell you every day how much Paul and I appreciate having you in our lives. You've been like a grandmother to our two girls, and Lord only knows, if you hadn't been here to take me under your wing and mother me, I would have been lost."

"I love you, too, Ruth Ann," Liddy said. "You've always been the daughter I never got to have, and I would have gone crazy if you and Paul hadn't come back to Bonnet when you did."

Ruth Ann stepped back around the counter and said, "Those were a tough couple of years. Paul was just out of law school. Y'all's daddy and his mama died within weeks of each other, and then Richie had the accident. Just remember this: we survived all that, so we'll get through Matilda's hissy fits."

"Seems like only yesterday," Liddy whispered. "Did I ever tell you that Richie and I argued? My last words to my son were that Matilda

Monroe was going to be the death of him." She laid a hand on her chest and bowed her head.

Lord, give me the strength to fight the battle ahead, she prayed silently, and then looked up at Ruth Ann. "He stormed out of the house, and I never got to tell him I was sorry. A mother never, ever gets over that kind of grief, and I will always blame Matilda for ruining my relationship with my only child."

"You did tell me," Ruth Ann said. "That was a horrible day. It still hurts when I think about it."

"I will never get over it," Liddy told her, "but a person has to live with it. Now, let's get this place dusted. The other volunteers that come in don't seem to know how to keep things all pretty in here."

"Amen to that." Ruth Ann started on the shelves with the baby gifts. "Do you think Matilda will try to take over the real estate business?"

Liddy tiptoed to reach the shelf of breakable items behind the cash register. "Now that she's divorced, it would be easy for Harry to bring her back to help him. I just hope that she doesn't come back with intentions of living here. That would be a nightmare."

"I hear her son, Nick, has his Realtor's license, so Harry might bring both of them into the business," Ruth Ann said.

"I expect you're right," Liddy said. "Since Harry doesn't have kids of his own, and he's been talking about retiring for several years, he might just turn the business over to Nick. The idea of attending two funerals with Matilda there is bad enough, but thinking about her living in Bonnet is enough to give me hives."

"Surely, Harry won't let her into the business. I've heard that they never did get along. They're kind of like you and Paul. There's a lot of years between them."

"Harry was sixteen when she was born, but they had the same parents. My mother died when I was sixteen and Daddy married Paul's mother a couple of years later. I loved Sally Ann, not as much as my own mother, of course. But she was so good for Daddy. Then they had

Paul, and Marvin and I got married and had Richie," Liddy said. "But why am I telling you all this? It's all old Taylor family history."

"Sometimes it's good just to bring up a sweet memory. Paul always said that Richie was more like a brother to him than a nephew, with the age difference between you and him," Ruth Ann said.

Liddy's head bobbed up and down in a nod. "They were inseparable. Sally Ann either had them both at her house, or they were at mine. But getting back to Matilda . . ." Liddy sighed again. "If Matilda's got a mind to return to this part of the state, there won't be a damned thing Harry can do about it. She's a manipulative bitch, and you know I'm telling the truth."

Ruth Ann dusted every bottle of lotion and bath gel on a shelf. "Every now and then Paul still needs to go over how he felt when Richie died, and what happened that night when he was killed."

"Every time I see that woman, I feel everything I did when I lost Richie—the guilt for arguing with him, the anger at Matilda for causing it, and the hole in my heart that has never healed," Liddy said with a long sigh. "I will never get over the feeling that I had when the policeman came to my door with the news, and I will never forgive Matilda Monroe for her part in his death."

"Of course you won't, because it's an unnatural grief to lose a child. We are born with the knowledge that we will lose our parents, and we can deal with that loss. But a child is . . ." Ruth Ann paused. "Well, we just don't have what we need to process that, and it stays with us forever."

"Amen," Liddy whispered. "And thank you for being such a good friend and sister-in-law all these years."

"Right back at you, and you know you can drop that in-law business. You might be twenty years older than me, but we're sisters." Ruth Ann smiled through misty eyes. "Now, let's talk about something else. Do you think this upcoming generation will even think about volunteering at the hospital?"

"I do not," Liddy answered, glad that Ruth Ann had changed the subject. "Most of them wouldn't even see the dust or know how to make change if they sold something." Death always made her think of Richie and her late husband, Marvin, who was never quite the same after they lost their son in the car wreck. "We should call Amelia and tell her what's happened. She's on spring break this week from the school, so she can help out with the funeral dinners. If we had about a dozen, or maybe even twenty, young women like her and Bridget to pick up the reins, we'd be okay to leave Bonnet in their hands."

Ruth Ann didn't look up from her cleaning job. "I'm just glad that they both came home to Bonnet when they finished their education."

"And Clovis," Liddy reminded her. "That boy just flat-out stole my heart away the first time I met him. He's been a perfect match for our Bridget. Speaking of education, has the school renewed Amelia's teaching contract for next year yet?"

"They rehire teachers in April," Ruth Ann answered. "I just wish she would find a good guy, fall in love, settle down right here in Bonnet permanently like her sister, and have a whole houseful of babies. Other women my age already have grandchildren, but my girls both seem to be career minded."

"I sure would like to rock a baby before it's my time to die. I can pretend it's a grandbaby, whether it really is or not." Liddy put away her dustrag and hiked a hip on the barstool behind the counter.

Ruth Ann shook her head. "Don't talk like that. You can't. What would Paul have to look forward to if you didn't make your lemon pies for funeral dinners and for his birthday?"

"I'm leaving my secret recipes to you in my will," Liddy said. "Then you'll have to choose who you leave them to in your will. As long as lemon pies are taken to funeral dinners, I'll be smiling down from heaven—providing I get there. With my attitude toward Matilda, I may not get past the pearly gates."

"I'll do my best to keep up the lemon pie works, but they won't ever be as good as yours," Ruth Ann said.

"Oh, hush!" Liddy giggled. "It's just lemon pie. It's not anything fancy. Folks need comfort food when they're mourning."

"That's the gospel truth," Ruth Ann agreed.

Liddy stomped the floor when she burned a skillet full of bacon and had to throw it out and start all over. She needed to get her mind off Matilda and the past and concentrate on what she was cooking. Good thing she hadn't already put the cut-up potatoes into the cast-iron skillet or she'd have to throw them out with the burned bacon.

She opened the back door to let the smell out, rinsed out the skillet, and cut up another half pound of bacon. When that was nice and crispy, she added a chopped onion and slid a pan of corn bread into the oven.

"There," she muttered. "Maybe all the burn smell will be gone by the time the family gets here." She poured the potatoes into the skillet and covered it with a heavy lid.

"Hey, I smell good old home cooking," Paul said as he and Ruth Ann came into the house through the open back door.

"And I can't wait to get into those beans." Ruth Ann hung her sweater on the back of a chair. "They smell like you dosed them up with a healthy bit of ham."

"Yes, I did. They're bland without the proper seasoning. So, what's the news? Have they figured out days and times for the funerals?" Liddy stopped stirring the beans and used an egg turner to flip the potatoes over.

"Wanda's funeral is going to be Friday at ten at the church," Paul said. "Lunch will be in the fellowship hall. Jack's is set for the same day at the funeral home chapel at four and they're having the dinner at the senior citizens building."

"Y'all talking about the double funerals?" Bridget asked as she followed Clovis into the house. "This place smells wonderful, Aunt Liddy. You should put in a café that specializes in good old common food."

"Yes, we were talking about funerals," Liddy said, "and family dinners are enough for me at my age."

"The folks at the hospital said that Matilda and her son, Nick, will be here tomorrow afternoon from Sweetwater. Harry is beside himself about losing Wanda and Jack the same day and told Wanda's husband that he is going to retire and turn the business over to Nick," Bridget said.

"And," Amelia said as she came in, "I heard that Matilda will be Nick's secretary, bookkeeper, and all-around helper like Wanda was to Harry. Think there will ever be a day when this feud ends?"

Liddy took in a long breath and let it out slowly. "No, I do not! We've had battles before, but this might be the beginning of the great war of Bonnet, Texas. This town will have trouble holding both of us. That woman will try to take over everything, and she'll be constantly trying to get us to sell pieces of our property to her. She's got money now since her husband didn't make her sign a prenup. She came out of the marriage a fairly rich woman."

"That ought to make her happy," Paul said. "I remember her very well. She would win class president or student council president, or even be named head cheerleader. Then she would gather her little best friends all around her and delegate the responsibilities to them. I don't know how in the hell Richie ever got mixed up with her to begin with."

"And she'd take the credit for everything all for herself. She'll do the same thing in Bonnet." Liddy sighed.

"You sit down right here, Aunt Liddy." Amelia pulled out a chair. "Bridget and I will finish putting supper together and get it on the table, and don't worry about anything. Matilda isn't going to get any of our Taylor land or property, no matter how rich she is."

"She will run Harry like a little toy train, or else he'll set his heels and tell her to drop dead. They never did get along." Paul took the plates from Ruth Ann's hands and carried them to the dining room table.

"I wonder if she'll move into his house and take control there as well as at the business?" Liddy asked.

Ruth Ann's phone rang, and she slipped into the living room to answer it. When she returned, she was pale as a ghost.

"Not another one," Liddy moaned.

"Not another death, but it's not good news. Matilda called Barbara and offered to spearhead Jack's funeral dinner, and Barbara agreed," Ruth Ann said. "I should have gone on out there and been with Barbara instead of sending Paul. I could have talked her out of that decision." She shot a look across the room at her husband.

"Hey, I had no idea that Matilda had already called, and the house was full. Don't blame me for this one," Paul said.

"No one is to blame," Liddy said. "Once Matilda sets her head to something, God can't even change it. Are you sure that Barbara agreed to such a thing, and it's not just a rumor? She's always been so good to help me with funeral dinners that it's hard to believe she'd let Matilda have that job."

"Why would Barbara do that?" Amelia asked. "Won't your regular ladies think we've slighted them by not asking them to bring their favorite dishes to Jack's funeral?"

"Probably because she's Harry's sister, and besides, we all know that whatever Matilda wants, she gets. This is her way of making a stand in Bonnet from day one." Ruth Ann removed an ice tray from the freezer and filled three glasses, then poured sweet tea over the cubes. "You know how wishy-washy Barbara is. She never could put her foot down about anything, not even if she disagreed with whatever it was. Matilda probably played the cousin card. I can't remember just how they're related."

"I forgot about Jack and Harry being distant cousins." Liddy dished up the potatoes. "Now I have to make all the calls and tell the ladies that they'll only need to bring food to one funeral."

"Don't worry about it, Liddy," Paul said. "Everyone in Bonnet knows you're the queen of funeral dinners. This will be just a onetime thing. Your grandmother and then your mother took care of that job, and you've done a fine job of organizing the dinners all these years. I bet the ladies show up at Jack's funeral with their casseroles and pies no matter what kind of affair Matilda tries to put on."

"If she tries to take over the funeral dinners, the next thing will be the Bluebonnet Festival and then the cookbook committee," Ruth Ann said.

"And the chamber of commerce, since she's going to be helping at the real estate agency, and maybe even the city council," Paul added.

"Holy smoke," Amelia said. "Surely she wouldn't do all that, would she?"

"Oh, yes, she would," Ruth Ann declared, "and I'm the head of the Bluebonnet Festival planning committee. If that woman thinks she's going to take that away from me, she better get her six-guns polished up. I've been working on my bonnet for the competition for a whole year. Do y'all have yours done?"

"She won't mess with that this year, since it's just two weeks from now," Paul assured his wife, "but you might have to bring out the big guns if she sets her sights on the festival for next year. I just hope she doesn't come in here and wiggle her way onto the city council. I hadn't planned on running again after my term is up this fall, but maybe I'd better rethink that."

"And about the bonnets for the competition, I figure I'll just add some fake flowers to last year's straw hat and maybe spruce up the ribbons," Bridget said.

"I've about got my bonnet done." Amelia set a roll of paper towels in the middle of the table. "I started all over from scratch. If I could talk all y'all into going to the Kentucky Derby with me, we could get double use out of our hats. Want me to get the corn bread out of the oven?"

"Sweet Lord! I'm letting things worry me too much. I forgot about the corn bread. Good thing you asked or we might have been eating burned bread," Liddy answered. "Yes, please get it out and cut it up."

"I'm glad to see pickled beets," Clovis said. "Bridget hates them, but they are my favorite. Do we have lemon pie for dessert?"

"Yes, you do, and I was so stressed that I made both lemon meringue and lemon chess."

"The idea that the name for your pie has stuck all these years is kind of funny," Paul said.

"I don't want my asparagus, Mama," Bridget whined like a little kid. "I want Aunt Liddy's lemon pie."

Liddy swallowed the iced tea in her mouth to keep from spewing it across the table. "That was a dang good imitation of Amelia when she didn't want to eat her vegetables."

"Aren't y'all ever going to forget that story?" Amelia asked.

"Nope, we are not," Paul answered.

Bridget burst out into laughter. "There's lemon pies in the stores and bakeries, but Aunt Liddy's lemon pies are the best. That's what you used to tell us all the time."

"Maybe we ought to take Matilda a lemon pie," Amelia said.

"That's a good idea," Liddy said. "Lemon would surely cover up the poison, wouldn't it?"

Liddy listened to the conversation with one ear while she ate, but she would need to buy lemons, and she'd have to make a trip over to Muenster because she was out of pie crusts and limoncello. Heaven forbid if someone ever saw her buying prepackaged pie crusts in Bonnet or knew that her secret to a good lemon pie was a tablespoon of liquor. Everyone in town thought that she made her famous pies from scratch—from the crust to the meringue. She did make the pie filling from her secret recipe, but she'd never mastered making a good, flaky crust. And who needed to when they could be bought and put into her fancy little floral pie pan.

"What do you think, Liddy?" Ruth Ann asked.

"Sorry, I was wool gathering," Liddy admitted. "Are we still talking about Matilda?"

"No, we ditched that topic a while ago," Ruth Ann said. "We're talking about the church cakewalk at the Bluebonnet Festival. Can I put you down for two pies as usual, or can I talk you into three?"

"I'll do three this year." Liddy nodded and then a wide grin spread over her face. "You think Matilda will donate a cake or a pie?"

"Lord, no," Ruth Ann said. "She's a vegetarian, don't you know, and all into healthy eating. Last time I talked to Harry, he said she turned fifty right before Christmas and she hated the idea of getting old, so she's on a healthy food and exercise program."

"Aging is something the poor girl *can't* control," Paul said.

"You never know what she might decide to do, but we do know that whatever it is, it'll be to benefit her. We'll just have to be ready for anything. So, polish up Grandpa's pistols," Liddy said with half a laugh.

Chapter Two

Nick Monroe couldn't get out of the SUV fast enough when they arrived at his Uncle Harry's place in Bonnet, Texas. Four hours in the vehicle with his mother was enough to cause the angels in heaven to belly up to the bar in a local honky-tonk and order a triple shot of cheap bourbon. And Nick was not an angel—not by any stretch of the word.

"God, I hate this house. If Liddy Latham hadn't been such a hard-ass, Daddy would have bought land from her and built us something modern, but oh, no, we had to live in this old house," Matilda grumbled as she pulled off her high-heeled shoes and put on a pair of flip-flops. "Harry could have at least had the driveway paved so it wouldn't ruin the heels of my shoes, but he wants to keep things just like they were when Mother and Father were living."

Nick ignored her rant, swung the driver's door open, and hit the button on the key fob to open the hatch. At the back of the vehicle, he picked up his single suitcase and one of his mother's half dozen and carried them across the accursed gravel driveway, set them by the back door, and went back for more.

By the time he had them all unloaded, Harry had come out of the house and immediately got busy helping carry them inside. "I see my sister still travels light," he teased.

Harry was a tall man with brown eyes and a thick crop of gray hair that he still parted on the side like he had his whole life. Nick often wondered whether his mother's hair would be the same color if she didn't have weekly visits to the beauty shop.

"Mother doesn't know what light travel is," Nick chuckled. "You should have seen what going on a cruise involved."

"Did you have to hire a moving van to get her to the docks?" Harry picked up the last suitcase and carried it inside to the living room. "You can take them upstairs later, after we have coffee and cake. My old knees aren't what they used to be."

"No problem." Nick wrapped his arms around his uncle and gave him a hug. "Right now, I want to tell you how sorry I am about Wanda and Jack. That's just crazy that they went on the same day."

"Thanks, Nick." Harry took a step back and clamped a hand on his nephew's shoulder. "We all need to talk. We'll have to run the business out of the house for a few days, maybe a couple of weeks. Paul Taylor and I talked about it, and since Jack and Wanda . . ." His voice cracked. "Anyway, we thought it best to have everything inspected to be sure . . ."

Matilda breezed past them on the way to the kitchen. "Well, I see that you haven't done anything with the house since I was here last. The bathroom should have been remodeled years ago, and that wallpaper Mother put up in my bedroom was ugly when she hung it forty years ago, and it has yellowed with age."

"Welcome home, Sis." Sarcasm dripped from Harry's tone as he followed her down the wide center foyer into the kitchen.

"Don't call me that. I hated it when I was a kid, and I still do." Matilda sat down at the table.

Queen Matilda has entered the room and taken a seat. Wait for it! Wait for it! The arguing will begin any minute, and then she'll start barking orders, Nick thought as he headed toward the coffeepot.

"Yes, ma'am, Tilly," Harry said with a grin.

"If you expect me to work with you, you'll never use that nickname again." Matilda shook a finger at her brother. The stones in her rings— one on every finger and her thumb—picked up the light from the overhead fixture and sent a rainbow of color flashing against the wall.

Harry poured one cup of coffee and cut himself a wedge of the triple-layer chocolate cake. "You won't be working with me. You will be working for Nick. Y'all help yourselves to the cake and coffee."

"I do *not* eat cake. It's made with eggs and butter. Is the coffee decaf?" Matilda asked.

"Nope, dark roast, and I used double the amount of grounds," Harry answered.

"Have you called a lawyer to file a civil suit against Liddy for killing Wanda and Jack?" Matilda demanded. "There's no way two people from the same office die on the same day without it being connected to the business."

Nick poured himself a mug full of coffee and added a spoonful of sugar and some powdered creamer, and then he cut a piece of cake twice the size of the one Harry had taken. "This looks great, Uncle Harry. We had supper in Wichita Falls, but no dessert." Hopefully that would set his mother off on a tangent again about the evils of caffeine, sugar, and fat grams, and she would forget the idea of a lawsuit that she'd talked to death all the way from Sweetwater.

"All that sugar, caffeine, and fat grams is going to kill both of you." Matilda pushed back her chair and went to the refrigerator. "Good God! There's nothing in here for a vegan."

"I guess you'll have to go shopping tomorrow. The grocery store is still just down the block. You can walk there and back, and I'll even let you borrow the little cart that I use to bring home the food," Harry said. "It is a little far to carry more than one bag, especially if you don't eat red meat."

Matilda shot a dirty look his way, picked up a bottle of water, and went back to the table. "I'll drive when I go. I refuse to look like an old bag lady pushing a cart down the street."

"It's not that kind of cart," Harry told her, "and you *are* past fifty now. You aren't a spring chicken anymore."

Matilda scowled at him. "That's enough out of you."

How could a brother and sister be so different in everything? Nick wondered. His mother had dark brown hair with gold highlights—compliments of an awfully expensive hairdresser—and green eyes, and she was uptight and controlling. Uncle Harry was laid-back—he didn't mind getting old, and his eyes were pale blue.

Matilda whipped around and directed the dirty look toward Nick. "Why are you looking at me like that?"

"I'm just wondering how you and Uncle Harry are even related to each other," Nick answered.

"He looks like Father, and I look like the other side of the family," Matilda said.

"Not just looks," Nick said. "You were both raised in this house. Uncle Harry loves it, and you hate it. It was my favorite place when I was a little boy, and now that I'm grown, it still is."

Matilda ignored what Nick had said. "If you aren't going to hire a lawyer, I will, Harry."

A big calico cat came wandering into the kitchen, and Matilda immediately covered her nose. "Where did that thing come from? You know I'm allergic to all animals with fur. Get it out of here."

Thank God for that! Either she or the cat will have to go. I vote that we keep the cat, Nick thought.

"Vera lives here." Harry shrugged. "She's not going anywhere, and you're not allergic to anything. Mama had you tested more than once. You just hate animals. I can't understand why you can dislike them and then turn around and love them too much to eat them."

Nick reached down and stroked the cat a couple of times and she jumped up into his lap. "Look, Mother. She's a sweetheart, and she's purring."

"You told me on the phone that you had made some decisions about the real estate company. Speak up, because I will not stay in the house with that horrid animal," Matilda said.

"All right then," Harry said with a grin, "I'll make it short and sweet. I've never married and don't have children—you know that. The business was started and this house was built by my grandfather, passed to my father and then to me. It's time for me to pass it on to you, Nick."

"But doesn't Mother own half the house, and part of the business?" Nick frowned.

"No, she doesn't," Harry answered. "When your grandparents died, they left the business to me and the house to Matilda. I bought the house from her at that time, so it's all mine."

Nick turned to focus on his mother. "Why would you sell your childhood home? And why didn't you ever tell me that Uncle Harry had bought your half of the estate?"

"Because I hated it, and I still do. The floors creak and all those flowers on the wallpaper in my room"—she shivered—"remind me of how unhappy I was when I lived in this wretched old place with its creaks and groans and rattling windows."

"Why would you ever have been unhappy?" Harry asked. "You were spoiled rotten and given anything and everything you wanted."

"I'm not having this conversation." Matilda crossed her arms over her chest. "I thought maybe I could stay here until after the funerals on Friday, but I can't, especially with that miserable cat roaming around. Nick, you can go put my bags back into my SUV. Just in case I couldn't bear to be here, I made arrangements at the bed-and-breakfast in Muenster where I usually stay. The cat just put the icing on the cake."

"That's fine," Harry said with a smile. "But before we load up your things, we need to talk some more. I was getting my affairs in order to retire when this happened. I had planned to call you"—he glanced over at Nick—"and see if you wanted to take over the business next month when I have my sixty-fifth birthday or if I should sell it and put the money in your bank account."

"Why would you do that?" Nick raked his fingers through his thick blond hair. This was an uncomfortable conversation, especially in front of his mother. "It's your property, not mine."

"I've got enough money saved to last me two lifetimes," he said, his voice cracking when he answered, "and I don't want to drop like Jack did. He was my best friend, and . . ." He pulled a white handkerchief from his hip pocket and wiped his eyes.

"Uncle Harry, don't make a big decision at a time like this. I'll stay here and work with you or for you as long as you want me to, but I think you should wait to hand it over to me for a few weeks at the very least," Nick said.

"That's nonsense," Matilda huffed. "If he wants to give it to you, then he should. I can help you run the place."

"With a cat in the house?" Harry chuckled, recovering. "We've got to do business out of this house until Paul is finished getting inspections done."

"And"—Matilda did a head wiggle—"I suppose you let him choose the inspectors. He'll pay them off to say there's nothing wrong in that office. Those Taylors are crooked, selfish, and they ruined my life."

Nick ignored his mother's comments and studied his Uncle Harry's face. "Why don't you take a little trip after the funerals are over? Maybe go to Florida and hang out on the beach for a couple of weeks until this office thing is cleared up. You used to tell me that you love the sound of the ocean."

"Son, are you not ready to take over for me?" Harry asked.

"Of course he is, and we're moving the office out of that building. I won't work in a place that the Taylors own, and I'm going to talk to a lawyer about suing them. I'm sure there's something in that place that caused these deaths. We may build a new office right here in the backyard. It doesn't have to be a big place," Matilda answered.

"We are not suing anyone, and we're not building another office. Paul has already said he'll have the place inspected. I planned to shut down for a few days anyway out of respect for Jack and Wanda. And you can't build an office here on this property anyway. This place is not zoned commercial," Harry protested.

"There's a grocery store and a snow cone stand across the street," Matilda argued.

"And that's where the commercial zone ends," Harry told her.

Nick shot a dirty look toward his mother and changed the subject. "Uncle Harry, I want you to be sure about this. How about between now and the weekend, we go get what we need from the office so I can work here at the house. All I need is the listings and your laptop. I can spend the time the building is being inspected figuring out where we are."

"I'm ready to retire, and this thing with Jack and Wanda has reinforced that," Harry said. "But you've got a good idea, Nick. I'll take a couple of weeks, hang out on the beach, get some of those massages, and then we'll talk when I get back. How's that?"

"Want me to make some flight reservations?" Nick asked.

"Nope, I'm going to drive," Harry answered. "Driving has always been peaceful to me."

"Have you gone bat crap crazy? You shouldn't be out running all over God's creation alone," Matilda barked.

"I have not lost my mind," Harry said, "and I'm not asking you to go with me, either. I couldn't stand five minutes in a car with you, much less whatever time it takes me to go from here to Florida. Hell, I might even get in some deep-sea fishing."

And now the arguing really gets started, Nick thought.

"What if you find a place that you really like? Will you settle down right there?" Nick tried to steer the conversation away from their argument.

"If I do find a place to put down roots, I imagine it would be by the ocean. If my dad hadn't left the business to me, I would have probably been a beach bum," Harry answered. "Funny thing, not ha-ha funny, but more like an omen, I guess. On Monday, Jack and I closed on the last properties we had contracts out on. Wanda was planning to take next week off to go see her grandkids in New Mexico. Reckon you can figure things out in two weeks? I could stay gone a month."

"When you called and told me about Jack and Wanda, you said you might need some help with the business. I thought you wanted *me* to help you." Matilda frowned.

"It all depends on what Nick wants at this point." Harry shrugged. "The way I see it is that he will have this house to move into and a business to slide right into. You"—Harry gave Matilda a brief glance—"could help him until you drive him up the walls and get fired or until you go over that list of folks interested in the job and help him hire someone."

Matilda slapped the table with so much force that the plates rattled. "I'm here to stay, and I'm telling you that I'm going to ruin Liddy's life, just like she destroyed mine all those years ago."

Again, Nick ignored his mother's temper tantrum. He'd learned years ago that to respond to her hissy fits just fed them and created a bigger problem, but after a few seconds he couldn't leave this one alone. "Why do you think Liddy destroyed your life, anyway?"

"If my only child is going to live in this godforsaken town"— Matilda let out a heavy sigh—"then I suppose I can manage. I'll just stay at the bed-and-breakfast until I can find a place to live. There's a new gated development going in out east of town. I understand there's already a couple of new homes out there that might be suitable."

"Just like the ones you wanted to live in when you were a teenager, right?" Harry asked.

"You didn't answer my question." Nick didn't take his eyes off his mother. She sighed again, this time even louder. He had heard her sighs of martyrdom too many times to let that one faze him. "Are you even going to answer it?"

"We had to live in *this place*, while she had that nice home right across the street, and she wouldn't sell Daddy a piece of property so he could build something nice for me to live in," Matilda growled.

"Daddy didn't have the money. We were in a recession back then, and . . . ," Harry defended his father.

"But *you* could go to college, couldn't you?" Matilda turned to shoot daggers at him. "Oh, yes, the boy child who never did a thing wrong went off to college and then came home, and Daddy helped you start up the real estate business, but I couldn't have a decent place to live."

"Daddy sent you to college, too," Harry countered.

"But did I get to join a sorority or go to the balls and parties?" She was focused on Harry now. "No, I did not, because there wasn't money for that, so I was the poor girl in college just like I was here."

"Poor, my ass!" Harry raised his voice. "You always had the best of everything Mama and Daddy could give you."

Nick felt like he was driving past a car wreck on the side of the road. He couldn't take his eyes off his mother or uncle, yet he didn't want to be in the middle of their war without a single weapon.

"Let's get you loaded up and on your way, Mother, before you go into anaphylactic shock from this cat." Nick could have kissed Vera right on her nose just for being there and giving his mother an excuse to go somewhere else. He would have reloaded twice that many suitcases to have this age-old argument done with.

"Yes!" Matilda pushed her chair back with such force that it fell on the floor, and the cat took off like a shot for the living room. "I'm sick of my only sibling taking sides with the Taylors, and"—she stormed toward the door but then turned and glared at Harry—"if you get in my way, I'll bury you in the same grave as I do Liddy when I take her down. I will not back down. Liddy should have sold that land to our family, and she shouldn't have embarrassed me by accusing me of Richie's death. Then Daddy would have had the oil drillers come in and we would have been too rich for anyone to dare say a word to me about anything. Money means power, and I intend to have both."

"Will you at least put one of her lemon pies in the grave with me?" Harry asked.

Her forefinger with its bright red polish shot up so fast that it looked like a streak of blood. "This is not a teasing matter. I've decided that I will own this town before I die. Daddy said there was oil out there on that property she owns east of town. That's the first piece of land I'm going to take from her."

"Good luck," Harry chuckled.

She crossed the room and stood beside the overturned chair. "Nick, pick this up. I'm not ready to go yet."

"Pick it up yourself," Harry told her. "Nick is not your slave, and as you've said, you are not old, and you are healthy." Then he turned back to Nick. "I'll be leaving the morning after the funerals to have a couple of weeks in Florida to recuperate from all this, like you suggested."

"You'd better have a doctor nearby," Matilda told him as she picked up the chair, slammed it down on the floor, and sat back down in it. "You are going to drop dead in a couple of days from whatever poison is in that office downtown."

"If I do, the business and this house you hate so much belong solely to Nick. You don't need anything in it anyway because you've got enough money to"—he paused and rubbed his chin—"put Liddy Latham in the ground as a pauper, right? I don't know why you keep this feud going. The Davis family wanted that land to put in a saloon, and the Taylor family refused to sell it. Then Daddy got it in his head that there was oil under the ground out there, but if there had been, Marvin would have asked the company he worked for to drill years before. It's a stupid feud that needs to be stopped. Give it up, Matilda, and get on with your life."

"I'm leaving. I don't have to take this from you." She turned toward Nick and barked, "Go get my things loaded up." Then she whipped around to Harry again. "If you die from whatever is in the real estate building, I may not even come to your funeral."

"First nice thing I've heard out of your mouth since you arrived. My will says that Nick will plan my funeral. I will be buried by Mama and Daddy in the Bonnet cemetery, and Liddy Latham is going to take care of my funeral dinner," Harry said. "I don't reckon you'll be missed."

Matilda stood up again, but this time she didn't knock the chair over. "I can't believe the day has come when a member of the Davis family threw in their lot with a Taylor."

"With a Latham. Liddy might have been a Taylor at one time, but she's a Latham now, and I'm sick of the feud, too." Nick got to his feet, knowing that his mother would have something else to say because she always had to have the last word and most of the time had to make a dramatic exit.

"Well, who thought I'd be back in Bonnet, Texas, and have to start over after your father got a dose of middle-aged crazy?" she said. "His new wife's not even pretty, and she piddles around in the flower beds like the old lady she is instead of letting the gardener take care of them. I can't imagine why he gave up me for *that*. It was like a kick in the teeth. But here I am, so I'll make the best of it, and it is, after all, my opportunity to right past wrongs. Liddy did me wrong by embarrassing me in this town when Richie died. She refused to even let me come to the funeral, and I graduated high school with him. I will right that wrong whether you two like it or not."

"Don't start on all that again," Harry said, "but do remember that you are working for Nick while I'm gone. And he will fire you if you try to control him."

"I'm his mother!" Matilda huffed. "He wouldn't fire me."

You are probably right, Nick thought. *I've inherited Dad's patience when it comes to you, but there came a time in his life when you used up all of his ability to put up with you, and it could happen with me, too.*

Nick started toward the living room with Matilda right behind him. "Well, aren't you going to agree with me?"

"No, ma'am," Nick answered. "You are my mother. That's a fact that can't be changed. I'm like Dad in that I'm not a hard person to work for, but you will not control me, Mother. So, let's get that straight from the beginning."

Harry chuckled. "Good for you, son, but take it from me: she will push you to the end of the world in an attempt to get her way."

"I'm standing right here," Matilda said, raising her voice, "so stop talking about me."

"Better to say what we've got to say to your face than behind your back," Harry told her. "Speaking of that, you might do well to remember that you are moving to Bonnet. This is a small town where everyone knows everything about everyone. There are folks who will remember what happened when you were young, and even—"

Matilda threw up both palms and butted in before he could finish. "You don't have to remind me. That's the reason I couldn't wait to move away from this place. I can't believe I'm agreeing to come back here, but I'm tired of seeing Nick's father with that woman every time I turn around. He could have been nice and quit the country club and gone to a different church, but oh, no! He told me if I didn't like seeing him with his new wife, I could change *my* lifestyle. All of our friends took his side, and I was left with nothing."

"Except an enormous bank account," Harry muttered.

Nick had lived in a house thick with tension his whole life, and he hated it. His mother slammed doors, threw things, and pouted if she didn't get her way. To try to keep some semblance of peace, his father gave in to her. The only time that Nick could remember being happy was when he came to Bonnet to visit Uncle Harry.

"Mother, you will be changing your lifestyle even more if you move to Bonnet," Nick reminded her. "There's no country club or fancy restaurants in this small town. I'm going to have another piece of cake. You sure I can't get you just a little thin slice to take with you?" He picked up the first two suitcases.

"I'd rather eat dirt," Matilda declared.

"That could be arranged," Harry yelled from the kitchen. "I just planted some spring flowers this week. The dirt is nice and soft, and I haven't seen Vera digging in it yet. That reminds me, Nick. She likes to go outside, but you need to keep an eye on her. She will disappear for a day or two if you don't watch her close."

Matilda rolled her eyes and ignored him. "I'm going over to Barbara's place to get an idea about where she wants to have the funeral dinner, and then I'll go to my bed-and-breakfast."

"Change your shoes, Mother," Nick said, "and I'll get all your things put back in your SUV. But if you're taking your vehicle, what am I supposed to drive until I can bring my truck up here?"

"The Jeep comes with the house." Harry came out of the kitchen and sat down in one of the ladder-back chairs in the foyer. "I plan to take my truck with me when I leave, but the Jeep is a company vehicle that you inherit with the business. You'll need it to drive through properties when someone lists land that doesn't have roads or lanes through it."

"Thanks, Uncle Harry." Nick headed out the door with the suitcases.

Harry popped out of the chair and picked up two more bags. "We can get her on her way twice as fast if I help you."

"I can hear every word you're saying," Matilda growled from the front porch.

"I hope so. It would be a shame if you started losing your hearing like Mama's sister did when she was about fifty," Harry chuckled.

"What is it about this house that you hate so badly, Mother?" Nick asked as he bypassed her on his way to her SUV. "Are there ghosts here, or bad memories?"

"It's old. It was old when I was a teenager. Can you imagine having your friends over to a house like this? They all lived in fancy places," she answered. "The one important thing I wanted Mama and Daddy to do was build me a new house, and they wouldn't do it."

Nick set the baggage down and opened the hatch. "Sounds like you should see my therapist."

"I don't need a shrink." Matilda marched across the gravel driveway to the SUV. "Dammit! I just ruined the heels on my shoes."

Nick shoved the baggage into the back of the vehicle as fast as Harry brought the rest of it out to him. "What time will you come by tomorrow?"

"I won't see you at all until the funeral," she answered as she fastened her seat belt. "I plan to spend the entire day with Barbara. She will need comforting, and we've got lots to do to take care of the family dinner. Then I'll need to stay with her until bedtime tomorrow night and plan what she's going to do now that she's a widow. You and I will have a lot to do over the weekend if we're going to get back here on Sunday night, so plan on being ready to leave by seven on Saturday morning."

"I thought we'd leave at six," he said.

"Good God! I'm not getting up that early," Matilda told him.

"It's your car, so I'll be ready at seven, but remember, I'll be driving my own vehicle on the return trip," he reminded her.

"What's that got to do with anything?" Matilda asked. "Do you think I'm too old to drive on my own?"

Nick smiled as he closed the hatch. "No, ma'am, I do not. I'm just trying to visualize how you're going to get all your gear from this SUV to your bedroom at the B and B without someone to carry everything for you."

"Don't be a jackass," Matilda snapped.

"At least you don't have to worry about furniture since Dad paid you for your half of the assets in the divorce," Nick said.

"You've always been on his side." She started the engine. "But then I shouldn't be surprised. Men *will* stick together, just like you and Harry when you ganged up on me in there. I thought Gregory was different when I married him, but that was one of the few times I've been wrong."

"What's that supposed to mean?" Nick asked.

"Nothing." Matilda slammed the door and drove away.

Nick sat down on the porch steps and watched the dust settle behind his mother's car. The snow cone stand across the street wasn't open for the season yet, or he might have walked over there. He could almost taste a rainbow with cherry, banana, and lime. As a kid, he would savor it to the last sugary drop of sweet syrup that always melted into the bottom of the cone.

Harry stuck his head out the door and whispered, "Is she gone? Do you want to enjoy that beautiful sunset alone, or would you mind some company?"

"She's gone and the dust has almost settled," Nick answered. "I hadn't even noticed the sunset until right now, but you're right, it's gorgeous."

Harry closed the door but quickly returned with two longneck bottles of beer. He handed one to Nick and twisted the top off his own before he sat down beside his nephew. "I'm glad the time has changed so that we get more daylight at the end of the day. It will make traveling so much better."

"Me too," Nick said. "Uncle Harry, what is this thing between you and Mother? Did you *ever* get along?"

"It's a long story. Our childhoods affected us each differently," Harry said. "With all that's gone on the past two days, I'd rather not dig up family skeletons tonight. Let's just enjoy our beer and the sunset."

If Uncle Harry was tired of all the tension, then Nick figured it wasn't the time to talk about it. Nick had heard about the battle over some land and a new house, but there was something deeper and more personal going on between his mother and Liddy—something over and beyond the feud itself, maybe something to do with Richie—and since he was going to live in Bonnet, he figured he had the right to know what it was.

"Are you really going to Florida?" he finally asked after a few minutes.

"I need some time to process all this and, like you said, to decide if I'd be bored to tears if I retire, so yes, I'm going to the beach for some R and R."

"Sounds like you've given this a lot of thought, even before Jack passed away so suddenly," Nick said.

"Retirement has been on my mind for a year," Harry confessed. "I had thought I'd wait one more year, but then yesterday, when Wanda and Jack both died, it hit me like a ton of bricks. I might drop just like they did without having ever done one thing on my bucket list. Don't just think you've got forever. Treat each day as if it was your last one, and"—Harry took a sip of his beer and paused for a long time before he went on—"find a good woman to share your life with. Don't let this thing with your parents sour you on marriage."

"Why didn't you ever get married?" Nick asked.

"It's another long story, but hey, I'm not too old to find someone. I might find me a nice middle-aged beach bunny who has kids and grandkids that she's willing to share," Harry said with a smile.

"I kind of know about the Davis and Taylor feud, but will you tell me the whole story someday?" Nick asked.

"I promise I will on your wedding day," Harry said.

"How about we make a deal," Nick said. "If I get married first, you have to tell me. If you get married first, you have to tell me."

Harry thought about that for a minute, then broke out in laughter. "I think you'd be getting the best end of that deal, but I agree. I'll be your best man, and you can be mine, and we'll talk about that subject on the morning before either of us says the vows."

"Sounds like a plan to me," Nick agreed, but after the chaos that came about when his dad left his mother, he thought that it would be a cold day in hell before he got married.

Chapter Three

Liddy brought her lemon chess pie into the fellowship hall, set it on a nearby table, and headed to the kitchen for three long cloths—one for each of the eight-foot tables: main dishes, salads, and desserts. She chose the white ones from the walk-in pantry and picked out a pink floral arrangement to go in the center of the middle table.

Ethel and Clara had bought miniature oil wells to use for centerpieces at Marvin's funeral and had arranged all the food on red cloths because that was his favorite color. Liddy and Ethel had decided on orange cloths with sunflower centerpieces for Clara's funeral. At Richie's service, Liddy remembered sitting in the front row staring at his casket and trying to brace herself for the last time she would be able to look at her only child. To this day, she couldn't remember a thing about the dinner, except that Ruth Ann and Paul were there to support her and Marvin.

"Hey, I'm here," Ruth Ann called out as she came in the back door. "I remembered to bring the extension cord with several outlets so we'd have plenty of plugs for the slow cookers and electric skillets. Amelia is coming in right behind me."

Liddy carried out the armload of tablecloths and the vase with pink flowers. "From the way Wanda had her office decorated, I thought the pink arrangement would be best."

"You're right." Ruth Ann set her electric skillet on a nearby table and took the cloths from Liddy. "I'll help you get these on the tables and straightened out; then we can set up the round tables and chairs for the folks. We need to get everything done before the funeral, since there won't be a graveside service in this weather."

"That's smart of Wanda's family." Amelia set a pan of brownies on a nearby table and relieved Liddy of the vase of flowers. Then she took a step back so she could eyeball the cloths and tell her mother and aunt when they were all even. When that job was done, she set the flowers in the center of the middle table and took her brownies down to the far end where the desserts would be put out.

Women had come and gone with their offerings, and there wasn't room to put another pot, platter, casserole dish, or dessert on any of the tables when it was time to go to the sanctuary for the service.

"Looks wonderful," Liddy declared as she led the way through a side door and down a hallway to the sanctuary. "It always comes together like a charm."

"That's because you keep a book of phone numbers and know who to call to help with funeral dinners, and we've all done this for so long that it's old hat," Ruth Ann said. "We never organize one of these that I don't think of Richie, Marvin, and Clara, along with the rest of our family that has gone on."

"Me too." Liddy forced a smile.

"And there was a lemon pie at every one of them, right?" Amelia asked.

"Even Richie's." Liddy nodded. "I couldn't let his spirit go without making his favorite pie."

"Speaking of pies, when the last amen is said, your brother will part the crowd like it's the Red Sea and he's Moses so he can get a slice of your pie. I believe he likes lemon chess even better than lemon meringue." Ruth Ann let Liddy go before her into the sanctuary.

Liddy suppressed a giggle over the visual of Paul hurrying to the fellowship hall for a piece of pie. Marvin had been like that when it came to lemon pie. She'd made them once a month for him whether there was a funeral or not.

"I've got to make a run to the restroom," Amelia whispered. "Save me a seat."

Liddy nodded and took a memorial folder from Rachel, the funeral director's wife. By luck the back pew was still empty, and since they would need to slip out of the church when the procession started to say last farewells to Wanda, that was perfect.

Liddy stood to one side and let Ruth Ann sit down before she did so that when Amelia arrived, she could slide in beside her. She adjusted the sides of the good black cardigan she wore over her basic black funeral dress in the spring and fall. She probably should go shopping for another dress, but folks didn't pay much attention to what she was wearing. They would, however, begin to plan her funeral if there weren't one of her two famous lemon pies on the dessert table at the family dinner. She had no illusions as to what was most important—looks or comfort food.

"Isn't that pink casket beautiful?" Ruth Ann whispered. "Wanda loved that color. She always had a pink carnation in a bud vase on her desk at the office, and all kinds of little self-help plaques and signs hanging everywhere."

"You can bet your sweet ass that Matilda will clean all that out as soon as they can get back in the office. So far, every inspection has turned up with no problems," Liddy whispered and changed the subject. "God, I hate pantyhose, but my only black thigh highs had runners in them. All this elastic around my waist is driving me crazy. Underwear, half-slip, and pantyhose. I wish I was brave enough to attend a funeral with my bare legs showing."

"I quit wearing those miserable things years ago, and so did Wanda," Ruth Ann said. "I hope they didn't put any on her. She doesn't deserve to have to wear them for all eternity."

"If y'all let the undertaker put them on me when I die, I'll come back and haunt you. And you better not take pictures of me in the casket, neither. That's not the way I want folks to remember me," Liddy told her. "Here comes Amelia. We all need to slide down so she'll have a place to sit. Where's Paul?"

"He was asked to be a pallbearer," Ruth Ann said out the side of her mouth.

"Thanks for saving me a seat," Amelia said as she slid into the pew. "I tried to redo my hair while I was in the bathroom. Thanks, Mama, for giving me curly hair that acts like a demon on steroids when it rains."

"I'd give anything to have curly hair. Mine was a deep brown color with chestnut highlights back in the day, but it's always been straight as a flat iron," Liddy said.

The preacher took his place behind the lectern and raised his arms. All conversation stopped, and everyone in the church rose to their feet. Wanda's husband and kids led the family in to sit in the reserved pews at the front of the room. Amelia nudged Liddy on the arm and said out the side of her mouth, "I can understand Harry being asked to sit with the family, but why would Matilda be coming in with them? She sure does put on airs, doesn't she?"

Liddy shrugged and shook her head in disbelief. "I told you that she would create havoc, and yep, that's always been her way."

"Shhh." Ruth Ann sent a dirty look down the pew. "Respect now. Gossip later."

Liddy bit back a giggle. Her mama would have come up out of her grave in the Bonnet cemetery and taken a switch to her, even if Liddy was seventy years old, for laughing during the reading of a eulogy. Or, for that matter, for even smiling too big at a funeral service.

The service was over in about thirty minutes, and then the funeral director opened the casket for friends and family to walk past and pay their last respects. Liddy, Amelia, and Ruth Ann all slipped out the back door and headed straight to the fellowship hall. Liddy made sure all the electrical appliances were plugged in and turned on the warm setting. Ruth Ann removed the plastic wrap from platters of ham, fried chicken, and barbecued ribs. Amelia checked to be sure that everything was where it was supposed to be—main dishes first, salads next, vegetables and bread after that, and then the desserts.

Amelia slipped a bibbed apron over her navy-blue sleeveless dress and handed one to each of the other two ladies.

Liddy put on her apron. "They'll be coming in here any minute, but they'll wait on the family to pay their last respects before they line up to eat."

"Family first." Amelia nodded.

"I like the idea of no graveside service." Ruth Ann removed the lids and covers from the main course dishes. "When I die, y'all have a regular service or a graveside, but not both."

Amelia shivered. "Don't talk like that, Mama. You are going to live forever."

Ruth Ann patted Amelia on the shoulder. "No one lives forever, *chère.*" Then she focused on Liddy. "I can't bear to think of you passing, but you need to tell us what kind of service and dinner you want."

Liddy patted her on the shoulder. "It's all in writing, along with my will. But the most important thing is that you or Amelia will have to bring lemon pie to my dinner. I just love it when everyone fights over my pies."

"And my gumbo." Ruth Ann smiled. "Think Matilda will put some of that on her plate today?"

"Yes, your gumbo, and honey, Matilda won't eat anything we've prepared," Liddy said.

"Unless she brings a taster," Ruth Ann whispered.

As if on cue, Matilda and Harry entered the fellowship hall with dozens of people right behind them. She took one look at the tables, sucked in a lungful of air, and let it out in a whoosh. "This is unacceptable, Harry."

"This is a southern funeral dinner. If you don't like it, the grass is turning green. You can go out there and eat all you want," he told her.

Liddy giggled despite her attempt to hold it in. So now, on top of everything else, Matilda was a vegetarian. Liddy had no problem with that, but the woman had rocks for brains if she thought for one minute that a funeral dinner was planned to suit her tastes.

"We do have salads," Ruth Ann said.

"But they all have eggs or cheese or other animal products in them. I'm so glad that Barbara and I are going to do things different this evening for Jack's family. If any one of you three"—Matilda included them all with a sweep of her hand—"are there, you'll see a proper, healthy meal laid out. We're having it catered with tofu turkey, plant-based shrimp scampi, and lots of good fresh vegetables and fruits."

Liddy looked Matilda right in the eye and said, "The three of us will be bringing brownies, gumbo, and lemon pie to the dinner, and other women in town will bring their favorite casseroles and dishes—things that Jack was real fond of. If folks don't want to eat what we bring, then we'll take our stuff home."

"That's so old school." Matilda glared at her. "Nowadays, most folks just go to a restaurant after a funeral. It's time y'all caught up with the times, and I'm moving to Bonnet to turn things around, Liddy, so say goodbye to everything as you know it now."

"Bless your heart," Liddy said in her best sarcastic tone, even though her body hummed with anger. "Don't you remember the story of David and Goliath?"

"What in the hell are you talking about?" Matilda hissed.

"I've got a slingshot and lots of stones gathered up. Goliath doesn't scare me, and neither do you," Liddy said with a smile.

Paul came in next with the rest of the pallbearers and sat down at a table right in front of the dessert, with a smile at Liddy. She sent a sly wink his way and tilted her head toward the kitchen. That meant if the rest of the pie was gone when the family went through the line, there was a slice hiding in the kitchen just for him.

The family finally arrived, and the preacher quieted everyone by tapping on a glass with a fork. "Instead of grace, let's all have a moment of silence and thank the good Lord for the friendship we had for Wanda." He waited for a second and then bowed his head.

Everyone followed his example, but after a couple of seconds, every hair on Liddy's arms stood up, giving testimony that someone was staring at her. She opened one eye and locked gazes with Matilda, who was standing in front of the dessert table. If that woman thought she was coming into Liddy's town and turning everything upside down, she had cow patties for brains.

"Amen!" the preacher finally said loudly and raised his head. "We will ask the family to lead the line for the buffet tables at this time, and then the friends and family can fall in behind them."

Matilda snubbed the first table and gave Harry a dirty look when he helped himself to not only a large slice of ham but also fried chicken. She held up the line for a good two minutes and then finally put a small amount of a green salad on her plate.

With a long sigh, she said, "I suppose I can pick out the bits of bacon and cheese."

"There's a Jell-O salad with peaches in it," Liddy suggested.

Matilda frowned and the look on her face said she would rather be talking to a chimpanzee than Liddy. "Don't you know that gelatin is made with animal bones?"

"Had no idea," Liddy answered. "I guess you could pick the peaches out and wash the gelatin off them."

Matilda leaned forward and threatened in a low whisper, "I don't care what Harry says. I'm hiring a lawyer to sue you for Jack's and

Wanda's deaths. It's your fault they are dead, and we are going to start at two million dollars. You should have sold that building to my brother years ago. We would have made sure it was safe, and"—her tone got even more evil—"I'm going to make your life miserable until you sell me that land that my family has been trying to buy from you for all these years."

"Wanda and Jack didn't die because of something in that building," Liddy said. "They probably heard you were coming to town and couldn't stand the idea."

"Prove it and decide how much misery you want. You can prevent all of it by selling me that land." She turned around and carried her salad to the table where Barbara and some of her family members were seated.

"Who put a burr in her britches? I couldn't hear what she said, but her tone sent chills down my back," Amelia whispered.

"Don't worry about her," Liddy said.

"Hello, I'm Nick Monroe, her son, but don't hold that against me." A tall, blond-haired guy with gorgeous green eyes stepped up to the dessert table. "That would be my mother who was just trying to create trouble. Harry is my uncle, and I like good food almost as much as he does. I apologize to you ladies for my mother's attitude. I could tell by her expression that she was not being nice. This is just a phase she's in. It'll pass in a few months, like all the others she's worked her way through."

"I'm Amelia Taylor, and I try not to judge anyone. I figure to each his own. Nice to meet you, Nick," she said.

Liddy hadn't thought about Nick and Amelia being in the same place, or that being close to the same age, they might get acquainted with each other. She took a very deep breath and let it out slowly. *When it rains, it pours,* she thought, *but this is a real toad strangler.*

"The pleasure is all mine." He flashed a bright smile and moved on.

"He's downright sexy with those green eyes and that cute little dimple in his chin," Amelia whispered to her Aunt Liddy.

In addition to worrying about whatever trouble Matilda would probably stir up, Liddy would have to think about how she would handle a romance between her niece and Matilda's son. That would surely be a disaster waiting to happen.

"They used to call that a cleft, but honey, that man is totally off limits." Liddy slipped the last piece of lemon pie onto a small plate for Paul.

"Why?" Amelia asked.

"It sure doesn't look like you've lost your touch, Miz Liddy," Harry interrupted with a grin. "Wanda and Jack both said more than once that you should put in a bakery, but I'm kind of glad you don't have one right now."

"Why's that?" Liddy asked.

"Because I'm leaving town on Monday on a little trip. If I knew you were baking these pies every day, I'd have trouble driving out of Bonnet," Harry said.

"Who's going to be our master of ceremonies and help judge the bonnet contest if you leave town?" Ruth Ann asked.

"Talk to Nick," Harry said. "That would be a good opportunity for him to start fitting into the community."

"I will," Ruth Ann said. "We'll miss you, but I hope you enjoy the trip."

"I wish I'd started marking off things on my bucket list when I retired rather than waiting," Liddy said. "Jack and Wanda sure enough taught us that we can't depend on the future, didn't they."

"Yes, they did, and that's why I'm doing this," Harry said. "Y'all be good to Nick. He likes this town, and I think he'll be a big asset to the community if he's given a chance." He glanced around the room, located his sister, and then said in a low voice, "And believe me when I say he's nothing like his mother."

"We will," Ruth Ann assured him.

"If I would have had a son, I would have wanted one exactly like Nick. He's a good man, and he even eats meat." Harry bypassed the table where his sister was sitting and went on to another one.

"Have y'all got something against vegans?" Amelia asked. "Two of my best friends at the school are vegans and another one is a vegetarian."

"Do they put you down because you like a good steak?" Liddy asked.

"Of course not, and I don't make fun of them because they don't eat anything that had a face," Amelia answered.

"It's not what Matilda does or doesn't eat that we have trouble with," Liddy explained. "It's the woman, not the food. If you're around her very long, you'll understand. You know part of the history between the Davises and the Taylors, and she's the worst of the lot. Harry's a pretty good guy, but Matilda is downright evil."

An hour later, when everyone had gone from the fellowship hall and things had been cleaned up, Amelia cornered Liddy and asked, "Why did you say that about Nick being off limits? Is he married or engaged?"

Liddy had seen the way they looked at each other, and the little flirty signs. Without a doubt, the attraction had started already with the first meeting. She sighed and headed toward the dessert table with Amelia right behind her.

"What's that sigh all about, Aunt Liddy?" Amelia asked.

"Let's eat these last two brownies in your pan. I don't know Nick well enough to know if he's engaged, but he's not wearing a ring, so he's probably not married. No surprise there." Liddy put the brownies on a napkin and carried them to a table. She didn't even want to think about Amelia and Nick together and sent up a silent prayer that her niece wouldn't get tangled up with him.

"Are you talking about his mother being so mean?" Amelia picked up one of the brownies and bit into it.

Liddy nodded. "When he takes a woman home to meet his mama, they probably drop him like a hot potato the very next day. I don't care if Nick is a knight in shining armor—you don't want to have to deal with Matilda, and you would if you got into any kind of relationship with him. She hates me, and you are kin to me. She would make life miserable for you. You've been down that road with Elliott, if you will remember."

"Why does everyone let her get away with being hateful?" Amelia asked.

"Liddy doesn't." Ruth Ann joined them. "That's what makes her dislike Liddy even more than the rest of our family. Plus she thinks there's oil under some property that we own, and she's determined to have it. Her father tried to buy it, too, but we're not selling it. Your father and I have other plans for that place after we retire. And honey, you just got over a really rough relationship with Elliott. Don't dive into another one."

"Aunt Liddy reminded me of that," Amelia said. "I learned my lesson there. Trust me, I won't make that mistake again."

Chapter Four

S o much sadness, and so much food," Amelia muttered as she followed her mother and aunt into the senior citizens building for the second funeral that day. A lit jar candle sat in the middle of each of more than a dozen long tables covered with white cloths.

"You got that right," Liddy said. "I can't remember the last time we were at two funerals in one day."

"Must've been back when those two brothers got killed out on Wolf Creek Road," Ruth Ann said. "They were seniors and the hushed-up rumors that went around town said that they were drunk and racing some of their cousins. But nobody talks out loud about the dead."

"Are you talking about Richie?" Amelia asked.

"No, honey, he crashed into a tree, and he . . ." Ruth Ann paused.

"It's all right." Liddy laid a hand on Ruth Ann's shoulder. "I still get a lump in my throat at the mention of him, but talking about him keeps him alive in my heart."

"Sweet Lord!" Ruth Ann gasped when she saw the table at the end of the room. "That looks more like something that you'd fix up for a party, not a funeral."

Caterers had set up an eight-foot table and were busy getting the food all arranged beautifully. One of the four ladies, who were all wearing fancy white aprons with the embroidered logo from a company located in Gainesville, smiled and pointed to another table over on the other side of the room. "Miz Matilda said that if food came in from the community, it was all to be put on that table."

Amelia's eyes darted from the fancy table with its three-foot-tall centerpiece made of fruit to the horrible old table that was across the room covered with dust. Nicks were taken out of it on all four sides, and the legs were covered in rust.

"What do we do, Aunt Liddy?" she asked.

"Pull out some of those chairs and set your food on them while I take care of this," Liddy answered.

"Can't we just put it on one of their tables?" Amelia asked.

"Oh, no!" Ruth Ann shook her head. "If we got a speck of anything on one of the fancy tablecloths, we might have to buy the thing."

"I am a member of this place, and I've supported it for years," Liddy declared. "We have had dinners here before, so I know where everything is located." She marched through the dining area and disappeared into the kitchen. She returned carrying a bright red tablecloth and handed it to Amelia. "Evidently the white ones are all in the laundry bin back there, but I did find this one."

"Are you sure about this, Aunt Liddy?" Amelia frowned. "It's red, and this *is* a funeral dinner. Are you doing this to get back at Matilda for all that fancy business she's having catered?"

"Nope, not one bit," Liddy answered.

"This is all for Jack and he wouldn't care what color it is, and it will cover up a multitude of abuse that old table has seen," Ruth Ann assured her. "At least we've got an electrical outlet underneath it. We can plug in my slow cooker, and maybe someone will bring an extension cord with more outlets on the end. Matilda isn't going to run us out of a funeral dinner."

"I'll help you get that cloth all even, Aunt Liddy," Amelia said. "I believe this is the very first funeral dinner I've ever been to that was catered. What they're putting out looks more like a wedding reception—"

Ruth Ann butted in before Amelia could finish, "That belongs in an upscale Dallas country club, not the senior citizens building in Bonnet, Texas."

Amelia and Liddy had just gotten the cloth situated when several women paraded in the door with dishes in their hands. "Do you think we'll need to set up another table, Aunt Liddy?"

"Yes, I do, so I'll go get another cloth." Liddy nodded.

"Jack always loved my potato salad," one of the ladies said. "I heard that Barbara turned the dinner over to Matilda and it was being catered, but I just couldn't let Jack leave us without making his ranch-style potato salad one more time."

"And he always asked for my baked beans." Another one set down a slow cooker and brought out a multi-plug extension cord. "I'll just crawl up under the table here and put this in place; then we should have enough plugs for all of our stuff."

Liddy returned with a hot-pink tablecloth. "This is the only one left back there. Amelia, will you help me bring a table from the other side of the room and set it up here?"

"I'll help Amelia. Liddy, you should organize the food as it comes in," Ruth Ann spoke up. "If he's looking down from heaven, Jack is probably getting a kick out of this."

More ladies came in with cakes, pies, casseroles, and platters of fried chicken and ham. When it was time for them to go to the funeral home for the service, both tables were covered from one end to the other. Amelia looked at the hodgepodge of cookers, skillets, bowls, platters, and pans on the tables covered in red and hot pink, and then at the gorgeous table on the other side of the room. One was solid southern tradition. The other was a new, modern idea. As they left the room, she wondered which one would be empty when the dinner was over.

"Is this a onetime thing?" Ruth Ann asked as she slid in behind the wheel of her SUV.

"Well, a person usually only dies once," Liddy answered as she fastened her seat belt.

"I think she's talking about the catered funeral dinner," Amelia piped up from the back seat.

"Nope," Liddy answered. "This is just the first battle of the war."

"Did we win or lose?" Amelia asked.

"We won't know until the end of the dinner," Ruth Ann answered, "but at least Matilda won't have the advantage she probably thinks she's going to have."

"Is that when we count the dead bodies in the fellowship hall?" Amelia asked.

"No, that's when we count how many of our dishes are empty and how much tofu turkey is left on that fancy-schmancy table on the other side of the room," Liddy answered. "I thought I might have some of those fresh strawberries and grab a chunk of cheese from Gladys Milton's relish tray. She makes her own pickled beets and sweet dills and then adds cheese and crackers to it for funeral dinners."

"Is that fraternizing with the enemy? Looks like Gladys might have gone over to the other side since her food is on that table." Amelia got out of the vehicle, popped up her big black umbrella, and handed each of the ladies one.

"No, it's called being neighborly," Ruth Ann said, "but I'm having Gloria Ann's chicken and dressing instead of tofu. I remember that Jack always had a double portion of it at any funeral dinner he went to."

"That's it!" Amelia stopped and gasped.

"What?" Liddy looked around to see if Matilda had arrived with a pistol.

"I just realized why the dinner after a funeral is important. Talking about the food kind of sparks memories of the newly deceased, and then folks get closure by talking about him or her. A catered meal just wouldn't have the same effect, would it? Why didn't I think of that before?"

"I should have thought of it myself," Liddy said with a nod, "but that pretty well sums it up, and kale salad and tofu turkey won't bring back a single memory of Jack."

Following the funeral, Nick drove his Uncle Harry and his mother from the funeral chapel to the senior citizens place for the family supper. Like Wanda's husband, Barbara had opted to forgo the service at the cemetery since it was still pouring down rain.

"I'm so embarrassed," Matilda wailed.

"About what?" Harry asked. "The funeral service was good, and Barbara held up really well. She told me while we were waiting to go into the chapel that she's going home with her daughter to Memphis, Tennessee, and might not come back until the end of summer."

"I know, and so I'd thought she might . . ." Matilda dabbed at her eyes with a white handkerchief with lace around the edges.

"She might what?" Harry asked.

"Never mind." Matilda tilted her chin up and tucked the hankie back into her purse.

"I know what you were thinking," Harry chuckled, "and those fake tears stopped working on me years and years ago."

"Oh, hush!" Matilda's chin went up a little more.

"I'd like to know what brought on the fake tears," Nick said as he parked his mother's SUV a block away.

"They weren't fake. Barbara is my friend, and I will miss her," Matilda protested.

"She's being dramatic because Barbara is leaving," Harry explained, "but not because she will miss her like she's saying. Barbara has always been laid-back and easygoing, so she'd be just the right person for my sweet sister to manipulate into being an ally for her against Liddy." Harry picked up an umbrella from behind the seat.

"I know about the land you want, Mother, but there's something more between you and Liddy, isn't there?" Nick got out, popped up an umbrella, and handed it to his mother, then got out a second one for himself.

"I'm not having that conversation today, and maybe never, but Liddy has ruined Jack's dinner that Barbara and I slaved over." Matilda carefully picked her way around puddles. "The caterer called and said that the local women had set up two tables and put a red cloth on one and a pink one on the other, and there's tacky-looking electric skillets and all kinds of casseroles covering them."

"Who cares about all that?" Harry asked. "This is small-town Texas, not the big city. Folks here do things differently. They just want some good old home-cooked food and a place to visit and pay condolences to the grieving family."

"I was trying to bring a little class to this place," Matilda declared as she waited for Nick to open the door into the building for her.

"Stand out there in the rain if you want to, woman. I'm going in right now. Hopefully, the lemon pie isn't all gone." Harry stepped around her, slung open the door, and went in ahead of her. "You were not trying to bring class to town; you were taking the first step to go to war with Liddy. Don't cover up your intentions with lies."

Nick heard feminine voices behind him, so he stepped to one side and held the door open. He had no idea who they were until the first three had gone inside the building, and Amelia's crystal-clear blue eyes locked with his for a moment.

"Thank you, sir," she said as she lowered her umbrella and set it inside the door on a mat.

"Not sir, just Nick." He followed her inside. "And you are very welcome. This has been a day, hasn't it?"

"Not the best for two funerals," she said, "but at least it's not bitter cold with the rain."

Nick motioned to an empty table. "Looks like the line is long, so we might as well sit down and wait awhile."

Amelia followed him across the room and eased down into a chair. "The folks don't seem to be having any trouble helping themselves, so maybe Aunt Liddy and my mama can manage without me. I understand you are taking over the real estate business?"

"At least for a couple of weeks. When Uncle Harry comes home, I might just be working as his assistant." Nick took a seat across the table from her. "You need a job? I'm in the market for an agent and for an office manager."

"I heard your mama was going to be the new office manager," Amelia said.

"Temporarily." Nick could feel his mother's cold stare all the way across the room. Her mouth was set in a firm line. Her perfectly arched brows were drawn down in a frown, and she was slowly shaking her head from side to side.

"So, Matilda isn't moving to Bonnet?" Amelia asked. "To answer your question, though, I have a job. I teach English at Bonnet High School."

"I see. Mother is not a small-town woman." Nick ignored the chill coming from across the room. "She'll be here for a while, but she's never liked this town."

"How about you?" Amelia asked. "Do you like it here?"

"Love it," Nick answered. "I plan to live here forever. My great-grandfather started the family real estate business, and it's been passed down to me. I studied business in college, worked in a bank for a while, and then settled into real estate a couple of years after that."

He could have drowned in her blue eyes and listened to her read the phone book in that slow southern drawl. "You weren't raised in Texas, were you?"

"Yes, but my mama is from Houma, Louisiana. That's way down south in bayou country. My grandmother, aunts and uncles, and cousins still live down there and we visit them every chance we get. The accent rubs off," Amelia said. "But I can tell from your drawl that you are Texan all the way from that bolo tie you are wearing down to the soles of your boots."

"Yep, I am." Nick grinned. "Do you like Texans?"

"Of course I do." She smiled back at him. "I might have inherited some Cajun accent from my mama, but I'm Texan by birth. Born and raised right here in Bonnet."

"Do you like living in a small town?" Nick didn't care if the line at the tables took forever. He would rather sit right there and talk to Amelia than eat.

"Every single bit of it, from the Bluebonnet Festival to the Friday night high school football games. I missed home so much when I went to college. I couldn't wait to get back here." Amelia glanced over at the table where Matilda was sitting.

"Do you have siblings?" Nick tried to draw her attention back to him.

"I have an older sister, Bridget, who is married to Clovis. They're both doctors and work in the ER at the hospital." Amelia flashed a brilliant smile his way. "They live out east of town, not far from where my parents live. But our big family is in Louisiana. Cousins, aunts, uncles by the beaucoup."

Nick raked his fingers through his blond hair. "That means *a lot*, right?"

"Yep, it does. Mama comes from a big family." Amelia nodded. "What about you, Nick? Got brothers and sisters?"

"I'm an only child, with no siblings and no cousins. I've always envied my friends that had those people in their lives."

"Well, darlin', anytime you want to be around a big family, I'll invite the Devereaux families up here for a weekend. Or better yet, I'll just take you down there for one of our get-togethers. Devereaux was Mama's maiden name, and she was one of twelve kids. We all call our grandmother on that side Granny Dee. That's the Cajun side of the family, but she's a throwback to the Irish blood we have from her DNA. There's a McCoy back in there somewhere on the family tree. And you didn't ask for a family history, so I'll be quiet now," Amelia told him.

"No, I like hearing about your family. It sounds like so much fun." Nick wondered if she was nervous because of him or because of the dirty looks coming from both his mother and her Aunt Liddy.

"It looks like everyone has gotten their food. I suppose we should go see if there's any leftovers for us." She stood up.

"From here, it looks like there's plenty of tofu turkey left, but the ham"—he nodded toward the table that was covered with a red cloth—"appears to be gone."

"I've tried that kind of turkey, and it's not bad," she said, "but it's just not the same texture as the real bird. I think I'll see if there's any chicken and dressing left, and maybe I'll have some fruit from that table for dessert."

Nick pushed back his chair. "Not me, I'm going for more of those brownies. I'm a sucker for chocolate. Do you know who brought them?"

"I did," Amelia admitted.

"Then, darlin', will you marry me?" he teased.

"Can I have some time to think about it?" She batted her long lashes.

"As long as you make brownies for me at least once a week until you say yes," he answered.

"Since we're discussing our wedding, what do you have in mind?" she asked.

"A trip to Vegas, a short ceremony at one of the chapels, and a honeymoon right here in Bonnet." He liked flirting with Amelia, even if it would never go anywhere. Nick Monroe was a self-proclaimed bachelor forever. He could never subject a woman to his mother.

"Why a Vegas wedding?" she asked.

"Because our relationship would be like Romeo and Juliet's. I've been getting dirty looks from my mother ever since we sat down, and your Aunt Liddy has been trying to get your attention for the past ten minutes." He ushered her across the room with his hand on her back.

"Then I guess maybe we'd better not look at gold wedding bands or wedding cakes just yet." Amelia picked up a disposable plate and scooped up some chicken and dressing from the slow cooker, then added some cranberry salad, one of the last twice-baked potatoes, and a spoonful of candied yams to her plate.

Nick had just finished loading his plate when Harry came across the room and sighed. "Hello, Amelia. Your Aunt Liddy is waving at you. I think you're supposed to join them at their table."

"I'm headed that way." Amelia gave Nick a sly wink. "Maybe we'll talk more later."

"Anytime." Nick followed his Uncle Harry to the table where he was sitting.

"I knew I should have been rude and gotten two pieces of Liddy's lemon pie on the first pass," Harry groaned. "Now it's all gone, and it could be years before I get another slice. Nick, your mother says you need to sit at the table with her. I'm not sure she can stand the sight of what you just put on that plate, but we can always hope the smell sends her back to the bed-and-breakfast, can't we?"

Nick chuckled. "Uncle Harry, where have you been all my life?"

"Hiding in Bonnet, Texas." Harry helped himself to a brownie and a scoop of blackberry cobbler.

Nick carried his plate to the table where his mother was sitting and sat down beside her. "Barbara, I haven't seen you since we got into town. I'm so, so sorry about Jack. He was always so good to me when I came to spend time with Uncle Harry."

"He was a good man." Barbara wiped away a few tears with a tissue. "Everywhere I look, I see him, so I'm going home with my daughter for a few months. She needs a sitter for her toddler, and I need a distraction." She stood up. "I'm going to go get a brownie. Can I bring you anything from that table, Matilda?"

"Lord, no!" Matilda gasped. "I'll have some fruit and a couple of those delicious-looking vegan cookies."

Nick knew his mother well enough that he could tell she was about to explode. He wasn't a bit surprised when she turned toward him and hissed, "I forbid you to talk to Amelia Taylor."

"Mother, I am thirty years old. You lost the power to forbid me anything years and years ago," Nick said under his breath. "Besides, I just proposed to her. I think it was love at first sight."

Matilda paled and laid a hand over her heart. "You did what?"

"Oh, don't get your underwear in a twist," Nick said, "and if you have a heart attack and die right here, I'll write up the obituary for the paper and will say that it seemed appropriate that you passed away in a senior citizens building since you are old enough to get a senior discount at restaurants. Then I will let Liddy Latham plan the funeral dinner. So, what do you say? Shall we eat, drink, and be merry?"

"You are just like your father." Matilda removed her hand and went back to eating kale salad. "He thought he was being funny, but he was crude, and if you ever let Liddy Latham near my funeral dinner, I will come back and haunt you every single day for the rest of your life. And I mean it when I say I will not have a relative of hers in my family."

"What about *my* family?" Nick asked. "Do I not get a say-so in who I fall in love with and maybe marry someday?"

"You've been around Harry too much already," Matilda whispered. "If anyone related to a Taylor ever becomes a part of your so-called family, then you can count me out of it. Not that I have anything to worry about. Liddy would never allow her kin to spend time with you."

Nick pushed his chair back, got up, and carried his plate over to the table where he and Amelia had been sitting. Being alone did have its benefits.

Chapter Five

The Bluebonnet Festival Committee held their monthly meetings at the Bluebonnet Café on Main Street, because they always served a lunch special of baked potato soup and a choice of sandwiches on Tuesdays. When Liddy heard Ruth Ann drive up, she slung her purse over her shoulder and headed out the back door.

"I always have two minds about the last meeting before the festival," Ruth Ann said when Liddy was in the car. "I'm excited to finalize everything, but then a little sad that another whole year has passed."

"Amen to that," Liddy agreed, "but I'm always excited to get to have lunch at the café and see everyone on the committee. It's always good to share a meal and a visit with folks that doesn't involve a funeral dinner."

"There's Gladys's car, and over there is Emogene's pickup," Ruth Ann pointed out as she parked her car in front of the café.

"And there's Ethel's truck." Liddy unfastened her seat belt and opened the door. "So it looks like we aren't the first ones here by any means."

Ruth Ann got out of her car and then picked up her tote bag from the back seat. "Shows that folks are excited about the festival, and it's a beautiful day, so lots of the folks are happy to get out and go somewhere."

"I know I am." Liddy headed toward the door with her sister-in-law right behind her. "Hello, everyone. Are we all excited about this weekend?"

"Yes, ma'am," several ladies chorused.

Ruth Ann sat down at the end of the table for eight and brought a thick blue binder that held all the festival notes from the previous two decades out of her tote bag. Before she could begin discussing the notes for that year's festival, the waitress came from behind the counter with a notepad.

"What can I get you ladies to drink?" she asked.

"Sweet tea for me," Ruth Ann answered and glanced down the table at the other five women. "Have all y'all ordered?"

Five heads bobbed up and down.

"Then bring me the special with a BLT sandwich, and sweet tea," Liddy said as she settled into a chair to Ruth Ann's right.

"I'll have the special and a club sandwich, Donna Sue," Ruth Ann said. "How's your grandma?"

"Still in the hospital, but she's stable. Thanks for asking. We're hoping she makes it to Mother's Day. She'll be a hundred years old that week," Donna Sue replied as she wrote down the order.

"Tell her that we're praying for her," Liddy said.

"Thank you, and I'll tell Granny you asked about her. She always loved being part of this committee when she was able to get around." Donna Sue smiled and then rushed off to the kitchen.

"Okay," Ruth Ann said as she opened the binder. "Let's get this part of the meeting taken care of while we wait on our food. It's too late to change the schedule, but I thought we'd go over it again to get everything fresh in our minds. Thank goodness COVID has died down, and we can have the festival. As usual, we will kick things off at ten o'clock with the festival of high school bands. At this time, I've got confirmation for fifteen area high school bands to be here to start us out with a parade, then like always the floats will make their way down Main Street to the park, where they will be parked on the side streets. Gladys, you've got the judges for the bands all lined up, right?"

"I've called in music teachers from Muenster, Gainesville, Nocona, and Lindsay," Gladys said. A short woman who was constantly dieting and had twice-weekly beauty shop appointments to keep the gray roots of her blonde hair from showing, she had always envied Ruth Ann's position as head of the festival planning committee, and it was no secret.

"And I've asked Don from the city council, our judge and one of his friends from Bowie, and Paul Taylor to judge the floats for us," Emogene said. "Same judges except for Harry Davis that we had last year."

"That's great." Ruth Ann nodded. "Then the kids on their decorated bicycles will come in behind the floats, and I've lined up judges for that from my Sunday school class."

Emogene giggled. "Remember back twenty years ago when we put the bicycles at the end of the parade?"

"Oh, yeah." Liddy laughed with her. "And then we got all kinds of complaints from their parents about them riding through horse crap. That's why the riding club on their horses come in behind the fire truck to finish up the parade."

"Sounds pretty traditional," Gladys said and then pointed toward the door. "Did someone invite Matilda Monroe to our meeting? I see her coming across the street."

"We did not!" Liddy declared.

"She's probably just coming in to get the lunch special," Gladys said.

"I invited her," Tina Adams, the newest member of the committee, spoke up. "I'm from Sweetwater. Matilda introduced me to my husband. They went to school together right here in Bonnet, and he thought it would be nice if we made her welcome in town."

"Holy crap!" Liddy muttered. "She got her hooks in before she even got here."

The battle of the funeral dinners had been just the first volley of the war, and Liddy wasn't sure she had the energy to mount a full-fledged strategy to put Matilda in her place.

Her deceased husband's voice popped into her head. *You don't have to do it all alone. You've got family.*

Who would have thought Max's trophy wife came from Sweetwater? Liddy argued. *We felt sorry for Maggie when he divorced her for the new woman thirty years younger than him, but I didn't know Matilda was behind the whole thing.*

You're falling down on your job, darlin'. She could swear she heard Marvin chuckle.

She kept her trembling hands under the table so no one could see how upset she was, but she couldn't stop grinding her teeth.

Ruth Ann laid a hand on Liddy's shoulder and leaned over to whisper in her ear. "We'll get through this. Don't stroke out on me. She's not going to win."

Thank God for family support, Liddy thought as she inhaled deeply and let it out very slowly. She took a sip of tea and managed a nod and smile toward Ruth Ann.

"Hello!" Matilda breezed into the café and sat down in the last empty chair right beside Tina. "Thank you, Tina, for inviting me. Sorry I'm a little late. What did I miss?"

Donna Sue—God love her soul—came to the table to get Matilda's order or Liddy might have given over to her desire to march down to Matilda's chair and knock her out of it. Liddy would gladly spend time in jail for assault for the privilege.

"You want sweet tea and the special, which is baked potato soup and your choice of a sandwich?" Donna Sue asked.

"No, I will have water with lemon, and a cucumber-and-tomato sandwich wrapped in a lettuce leaf instead of bread and no mayonnaise," Matilda said. "If you have avocados, you may slice one and lay it on the side of the sandwich."

Liddy appreciated the fact that Donna Sue kept a straight face and read back the order to her without even a hint of a giggle.

What did you expect her to order? the pesky voice in Liddy's head asked. *She wouldn't touch the loaded potato soup. It's got bacon in it.*

Do you think she would leave town if I turned a couple of good-sized hogs loose in her bedroom over at the B and B? Liddy's hands knotted into fists under the table.

"Since I was raised here in Bonnet and have been back to visit through the years, I know all of you ladies, but in case you don't recognize me, I'm Matilda Monroe, Harry Davis's sister. Nick Monroe is my son. Since *my* real estate business is part of the chamber of commerce, and Tina thought I might offer some suggestions to help out with the festival, I'm here to be of help to y'all." Matilda's gold bracelets clinked as she moved her hands with every word.

"*Your* real estate business?" Liddy raised an eyebrow.

"Well!" Matilda pasted on a fake smile, but the look in her eyes told Liddy to drop dead right there in the café. "Technically, it still belongs to my brother, but he's turned it over to my son, Nick, while he's gone on a vacation. Nick is much too busy settling in to attend this meeting, and besides, all of you know that it's a *family* business, and *my* family helped build this town. I've been told that the bands will be marching, one after the other, at the beginning of the parade that kicks the festival off. I suggest that you have a few floats in between the bands so one band doesn't drown out the next one. And really now, you should have the fire engine start off the parade."

Her smile was so saccharine that it made Liddy's teeth ache. "Who gave you the lineup?"

"I just asked Kayla Paulson, the secretary at the chamber of commerce, this morning when I went in to introduce myself," Matilda answered. "She agreed that the festival has gotten kind of boring and needs some revamping. I know we can't change a lot of what is already planned, but we could tweak it just a little." She held up a forefinger and thumb to measure about an inch.

I wouldn't give you a fraction of an inch, Liddy thought.

"That's something we could consider," Gladys said.

"The bands know that they play one after the other," Ruth Ann said. "No two play at the same time, and we've already printed and sent out the order of the lineup."

"Since it's only a few days away, I vote that we keep things as they are to avoid confusion," Ethel said.

"I second that motion," Liddy said.

"All in favor of leaving everything as is this year, raise your hand." Ruth Ann's hand shot up first.

Everyone around the table except Gladys and Tina raised a hand.

"Can you give us a reason you aren't voting with the majority, Miz Gladys?" Matilda asked.

"I think there's always room for improvement, and maybe the parade is getting to be boring," Gladys said.

"And you, Tina?" Matilda asked.

Tina tucked a strand of platinum-blonde hair behind her ear. She was so thin that a good strong gust of north wind would blow her all the way to the Gulf of Mexico. Liddy wondered what she looked like without that perfect makeup job she must have spent hours on every morning.

Tina tilted her chin up just enough to give the impression she was looking down on everyone at the table. "I think the Bluebonnet Festival is a great idea, and maybe Ruth Ann is right about not being able to do much about it this year. But I would like to see the bonnet contest done away with, and maybe instead we could have a Bluebonnet Bridal Show in conjunction with the festival to dress it up a little."

Matilda laid a hand on Tina's shoulder. "That's a brilliant idea. There are so many ways we can put new life into this age-old festival, and that would be number one in my book. It would draw all kinds of folks into town."

"Thank you," Tina said. "I had to go all the way to Dallas to attend a bridal show when Max and I got married last summer. March is a lovely time of the year to have one, and we could decorate the venue with bluebonnets to keep the theme."

Matilda removed her hand and took a sip of the water Donna Sue had set in front of her. "In my opinion high school bands are a little outdated, so maybe we could just do away with the parade and focus on the vendors and the carnival in the park next year and see how that works. And we really need a new banner to put up over Main Street. That one with the bluebonnets is kind of cheesy."

"I suppose you'd want to change the name of the festival to the Bridal Show Weekend?" Liddy asked.

"That would certainly be something to consider in the future," Gladys chimed in. "Tina and Matilda have a good point. Since the festival began, everything has been updated, so we should consider shaking things up a little. Just think about telephones, for instance, and computers, and vehicles—just to name a few."

"The festival is tradition. People come from miles around expecting and liking the fact that they can depend on it being pretty much the same year after year," Ruth Ann declared.

"I vote that we table all those suggestions until fall, when we begin to work on the one for next year," Liddy said.

Do not let her get under your skin, the voice in Liddy's head yelled.

Everyone started talking all at once, sounding like a bunch of buzzing bees in Liddy's ears. She glanced down the table to find Matilda smiling right at her. The feeling Liddy got was that the woman was bragging about causing a stir in what had always been an amicable meeting.

Ruth Ann tapped a spoon against her tea glass. When she had everyone's attention, she said, "We've voted to leave our traditional festival alone for this year, but I would like to suggest that if you think our festival is boring or needs updating, then"—she paused and focused on Matilda—"maybe you should start a bridal fair weekend. It could be a whole separate event from what us old-timers have come to love and respect in the Bluebonnet Festival and would possibly bring folks to Bonnet two weekends in March. Or you could bring the bridal fair to Bonnet in April, and that would give folks events to enjoy and look forward to for two separate months."

"People wouldn't come to a backwoods town like Bonnet two weekends in a month," Matilda said with half a shrug.

"If you feel like that about our town, then why are you moving here?" The whooshing noise in Liddy's ears told her that her blood pressure was rising.

Matilda lowered her chin just slightly and glared at Liddy. "Because I intend to turn this town around, and make it grow into something respectable."

"We're talking about two different dynamics here," Ethel said, jumping into the battle. "Brides would come from all around to your show, and the folks who are used to boring parades and bonnet competitions would come to our festival. I vote that we make Tina the chairman of a future committee for the bridal fair, and we will stay out of her business. Ruth Ann can remain the chairman of our regular Bluebonnet Festival, and since Tina will be so busy with her idea, she can step down and out of this committee."

"I second that vote," Liddy said.

"All in favor raise your right hand," Ruth Ann said.

The same hands went up that had a few moments before. "Let it be entered into the record that we have voted," Ruth Ann said. "Tina, I might suggest that you get a binder to keep all your notes in, and you probably want to start right now by finding a venue big enough for your bridal fair. Maybe it could be an open-air event at the park."

"I can take care of everything on my phone and my computer. I don't need an old-fashioned binder with papers in it," she grumbled as she pushed her chair back.

Matilda stood up and shot Liddy another go-to-hell look. "I'll be glad to sit on that committee with you, Tina."

"So will I." Gladys followed their lead and pushed her chair back. "And since Kayla, the chamber secretary, is my granddaughter, I reckon I can talk her into joining us. I hereby resign my position on this committee, Ruth Ann, so take my name off the roster. I'm disappointed in the whole lot of you here at this table for refusing to move on with the times, but then, at the same time, I'm not surprised."

"Thanks, Gladys and Matilda. Let's take our new committee to my house and discuss ideas," Tina said.

All three of them marched out of the café without even leaving money on the table for the meal, but Matilda took a moment to bend down and whisper in Liddy's ear, "Sell me that property out east of town and the building my brother's business is in, and I'll back off a little."

"Not over my dead body, but yours," Liddy said through gritted teeth.

"What did she just say?" Ruth Ann asked.

"That she would back off if I sell her the land," Liddy said out the side of her mouth and then turned toward the others. "Now, is there any new business?"

"Do you think Amelia and her friend from the school, Daniel, would take Tina's and Gladys's places?" Ethel asked. "We could use some young folks, and it would be nice to have a guy on the committee with us."

"I will ask them. All in favor of Amelia and Daniel joining us if they are willing, raise your hand," Liddy said.

All hands went up.

Donna Sue brought out the food and frowned as she glanced around the table.

"Just put what they've ordered on my ticket and then put it in the dumpster," Liddy told her.

"Shall we order dessert while Donna Sue is here?" Ethel asked.

"I think we deserve it," Ruth Ann fumed. "The very idea of turning our festival into a bridal show! That beats all I've ever heard."

"Honey, that's just the beginning of what we will have to fight for if we intend to keep our town like it is now," Liddy said with a long sigh.

Ethel nodded. "I figure there will never be a bridal show because Tina would have to work at it, and that woman is too involved with being pretty to work at anything."

"Or if she does succeed in starting one, Matilda would delegate all the work out to her recruits and then take all the credit if the show was a success," Liddy said.

"Or lay the blame on them if it wasn't," Ethel added.

"You got that right. We all know Matilda, and I, for one, feel like we have met the enemy head-on today, and we didn't lose an inch of ground. Let's all order blackberry cobbler with ice cream." Liddy told Donna Sue what they wanted. "And put the desserts for all of us on my ticket, too. I'm treating these folks today for standing for our traditions."

"Thank you," Emogene said with a smile that put even more wrinkles on her face, but it sure lit up her brown eyes. "This is just round one, ladies. When I heard Matilda was coming back to town, I figured we'd have to weather some storms. I just didn't think we would have a class-five tornado two days after she arrived."

"Oh, honey," Liddy chuckled, "that was just a little dust storm so Matilda could see where she stands. There will be a whole cluster of tornadoes before it's all finished."

Emogene heaved a heavy sigh. "I hate conflict."

The other women around the table nodded in agreement.

"I wish she would decide to go back to Sweetwater," Ruth Ann said. "From what Harry has said, Nick is a fine young man and nothing like his mother. I just hope he's not like his grandfather."

"Amen to that," Ethel said.

While they whispered about forty-year-old rumors, Liddy let her thoughts go back to the funeral dinner where it had been so evident that Nick was flirting with Amelia. She needed to have another talk with Amelia and remind her which side of the feud she had been born into. Nick was every bit as handsome as his grandfather Floyd Davis had been. Floyd could walk into a room, flash his smile, and women would begin to move toward him as if he were a magnet and they had metal underpants.

Besides being Matilda's son, Nick might have inherited a wandering eye and a penchant for cheating from his grandfather. That meant Liddy didn't want him anywhere near her precious niece.

"Do you ever wonder why his wife, Linda June, put up with him?" Emogene whispered.

"Probably because she was just as unfaithful to him as he was to her," Ethel answered. "The whole town always had doubts that Matilda belonged to Floyd. I wonder what she'd do if she ever found out about that little tidbit of gossip?"

"Maybe that's why Floyd left the business to Harry and the house to Matilda," Ruth Ann said. "Even if he was a philanderer, he would have wanted to be sure the family business was kept in the real family."

"Think she knows?" one of the other ladies asked.

"No, but she will if she ever has one of those fancy-schmancy DNA tests done," Ethel answered. "But then it might prove that she *is* Floyd's daughter after all, and she would figure out a way to say she was a Daughter of the Republic and her ancestors came over on the *Mayflower*."

"Long as she don't mess with our festival, she can claim she's a descendant of the queen of England," Liddy said.

"I taught world history, as you all know," Ruth Ann said, "and Matilda really was the name of one of the queens of England, though, boy, did she have a fight."

"Lord, don't tell Matilda that!" Liddy gasped. "She'll want the city council to buy her a crown and have a huge parade in her honor."

Aunt Liddy had told Amelia a while back that she was grooming her to help with the planning committee, so Amelia had planned to attend the meeting at the Bluebonnet Café that day. But just as she was walking out the door, she got a request from the principal to fill in for noon detention. The history teacher who normally took care of that had to rush his kindergarten-age son to the emergency room to have a rock that the boy had picked up on the playground removed from his nose.

"How does a kid get a rock in his nose?" she asked as she turned around and headed back to the detention room.

"Evidently, with great determination," the principal said with a chuckle. "Thanks for agreeing to monitor detention today."

"No problem." Amelia opened the door to the room and recognized the student sitting in one of the dozen cubicles. "All right, Creed, you know the drill. You are here for fifteen minutes of your lunch break. You are to face forward at all times and raise your hand if you want to speak. You may not lay your head down on your desk, and it would be best if you work on an assignment."

He nodded and opened a book.

Amelia checked her phone, allowed for the two minutes it had taken her to get to the room, and set an alarm for when he would be set free. She had really looked forward to having baked potato soup and a BLT sandwich from the café that day, but the job came first. She would just grab a pack of crackers and a container of milk from the teachers' lounge as soon as Creed was gone.

While she waited for the alarm to go off, she scrolled through her messages and found a message and a picture from Aunt Liddy: Guess who just showed up to our meeting? And there was a photo of Matilda Monroe. The woman looked like she had just walked out of a soap opera in her white pantsuit and all that gold jewelry.

What happened? Are you and Mama all right? Her thumbs were a blur as she typed.

She had barely gotten that sent when an answer came back. We are fine! Chalk up another one for us, zero for Matilda. Meet me for ice cream at the Dairy Queen right after school. I've got something to ask you.

Amelia typed a message back: I'll be there.

She was still staring at the screen when the alarm went off and startled her.

"That mean I can go?" Creed asked.

"Yes, it does," Amelia answered. "You may leave."

The tall, lanky kid with bright red hair and a face full of freckles stood up and shuffled slowly out of the room without a word. Amelia pushed back her chair, picked up her phone and car keys, and was closing the door when her phone pinged again. She kept walking toward the lounge but stopped dead in her tracks when she saw an unknown number pop up on her phone.

She hit the accept icon and read the short message: This is Nick Monroe. Is it all right if I call you?

She reread the message a dozen times and answered: Sure, but how did you get this number?

While she waited for his answer, she added his name and number to her contact list.

A door opened across the hall and Daniel Patterson, the high school chemistry teacher, smiled at her. They had both been newbies at Bonnet High School five years before, and over the years, they had become good friends. His fiancée taught kindergarten at the elementary school, and the two of them were constantly trying to fix Amelia up with one of their many friends.

"Everything okay?" he asked. "You look a little annoyed."

"I had to work detention and give up lunch, and I was planning to have hot potato soup and a BLT at the café with the festival planning committee," she answered.

"Then that's beyond annoyed. It's downright cranky, with hunger added to it. I wonder if that could be called cranger?" He headed on down the hallway toward his lab room and then turned around to say, "There's a pineapple upside-down cake in the lounge, and there's always bread and peanut butter in the cabinet."

"PB&J is a poor substitute for a hot lunch," she muttered as she made her way to the end of the hallway and went into the teachers' lounge.

She had the place all to herself, and Daniel had been right about the cake. There were two pieces left—one with a slice of pineapple, the other with half a slice. She eyed them both for a few seconds and then put the large square on a paper plate.

"Forget the peanut butter," she muttered. "If I can't be there to slap Matilda at least once, then I deserve this."

What about Nick's message? that pesky voice inside her head asked. *You know you can't encourage that.*

She went back to the countertop and put the last of the cake on her plate. Knowing that Matilda had crashed the committee meeting, plus dealing with Nick Monroe, was enough to earn her extra cake. Bridget claimed that stress ate up calories and fat grams. If that was true, then Amelia shouldn't even have to go for her evening jog.

Nick didn't seem like the jackass that her former boyfriend had been, but then neither had Elliott in the beginning. He had been so charming when she first met him, and then through a couple of years had worked his wiles on her, creating a woman to jump to his every whim and whisper. Maybe she shouldn't trust her own judgment when it came to guys. She'd dang sure messed up the last time that she did. She swallowed the last bite of the cake and then went over to the pan and scraped the edges. She checked the clock on the wall and found she still had ten minutes until the bell rang, so she called Bridget.

"Is everything all right?" Bridget answered in a worried tone. "You never call me during the day."

"Everything is fine, or at least I think it is. I've only got a few minutes. Have you heard from Aunt Liddy or Mama?" Amelia asked.

"Got a text from Mama," Bridget answered. "Can you believe the nerve of that woman?"

"She's out for war, but that's not why I called . . ." She went on to tell her sister all about the text she'd gotten from Nick, ending with, "What do you think?"

"That's a no-brainer," Bridget told her. "Number one, it's taken you two years to get over the Elliott fiasco. Number two, are you ready to meet your maker or maybe be committed to the *couyon* place? You know the history behind Matilda and Aunt Liddy. Do I need to say more? The devil can transform himself into many forms according to Granny Devereaux, even a sexy blond-haired guy with a smile that draws you to him like a moth to a red-hot flame. The answer is back away and leave that alone. My lunch break is over. Call me later tonight."

"Thanks, Sister," Amelia said as she ended the call.

She was digging out the last bite of cake that had hidden in the corner of the pan when her phone pinged. It was another text from Nick: I'd rather tell you face to face. Can we meet for ice cream?

"If I ate ice cream twice in one day and after all that cake, I'd have to jog from here to Dallas," she whispered, "and besides, if I was seen in public with Nick, Aunt Liddy would stroke out."

"Are the kids driving you crazy?" Daniel came into the lounge. "I see the cake is all gone. You must have had cranger for sure. Thank goodness Savannah sent me some cookies in my lunch or I'd be mad at you for even scraping out the pan." A short guy, with a crop of curly brown hair and a beard, he and Savannah, his fiancée, made the cutest couple.

"Why would you ask that?" she asked.

"You're talking to yourself," he said with a grin. "You only do that when you're ready to rain down Irish temper on someone."

"I guess that is the first sign," she agreed, "but I don't think I'm dangerous now that I had all that cake."

He put coins into the drink machine and hit the button for a root beer. "I'm taking this to the lab, but don't tell the kids. I don't let them bring anything to eat or drink into that room," he said as he headed for the door.

"I'll keep your secret if you don't tattle on me for talking to myself," she agreed.

"It's a deal." Daniel disappeared out into the quiet hallway.

What would Daniel say about Nick? she wondered as she headed back to her classroom.

The same thing I did, Bridget's voice in her head almost yelled.

Granny Dee had been right about the devil transforming himself into all forms. Elliott had proven that with his manipulation and control that had almost sent Amelia to that place Bridget mentioned. She hadn't heard the word *couyon* in a long time. It meant crazy, and her Louisiana cousins used it often when describing a person or even an event.

"I would be crazy to meet Nick anywhere at any time," she muttered as the bell rang and kids began to file into the classroom.

But that didn't mean she couldn't find out exactly where he got her phone number, now did it? After Elliott, she still had trust issues, and it would just be a onetime phone conversation with Nick Monroe. After all, Matilda was his mother—that alone was warning enough.

She sent a text that said: Call me after five.

Chapter Six

*L*iddy slid into a booth on the left side of the Dairy Queen so she could watch the people come and go outside the window. If Matilda showed her face, Liddy planned to send Amelia a text and tell her to come to Liddy's house, and they would make chocolate sundaes in her kitchen. She'd already put up with Matilda for fifteen minutes that day, and that was just about the limit of what she could stand for a year.

She remembered sitting in the same booth almost thirty years ago, watching for Richie. He'd come into the café with an expression that told her he wasn't going to listen to anything she had to say, but it was her job as his mother to be honest with him. He had crossed his arms over his broad chest and said, "If this is about Matilda, don't waste your breath, Mother."

That he had called her Mother, rather than Mama, had pricked her heart and put tears in her eyes. "She's using you to get back at me. She's never leaving Gregory and his money," Liddy had told her son that day.

"I love her, and she's promised me that she would divorce so we can be married," Richie had said.

"Hey!" Don Hollis, the president of the Bonnet City Council, interrupted her thoughts and brought her from the past to the present. "I've been meaning to call you. Got a minute?"

"Of course," Liddy said. "What's on your mind?"

Don slid into the other side of the booth. "We need to be thinking about filling Harry Davis's seat on the city council. It'll only be until the election in November, and he'd already told me that he wasn't running again this year. Is Paul going to leave office or run again?"

"He'd thought about packing it in, but with everything that's going on, he might change his mind," Liddy answered.

"He's sure been an asset to the community. When all of us old dogs retire, and I'm talking about myself since I qualified for Medicare this past month, I'm hoping the upcoming generation respects our traditions," he said.

"Then you'd better hope that Matilda Monroe doesn't have her way," Liddy told him.

"Ethel is my mother-in-law, as you well know, and she told me about the festival committee meeting. Looks like we could have a problem on our hands," Don said.

"No, sir!" Liddy shook her head. "What we've got goes beyond a problem. It's a full-fledged battle."

"Mr. Hollis, your order is ready," the lady behind the counter yelled across the room.

"Be thinking of someone to nominate at the next meeting"—Don slid out of the booth—"and call me if you get a good idea."

"I will do that." Liddy nodded. "If you decide on someone, let us know. I'll visit with Paul and Ruth Ann, but last I heard"—she lowered her voice—"Paul hadn't made up his mind about running again."

"I understand," Don said. "My youngest brother went to school with Matilda and your Richie. I remember that woman very well."

He went to the counter, got his order, and opened the door for Paul on his way out of the place. Liddy waved at her brother and motioned him over to her booth.

He sat down on the other side of the table from her and laid a hand on hers. "Are you all right? Ruth Ann is pretty steamed up over what happened. She's afraid your blood pressure went sky high. Have you checked it since the meeting was over?"

"Nope." Liddy used her free hand to pat his. "I can tell from the whooshing sound in my ears when it's high, and that's all gone now."

"I'd feel better if Bridget checked it, so I told her to drop by your house on the way home," Paul said. "Ruth Ann told me what Matilda said. That woman won't even get that land over my dead body. We've got it in our wills that the girls will inherit it, but it can't be sold. Besides, when I retire, Ruth Ann and I still plan to put in a catfish farm."

"She mentioned that you had other plans for it. I think that's a great idea."

"Why does Matilda think there's oil under that ground anyway?"

"Her daddy got that harebrained idea and she's still running with it," Liddy answered. "The company Marvin worked for believed that he could walk across a field and smell the oil under the ground. I don't know what his gift was, but if he told them to drill, they did, and if he told them not to waste their time, they listened to him, so he would know if there was oil under there. Marvin said that Floyd had drank too much of the moonshine his father made, and it affected his brain."

"I can hear Marvin saying that," Paul chuckled, "but I wouldn't care if there was oil out there. After the deal with Richie, I wouldn't sell her a blade of grass from that acreage. She can choose another place. There's land for sale all around here."

"But it's not the last big chunk of Taylor land, and she wants to lord it over me," Liddy told him.

"It's you who should be lording things over her," Paul said. "She's the one that led Richie on in high school, broke his heart, and then came back for the second time to break it again."

"I don't want to fight with her," Liddy said, "but I will."

"You won't be going into the battle alone," Paul said. "This whole family will put on our armor, load our weapons, and fight with you. If Matilda thinks she can whip the Taylor family, then she's got rocks for brains. I see Amelia parking out there, so I'll get on out of here and let y'all visit."

"Thank you for everything," Liddy said. "I don't think I could have made it through Richie's death without this family, and then for you and Ruth Ann to share the girls with me . . ." She pulled a napkin from the dispenser and dabbed at her eyes.

Paul stood up, and then leaned down to kiss her on the cheek. "Those were some tough days. Thank goodness we had family to lean on. You've always been like a second mama to me, and no one, especially not Matilda Monroe, is going to run roughshod over you."

"I've loved you more like a son than a brother." Liddy smiled up at him. "Family support means everything to me."

"And me." Paul crossed the floor and opened the door for Amelia. He said something to her, but Liddy couldn't hear it. Amelia nodded, so evidently she agreed with him.

Amelia slid into the place where her father had been sitting and eyed her aunt carefully.

"I feel like you are putting me under a microscope," Liddy chuckled.

"Are you okay?" Amelia asked. "Daddy said that Bridget is going to check your blood pressure, but should we just drive out to the ER and let her do it now instead of waiting? You look a little flushed."

"Like I just told your father, I'm fine. I love you all for worrying about me, but Matilda Monroe is not going to have the satisfaction of putting me in the grave." Liddy reached across the table and patted Amelia on the hand. "I was waiting for you to put in an order. I was too angry to eat very much at lunch, so I was thinking maybe I'd start with a burger or some tacos."

"I had to skip lunch and ate two pieces of pineapple upside-down cake, so I'm ready for some solid food. I think I'll have a double bacon cheeseburger and fries." Amelia stood up and headed toward the counter. "Matilda sure didn't put you in the ground today—just saying that makes me shiver—but she upset you if you didn't eat lunch. You love the potato soup they serve there."

Liddy walked along right beside her. "Matilda not only crashed our festival committee meeting, but before it was all over, she got Tina and Gladys both to resign. We thought maybe you and Daniel might take those positions. What do you think?"

"I'd be glad to help out, and I can ask Daniel tomorrow, but don't y'all usually meet on Tuesdays? That would be an iffy thing for me and Daniel," Amelia said.

"Can I help you?" the teenager behind the counter asked.

"I want the double bacon cheeseburger basket and a medium Diet Coke," Amelia said.

"Make mine the same, only I want a real root beer, not one of those diet things," Liddy said.

"But, Aunt Liddy, don't you know if you drink a diet soda pop with your meal, it cancels out all the fat grams and calories?" Amelia asked.

"At my age, honey, we don't count those things. We eat whatever we want," Liddy chuckled as she got out her billfold and laid two tens on the counter. "You can buy the ice cream if we are still hungry. I know what teachers get paid, so I'm buying supper tonight."

"Thank you." Amelia tucked her money back into her pocket, picked up the number the girl handed her, and headed back to the booth.

Liddy pocketed her change and followed Amelia. "You are very welcome, and the festival committee can meet for lunch on Saturdays if you and Daniel will join us. Or, for that matter, we can meet on Sunday afternoons after church, and if his fiancée, Savannah, will come, we'll add her to the group. I like that young woman. She's been a blessing to the church and even took on the job of teaching the five- to seven-year-old Sunday school class. We need some young folks to help out with civic events. Want to run for city council? I'll be your campaign manager and back you all the way."

"One thing at a time," Amelia said. "The festival will be enough for this year, and Daddy hasn't decided to give up his seat yet. I would never, ever run against my daddy."

"You might think about it when he does get tired of the position. He's been on the council for more than twenty years." Liddy slid back into her place in the booth.

"How many years *did* you work as the school secretary?" Amelia asked as she sat down across the table from Liddy.

"Forty." A visual popped into her mind of those first days. They were all so young looking with their big hair and short skirts. "I got the job when Richie started kindergarten. Clara was already working in the cafeteria, and Ethel had been teaching for several years. We became good friends. I sure miss Clara since she passed a few years back. I was glad to still have Ethel and your mama there today, though, when Matilda and Tina Adams tried to redo our whole festival. I sure wish you had been there."

"Me too," Amelia said. "Mama says when Daddy retires that she's turning the whole festival thing over to me, like you did to her when you quit working at the school. Hopefully, if I sit on the committee, I'll be prepared for it in another ten years when she and Daddy start catfish farming." She then told Liddy what had happened with detention. "Just why would a kid shove a rock up his nose?"

"Bless their little hearts." Liddy giggled. "They don't think before they act at that age, and sometimes other kids will dare them, and they just have to prove themselves. I remember when Richie put a bead up his nose. He was about four, and it was one of those three-sided things. The doctor had a devil of a time getting it out."

"Makes me wonder if I ever want to have kids, and the very thought of losing a child like you did . . ." She shivered. "I can't imagine the heartache and pain." She clamped a hand over her mouth. "I'm so sorry, Aunt Liddy. I didn't mean to bring up bad memories."

"Losing Richie in that accident just about killed me, but I wouldn't trade the experience of being a mother for anything. So, don't be afraid to have children." Liddy reached across the table and laid a hand on Amelia's arm. "But back to the festival meeting. Matilda came in with an attitude that said, 'Look at me. I'm important in my expensive clothes and jewelry, and I'm going to run this festival whether y'all like it or not.'" She then told Amelia what Matilda had said. "It looks like she's gathered a posse for herself right now to try to shatter all of our traditions. Gladys has joined her, and Tina, and I'm sure she's added Kayla from down at the chamber. Poor folks don't know that they're victims, not friends."

"Is she crazy?" Amelia asked. "Daddy would never sell a piece of Taylor property, and why does she want it anyway?"

"She doesn't leave a string of dead bodies everywhere she goes, but she does walk all over anyone in her path to get her way, which is about the same thing." Liddy almost recanted that statement when she remembered her own son's body in that casket—and all because of Matilda.

"And?" Amelia asked.

"And," Liddy replied, "I could be wrong, but I believe she blames me for her not being rich. Her granddad and her father both wanted that piece of land, and Floyd—that would be her father—was convinced there was oil on it. She must have the mistaken idea that if they'd had oil money, she would have been superrich. I don't understand why she would want more than she had. Floyd and Linda gave her everything she wanted when she was growing up."

The teenage girl from behind the counter brought their food out on a tray and set it in the middle of the table. "Anything else I can get you?"

"Not that I can think of, but maybe later we'll order some ice cream. Thank you for bringing this to us," Amelia answered.

"Just holler if you need anything." She left to wait on a bunch of schoolkids that were lining up in front of the counter.

Amelia popped a french fry into her mouth and ate it while she removed the wrapper from her cheeseburger. "I never knew about the land, but I did hear that she was the cause of Richie's death. Mama said we weren't to talk about it because it would upset you, but what happened?"

"He was twenty-two," Liddy answered. "He had graduated from college in May and the wreck happened in June."

"Was Matilda in the car with him?" Amelia took the first bite of her burger.

"No, she wasn't," Liddy answered.

"Then why—" Amelia started.

Liddy butted in before she could finish. "She and Richie had dated in high school, and she was spoiled and wild even back then. I was so glad when she broke up with Richie, even though it broke his heart. He really thought he was in love with that girl. Then she moved to Sweetwater and got married, and I thought all my problems were over, and everything was going to be fine. A year or two after she married Gregory, she gave birth to Nick. I even hoped that maybe motherhood would settle her down and she would think of someone other than herself. I was wrong on all counts. She had come back to Bonnet to visit her folks when Nick was just a toddler. I remember seeing Harry toting him around town."

"Aunt Liddy, it makes me hurt for you just hearing the sadness in your voice," Amelia said. "Let's talk about something else."

"It's all right," Liddy assured her. "Sometimes it helps to talk about things and not hold them inside. You know that even better than I do since you had a therapist after the Elliott ordeal."

"Absolutely," Amelia agreed. "I didn't realize that he was even telling me how to style my hair and what to wear until I talked to the therapist. I should have seen how he was tearing down my self-esteem and turning me into his own puppet."

"We were all so busy with our own lives that we didn't see it either until it was almost too late." Liddy gave her arm a gentle squeeze. "Right now, though, I want to tell you what happened so you understand why you should stay away from Nick. It doesn't matter what kind of person he is. His mother would be horrible to deal with." Liddy hoped that Amelia was listening to every word. "That year that Richie came home from college, I found out she had been calling him, and they were meeting on the sly at the park, at a motel, anywhere they could be alone. I confronted her about it. I'll admit that I didn't want Richie to date her in high school, and I damn sure didn't want him mixed up with a married woman. She told me to go to hell, that she would ruin my family any way she could because the Taylors kept her family from getting rich. I called Richie, had him meet me right here in this same booth, and told him exactly what she said."

"Oh! My!" Amelia felt like leaving the booth. "We shouldn't be sitting here. We need to go across the room. That's too much for you after the day you've already had."

"It's okay, sweetie." Liddy assured her with a smile. "It's just a booth. I told him, and he didn't believe me."

Amelia swallowed fast to keep from spewing Coke all over the table. "No wonder you don't like her."

"That's putting it mildly," Liddy said. "The way I felt about her started when she and Richie were in high school. They had been dating for several months their senior year, and he invited her to the prom. He had ordered her corsage and had even gotten his tux vest to match her dress. Two days before the prom, she broke up with him to go with another boy. Richie refused to go at all, and I wanted to wring her neck and then throw her out in the pasture for the coyotes."

"And then?" Amelia leaned forward, hanging on every word now.

"Then he went to college, dated a few girls, even brought one home that I actually liked. I hoped she was the one that would make him forget all about Matilda," Liddy said, "but then Matilda brought her son to Bonnet for a visit. When I found out she had Richie wrapped around her finger again, I cornered Matilda. She informed me that she just wanted a fling and then she was going back to her husband. She said that Richie could never support her in the lifestyle she was accustomed to since she had married Gregory, and that money was better than sex any day."

"Did you tell Richie?" Amelia asked.

"I did, and from what I learned later, he had gone straight to the house and talked to her. She basically told him the same thing. He drove over to a bar near Muenster, got drunk out of his mind, and wrecked his car on the way home," Liddy said. "I never forgave her and probably never will."

"But why would she still carry a grudge against you?" Amelia asked.

"Because I just might be the only person who ever stood up to her, and honey, I was not kind when I confronted her," Liddy answered. "And then there's the issue with the land, and the family owns the building where Harry has his real estate office, which, by the way, has been fully checked out and is safe. There's nothing in the place that could have caused Jack's or Wanda's death."

Amelia saw the pain still in Liddy's eyes, even after nearly three decades had passed. She loved her aunt so much that she fought tears in her own eyes, and her heart was heavy with grief for a cousin that she hadn't even known.

Pain and guilt mingled together would probably always haunt Liddy. If she hadn't cornered Matilda, if she hadn't told Richie what was said, he might be alive today. Granted he wouldn't be married to Matilda, because like the woman had said, money was more important to her than Richie. But things might have turned out different if he'd found out on his own what kind of woman she was. For that, Liddy would always have to carry part of the burden of her only child's death.

"Oh, Aunt Liddy, I'm so sorry," Amelia said, "but I'm sorrier for Richie because he got duped so badly."

"She came from a long line of"—Liddy paused and wondered if she hadn't already told Amelia more than she should, but she went on—"folks who didn't value their marriage vows. Rumor had it that she might have been fathered by one of her mother's many affairs."

"Good grief, Aunt Liddy! This all sounds like a bad soap opera."

"Yes, it does, and that's the background that Nick comes from. Cheating grandparents, a cheating mother, and evidently a cheating father, since Gregory divorced Matilda for another woman." Liddy nodded.

"But maybe he's a good man and not at all like his relatives. Daddy has said that Harry was the only good Davis. Nick could be more like him," Amelia said.

Liddy dipped a french fry in ketchup, started to put it in her mouth, but laid it aside for a moment. "Honey, the apple does not fall far from the tree. Harry was a philanderer, but at least he never married. I heard that he said the Davis line would end with him. Everyone in Bonnet knows that his grandfather was a womanizer, too, but that Harry's grandmother—that would be Nick's great-grandmother—was a religious woman who just looked the other way."

"You might be right about that apple business. Daddy always told me that I didn't fall far from the Irish tree," Amelia said. "Ever think that maybe Nick takes after his great-grandma?"

"You got a double dose of sass and temper from your mama and from me, but I don't know where that sweet and kind heart of yours comes from unless it's from your Granny Devereaux. But honey, I wouldn't take a chance on Nick getting any DNA from his grandma's side of the gene pool. Now that you know why I can't stand Matilda, and how she behaves herself, you beware of her. Even if Nick is a good man, I wouldn't want you saddled with that woman for a mother-in-law."

"Yes, ma'am." Amelia nodded.

Nick leaned back in his office chair and watched a couple of squirrels playing chase in a live oak tree in the area between him and the next building. Years ago, there had been a liquor store there, but it had burned to the ground when he was a teenager. He envied those two squirrels and their freedom that afternoon. They didn't have to worry about a mother who tried to run their lives or tell them who they could flirt with or not. All they had on their minds that sunny day was chasing each other and maybe stopping long enough to dig up a pecan to eat.

"Nick, where are you?" His mother's voice cut through the peace and contentment like a hot knife through butter.

"I'm in my office," he replied, raising his voice.

His mother was a force, no matter where she went. Not in a good way, either, but more like flat-line winds or even a tornado ripping up emotions and leaving a mess in her wake.

"I swear!" She burst through his door without so much as a customary knock and sat down in one of the chairs across the desk from him. "This town is so stuck in its damned old traditions that a jackhammer couldn't shake them loose. Tina invited me to the festival meeting, so I went."

"Oh my God, Mother!" Nick sat up straight in his chair. "You know very well that Ruth Ann Taylor and her family take care of the festival. That would be like slapping a hornet's nest with your bare hands."

"I'm going to bring Liddy Latham to her knees before I die, and I dug part of the hole I intend to bury her in today," Matilda said.

"Why do you hate Liddy so much?" Nick asked.

"I've got my reasons." Matilda stood up. "Did you even notice that I've finally got the last of all the sentimental crap Wanda had hanging everywhere boxed up and ready to take to the dumpster out back?"

"I saw some boxes beside the desk in the front office." He was still stunned that his mother had gone so far as to bait Liddy in public, and now he was overly curious about why those two women despised each other. Nick was determined to find out the whole story if he had to march over to Liddy's house some evening and ask her to tell him what happened.

"Just like a man," Matilda huffed. "You don't really see anything."

"What's that supposed to mean?" Nick asked.

"Men are blind for the most part," she snapped. "I've called a painter to come and redo these walls next week, and I've ordered a decent desk—one that's got a lovely glass top and black metal legs."

"Are you paying for a new paint job and for the desk?" Nick asked.

Her bracelets rattled when she popped her hands on her hips. "I am most certainly not. The business can purchase the desk and pay the painter."

"The business—that would be me—will not be paying for anything right now. I'd suggest that you cancel both the hired help and the order, or else *you will* be writing a check for them out of your personal account," Nick said, "and I will be going over the finances each evening, so don't try anything shady."

"Working with you is as bad as I imagined it would be to work with Harry." Matilda gave him a dirty look and picked up the phone.

"You're working *for* me, Mother, and that's just until I find a full-time office manager," Nick said. "We both know that neither of us would ever survive a long-term office relationship."

"I might just start my own real estate firm and run you out of business. Wouldn't it be a shame if you were the cause of Harry's precious family real estate business finally closing its doors? It's not fair that he got all of Daddy's support, and I had to get married to get ahead." She waved her hand around the office.

"You just jump out there, rent a building, and put in a real estate business if that's what you want to do," Nick said, "but before you do, cancel that desk order and tell the painter not to come. And as for Uncle Harry, I want to grow up and be just like him."

"You don't have to grow up for that—you are already like him and your father, and you can write that down in stone," Matilda said.

"Maybe I'll just have it fixed on a plaque and hang it in my office," Nick suggested. "It will say something like, 'Uncle Harry is a fine man. I want to be like him.'"

Matilda set her jaw like she always did just before she spewed out something about how he was a worthless son. "I could have been the queen of this place if—"

"If what?" Nick butted in. "How was that land going to make you rich? According to Uncle Harry, y'all weren't dirt poor, anyway, so why did you want to have more?"

"You can never have too much money, and money is power. And you mark my words, I will own that land and drill for oil before I'm dead," Matilda said. "And when I do, I'm going to rub it in Liddy's face. And while I'm waiting to buy it, I might start a gym. God knows there's enough women in this backwoods town who need to shape up their bodies. Most of them look like they've been eating Liddy's lemon pie for breakfast, dinner, and supper every day."

"I love both of her pies, but I've got to admit that her lemon chess is my favorite. But if you're going to put in a gym, why don't you make it double duty and add a vegan store in the same building. That would guarantee that you'd be broke in six months," Nick suggested. "This is small-town Texas, Mother. People like the way they do things, and they don't want to change. Get used to it or go back to Sweetwater."

"Some days I don't like you at all," Matilda told him.

"Only some days?" Nick asked.

She ignored his remark and slung her purse over her shoulder. "I'm going to the B and B, and if I don't come in tomorrow morning, you can blame yourself for being so hateful about me redecorating the office."

"I'm surprised that you're even coming in this place at all after all that fuss about getting a lawyer and suing the Taylors for causing Jack and Wanda's deaths," he said.

"Don't you even get me started on that," she growled. "I don't believe those inspectors, and I do not intend to stay in this building more than a couple of hours at a time. The only reason Harry isn't dead is because he has that milkshake habit and left this place twice a day to walk down to the Dairy Queen for his chocolate shake. The milk probably coated his insides and kept the poison from seeping into his brain and heart."

"Maybe I'll start having a milkshake twice a day," Nick teased.

"Don't you"—Matilda shook her finger at Nick—"joke about something this serious. I would have gladly paid a lawyer if he could have won a case against those damn Taylors. I've got one hired now to go back through all the paperwork on that land I want. If there's one discrepancy in the titles, I'll figure out a way to take it from Liddy, and the next week, there'll be drillers out there."

"Good Lord, Mother!" Nick gasped. "That's downright mean."

"Yes, it is, and I don't give a damn. It's a sin to waste land like that." Matilda stormed out of the building.

Nick stared at the walls that looked bare and slightly stained where the pictures had hung. Then he picked up the screwdriver lying on the desk and hung every single picture back up.

"Like I said, Mother," he muttered, "this is a small town. They don't want to change, and neither do I. I like things just the way they are here in Bonnet. Take it or leave it. I can manage to run this place on my own until I can hire some help if I have to. And you're one to be talking about sinning, now, aren't you?"

Just before he closed the door, he took one more look at the office and smiled at the picture that had hung on the wall since he was a child. It showed big black clouds on one side and a bright sunset on the other, and below the picture was written, "This, Too, Shall Pass."

"I sure hope that it's right," he muttered as he got into the old company Jeep. He started the engine and wondered, like he had done so many times through the years, if the storm would pass or if it would destroy the lovely sunrise. Stepping into the office, being his own boss was like watching a brand-new dawn, but his mother was like dark storm clouds threatening to ruin the day.

"Always been like that," he reminded himself, "and probably will never change."

He didn't feel like cooking, so he drove to the Dairy Queen and ordered half a dozen tacos to go. Then he went home to his new house that probably wasn't far from being a hundred years old. Vera met him on the porch and rubbed around his ankles as he unlocked the door.

"Where have you been?" he asked as he reached for the phone and scrolled down the contact list until he found his Uncle Harry's name. "I looked all over this place for you last night."

"Hello, how are things in Bonnet?" Harry answered on the first ring. "Has Matilda come close to driving you crazy yet?"

"That happened the first hour on Monday morning," Nick answered. "Vera must've slipped out past me yesterday. She just now came home. When did you get her, anyway? She wasn't here when I came for Thanksgiving."

"She arrived on my doorstep one stormy night at Christmas. Poor thing was wet and hungry. I adopted her and got her fixed at the vet, so you don't have to worry about kittens. I should have done that to your mother." Harry chuckled and then went on. "Course then if I'd had Matilda fixed, I wouldn't have a nephew to leave the business to, so I guess it all worked out all right."

"Things sometimes do work out right, Uncle Harry. Miz Vera is pretty sneaky about getting in and out of the house, isn't she?" Nick asked.

"Yep," Harry said. "I bet she snuck out when I left yesterday morning."

Nick stooped down and petted the cat while she ate. "I'll have to be more aware of this critter. I like her too much to lose her."

"I should fess up. I didn't really want or need a cat, but I got to thinking about Matilda and how much it would aggravate her if I had one, so I kept her, and I named her Vera after an old girlfriend. My first love, and like they say, you never forget your first," Harry told him. "But that's a whole nother story."

Nick straightened up, got a beer from the fridge, and carried it to the living room with Vera right behind him. "Uncle Harry, what is this thing between you and Mother? Do you know why she hates Liddy Latham so much, and why she would forbid me to call or see Liddy's niece? I knew about the land dispute. Mother bitched about it pretty often, and she blamed Liddy for the fact she wasn't rich, but this thing seems to be a lot more personal than even that."

"It would take more than one conversation to tell you about me and Matilda, but I can tell you that Liddy Latham blamed Matilda for her son's death. You were almost two that summer, so you won't remember any of what went on. Matilda came home for a visit. She had a fling with Richie—that would be Liddy's son and Matilda's old high school flame. Liddy begged her to break it off with him, but"—Harry paused—"your mother broke that boy's heart. He got drunk and died in a car wreck. She didn't pour the alcohol down his throat, but she caused that wreck just the same. She and Liddy . . . well, it was better when Matilda stayed out of Bonnet."

"Were Mother and Daddy separated or getting a divorce at the time?" Nick asked.

"No, they weren't," Harry said. "Your daddy had and has money. Matilda said that a fling was good for a marriage, but that money was better than sex, so she would never leave your father."

"Then she cheated long before he did?" Nick frowned.

"I wouldn't know about that, but most likely that's the way it went. Matilda does what she wants, when she wants, uses people to get her way, and not many people have ever stood up to her. Liddy Latham and I might be the only two," he answered. "She can't stand it when anyone doesn't agree with her. You should know that by now, son."

"No wonder she forbade me to go out with Amelia," Nick said.

"Don't drink the poison," Harry chuckled.

"What's that supposed to mean?" Nick asked.

"Remember the story about Romeo and Juliet?" Harry asked.

"Oh, I see what you mean," Nick said. "Or maybe this is the Hatfields and the McCoys?"

"You might do well to back off from Amelia. Either Liddy will kill you, or your mama will shoot Amelia. Either way, one or both of you will end up dead," Harry cautioned.

"Thanks for the advice and for telling me." Nick felt more than a little bit numb at the idea of his mother, even with all her narcissistic ways, cheating on his father.

"You need to know since you're going to be living in Bonnet," Harry said. "Now let's talk about something else. Are you back in the office yet? What did the inspectors find?"

"They cleared the building, and I'm working out of the office." Nick was still trying to process what had happened in his mind. He wanted more details, but Harry was clearly through talking about what happened all those years ago. "Mother is livid that they couldn't find anything. She was going to sue the Taylor family for two million dollars."

"I never thought there was. If something had been that deadly in the building, I would have gotten it, too," Harry said. "I bet my sister really is madder'n hell that she can't bring a suit against the Taylors. Serves her right for being so ugly to Liddy."

"I'm not sure that there's anyone in hell that's as mad as she is," Nick answered. "Did you know that she's hired a lawyer to check everything on the land the Taylors own? She swears she will take it away from them if he finds any kind of discrepancy."

"My dad tried that forty or fifty years ago. There's nothing to find, so she's throwing her money away on a wild-goose chase," Harry said. "But enough about Matilda. That's a depressing subject. I'm in Mississippi in a sweet little hotel. Got a pizza and a six-pack of beer right here beside me, and I'm looking forward to watching the sun set over the Gulf of Mexico tomorrow night in Florida. You have a good night, son, and if it rains this week, you might ought to practice running between the raindrops."

"Why would I do that?" Nick asked.

"So that you can be really good at dodging bullets. Bye now." Harry ended the call.

Nick smiled at what Harry had said even though he'd heard it dozens of times through the years. Every time he called his uncle to vent, Harry would tell him to dodge the bullets coming from his mother when she was on a rampage about something.

He walked to the table, sat down, and unwrapped his first taco. "Well, Vera, it looks like this little town has a lot of secrets, and some of them put me smack in the middle of a big mess."

Chapter Seven

When the phone rang, and Amelia saw that the caller was Nick Monroe, she was two ways about answering it. Why start something that had no finish line in sight? But then, why judge a man by his parents and grandparents? On the fifth ring, she picked it up.

"Hello," she said.

"Hi, this is Nick. It's after five, and—"

She butted in before he could finish. "Are you aware of the history between your mama and my Aunt Liddy? And, for that matter, between the Davis and Taylor families?"

"I knew part of it, and I found out some of the rest about five minutes ago," he answered. "How long have you known?"

"An hour," Amelia said.

"Why did you answer the phone?" Nick asked.

"The same reason you called," she told him. "To tell you that it would probably be best for us not to have ice cream or even be talking to each other."

"Then how about dinner?" Nick asked. "I know a funeral is a crazy place to meet a woman. Yet are we going to let some old history ruin what might be a great friendship?"

Hell yes, you are! Aunt Liddy screamed loudly in her head.

"I can't hurt Aunt Liddy's feelings, and I refuse to sneak around at my age. And I came out of a bad relationship two years ago," she said.

"Hey, I'm not down on one knee with a ring in my hands." Nick thought of the expression on his mother's face when he jokingly told her that he had proposed to Amelia. "I'm not in the market for a relationship, either. My mother is worse than the bubonic plague. I'm just looking for someone to talk to, maybe grab a beer or a pizza with occasionally, but no strings attached." After his mother had sabotaged two relationships, he'd dubbed her an emotional vampire and decided to become a bachelor like his Uncle Harry.

"Tell me, Nick Monroe, how does a friendship work between us? Have you ever heard of the Hatfields and McCoys?" Amelia asked.

"Well, we could talk on the phone," he suggested.

There was a lull in the conversation. Amelia already had a guy friend in her life. Daniel was nice and safe since he was engaged, and she loved Savannah. She visited with Daniel at school, and since she, Daniel, and Savannah all lived in the same apartment building, they were all in and out of each other's places through the week.

"Well? I could use a friend," Nick finally said. "I'll buy you a pizza supper on Friday night."

"Are you *couyon*? That means crazy in Cajun," she explained. "We can't be seen in public together, not even as friends."

"Then let's do a virtual supper. I'll have a pizza delivered to each of our houses, and we can talk while we eat," he suggested.

"And how are you going to do that? The minute you send a pizza to my apartment, the rumors will start, and everyone will know that you did it, and besides, you never told me how you got my phone number." Amelia seemed to run out of breath. "So, fess up. Did Daniel give it to you?"

"Nope, and who is Daniel?" Nick asked.

"He's my friend who teaches at the school with me," she answered.

"Don't know him, but if you're involved with someone . . ."

"He's engaged to Savannah, who teaches kindergarten. We're not involved in anything other than a very good friendship," Amelia answered.

Nick didn't realize he was holding his breath until it all came rushing out. There had definitely been flirting with Amelia at the funeral dinners, but to get involved with her would probably send the whole town of Bonnet up in flames. Fate, or destiny, or the universe was a real bitch to put a woman in his path who caused such an attraction. He was playing with fire to even talk to her on the phone, but he was drawn to her like the old proverbial moth to the candle flame.

"Okay," Amelia agreed. "One virtual type of supper, but only if we each order our own pizza. Anything else and the gossip would reach my family's ears, as well as your mother's, before they even delivered our food. They would both be knocking on our doors before the pizza man even got the pies out of the oven."

"It doesn't sit well with me to ask you to have supper with me and then not treat," Nick said.

"That's what friends do," Amelia answered. "We can talk while we eat, and then at seven, I have to go over to Aunt Liddy's place and help take care of some final stuff for the festival."

"Where does she live?" Nick asked.

"Diagonally across the street from you," Amelia answered. "She kept me a lot when I was a little girl, and we'd have a snow cone every day."

"Then I will be on the porch and wave at you when you drive by," Nick said.

"You are a daredevil," Amelia said with half a giggle. "Even that might get one or both of us shot. Good night, Nick."

"Are we getting dressed up for the evening?" He didn't want the conversation to end.

"You'll be able to recognize me. I'll be wearing a pair of bibbed overalls, a T-shirt with Daisy Duck on the front, and flip-flops," she answered, "and my hair will be in a ponytail. And you still haven't answered my question. How did you get my number?"

"That sounds downright sexy." Nick visualized her wearing such an outfit and loved the picture.

Good God, Son! Matilda's voice popped into his head. *I've raised you better than that. Besides, I will disown you if you have anything to do with that woman. Don't do this if you love me.*

"That proves that you are crazy, and that's not something a friend would say," Amelia scolded. "Now, this is really good night."

"Whoa! Don't hang up just yet. Let me answer your question so you don't think I'm a stalker, and since I've never had a girl-type friend, I'm not real clear on the rules. A few months ago, you came into the real estate agency looking for a small house preferably in town to purchase," he said. "I found the file today when I was looking through things at the office. It surprised me that a Taylor would even consider doing business with a Davis."

"I remember filling out a form. You still have it on file?" she asked. "And Harry ran the only real estate business in Bonnet. I didn't have a lot of choice."

"Yes, ma'am, and for some reason, it was still in my Uncle Harry's tray on his desk. I guess, since he hadn't followed up on finding something to show you, he just never gave it to Wanda to file. Is that an omen or what?" he asked.

"And my phone number, as well as Aunt Liddy's, was listed," she said. "I can't imagine why the form was still there. I called Wanda and told her that when my dad found out I was thinking about buying a place, he offered to give me an acre out on our property where he and Mama live, and where Bridget and Clovis have built a home."

"Just one of those things, I guess." Nick cleaned up the trash from his tacos and headed to the living room.

"Well, that clears that up," Amelia said. "Good night, again."

"Good night, Amelia." Nick sat down on the sofa beside Vera, who yawned and moved over into his lap. He stroked her long fur and said, "It's just me and you from now on, girl. Mother is probably about to disown me for even just talking to Amelia, but it feels right, and who knows? Maybe I'll change my mind about being a bachelor if she does toss me to the curb. Then in a year or two I'll find a good woman like Uncle Harry told me to do."

Amelia tossed and turned, counted sheep, and even tried singing the old thing about beer on the wall in her mind, but nothing worked. The next morning, she parked beside Daniel and they got out of their vehicles at the same time.

He waved and walked over, and they crossed the parking lot together. "Girl, you look like you had a rough night."

"I did." Amelia covered a yawn with the back of her hand. "I did something stupid."

"You didn't!" Daniel stopped in his tracks.

"I didn't what?" Amelia took one more step and then turned to face him.

"Did you go over to the bar on a school night and pick up a guy?" Daniel asked.

"No, I did something even worse." She laughed at the very idea. "It would take at least two hours to tell you the story."

"Then let's go to your room and you can give me the shortest version possible." He led the way to her classroom and stood to the side while she unlocked the door. "Is this a past or present guy?"

"How do you know it's about a guy?" Amelia turned on the lights, adjusted the thermostat, and then sat down behind her desk.

"Because you've got bags under your eyes, just like you did after the Elliott thing," Daniel said. "Please tell me that you haven't let him back into your life. If you did, I'm telling your mama and Liddy. The way he controlled you, down to telling you that you couldn't be friends with me and Savannah anymore, was horrible."

"It's not Elliott," Amelia sighed, "but in some ways it's even worse."

"I don't see how it could be." Daniel slumped down into a desk in front of her and pointed to the clock. "Ten minutes now. Talk to me."

"There's history—Romeo and Juliet or maybe Hatfield and McCoy history involved—and dating is out of the question. Friendship might not be, and so I agreed to talk to him on the phone Friday night while we eat pizza at the same time." She gave him the shortest version she could of the story and watched his eyes widen out further and further with each sentence.

"Holy smoke, Amelia!" Daniel gasped when she finished. "You've told me about Matilda and the feud, so you know you can't do this, don't you? Have you talked to Bridget, or your parents? I know you haven't said anything to Liddy because the town is still standing."

"He doesn't really know anyone in town," Amelia said. "Maybe I can tell him that you'd be his new buddy?"

"Oh, hell no!" Daniel shook his head. "I'm not getting in the middle of the battle. Savannah would shoot me. She's good friends with your mama and Aunt Liddy."

"You ever think about what would have happened if a Hatfield had fallen in love with a McCoy, or if Romeo and Juliet had left the poison alone? Maybe if Nick and I were friends, Matilda and Aunt Liddy would bury the hatchet."

"That will happen three days after hell freezes over," Daniel told her. "Your Aunt Liddy won't ever forgive Matilda for causing her son's death, even if it was in a roundabout way."

"Then tell me not to do this, Daniel. Be a good friend and tell me that I'm playing with fire," Amelia said. "You helped me see that Elliott was bad for me."

"You got to figure that out, but you know the answer already." Daniel glanced up at the clock and stood. "I've got my own Romeo and Juliet going on, and that's why Savannah and I are going to Vegas to get married." He took the first step toward the door just as the bell rang. "You've got to do what your heart tells you."

"Thanks for listening and for reminding me of that," Amelia said.

"Anytime," he said as he crossed the room. "That's what friends do."

She made it through the three classes before noon, but within a minute after the bell rang and the kids headed for the cafeteria, Daniel knocked on her door. She motioned for him to come in, and he brought a brown bag with him and sat down in one of the desks in the front row.

"Savannah sent me a text saying that she has a meeting with the other kindergarten teachers, so I'm alone. Thought maybe I'd have my lunch in here unless you've got other plans." He tore into an individual package, took out a wet wipe, and cleaned the desk. "Never know what these kids might leave behind."

"Glad for the company." Amelia picked up her tote bag and took out a thermos of soup.

"I've thought about your predicament all morning," Daniel said between bites of his sandwich. "If you need a woman's opinion and you're afraid to talk to Bridget, Savannah might be willing to help out."

"I appreciate the offer. If I get to feeling like I'm drowning, I might show up on her doorstep." She smiled as she removed a bowl of salad from her tote bag and wished for a pizza—something loaded with fat grams and calories—to take her mind off all the vibes she felt when she got the messages from Nick. Food, she had discovered, after Elliott controlling that aspect of her life, too, was her go-to when she was either nervous or angry.

Daniel laid a baggie with two cookies on her desk. "Savannah knows how I love sweets, so she always sends extra. And with what's weighing on your heart, cookies might help."

"Tell her thank you." Amelia pulled the bag closer to her and had a cookie instead of her salad. "Aunt Liddy says that life is short, so eat dessert first."

"Smart woman," Daniel said.

Amelia had really planned to go home as soon as school was over and call Bridget. Her sister had been her rock when she had finally broken up with Elliott and had even adjusted her schedule to go along to her weekly therapy sessions over in Gainesville for more than a year. But as she was walking across the parking lot, she got a text from Liddy: I need to go to Gainesville. Amos Denton died. I'll need to make pies, and I'm out of supplies. Will you go with me?

She sent one back: Just leaving school. Be there in five minutes. But we're not going anywhere until Bridget checks your blood pressure. She'll be leaving the hospital in just a few minutes.

Amelia and Bridget pulled into the driveway at the same time.

"How is she?" Bridget asked before she even closed her car door.

"Angry at the memories Matilda has brought back to the surface," Amelia said as the two sisters started toward the front porch.

Liddy stepped out and held out her arm. "Get it over with so Amelia and I can go shopping for groceries."

"Oh, no!" Bridget shook her head. "You march yourself back into the house and sit down in your recliner. Prop your feet up for fifteen minutes and get all calmed down. Then we'll take your blood pressure."

Liddy let out a lungful of pent-up air so hard that she snorted. "This is ridiculous. I know my body, and I know when my blood pressure is up. My ears get a whooshing sound."

Bridget pointed. "In the house. Feet up. If it's low enough, you can go shopping, so you better put Matilda out of your mind and think happy thoughts."

Liddy marched into the house and plopped down in her favorite recliner. "What would give me happy thoughts is making a lemon pie with extra eggs and sugar for Matilda's funeral."

"Legs up so you are relaxed." Bridget and Amelia sat down on the sofa.

"We could be halfway to Gainesville in the time I have to sit here and wait. I've got better things to do than watch the bluebonnets grow," Liddy fumed.

From a distance, her aunt always looked small and frail to Amelia. Up close was a different matter. When she was right there beside her, Amelia thought that her aunt was ten feet tall and could probably bench-press an Angus bull. Right then, with all the anger in her aunt's little body, Amelia figured Liddy could probably throw an elephant from one end of Bonnet to the other—especially if the critter was named Matilda.

"I saw Amos's name on the funeral home marquee as Ethel and I were coming back from our water aerobics class," Liddy said as she popped the leg rest up. "I'm all out of my secret ingredient since we had two funerals recently, and I'm flat out of pie shells. If either of you ever breathe a word of what I just said, I'll never make you a pie again. Folks in town think I have a special recipe for my pie dough as well as the filling."

"Wouldn't dream of it, and Clovis would divorce me if you made that promise good." Bridget stood up, took Liddy's wrist in her hand, and looked at her watch. "Pulse is pretty good."

Liddy cut her eyes over at Amelia. "You called her, didn't you?"

"If I didn't love you, I would have let you drop in aisle four of the Walmart store with a stroke." Amelia shrugged.

"So, you and Mama have another funeral dinner to plan?" Bridget asked.

"Yes, we do," Liddy answered. "Were you the attending when they brought Amos to the hospital?"

"No one brought him," Bridget told her. "He died at home. Clovis went out and pronounced him dead."

"Poor old Amos," Liddy sighed. "He was a good guy. Supported the church and was always trying to do good for the town. Fifteen minutes is up. Get that thing on my arm and prove that I'm fine."

"Aunt Liddy, my blood pressure probably was jacked up when I heard about Matilda trying to sabotage the festival," Amelia said.

"Mine was." Bridget slipped the armband on Liddy's upper arm and pumped it up. "Clovis took it, so I know that for a fact. Well, you get to go shopping instead of to the hospital."

Clovis knocked on the door and then came inside without waiting. "Is she all right?"

"She's better than I was," Bridget told him.

He came on into the living room and checked her pulse. "How do you keep so calm in all this turmoil?"

"Easy, I just picture Matilda leaving Bonnet." Liddy popped the footrest down and stood up. "Now, you two have worked long hours. Go home and get some rest. Amelia and I are going to Gainesville. I need to buy fresh lemons to make a pie for Amos's funeral dinner."

Clovis gave her a quick hug. "You will call me and Bridget if you get to feeling bad, won't you?"

"I promise." Liddy slung her big black purse over her shoulder and headed for the door.

"She's one salty old gal," Clovis chuckled under his breath.

"She's made of steel. They don't make 'em like her and Mama anymore." Bridget picked up her equipment and followed Clovis outside.

"I kind of feel sorry for Matilda," Amelia whispered. "She thinks she's Goliath, but Aunt Liddy is just like David with his slingshot and stones."

"Amen," Clovis and Bridget said at the same time.

Liddy was already in the car with her seat belt on when Amelia slid in behind the wheel. Amelia didn't even realize that she'd been so worried until her muscles began to relax, and only then when she pictured Matilda leaving a trail of dust behind her as she left Bonnet.

She backed out of the driveway and drove to the stop sign, then pulled out onto the highway and headed east. Determined not to talk about Matilda or the feud for fear it would really raise Liddy's blood pressure, she tried to clear her mind and come up with something neutral when a picture of a lemon pie flashed through her mind.

"You should just buy a bottle of limoncello instead of getting those little single-shot things," Amelia said. "Why don't you let me go into the liquor store for you today instead of going through the drive-up window? I'm all out of Jose Cuervo, so I should buy some of that."

"Do you think it would fit in my purse?" Liddy asked. "I can't be carrying in a brown paper bag that looks like it's holding a bottle of liquor. Folks are keeping an eye on me lately. I wouldn't be a bit surprised that they don't have a bet going as to whether I will serve a lemon pie at Matilda's funeral, or if she'll make all y'all eat tofu turkey at mine."

Amelia's giggle turned into full-fledged laughter that had both women hiccupping when it was over.

"Not to worry, Aunt Liddy. If it doesn't fit in your purse, we can put it in my tote bag. And don't talk about your funeral. You're going to be like Methuselah and live to be almost a thousand years old. There's no way you would die and let your friends eat tofu turkey or kale salad." Amelia laughed out loud.

Aunt Liddy hides liquor. I hide the fact that I told Nick we could talk in a couple of days. I guess we all have secrets, Amelia thought.

Everyone hides something. There's no such thing as a totally transparent person in this whole world, the voice in her head said.

"That would be great, but I usually just use the little sample bottles so I can get rid of them easily," Liddy agreed. "I guess I could hide a bigger bottle in my closet when I'm not using it. Think you could maybe get two bottles for me?"

"Sure." Amelia nodded.

"You know, when me and Clara and Ethel were first working at the school back in the sixties, the administration would have fired a teacher if she was seen in a liquor store," Liddy said. "Now, a teacher can walk right into a liquor store and not even think about consequences."

"Man, I wouldn't have wanted to be teaching in those days. I'm sure glad that times have changed," Amelia said.

"Me too." Liddy nodded. "Speaking of that, the weekly newspaper came out today, and guess who's on the front page?"

"I haven't seen it yet," Amelia said.

"Matilda and Nick are right there with big smiles on their faces, and they're standing in front of the real estate office. The article tells about how Harry has taken some time off and how Nick is taking over the business while he's gone. It gives a long list of all the community organizations he was a member of down in Sweetwater. If I had to read all that out loud, it would have taken every bit of the breath the good Lord gave me for a whole month," Liddy told her.

"How did that make you feel?" Amelia asked.

"I drew a moustache on Matilda and cut the article out," Liddy answered.

"I didn't ask what you did with it," Amelia said. "I asked how it made you feel."

"It made me mad as a wet hen after a tornado tore up the henhouse, so I carried it out to the backyard and set it on fire," Liddy said and then pointed out the window. "Oh, look at that field of bluebonnets. I just love this time of year when everything is blooming."

Amelia glanced over that way. "So do I. I remember picking them for my mama and asking her if we could mail some to Granny Dee. She told me that they would wilt and die before they got to Louisiana."

"First time she told you that, you cried," Liddy said.

"Yes, I did, but what about the fire you set in your backyard? How did that make you feel? I would have felt good about burning Matilda's picture, but I'm not sure about Nick's. He's kind of like an innocent bystander, isn't he?" Amelia asked.

Liddy eyed her carefully. "Are you studying to be a school counselor or something?"

"I've thought about it, but I haven't started really looking into it yet." Amelia could feel the heat from her aunt's glare. If just taking up for Nick could bring on that kind of response, then she didn't even want to know what kind of fire she'd be under if she went out with him.

"Watching Matilda's face go all black was exhilarating," Liddy said.

"Aunt Liddy!" Amelia scolded. "That's not very Christian of you."

This is not the time to come clean about talking to Nick, Amelia thought.

"Nope, it's not," Liddy agreed. "I never believed in witchy stuff, not even that good kind, but I found the black candles that we put on your Uncle Marvin's fiftieth birthday cake and burned them."

"Why would you do that?" Amelia shivered at the idea. "And why would you keep candles for more than twenty years?"

"Because they came twenty-four to a box, and I had to buy three boxes to get fifty, so there were leftovers," Liddy answered. "And you burn a black candle to ward off all negative or evil spirits. I figured one might not be enough to send Matilda packing, so I burned all the ones left in the box. And don't be tellin' me it's not Christian," Liddy argued. "A non-Christian wouldn't ward off the evil and burn her picture."

"What would they do?" Amelia asked.

"Hypothetically speaking, of course, that person would send her a nice big bowl of tofu soup with a sprinkling of arsenic in it, and then not take a lemon pie to her funeral dinner," Liddy told her.

"Well, now, that would be pretty unchristian for sure," Amelia said. "I'm glad you didn't do something like that. If she died, would you really not take a lemon pie to the dinner?"

Liddy's shoulders raised in a shrug. "The way I feel about her, it would be downright hypocritical to take one of my famous pies to her dinner. God might strike me graveyard dead if I did something like that. And if her spirit was hovering around, she could hear all the folks fussing about not having lemon pie."

"What would you take?" Amelia asked.

"Nothing. Not one blessed thing, because I wouldn't go to the dinner. I would attend the funeral just to be sure she was dead, and to have a talk with God," Liddy answered.

"Would you pray for her?" Amelia saw a faint sliver of light at the end of the dark tunnel.

"Yep, I would pray that God would send her straight to hell." Liddy's tone had gone ice cold.

"Ever wonder if she might pray the same thing about you?" Amelia asked.

"She probably does." Liddy finally grinned. "I hope that I make her miserable. She's damn sure caused me enough pain through the years."

There was no way Amelia was going to get her aunt to forgive and forget, not this side of eternity, and quite possibly not on the other side, either. So, she changed the subject. "Look at that field, Aunt Liddy. It's even thicker with bluebonnets than the last one we saw."

"Bull shit," Liddy laughed.

"Why would you say that?" Amelia couldn't figure out why her aunt thought it was funny. "It really is a pretty pasture."

"They are beautiful because of bull crap, or cow crap, or even newborn calf crap," Liddy answered, "just like I said. The bull shit fertilizes the ground and makes a thicker crop of bluebonnets. Think about the few you see in town, girl. They struggle to even survive a day or two."

Amelia chuckled. "Never thought of it that way."

"We had lots of rain to wash the crap down into the soil, and now sunshine. That's what makes for a good crop of them," Liddy answered, and then said, "I got to admit, I looked up a recipe for both kale salad and for tofu turkey and then I went on the internet to see where I could buy some arsenic. Did you know that I could get it at Walmart in the form of rat poison? Seems kind of a fitting thing to do to Matilda, don't it? But"—she sighed—"I guess the black candles cleared out the evil spirit from me, too, because I erased all the ingredients from my grocery list."

Amelia pulled into the parking lot of the liquor store in the small town of Lindsay on the way to Gainesville. "I'm glad to hear that you aren't going to poison Matilda. I'd hate to have to visit you in prison, and besides, you don't look good in orange. Two bottles of limoncello? Anything else for you?"

"I don't suppose they sell black candles in there, do they? I might need some more if my fingers start itching to buy rat poison," Liddy said with a grin.

"Not that I know of, but I'll check." Amelia winked as she unfastened her seat belt.

Her hands shook and her knees felt slightly weak as she crossed the gravel lot and went into the liquor store. Compared to this thing between her aunt and Nick's mother, the Hatfield and McCoy feud looked like a kindergarten playground fight.

"I can't imagine why the kids decided to bury Amos so fast," Liddy said as she spread out a cloth on one of the tables on Friday afternoon.

"I guess it's because the festival is tomorrow, and usually no one has a funeral on Sunday." Ruth Ann set down her slow cooker of shrimp alfredo on one end of the table.

Liddy finished what she was doing and moved her lemon pie from the kitchen to the far end of the table, where the desserts would go. Three other ladies brought in more food and then headed to the kitchen to help bring out disposable plates and cutlery.

Gladys came in next with her bowl of garden salad. "Tina, Matilda, and Kayla are on their way. They're all together in Matilda's vehicle."

She leaned over the table and whispered just for Liddy. "This is a funeral dinner. You should treat her with respect, Liddy."

"Oh, honey." Liddy's smile was pure saccharine. "I respect Amos too much to have a catfight at his funeral, but if she starts something, I will finish it. Amos would understand, I'm sure."

"For God's sake, Liddy, that's no way to act," Gladys almost hissed and then focused on Tina, Kayla, and Matilda, who were crossing the floor. "We're so glad y'all could help out today. It's good to see the young folks stepping up at funeral dinners."

"He's my husband's third cousin," Tina said without a hint of a smile. "I brought a fruit salad."

"And I've got some marinated vegetables," Kayla said. "Since I've been eating right, I've lost forty pounds, and I have so much energy."

"Well, ain't that nice," Ruth Ann muttered.

Liddy stifled a giggle. That was the phrase she and Ruth Ann used rather than saying, "Screw you!"

"Amen," Liddy said.

Gladys actually smiled.

Matilda was dressed in a simple black dress, but she'd added a lace duster with red roses printed on it, and her high heels had red soles. Liddy couldn't remember which designer used that for his signature, but she did know that they couldn't be bought for a dollar ninety-nine at the shoe store.

"Where do I put my tofu chicken and rice?" Matilda asked. "Does it go with the main courses or with the vegetables, or would you rather we kept our healthy foods all in one place?"

"It can go down there with the ham and the barbecued pork chops," Liddy answered. Then she said in a sugary voice, "Thank you all so much for thinking of the family. If you're not going to the funeral, we can always use some help putting the tablecloths on the rest of the tables and arranging the chairs around them."

"I couldn't miss Amos's graveside service." Tina was already on her way across the room. "And of course Gladys, Matilda, and Kayla are coming with me for support."

"Well, then maybe you all can help out by washing the empty slow cookers and casserole dishes later," Liddy suggested.

"I don't do dishes," Matilda said just loud enough for Ruth Ann's and Liddy's ears. "Have you made a decision about that land?"

"Yep, I have," Liddy answered.

"And it is?" Matilda almost smiled.

"That Paul and I would give the land to a pig farmer before we'd sell it to you for ten million dollars," Liddy told her.

"Is that your asking price?" Matilda asked.

"No, ma'am, but we do have a pig farmer lined up," Ruth Ann said.

"I intend to keep you so tied up in court that you lose everything in lawyer fees," Matilda growled.

"Paul works for free for the family," Ruth Ann reminded her. "So bring your best game. We're ready for you."

"Go to hell!" Matilda tipped her chin up, turned around, and stormed out of the room, followed by Tina, Kayla, and Gladys.

"I kind of feel sorry for them." Ruth Ann set about getting things organized.

"Why?" Liddy gasped.

"It's going to hurt like hell when they fall off those pedestals," she answered. "To tell the truth, I never thought Gladys would turn on tradition the way she has."

"Amen!" Ethel brought out her electric skillet full of potatoes. "Be right nice if they would change their ways and just enjoy living in a small town, but I don't see that happening. How about you, Liddy?"

"I was trying to figure out how tall those pedestals are, and if there was a slight chance a fall from them could break a person's neck," Liddy said.

"You have to forgive if you expect Jesus to forgive you," Ethel reminded her.

"I can't do it," Liddy said. "Don't know if I ever can."

Liddy wasn't sure God Himself would forgive Matilda. If He could, that was between Him and Matilda and none of Liddy's business. But she could not forgive someone for taking her son from her. She fought back a tear at the picture of Richie's face when he walked out of the Dairy Queen that evening. His heart must have been shattered when he confronted Matilda.

Liddy wondered, for the thousandth time, what kind of hold Matilda had had on Richie. Or for that matter how she drew people like Tina, Kayla, and Gladys to her side to do her bidding.

"A long time ago," Ethel said, "when I was a little girl, I would come in from school stomping around all mad at one of my friends. My grandmother would tell me that I had to go into my bedroom and pray for the child. I told her that I'd rather shoot them as pray for them."

"I can damn well . . ." Liddy rolled her eyes up toward the ceiling. "Forgive me, Lord, for swearing in the church fellowship hall." She brought her focus back down to Ethel. "You have to understand the situation, Ethel. If Matilda hadn't had a small son of her own, I might have been wearing an orange jumpsuit for the past twenty-eight years."

Ethel moved some casseroles closer together so that the next women coming in could find a place for their food. "When I prayed for the person, it helped *me*, not them. It took the anger out of my heart. I doubt that Matilda would change any at all, but if you pray for her, it might remove that burning desire to do her bodily harm."

"Okay, I will pray for her." Liddy bowed her head and prayed out loud. "Dear Lord, I am here to lift Matilda Monroe up before your face. Since I'm convinced that you know her even better than I do since you see all things from your throne in heaven, I'm sure you will understand my petition for the woman. I would ask that you strike her with boils to humble her. I don't know her son, Nick, all that well, but please put a woman in his pathway that Matilda can't stand. If you could make everything she touches turn to crap, I would be much obliged. In our sweet Jesus's name. Amen."

"Good grief!" Ruth Ann giggled.

"You are so right, Ethel," Liddy said as she raised her head. "Thank you for telling me that story. I do feel much better now that I've prayed for Matilda."

Chapter Eight

*n*ick had been fortunate enough to attend a couple of festivals in his lifetime and had enjoyed them. But what he looked forward to more than the big event on Saturday was getting to talk to Amelia that Friday evening.

He whistled as he drove from his house to the office that morning and parked out behind the building. Sunshine warmed his face when he got out of the Jeep. The sounds of birds chirping in the old scrub oak tree at the back of the building filled the air, and a butterfly lit on Nick's shoulder. The day was starting out every bit as good as he hoped it would end.

The aroma of coffee rushed out to meet him when he unlocked the back door. That meant his mother was already there—the whistling stopped.

"Oh, Nick!" she yelled from the front office. "I've got wonderful news."

You're going back to Sweetwater? He almost crossed his fingers behind his back but poured a cup of coffee instead and vowed that nothing was going to ruin his good mood that morning.

She didn't wait for him to say anything but went right on. "Tina told me after the funeral yesterday that Amos's house will be on the market soon, possibly as soon as next week, since he left all his belongings to her husband. I've coveted that house since I was a little girl, and I've decided to buy it before it even gets listed."

"What house is that?" Nick asked.

"The one south of town, a block or so past the cemetery. It's the huge stone one that you used to tease me about. The one you called the haunted castle. It's just so English looking that I can imagine royalty staying there." Matilda sipped on something green. "Of course, it's not haunted at all, but it is close to being eligible for the historical register, which makes me like it even more."

Nick had to swallow fast to keep from spewing a mouthful of coffee. "Why on earth would you want a house that big?"

"I love staying in bed-and-breakfast places, so I'm going to turn that place into one. Tina says that there are six bedrooms upstairs and the attic has been made into a library of sorts, and there is a master suite on the ground floor that can be mine. I'm so excited about this new page in my life!" Matilda rattled on. "And the good thing is that I can live there while I'm remodeling and getting it ready to open. If all goes well, a grand opening right before Thanksgiving is my goal, and then when folks come to Bonnet for the holidays, they won't have to go to Muenster or Gainesville for a hotel."

"I thought you hated this town," Nick said.

"I do, but there's nothing for me in Sweetwater, and I've made some new friends who are begging me to stay here." She smiled.

"Mother, you don't cook, which you'd have to do at a B and B," he reminded her.

"Stop throwing ice water on my idea," she snapped. "I plan to steal Kayla away from the chamber of commerce. She is an amazing cook, and I can easily hire a couple of women to clean the rooms. Just think, that will even be helping the town by giving a few people jobs. I will serve as the welcoming hostess, and maybe even help Kayla set up the buffet table for the guests' breakfast. I have quite the eye for decorating."

"You have quite the eye for hiring a decorator," Nick reminded her.

"Why can't you be happy for me?" Matilda asked.

Nick ignored the question and asked, "Is this going to be a vegan bed-and-breakfast?"

"We will serve healthy food with a vegan option." Matilda glared at him.

"You do realize that any business will take at least a year to get out of the red and start making a profit. You and Kayla might have to clean the rooms yourself until you get the finances out of the red," he offered.

She glared at him. "I will be a perfect hostess, but I don't intend to clean and cook—ever. I will charge enough that I can afford to pay someone to do those jobs."

"Do you think people will stay at an expensive B and B when they can drive a few more miles for one that probably charges half as much? You need to think this through rather than doing something impulsive like you always do." He knew that would make her mad, but he had to try to make her see the folly in what she was thinking about doing.

"You can't talk me out of this," Matilda declared. "I'm going to own a business. That way I'll have a leg up on those Taylors, and then I'm on my way to leading this town."

"I wish you the best"—Nick took a couple of steps toward his office—"but you have champagne tastes, and it will take a lot of money to refurbish an old place like that."

"I've got money from the divorce settlement. Thank God your father didn't make me sign a prenup. I can do this. Be happy for me instead of throwing negative vibes my way," Matilda said.

Think of it this way. Harry's voice was so real in Nick's head that he glanced over his shoulder to see if his uncle had snuck in the back door. *If she's all wound up with her new young friends and the B and B, she'll be out of your hair.*

"I am happy for you, but I still think you are rushing into something without putting a pencil to all the financial details of such a big venture," he said. "Owning and operating a business, especially a new one like that in a small town like Bonnet, will require a budget and careful planning."

"I ran an office for years. I know how to manage money." She finished off her smoothie and rinsed out the tall glass.

"Then I hope you are happy with your decision ten years down the road," Nick said. "Just one more word of warning. Be sure to have it inspected for termites, and have the wiring and plumbing checked."

"It's rock, for God's sake," Matilda told him. "Termites don't eat rocks."

"But the studs, the ceiling joists, and the drywall are not rock," he said.

"Okay! Okay! I will have it inspected before I buy it," she sighed. "This means that you need to get very serious about finding an office manager for this business. I will stay through next week, but next Friday will be my last day. I will have too much to do to run this business for you."

"I can do that." Nick topped off his coffee mug and headed across the room.

She waved a hand around to take in all of Wanda's office. "I'll be so glad not to have to look at all this crap on the walls that you insisted on putting back up."

"So, you aren't going to go with an antique theme for your B and B? The old stone house kind of lends itself to that idea," Nick said, to tease.

"Good antiques are different from all this." She sneered at the plaques hanging on the pink walls. "This is just cheesy and cheap looking. Tina and I will begin scouring the *real* antique shops and markets for what we want to use in the B and B."

"Are you going to name it the Bluebonnet B&B?" Nick asked.

"No, I am not!" she declared. "It will be known as the Grey Manor, and I'll spell it G-R-E-Y, in the English way," she answered.

Nick could imagine his mother sinking too much money into a place where the rooms would be very costly to book for a night or two.

Bonnet was not a tourist town, and when folks came to town they usually stayed with their relatives. Matilda would be bored with her B and B in less than a year and then she wouldn't be able to sell it for what she had in it.

"That's a little pretentious for a town with less than three thousand people, don't you think?" he suggested.

"I'll be bringing a little class to this place," Matilda said.

"After what happened with Liddy Latham's son, I doubt this town wants any of your class," Nick said. "I just hope that folks continue to list their properties with me since I'm your son. Liddy is an upstanding member of the community. What makes you think people will forget a scandal like that?"

Matilda's mouth set in a firm line, and Nick imagined steam coming from her ears and fire shooting from her eyes.

"Who told you about that? Did Liddy tattle, or was it that niece of hers?" Matilda hissed.

"Neither of them told me anything, and it doesn't matter how I got the information." There was no way Nick would throw Uncle Harry under the proverbial bus. "You had to have known that I would find out when we moved here."

"Richie was a nice guy, and your father and I were going through a rough patch," Matilda said. "To me, it was just a fling. If it was more to Richie, then that was on him. I didn't make him go to a bar and get drunk or make him drive in that condition, so it wasn't my fault that he died."

"Just a fling?" Nick asked.

No wonder people feared that he would be like his mother. He couldn't blame them for wanting to lock up their daughters and protect them from a man like he might be. He should probably call off even talking to Amelia that evening.

"Your father left me for a dumpy older woman. That made me a laughingstock," she protested.

"Would it have been better if he'd left you for a woman half his age?" he asked. "And he didn't have an affair and leave you until a couple of years ago. You were having 'a fling' twenty-eight years ago. How many more did you have?" he asked.

"If your father would have made me happy . . . ," she started.

"Whoa!" Nick said. "I'm calling bullshit on that, Mother! I was there in the house until I went to college. Dad gave you everything money could buy."

Matilda shrugged. "Everything except excitement. You're just like him. You are boring, and any woman who marries you will do it for security. Then she'll go looking for excitement in other places."

Nick opened his mouth to smart off but then snapped it shut and counted to ten—very slowly.

"I guess by your silence you know I'm right," she sneered.

"I hope you aren't, but then I don't plan to find a woman like you if and when I ever get serious," Nick said. "Why did you even marry Dad in the first place?" Nick wished he could go back outside and recover the feeling he had before he ever walked in the building.

"Like I said, I married Gregory for stability and security, and I had you as quick as I could to double up on that security issue. If we had a child, then he would never leave me, or so I thought at the time. That might be the only time I was wrong. Any woman who is as smart as me will be sure to finagle things so there is no prenup. That's marriage in a nutshell to any intelligent woman. Lust is a whole different matter. The trouble with Richie was that he thought marriage and lust went together," Matilda said. "My advice to you, since you are a man, is to demand a prenup."

"How can you take something so sacred as marriage and just explain it away like that?"

Nick had looked up the word *narcissism* when his father accused his mother of being the poster child for that. He'd agreed with his dad's armchair diagnosis, but that morning he felt like he was getting the full effect of the definition. The symptoms went through his mind like he was listening to a podcast—an extreme sense of self-importance and an inflated ego. Thoughts and fantasies of power, success, intelligence, and high status. Only associating with folks they consider to be special or in good social standing. Seeking constant attention and an entitled attitude.

Matilda shrugged and then said, "Don't give me that look. It reminds me of your father when we argued, and he would just clam up and walk away. I'm the way I am because of the way I was raised. Daddy cheated on Mother. Mother had her flings, but she was discreet where Daddy wasn't. When I was ten, one of my friends came to spend the night with me and told me that Floyd wasn't really my daddy. She said that I belonged to a man who had bought a house from my daddy," she said in a matter-of-fact tone. "I didn't give a damn who fathered me as long as I got what I wanted."

Nick felt as if someone had slammed a boulder against his chest. For a full minute he couldn't breathe, but then he inhaled deeply and let it out slowly. With an inheritance like his, there was no way he could ever be anything but a bachelor. If fate had a name, it was Matilda, for being the mother that he had.

"Don't look so shocked. Did you think everyone in your family tree was perfect?" Matilda asked.

"No, but I didn't know the tree was rotten at the core," he muttered.

The bell above the door dinged, and Matilda pasted on her best smile when she saw Tina entering the office. "Good morning. Did you come to talk about the house?"

"Yes, but if you're serious about buying, we won't list it," she said.

Nick closed the door to his office, sat down at his desk, opened a drawer, and popped three aspirin into his mouth. A brutal headache had suddenly hit him in the eyes.

The business phone rang and caused another wave of pain to slap him, but when his mother didn't answer the jangling thing on the fourth ring, he reached for the receiver. "Good morning, this is Nick," he said.

"You sound like hammered owl shit," his father chuckled. "Your mother driving you up the walls?"

"Did you cheat on Mother your whole married life?" Nick blurted out.

"What on earth brought on that question?" Gregory asked.

"Did you?" Nick asked again.

"No, I did not. The only affair I ever had was with Betsy, and as soon as the divorce was granted, we had a simple ceremony here at the house. We are very happy, Son, and I believe that I've found a woman who believes in real marriage."

"I found out—"

"About your mother's infidelities?" Gregory asked. "I tried to make her happy. I really did, but it was impossible. Look, I just called to check on you, not drag skeletons out of the closet. You've been at the business for a week now. How's it going?"

"Great," Nick said. "I'm settling in a lot faster than I thought I would, and I met a wonderful girl, but there's this big problem."

"You want to talk about it?" Gregory asked.

"You ever hear about the business with Liddy Latham's son?" Nick asked.

"That's old news," Gregory said. "I'm surprised Harry didn't tell you that story a long time ago."

"Well, this woman I met is Liddy's niece." Nick rubbed his temples.

"Now that's a nuclear bomb just waiting to go off. I can't do much about that, but I'm here if you need to talk," Gregory told him.

"Why did you stick with Mother so long, Dad?" Nick continued to massage his head.

"We didn't have a prenup, and well"—his father paused—"the truth is I had to take care of the finances. Matilda is reckless when it comes to money, but she is your mother, and I shouldn't be talking about her at all. Besides, I wanted to be around to give you one stable parent; then the years went by and suddenly you were grown. I didn't think I'd ever find anyone to be happy with, so why not just be married to my job?"

"Do you think I'm like her side of the family?" Nick asked.

"You are you, Son. Every choice a person makes has a consequence. Make the right one and don't let all that old history define you," Gregory said. "If you really feel something for this niece of Liddy's, then go for it, and be damned to both sides of the family."

"Thanks, Dad. I've got a showing at a house in five minutes, so I suppose I should go." Nick's headache was much better already. "Tell Betsy hello for me."

"I sure will," Gregory said. "Don't be a stranger."

"I won't," Nick said. "I'll try to get down to Sweetwater one weekend to see you. I'd invite you to Bonnet, but there would be too much drama."

"I don't have any desire to be anywhere close to Matilda, but our door is open to you anytime," Gregory said. "Bye now."

Nick put the phone back on its base, picked up a folder with all the details on the property he would be showing, and walked through the front office where Tina and Matilda had their heads in an estate sale bill. The whole way out to the acreage he thought about what his mother had said and decided that, like his dad, he would take boring over dangerous and exciting any day.

"Hey, Amelia," Daniel yelled down the hallway.

She turned around and waved. "You got plans for lunch?"

"Nope. Savannah is on a field trip with her class, so I'm free, and I've got half a dozen of her famous pecan sandies I'm willing to share for some company," Daniel answered.

"Bring it on," Amelia told him.

Daniel brought his brown bag lunch into her room, sat down at a desk, and like always cleaned the top with a sanitizing wipe before he laid out his food on a paper towel. "Are you nervous about tonight? You are going to at least FaceTime it, aren't you?"

"Of course." Amelia didn't admit that she hadn't even thought of FaceTiming, but that did make more sense. Still, what if she dropped a chunk of cheese or a piece of pepperoni on her shirt? Or worse yet, if she got tickled and snorted beer out her nose?

"You hadn't thought of FaceTime, had you? Now you're worried you'll do something stupid, right?" Daniel asked. "I can tell by that smell-the-skunk look on your face."

"Busted," Amelia said. "I was worrying about laughing and snorting beer out my nose."

"I did that when Savannah and I had to FaceTime a year ago, so it's possible," Daniel admitted.

Amelia's giggles turned into laughter, and then she grew serious again. "I'm nervous for more reasons than that, but it helps to know I'm not the only one who does stupid things." She dabbed her eyes with a tissue. "I can't get that picture of you doing that out of my mind. I wonder if Savannah jumped back when the beer hit the screen."

"Yep, she did," Daniel laughed with her.

"You have to tell your kids that story someday," she said. "Seriously, though, I feel like a teenager sneaking around behind my parents' backs even just talking to Nick."

Daniel finished off his sandwich and opened a bag containing three cookies. "You got to eat your food before you get cookies."

"Yes, Daddy!" Amelia teased as she popped the last bite of her sandwich into her mouth.

Daniel passed the second bag over to her. "Here's the way I see it. If you don't like Nick after talking to him for an hour tonight, then don't agree to let him call you again. But if this talking turns into a real date, then you need to tell your family before the third date."

Amelia opened the bag and took out a cookie. "Why the third date?"

"Come on, girl." Daniel turned a slight shade of pink. "Everyone knows the third date rule."

Amelia felt the heat coming from the back of her neck to flood her cheeks. "The sex date, right?"

"Yep, that's the date where you seal the deal, or else you end the relationship," Daniel told her.

"It's friendship, not a relationship," Amelia reminded him.

They had just finished their cookies when the bell rang, and Daniel tossed all his trash into the can at the end of her desk. "See you Monday, and good luck."

"Thanks for the cookies," she said with a smile.

I'm going to need more than luck, she thought as she watched the next class of freshmen pour into her room.

That afternoon, minutes seemed like hours, and no matter how often Amelia looked at the clock, the hands seemed to never move. When the last bell finally rang, she grabbed up her tote bag, slung her purse over her shoulder, and drove straight to the grocery store to buy a six-pack of beer and half a gallon of rocky road ice cream.

She grabbed a cart at the front of the store, gathered up her beer and ice cream, and then remembered that she needed a box of oatmeal, so she whipped into the cereal aisle to get it and was on her way to the checkout counter when she bumped smack into a cart that Matilda Monroe was pushing.

"Miz Monroe," she nodded and pasted on a fake smile.

"Andrea," Matilda said without even a hint of a smile.

"It's Amelia, ma'am."

"Don't call me that. I'm not an old woman." Matilda shot her a dirty look.

"Sorry, ma'am," Amelia stuttered. "I mean Miz Matilda."

"Don't call me that, either." Matilda glared at her. "You may call me Miss Monroe, and you may also stay away from my son. I saw the way you were flirting with him at Wanda's funeral."

Amelia could accept that she had offended the woman by making her feel old, even if that wasn't her intention, but for Matilda to presume that she could tell her what to do brought her Irish temper right up to the surface.

"Your son, ma'am"—she dragged out the last word in true Louisiana fashion—"and I are both consenting adults. If we want to flirt, that would be our business and none of yours."

"I'll disown him if he goes out on one date with the likes of *you*," Matilda hissed, and then smiled sweetly at a woman who passed by them before turning her cold glare back toward Amelia.

"That's your problem . . . ma'am." Amelia shrugged and met Matilda's gaze. "You have a great day. I've got plans for the evening, so I have to get home."

"You are just like your aunt," Matilda whispered.

"Why, thank you, ma'am." Amelia raised her voice slightly. "Aunt Liddy is my hero. She has even willed me the recipe for her lemon pie. I hope to continue the tradition of taking one to every funeral dinner that's ever held right here in Bonnet."

"I'll turn this town around if it takes me ten years, and you can mark my words, I will bring Liddy Latham to her knees," Matilda said as she pushed past Amelia.

"Aunt Liddy has seen folks like you come and folks like you go. Most of them come with intentions of changing the way we do things here in Bonnet and leave without having accomplished a single thing. You have a blessed day now, ma'am." Amelia pushed her cart around the end of the aisle, went straight to the freezer section, and grabbed another container of ice cream. After what she'd just experienced, she felt that she deserved more than one.

The pizza arrived with ten minutes to spare before the date was to begin. Nick gave the delivery guy a tip and then rushed up to his bedroom to run the electric razor over his face, slap on some aftershave, and put on a fresh shirt. Then he scolded himself for all his efforts—this was a virtual date, not a real one.

At exactly six o'clock he set his phone up on a stand and called Amelia. She answered on the second ring, and she hadn't been teasing about wearing bibbed overalls and a T-shirt. He wished that he could reach into the phone and give her a hug, or better yet, kiss her on the cheek, but that would be considered friends with benefits. Neither of them was ready for that—not by a long shot, if ever.

"Hello," she said. "You are right on time."

"And you look beautiful," he said. "Has your pizza arrived?"

"Yep," Amelia said. "Shall we eat? I'm starving. How did your day go, Nick?"

"I've got the promise of my first sale. A guy from over around Gainesville looked at some acreage between here and Saint Jo. He's a rancher who wants to buy a place for his son to start his own ranch." Nick saw that she had picked up a slice of pizza and started to eat, so he did the same. It was refreshing to have someone ask about his day.

"That has to be exciting," Amelia said.

"Yes, it is. It means a lot to me. How about your day?" he asked.

"Slow, but that's not unusual for Friday," she answered. "The kids are always rowdy at the end of the week, and especially so for the days after spring break. Then . . ." She paused and rolled her eyes toward the ceiling. "I suppose we should be honest with each other from the beginning of this friendship."

"Yes, ma'am, that's always the best route to take," he agreed.

"I ran into your mother at the grocery store, and I do mean ran into her. I came around the end of an aisle and bumped carts with her," Amelia said. "She said that she would disown you if you even talk to me."

Nick chuckled. "I've heard that for years, and she hasn't done it yet. I imagine I would get the same reception from your aunt if I crashed into her grocery cart. Shall I start calling you Juliet?"

"Might be a good idea, Romeo," she said. "Would you be Nicholas Romeo Monroe on your birth certificate?"

"No, I'm Gregory Nick Monroe on that piece of paper," he answered. "Are you Amelia Juliet Taylor?"

Her laughter made the whole kitchen brighter. "You're not going to believe me, but my name really *is* Amelia Juliet Taylor. My mama loves all things literary. My sister is Bridget Louisa."

"Your folks must really be special," Nick said.

"They are," Amelia confirmed, "and I'm remembering that there was a Nick Hatfield in that family, so we're pretty much the same as those feuding families, aren't we?"

"Do you think we've got a chance of ever being friends with those kinds of omens behind us? Romeo and Juliet plus the Hatfields and McCoys?" he teased.

"I'm willing to give it a try if you are," she answered, "but let's keep it between us for a little while before we go public with it. Let's see if we really do like each other before we cause another war."

"Or drink the poison?" Nick asked.

"You got that right." Amelia's blue eyes twinkled. "We now know each other's full names, and I don't intend to drink any poison. So, tell me, what made you go into the real estate business?"

"Uncle Harry," Nick said. "I've idolized him my whole life. But then my dad is into something similar. He doesn't run a real estate business, but he buys things that are going under—like big apartment complexes, corporations, and that kind of thing—builds them up, and resells them. I guess it's in the blood, so to speak. What put you into the teaching profession?"

"Mama did," Amelia answered. "She was a teacher right here in Bonnet until she quit last year. She put a love of learning into both of us girls."

"And your dad is a lawyer, right?" Nick asked.

She tipped up a bottle of beer and took a small sip. No way was she spewing it all over the screen like Daniel had done. "Yep, so we've got two doctors, a lawyer, and a couple of teachers in the family."

"Why didn't you go into the medical field like your sister?" Nick asked.

"I'm not that ambitious," she answered. "Do you have pets?"

Nick shook his head. "I always wanted a brother, a sister, or a dog," he chuckled. "But instead, Uncle Harry left me a cat."

"I'm not much of a dog person, but I do love cats. I can't have one in this apartment, which is probably a good thing because I would adopt half a dozen," she said.

Nick reached over to the chair next to him and picked up Vera. "Meet my new pet. I inherited her from Uncle Harry if he decides to really retire, along with the house and business. Her name is Vera."

"Oh, I would love to pet her," Amelia said. "She looks a little like my Granny Dee's cat back in Louisiana. Boss Lady is her name."

"You are welcome to come over anytime and pet her all you want." Nick kissed Vera on the nose and put her back on her own chair.

"Why did Harry name her Vera?" Amelia asked.

"She's named after a woman he loved sometime in the past," Nick explained.

"When I get my own house, I'm going to have a cat and name her Buttons or maybe Callie if she's a calico, or Bootsie if she's a tuxedo girl and has four white feet. I like whimsical names." Amelia finished off her slice of pizza and reached for another one.

Nick did the same, and part of the topping fell off and landed smack on his shirt. Amelia giggled, and then a chunk slipped off her slice and dropped right into the pocket on the bib.

"Guess I should've worn overalls," Nick said with a laugh as he grabbed a paper towel and wiped the glob from his shirt.

"The pockets do come in handy," Amelia told him.

Nick didn't realize how much fun a virtual date could be, but he wished they were sitting across from each other in a booth—or even right next to each other.

They'd both finished a third slice of pizza when Amelia finally said, "This has been fun, but I promised Aunt Liddy I would be at her house at seven, so I should go."

"Can we do it again?" Nick was startled that the evening had passed so quickly. He checked the time on his phone and, sure enough, they'd been talking for almost an hour.

"You know that isn't going to happen," Amelia told him.

"Why not? I'm not interested in a relationship, not with the mother God gave me, and you don't seem to be, either, but it's nice to talk to someone my age," he said.

"Can I think about it?" she asked.

"You've got my number," Nick answered. "Feel free to call anytime."

Chapter Nine

*P*ies, cakes, platters stacked high with cookies, cupcakes, and cobblers were all set in a row to tempt people to buy tickets for the cake walk at the festival that Saturday afternoon. Main Street was lined with folks either sitting in lawn chairs or standing behind them to watch the parade. Men and women alike of all ages wore wide-brimmed hats to keep the hot sun off their faces.

Little children darted out behind the fire engine to gather up candy that the firemen threw out. Then everyone moved their chairs and cars to the city park, where the carnival was ready for business. Vendors of every kind, from funnel cakes to jewelry, were set up on two sides of the park. The other two sides were for fun things like cake walks and a dunking booth. Music from the Tilt-a-Whirl, Ferris wheel, and a carousel—along with almost a dozen more rides—filled the park.

Liddy imagined that, from the sky, the whole crowd would look like a bunch of ants running from one attraction to the other. She and Ruth Ann manned the bake sale for the hospital from noon to two, but they sold the last platter of cookies half an hour before their duty was done.

"Looks like Gladys and Delores got off easy this time. They won't have to do anything at all except collect the money. Ever wonder how long it will be before Gladys decides to step down from the volunteer committee and turn it over to Matilda?" Ruth Ann asked.

"I shudder to think about it, but I can see it coming." Liddy folded her chair and headed to Paul's truck with it.

Ruth Ann did the same and picked up the money bag on her way to the truck. "I keep hoping that Matilda will get bored in our little town and go back to Sweetwater."

"Or maybe even Paris, and I don't mean Paris, Texas." Liddy laid her chair in the bed of the truck. "I might be able to tolerate her if there was an ocean between us."

"Same," Ruth Ann said.

Liddy started back to their empty table to help get it broken down and loaded. "But it would be a start, and there's not a bullet that will travel that far, so she would be safe over there."

"You got that right." Ruth Ann laughed.

"I love quiet," Liddy said as she and Ruth Ann broke down the table and loaded it into the bed of the truck, "but there's something about the carnival music and seeing so many folks out and about that makes me feel young again."

"And the aromas floating around." Ruth Ann paused in loading. "Remember when I met Paul right here? That's such a good memory and I get to relive it every year. You and Marvin were riding the Ferris wheel that day, and then Paul introduced me to you. I thought he was joking when he said you were his sister."

"I'm twenty years older than him, and his mother was only five years older than me when she married my dad," Liddy said, "but you know all that old history. I miss Marvin, but I really miss him at the carnival. We always had a ride on the Ferris wheel, and we always shared cotton candy. You should go find Paul so you two can ride the wheel."

"And leave you alone out here with Matilda on the prowl?" Ruth Ann said. "Paul and I will have our ride and our cotton candy when one of the girls gets here to keep you from going to jail."

"That might be a good idea, but I believe I could take her," Liddy said.

"I know you could," Ruth Ann agreed.

"If I couldn't, I could pick up a big stick," Liddy chuckled.

"Hey, what are y'all doing?" Gladys yelled from a few feet away as she and her friend Delores walked toward the truck. "Did you already sell everything?" She stopped at the railroad ties that circled the entire park to keep folks from driving their vehicles onto the grass.

"Yep, and next year, you two get to take the first shift," Liddy answered.

"Here's the money." Ruth Ann handed off a zippered bag to Gladys. "You're the president of the volunteer committee at the hospital, so *you* can take care of it. There's somewhere between three and four hundred dollars in there, mostly in fives and ones. Liddy's lemon pies went first, but that's no surprise. Folks would beat a path to her door every morning if she would sell them out of her house."

Gladys took the bag from her hands. "I'm not surprised. Seems like no one cares about calories, fat grams, or even if they're on their way to a heart attack or stroke. Next year Matilda is going to prepare a few healthy items for the sale."

"And," Delores said, "we're going to donate the money to the senior citizens center, where Matilda is going to offer to give some classes on healthy eating as soon as she gets settled."

"Then next year, y'all can help Matilda take care of the church booth from noon until closing. You'll have lots of time to visit while you sit behind the table all afternoon. Folks come to the festival to throw caution out the window when it comes to healthy eating," Liddy told her, "and the church probably won't have a sellout. Maybe after five o'clock, when the carrot and celery sticks that are left are going limp, you can put them on sale for half price. I doubt she even goes through with her ideas. She's mainly just a bunch of hot air—she'll delegate to others and do very little herself. Then if it goes well, she'll take credit. If it doesn't, it will be y'all's fault."

"Why are you so mean to Matilda?" Delores asked. "She means well, and she's just trying to help."

"Yeah, right." Liddy almost felt sorry for the two women. They were getting fleeced and didn't even know it.

"No, she's trying to undermine anything that Liddy does," Ruth Ann protested. "She steps on people to climb up to glory for herself."

"I don't see it that way," Gladys said.

Ethel walked up behind Liddy and leaned on the fender of the truck. "I see that you've loaded the table and chairs, so you've sold out. I bet Liddy's lemon pies went first, didn't they? Ira might even divorce me after fifty years of marriage because I didn't get here in time to buy one."

"They were gone in fifteen minutes," Ruth Ann told her.

"We did really good this year, too," Ethel said, "but my feet hurt from standing on them for two hours, and Ira didn't win a single one. He wanted to take home one or both of your lemon pies."

The tension was so thick that Liddy didn't think anyone could cut through it with a machete, and from the expression on Ethel's face, she finally realized that she'd just walked into the middle of it.

"Did I interrupt something here?" she asked.

"They were bad-mouthing Matilda—again!" Delores said.

"No," Liddy disagreed, "we were stating the truth, but you two will have to figure it out for yourselves."

"That's right," Ethel agreed. "Some folks have to find out the fire is hot by putting their hand in it. I see Ira and he's waving at me, so I better go talk him into funnel cakes and cinnamon rolls."

"Come on, Delores." Gladys took the woman by the arm. "We'll go lock this up in my car. I don't want to carry it around all day." She turned toward Liddy. "You might as well get used to her being here in Bonnet, because she's buying Amos's old stone house, and she's going to turn it into a bed-and-breakfast. She'll be a regular old business owner in town, and she's talking about running for city council this fall. Harry's position will be open, and talk has it that Paul might not run again."

"Does Matilda realize how much remodeling will have to be done on that place to put a bathroom in for every bedroom?" Liddy asked.

"She's got money, lots of it." Delores tipped her chin up just a little. "She took that cheating husband of hers to the cleaners."

"Oh, really." Liddy raised an eyebrow.

"Seems kind of hypocritical that she would do that to Gregory," Ruth Ann said, "since she's never been faithful to him."

Liddy could almost feel Ruth Ann's Irish temper hitting the boiling point, and hers wasn't far behind. If it wasn't for missing all the good food and reliving the memories, she might have tied right into both of them. A good old catfight would almost be worth it, but then Ruth Ann would think she had to help her in the battle, and they'd both end up in jail.

Delores's already thin lips disappeared as she pursed them. "Y'all need to be nice to her. She was devastated that he would leave her and marry that *old* woman."

"At thirteen and eighteen, five years' difference would matter a lot, but not at fifty-three and fifty-eight," Liddy argued.

"Well," Delores sighed, "I'm glad that old stone place is going to be a bed-and-breakfast. Maybe other businesses will see that we're making some kind of progress and come to town, and we'll owe it all to Matilda. We could use a gym with one of those spa things. My daughter took me to hers in Dallas and it was fantastic. And maybe a car dealership, and—"

"And a unicorn farm," Liddy snapped at her.

"They're always going to be hateful because they can't stand the idea of bettering our town. Let's just go, Delores." Gladys headed for her vehicle. "It's in their nature, and you can't make a coyote be anything but a coyote."

"Or a vulture be anything but a vulture," Ethel muttered.

Delores's short legs had to really churn to keep up with Gladys, but she managed, and the buzz of their whispers floated over the breeze. Even though they couldn't hear the exact words, there was no doubt in Ruth Ann's and Liddy's minds that they were raking them over the hot coals.

"She's gathering a posse. We better polish up our armor and swords."

"Armor and swords, my butt," Ruth Ann declared. "I'm going to polish up my pistol and sharpen up every shovel in my garage."

"Don't be so hard on Matilda. She means well, and she does have the town's best interests at heart. Gladys and Delores just said so, and they wouldn't lie or allow themselves to be manipulated by Matilda, now, would they?" Liddy tried to make a joke, but her words dripped with sarcasm.

"That woman doesn't want a compromise. She wants a hostile take-over," Ruth Ann declared. "Paul says that Remington makes a one-shot dose that will keep a coyote from ever trying to get into the sheep pen a second time. It should work on two-legged coyotes just as well."

"Do they sell that kind of one-shot dose at the drugstore?" Liddy asked through clenched teeth as she watched Gladys and Delores keep glancing over their shoulders as they walked away. She had to hold her hands to keep from making a pistol with her thumb and forefinger and pretending to shoot them.

"No, but they do at the ammo store," Ruth Ann answered. "But for now, let's go find food. I hear a caramel apple calling my name after we have a gyro. I want to sit under a shade tree and eat every bite of it. Delores is probably itching to find Matilda and tell her, word for word, what you said."

"That was my intention," Liddy said.

"Well played, Sister, well played." Ruth Ann patted her on the back. "Now, let's forget about Matilda and her band of followers and enjoy this festival."

"Hey, Aunt Liddy!" Amelia waved from a table where she sat with Daniel.

Liddy veered off the path and stopped by the nearly empty table. "Looks like y'all are about done here, too."

Daniel nodded. "I'll be glad when ten more people come by and buy these last lollipops. Our goal was to sell a hundred, and we've got these last ten to go."

"It beats going door to door for the junior-class fundraiser," Amelia said.

"How much are they?" Ruth Ann asked.

"Dollar each, and the kids get to keep a portion of the proceeds for their prom," Daniel answered.

"I'll take all of them." She took a ten-dollar bill from her purse and handed it to him. "That's exactly how many kids I've got in my Sunday school class, and I try to take them a little treat every few weeks."

"You are a sweetheart, Mama!" Amelia put the last lollipops into a brown paper bag.

"Yes, you are." Daniel took her money and put it in a ziplock bag. "Now I can go enjoy the carnival with Savannah. Her booth was selling cookie dough, and they ran out in the first hour. You can go, Amelia. I'll put this table and our chairs in my truck."

Amelia pushed her chair back and stood up. "I'm not even going to argue with you. Where are we off to, Aunt Liddy?"

"The gyro wagon," Liddy answered. "None of us had time for lunch."

"Me either, and that sounds so good," Amelia said. "Let's get cotton candy afterwards, and then wait a little bit and have funnel cakes."

"And after that, a caramel apple," Liddy said. "I'm convinced that a caramel apple every year at the festival brings me good luck until the next year, and Lord knows I need some good luck the way this year is going."

"We might ought to eat two," Ruth Ann suggested.

"Core and all." Liddy giggled. "And maybe the wooden stick just to be sure."

"Y'all are too funny," Amelia said. "I want to grow up and be like both of you. I'll treat all of us to a caramel apple. Maybe if we all have one, Matilda will go away in a puff of smoke, never to be seen or heard from again."

"Amen to that," Liddy agreed.

Ruth Ann looped an arm into her daughter's and the three of them headed for the gyro wagon.

"I just love the festival. I hope it's still going on when I'm eighty years old," Amelia said.

Liddy did the math in her head and then said, "That would be fifty-two years from now. If you want it to be around that long, you might have to take over the planning committee when your mama decides to step down."

"We've already talked about that, and I'm looking forward to it," Amelia agreed, "but not for a long time, because Mama does a fantastic job, and it will take me years to learn how she gets it all done."

"What would you change about the festival if you did take over?" Ruth Ann asked.

"Not one thing," Amelia said. "If it wasn't the same, then folks that come would be disappointed."

A Realtor didn't keep the same hours as a banker. Sometimes, Nick had to show a property on a Saturday or even a Sunday because that was the only time folks might have to look at a house, a farm, or an acreage. That morning, he had missed the parade because a potential buyer from Oklahoma City could only fit a couple of hours into his schedule to look at a large ranch that was for sale south of Bonnet.

He had made a round at the park and noticed Amelia sitting with some guy at a table. A little jealousy streaked through him before he realized that it had to be her friend from school when another lady stopped by and kissed him.

"What are you thinking about?" Matilda and her new friends sat down at the table where he was having tacos and a beer.

"Whether or not to get another beer or a soda pop, or to forgo both and go have some funnel cakes," he answered.

"Don't lie to me. All that unhealthy food does not put that kind of smile on your face," she declared.

"I was thinking about Dad," he told her.

"Why would you even let that man cross your mind after the way he's treated me?" Matilda was careful not to let the trained tear hanging on her lashes drop and ruin her mascara.

"You poor dear. Do you need to sit down for a spell?" Gladys gave Nick a dose of stink eye, but down through the years he had had far worse than whatever that little lady could produce.

"Yes, I do," Matilda sighed. "I don't want to talk about Gregory or even think about him. I want to talk about the Grey Manor to take my mind off my broken heart. That's why I'm working so hard to try to help this little town become a nicer place to live. I need something to fill the horrible void that Gregory created when he left me."

Matilda and her friends started talking about how they were going to change things in the old stone house. That went right into their plans to buy a couple of the empty buildings in town so that there could be a spa and a gym in Bonnet. Then he noticed Amelia, Liddy, and Ruth Ann ordering from the gyro wagon. He waited until they had their food, then sent a text to Amelia: It's good to see you again.

He watched her take her phone from the hip pocket of her skinny jeans that hugged every curve and smile when she saw the message. Then she took a bite of her gyro and typed: You too.

"What are you doing? It's rude to text when I'm talking to you," Matilda broke into his moment.

"I'm not really interested in your ideas for the Grey Manor, and I think a gym and a spa in a town this size is more than a little stupid," Nick answered.

"See what I have to put up with?" Matilda sighed again, just for her friends' benefit, though. She kicked Nick under the table and frowned at him.

"We weren't talking about the new businesses," Tina told him in a tone that dripped with icicles. "Your mother was asking you if you wanted to go with us to get a snow cone. She was remembering how much you love them."

"No, thank you," Nick said.

"Why not?" Matilda asked. "Does it have something to do with the fact that you are messing with your phone and not paying a bit of attention to me?"

You'd drop with cardiac arrest if I answered that truthfully, Nick thought.

"I'm going to have another beer and watch the people," he said. "I'm not sure they have sugar-free snow cones, but you can check."

Matilda stood up and glared across the table at him. "I have already checked, and they have sugar-free cherry, which is my favorite flavor. And for your information, there will be more healthy food wagons at this festival next year. Liddy Latham can't live forever."

"I wouldn't hold my breath about that if I was you, Mother. Kids are always going to spend their money on tacos and cotton candy, not little cups of carrot and celery sticks," Nick said.

Matilda sighed, this time even more dramatically than before, and turned to her friends. "When a child is little, they walk on your toes. When they grow up, they stomp on your heart."

Toes, nothing, Nick thought. *I wasn't ever allowed to get close enough to you to put a footprint on your fancy high-heeled shoes. You were always afraid I would put my dirty little hands on your clothes. And I'm not sure anyone has ever gotten close enough to your heart to put a fingerprint on it, let alone stomp on it.*

"Y'all go on and enjoy your snow cones," he said with a sideways glance over toward Amelia. Why, oh, why were there sparks and electricity between them when even so much as a friendship seemed impossible? *Time to make the women speed up their departure.* "I'm going to sit right here, rest my taco-filled body, and have one more beer. Then, when I get hungry again, I'm having one of those great big cinnamon rolls with all the buttery icing on top. You're sure y'all don't want to share?"

"I'm not sure he's even my son," Matilda said in a half-joking tone. "I think maybe they mixed up my baby with another one in the nursery when he was born."

Nick let her have the last word, went back to his phone, and typed: Look to your left at the taco wagon.

She read the words and then their gazes met somewhere in the middle of the distance between them. She nodded slightly and sent another message: Huh-oh!

He read the one word and glanced up to see his mother and her entourage stopping in front of the table where Liddy was sitting with Amelia and her friends.

His thumbs flew over the keys, and he stood up. No way was he going to let his mother make a big public scene: I'm on my way.

Whoa! she sent back. All is good.

He sat back down and finished the rest of his beer, glad that whatever went on happened fast and was done with. Then he typed: What happened?

He chuckled when he read: A few barbs and I got a few dirty looks.

He glanced that way out the corner of his eye to find Liddy glaring at him. She certainly had a right not to want him around her niece with all the history between the Davis and Taylor families. He typed: It's my turn now.

With his eyes glued to the phone screen waiting for a reply, he didn't even realize that Amelia was coming toward him until she was right there. The hair on his neck got all prickly just like it had the first time he saw her at Wanda's funeral.

She continued right past him without even a glance, ordered a beer at the wagon, and then brought it to the table where he was sitting.

"Hello, Nick." She smiled. "Did you enjoy the parade? I looked for you but never could find you."

"I didn't get to go to the parade," he answered. Then he asked out the corner of his mouth, "What are you doing here? Do you want to get us both killed?"

"I ordered a beer and happened to see you here sitting alone. Thought I would stop and visit with you. Mind if I sit down?" she asked with an impish grin. "And neither Aunt Liddy nor your mother will kill us when we're together. The gossip would be more than they could stand. Think about the newspaper headline in the *Bonnet Weekly News*: Two Prominent Bonnet Citizens Dead: Taylor and Davis Feud Alive and Well. 'The couple was sitting at a wooden picnic table when daggers, shot from the eyes of Liddy Latham and Matilda Monroe, pierced their hearts and killed them graveyard dead.'"

Nick laughed out loud. "Please sit down and tell me more about this article with our obits in it. I'm about to get myself another beer. Do you want one?"

"I'm good," she answered.

He bought a Coors longneck bottle and brought it to the table where she was waiting. He twisted the top off and set it down. "The cold air that's flowing from the gyro wagon to this table might freeze the beer."

"Could happen," she agreed. "Way I see it is that it's rude to ignore a newcomer in town."

"Well, thank you." Nick nodded.

"Why didn't you get to the parade?"

"I had to show a ranch south of town. The possibility of a sale looks promising," Nick said. "Was that your friend Daniel sitting with you at the table where you were selling lollipops?"

"Yes, it was," she answered. "He and I started working at the high school at the same time five years ago. So, you saw us selling lollipops?"

"I walked right past your table, but you were waiting on a family with a bunch of little kids," he answered. "Does this mean we can actually talk face-to-face when we just happen to be in the same place? Like church tomorrow morning?"

Amelia took a sip of her beer. "I would think so since I would never be rude—except maybe a little catty to your mother. My Granny Dee would make me sit in a corner if I was hateful and rude to anyone, and I really did not like sitting with my nose in a corner."

"Drink slowly," he said.

"Why?" she asked and sipped at her beer again.

"Because when you get finished, you'll leave," he answered.

"If I stay longer than it takes me to drink this . . ." She paused and set her beer on the table. She looked up. "Huh-oh, we're about to have company. Afternoon, ma'am. That snow cone sure looks good. I might hit that wagon when I finish my beer."

Nick looked up from his own beer into his mother's angry eyes. "Hello, Mother. That didn't take long. Where's your friends?"

"They went to check out a jewelry vendor." At her tone, he could have sworn the temperature dropped ten degrees. "What's going on here?"

"I came over for a beer, and Nick and I've been talking about the festival." Amelia put on her best fake smile. "Are you enjoying the fun, ma'am?"

"I was until this moment," Matilda answered. "And I told you not to call me ma'am."

"I was brought up to be respectful to my elders—to call them ma'am, or sir if it happens to be a gentleman. I believe you are female and you're certainly older than me, so I should call you ma'am," Amelia said.

Matilda tipped her head up and looked down her nose at Amelia. If looks could kill, there would be nothing left of Amelia but a greasy spot beside a half-empty longneck bottle of beer.

Nick saw Liddy and Ruth Ann walking right toward them and raised an eyebrow. Amelia motioned them over to the table. "Aunt Liddy, Mama, come on over here and meet Nick. I was just telling Miz Monroe here about the manners my Granny Dee taught me—the ones you two reinforced my whole life."

"I've known Nick since he was a toddler." Liddy's tone was every bit as cold as Matilda's.

"Well, then, Nick, this is my mother, Ruth Ann." She pointed to her left. "I've just got a bit more of this beer left. Are y'all ready to go check out the rest of the carnival?"

"I'm pleased to meet you, Miz Ruth Ann, and to see you again, Miz Liddy." Nick could tell by her expression that she would rather be talking to a rattlesnake, but he flashed her a bright smile and looked right into her eyes. "I remember you coming by the shop to bring Harry a lemon pie on his birthday when I was about ten years old. That was the best pie I ever ate, until I got a small piece of one of your pies at Wanda's funeral. You certainly haven't lost your touch," Nick said.

Nick noticed that Liddy's hands were knotted into fists. Ruth Ann looked like she could chew up a full-grown Angus bull and spit out hamburger patties. His mother had crossed her arms over her chest and was tapping her foot. That always meant he was in big trouble.

Amelia polished off her beer. "Thanks for the visit, Nick. I'm sure I'll see you around."

"Hope so," Nick said with another brilliant smile.

Matilda waited until they were completely out of hearing distance, and then she sat down across from Nick. "What the hell was that? I told you to stay away from that woman."

"We met at the funerals, and she was just being friendly," he said. "Like I told you before, this is a small town, and people do tend to be nice."

"You know what's going on between me and Liddy." Matilda shook a finger at him. "Why are you staring at me like that?"

"Your snow cone just leaked out the bottom and onto your white silk blouse, and now it's dripping on your slacks. I guess you got cherry flavor, and now it looks like you're bleeding." Nick didn't want to hear anything more about the feud, but he did want to talk to Amelia some more.

Matilda looked down at the ruined shirt and slacks and growled, "You caused this. Now I'll have to go change. Thank goodness I brought extra things in my SUV." She tossed the rest of the snow cone on the ground and stood up. "I mean it, Nick. I won't have you talking to that woman."

"I do not intend to be rude to anyone. I like talking to Amelia. Besides, this is a small town. Being hateful could ruin the business," Nick told her.

"You can be friendly without buying her a beer," Matilda replied.

"That's not my style, Mother." Nick shrugged. "Your friends are all coming this way. They look like they're about to call the EMTs and have the ambulance haul you off to the hospital."

Matilda turned around and stormed away toward the four women. "This isn't over," she tossed back to them.

"No, Mother, it's not." Nick agreed with her for the first time in weeks, but inside he was fighting the desire to laugh out loud, raise a forefinger, and say, "Score one for me, zero for Mother."

Chapter Ten

*L*ike always, Amelia made her way past Clovis and Bridget to sit between her sister and her aunt that Sunday morning. She leaned forward and smiled at the rest of the family, who were lined up on the other side of Liddy.

"You look harried," Bridget whispered. "What's going on? Do I need to check *your* blood pressure?"

"I changed clothes five times this morning. Nothing seemed to be right," Amelia answered. "I thought I was going to be late and got a warning from a town cop because I was driving too fast."

"Why are you so worried about what you are wearing?" Bridget asked.

Amelia shrugged. "Don't you ever have a day like that?"

"Only when I'm trying to impress someone," Bridget answered. "Is there a new man in your life? Please tell me there is because Mama and Aunt Liddy are worried about you and Nick."

"Not right now." Amelia figured it wasn't a lie because she and Nick were just talking, not dating.

"Shhh . . ." Aunt Liddy shook her head at her nieces.

Amelia caught a word or two of the conversations behind her as the sanctuary buzzed with whispers. About half of what she heard was about Matilda and the other half was about Liddy. Amelia smiled when she heard someone say something to the effect that Liddy would live long enough to serve lemon pies at Matilda's funeral dinner.

Liddy nudged her on the arm. "What are you grinning about?"

"I'm just happy," Amelia answered in a low voice. "You shushed me and Bridget. Why are you talking?"

"I read the time wrong for the start of the service," Liddy said. "Guess I might need to get me some reading glasses."

Bridget leaned around Amelia and said, "It's springtime, Aunt Liddy. Birds are singing. Bluebonnets are in bloom."

"I can't hear the birds singing," Liddy said.

That's a good thing, Amelia thought, *because if you could you'd hear all the gossip going on about you and Matilda. And then you'd be standing up and preaching a sermon right here before church.*

"If everyone was quiet, you could." Amelia's smile got even bigger.

"Probably so, but are you in such a good mood because your hormones are in overdrive, like the birds and the bees? Don't you tell me that you've got a hankering for Nick Monroe." Liddy eyed her closely. "I saw the way he was looking at you yesterday over at the taco wagon. I might've said something more about it right there, but that would have meant I was in league with Matilda. It's plain as the nose on a hog's face that she doesn't like him talking to you, and I wouldn't throw in with her for half the dirt in Texas."

"What I was thinking," Amelia said as she leaned closer to her aunt's ear, "is that you should shed those pantyhose. No one wears them anymore. You don't need them for warmth like you might in the winter. Lord only knows you would be a lot more comfortable without them. Throw them away and be free to enjoy the spring. I bet the reason you can't hear the birds is because those things have prevented your blood from circulating to your ears."

"Honey, my pantyhose hide a multitude of ugly veins," Liddy whispered, "and I buy the ones with a control top so I don't look like ten pounds of potatoes stuffed into a five-pound bag."

Amelia felt Nick's presence at the end of the pew and got a whiff of his woodsy aftershave. Her heart threw in an extra beat and her pulse raced when she looked up into his mossy green eyes. That was the first time she'd noticed the golden flecks, and for some crazy reason, she thought of the pot of gold at the end of a rainbow.

"Good morning." Her voice sounded strange in her own ears, but dammit, his touch made her mind go places that shouldn't even be thought about in church.

"This is a beautiful day, but not as beautiful as all you ladies." He included all of them in the statement.

Nice work, she thought.

Liddy barely nodded at him. "Thank you, Nick. It's good to see you again."

"What about us two guys?" Clovis asked from the other end of the pew, where he sat next to Paul.

"I probably shouldn't call you beautiful." Nick smiled.

"C'mon! I changed shirts three times this morning just so I'd look pretty," Clovis teased.

Amelia's emotions were on a roller coaster, and she couldn't grab on to even one of the top two—guilt and attraction. In all the spinning thoughts, she made a mental note to make Clovis a pan of her brownies next week to thank him for nipping what could have been a bad situation in the bud.

"The festival was great yesterday," Nick said. "Just like I remembered it from the last time I visited Uncle Harry. I got up early this morning and helped the volunteers pick up trash, so now the park looks all pretty and clean again."

"That's really sweet of you," Amelia said.

"Thanks," Paul muttered.

"Looks like I'd better take a seat. If y'all need anything for next year's festival, just let me know. I enjoyed sitting on the panel that judged the bonnets. Congratulations on winning it, Bridget," Nick said.

"Thank you," Bridget said. "That's my first time to win. I'm excited to have the trophy."

"She's not going to let me forget that she beat me out with a hat she's worn for the past five years," Amelia giggled.

"The vote was unanimous, but your bonnet was really nice, too, Amelia." He sat in the pew where his Uncle Harry always sat—right across the aisle from them.

"That's Matilda's son?" Paul leaned around Ruth Ann and whispered to Liddy. "Hardly seems possible."

"He does seem to be a sweet person, doesn't he?" Amelia said out the corner of her mouth.

"Looks can be deceiving," Liddy muttered, "and if Matilda saw him talking to us, he might not survive the day."

"He picked up trash. Got to give him credit for that," Amelia said.

"That was just so everyone would know he's trying to be part of the community. He's probably just as conniving as his mother. The apple doesn't fall far from the tree," Liddy whispered.

"Then heaven help *me*," Amelia said with half a giggle.

Liddy always tried to think of something she was grateful for when she arrived at church, and that morning she had thought about how wonderful it was to have had so much family support through the years. Matilda had brought back so many memories, and through it all, Liddy had had Paul, Ruth Ann, and their girls right there to support her.

She was determined not to let Matilda get under her skin—if she even showed up for church that morning—and then Nick arrived. Sure, he had picked up trash, and he was a good-looking guy in those khaki slacks and that dark green shirt. If Liddy had been fifty years younger, she might have even thought he was sexy, but he was Matilda's son, for

God's sake. And there was no doubt in her mind that he was flirting with her Amelia.

The preacher stepped up behind the podium and cleared his throat. As if on cue, the whole sanctuary went quiet, and the preacher smiled. "Good morning, everyone. What a blessed day this is. Spring is here, and Easter is right around the corner. I'd like to remind all of you that we will be having our church egg hunt for the kids on the Saturday before so that each of you can have Easter Sunday with your own families. The hunt is scheduled for ten o'clock that morning, and we'll have a potluck out on the church grounds if it's not raining, so bring your quilts and join us for a fun day. If it does rain, the hunt will be held in the sanctuary and all the Sunday school rooms, and the potluck will be held in the fellowship hall. Anyone who wants to donate plastic eggs filled with candy or whatever you want to put in them should get in touch with Ruth Ann Taylor. She will be spearheading that event for us." He stopped, looked toward the back of the church, and nodded. "Before we begin our congregational singing, I'd like to announce that Delores has decided to retire from playing piano for us and has given her post to Matilda Monroe. After services, all y'all welcome Matilda back to Bonnet, and shake her hand for agreeing to take over for Delores."

"Hmmph," Liddy snorted, "it ain't got *that* cold in hell."

"Aunt Liddy!" Amelia scolded.

"I'm just tellin' the truth," Liddy said. "I had a visit with God when Richie died. I told Him I wouldn't shoot that woman since she had a son to raise, but Nick is a grown man now, so she's walkin' on thin ice."

The noise of folks turning around on the old wooden pews filled the sanctuary. Liddy heard what the preacher said, but she could hardly believe it, and yet when she turned, there was Matilda, making a grand entrance, almost strutting down the aisle. She must've wanted to give the impression that she was an angel in her white dress with a lace shawl around her tanned shoulders. The gold-and-diamond cross that hung around her neck flashed with every slow and mincing step she took. As if she were riding on the hood of a car in a parade, she waved and smiled at the folks when she passed each pew.

"So everyone can see her," Liddy muttered under her breath.

"Looks like she's snuck one in on us," Paul whispered.

Matilda sat down at the piano, smiled once again, this time for the benefit of the whole congregation, and turned the pages of the hymnal in front of her. The preacher stepped away from the podium and took a seat on the deacon's bench as the song director took her place.

"Miz Monroe has asked that we sing number one seventy-nine, 'Abide with Me,'" she announced.

"That song talks about the helping of the helpless," Liddy whispered as she found the page. "Seems like an oxymoron to hear those words out of Matilda's mouth."

"She will bend the helpless to her will for sure, just like she did Delores," Ruth Ann told her.

"Aunt Liddy!" Amelia scolded. "You should love your neighbor."

"I do. I love all my neighbors, and sometimes I even like them. But Matilda is living in Muenster so . . ." Liddy shrugged. "Besides, God *is* abiding with me. That woman is still alive, isn't she?"

Matilda played a prelude to the hymn, and then the song director started the congregation off with the first words.

What next? Liddy wondered. *It looks like she's here to stay, since she's buying the old stone house.*

Think you'll ever be even cordial to each other? The voice in her head asked.

Ain't damn likely, Liddy answered as she sang along with the rest of the folks.

As soon as the benediction was over, Amelia stood up and stepped out into the center aisle at the same time Nick did. His hand brushed against hers, and the vibes were so heavy between them that she was amazed her Aunt Liddy couldn't see them dancing around like hot little flashes from a Fourth of July sparkler.

Nick just smiled and moved on in the line of people headed toward the door to shake hands with the preacher.

She smiled back and then lingered with the rest of her family, who were talking to Don Hollis. She got in on the tail end of something to do with replacing Harry Davis on the council, and then Don moved on.

"What was that all about?" she asked.

"City council stuff," Clovis answered. "Don wants Paul to run again, and they're both trying to talk me into throwing my hat into the ring."

"You'd be good at that," Amelia said.

"Bridget and I will have to talk about it," Clovis answered, "but for now, I'm starving. Think we could sneak out the side door and skip shaking hands with the preacher?"

"Suits me just fine," Liddy agreed with a nod. "Matilda is ahead of us, and unless he squirts some of that sanitizer on his hands, I don't want to take a chance on her germs transferring from her to him to me."

"I hear you," Paul said.

Amelia bit back a sigh. Attraction or not, anything at all with Nick was not happening.

"Follow me." Liddy led the whole family out the door and into the parking lot. "Clovis, you better be in line for dinner before me. I love Ruth Ann's shrimp alfredo casserole, so there might not be any left after I fill my plate."

"Everybody best watch out or they might get a fork in their hand when it's my turn to get at it," Clovis teased.

Amelia would have never thought Bridget would fall in love with a guy like Clovis Doucet. Her sister had always gone for the tall, dark, and handsome guys until Clovis came along, but then there was that old saying about opposites attracting. Just like Amelia, Bridget was five feet, three inches tall, but she had green eyes and maybe just a few more curves than Amelia had. Her hair was a bit redder and was straight as a flat iron, whereas Amelia had to fight curls—especially in rainy weather.

Clovis had dishwater-blond hair and a round baby face. He wore wire-rimmed glasses that he was constantly misplacing. He was one of those guys that kind of disappeared in a crowd because there was nothing outstanding about him. Except for his sense of humor. After spending half an hour in the room with him, a person couldn't help but love him. Amelia always thought that was why he was so good in the ER.

"The way Nick was flirting with you, I thought maybe you had plans with him," Clovis whispered.

"I thought he was flirting with you." Amelia nudged him on the shoulder.

"You do know he's off limits, as in never, ever, not in a million years, right?" Clovis asked as they approached their vehicles.

"Yep, I know that." Amelia sighed as she slid in behind the wheel and started the engine to her car. She loved Sunday dinners at her folks' house every week. That was one thing she missed when she was in college and couldn't get home every single weekend.

About once a month Aunt Liddy brought a lemon pie, and today was one of those times when she'd made one of her lemon meringues. Liddy had a theory that if a person ate lemon pie every day, they would soon get tired of it, so it should be an occasional treat.

"Does that work with attractions like the one I've got for Nick? If I saw or talked to him every day, would I soon see something in him, like I did with Elliott, that I couldn't stand?" she muttered as she drove through town toward her folks' place.

Clovis was setting the table and Bridget was taking a salad from the refrigerator when Amelia entered the house. The whole place smelled like the loaf of fresh-baked bread waiting to be sliced.

"What can I do to help?" Amelia asked.

"Pour the tea." Paul plugged in the electric knife. "I'm going to take care of the bread. Liddy is putting out garlic butter and the stuffed mushrooms. I think Harry Davis is a fool."

"But, Daddy"—Amelia stopped taking glasses down from the cabinet—"you always said he was the only one of the Davis family worth anything."

"Because he might not come back to town, and he'll never get another of Liddy's lemon pies if he doesn't," Paul said. "And while we're talking about the Davis family, what was that all about this morning in church?"

"Harry has probably got his toes in the warm sand, watching cute women in bikinis, and having shrimp po'boys for dinner." Amelia ignored the question.

"But he's not having lemon meringue pie or your mama's shrimp alfredo casserole," Paul answered. "And you didn't answer my question."

"I was nice to Nick at the festival," Amelia answered. "He was at the taco wagon when I went over. He's new in town, and we talked a few minutes. To be honest, though, Dad, he did offer to buy me a beer."

Paul finished his job and draped an arm around Amelia's shoulders. "Speaking to a person is one thing, but letting him buy you a beer might give him ideas. You've always had a soft heart, but be careful, darlin'. Nick could be a good person in spite of who his mother is, but I couldn't bear to see you go to that dark place you were in two years ago," he told her.

"I'm over Elliott, and I learned my lesson about men like him, Daddy." She tiptoed and gave him a kiss on the cheek. "I won't make that mistake again. I can spot a controlling narcissist a mile away."

"Well, thank God for that," Bridget said. "Did you see the way Matilda practically danced up the aisle to the piano, and she's not even as good as Delores. She messed up several times. Delores never did."

"She won't be here long," Liddy assured Bridget as they all took their places around the table. "When she figures out that she can't run roughshod over our family, she'll move on."

"But she'll leave Nick behind." Ruth Ann caught Amelia's eye.

"At least he seems like a decent-enough guy," Paul said. "Long as he doesn't flirt with my daughter, I don't care if he's here. Clovis, will you say grace for us today?"

"Yes, sir," Clovis said, "be glad to."

Amelia bowed her head with the rest of the family, but she couldn't resist opening one eye and studying each of them. When she was with Elliott, he had slowly pulled her away from her family, and she seldom spent time with them, even though she lived in the same town. Elliott drove over from Wichita Falls several times a week and expected her to be at his place from Friday after school until Monday morning.

If she continued to talk to or even possibly date Nick, it would mean an instant break with the people around the table. She couldn't have both, and she'd been absolutely miserable when she'd lost her family relationships, especially with her mother.

Amelia dried the last dish and put it away, then yawned. "Excuse me. Not bad company, but too much good food and fellowship," she said. "It's time for me to go home and get a nap. I can't keep up with you folks. A whole day at the festival and then this much excitement today is too much for me."

"Don't go yet," Bridget said. "Mama and Aunt Liddy are going to her house to talk about the cookbook stuff for the church. Daddy and Clovis are headed out to the golf course to knock a few balls around. Stay and sit on the porch and talk to me. We haven't had a couple of free hours to spend together in a long time."

"Only if you promise that if I fall asleep you won't pinch me," Amelia agreed.

"Cross my heart." Bridget made the sign across her chest like she and Amelia did when they were little girls.

Amelia hung the damp dish towel on the rack beside the refrigerator and followed her sister out to the porch. She slumped down in a bamboo settee and propped her feet up on a matching hassock.

Bridget sat down beside her. "Move your feet over a little so I can use the hassock, too."

Amelia shifted her legs to one side. "You are welcome."

"Okay, okay!" Bridget giggled. "Thank you for doing that, Sis. Now that we're alone, tell me what was going on this morning. I could feel the heat between you and Nick all the way down the pew."

"I'm attracted to him, and I think he is to me, but like Daddy and Clovis both said, it won't ever work. Strange thing is that they liked Elliott when I brought him home to meet them, and he was . . ." Amelia frowned.

"And he was a manipulative chameleon," Bridget finished, "but you're right. We all thought he was wonderful until he almost took you away from me. I can't even begin to tell you how glad I am to have you back to normal. If this Nick guy is anything like his mother, you might be getting right back into a situation like you had with Elliott. From what everyone says, Matilda is controlling and manipulative, just like Elliott. They both change who they are to fit the group, and then use people."

"What if he's like his father?" Amelia asked.

"Do you know his dad?" Bridget raised an eyebrow.

"No, but Aunt Liddy says he is a decent guy, and do we really know anyone? You went to college and then medical school, clinicals, and internship. When you came home, did you know those people you went to high school with anymore? You had all changed, just like the kids who were my classmates. Everyone changes. I'm sure Nick has a past, just like all the rest of us. I hope no one judges me by the mistake I made with Elliott," Amelia answered.

"That sounds like an excuse wrapped around shaky reasoning. Granny Dee always said that, and I'm not sure I understand what all this beating around the bush has to do with Nick or answering my question about knowing his dad, for that matter," Bridget said.

"I do not know Nick's father," Amelia said. "It's not fair to judge him by his mother any more than it would be to judge me by my mistake in letting Elliott control everything in my life. What if I'm throwing away the one person who could make me happy for the rest of my life?"

"With Elliott, you didn't realize what you were throwing away until he almost had you totally brainwashed. With Nick you'd go into the relationship knowing how much it will upset everyone. You are a grown woman, and I can't talk you out of anything, but think twice, then sleep on it and think again. This is some serious stuff, little sister. Promise me you won't go into it without a lot of thought and maybe some prayers," Bridget advised.

"I promise I will do that," Amelia agreed.

"Now on a different note," Bridget said, "I've been dying to tell someone that Clovis and I are going to start trying to have a baby next month. I can't tell Mama or Aunt Liddy because if we can't have children, or I don't get pregnant right away, then they'd be disappointed. But I just had to tell someone."

"Oh, Bridget!" Amelia jumped up and rounded the hassock to hug her sister. "I can't wait to be an aunt."

"Think we'll be able to say Aunt Amelia? Or will it come out Aunt Liddy, because *Liddy* just naturally follows *aunt* in our minds?" Bridget giggled.

"I don't care if she calls me Aunt Mellie or just Auntie. I'll be her favorite aunt." Amelia stepped back, happy that she was going to be an aunt for sure, but maybe just a tad bit even more joyous that they could talk about something other than Nick and Matilda.

"You will be the only aunt on this side, but remember Clovis has three sisters who are all older than him, so they might fight you for the title of favorite," Bridget told her.

"Bring it on!" Amelia struck a boxing pose. "I'm also the meanest aunt she'll have."

"She?" Bridget teased. "What if we have a boy? I was thinking that Daddy might really love a grandson."

"Girl or boy makes no difference to me. I'll be an aunt either way," Amelia said.

A clap of thunder brought on instant rain that came down in sheets and drove the sisters inside the house in a hurry.

"Granny Dee says that hard rain don't last," Bridget said.

"So does Darryl Worley in his country song, but it doesn't matter if it lasts or not, Daddy and Clovis won't be playing golf this afternoon," Amelia said.

"You're right," Bridget said. "I hear truck doors slamming already. Guess the storm reached the golf course before it got here."

Amelia thought of the family storm going on with Matilda and Nick Monroe and wondered if that one would ever pass over like the rain of that moment.

"I'm going to run between the raindrops and go home for a nap." Amelia gave her sister a quick hug. "I've got papers to grade this afternoon, and I'll have trouble keeping my eyes open if I don't have a thirty-minute power nap."

"Love you," Bridget said. "And keep your fingers crossed for us."

"I definitely will, and I'll be the first to know, right?" Amelia whispered.

"Right after Clovis," Bridget told her.

Chapter Eleven

S orry, girl"—Nick bent down to pet Vera at the back door—"but you can't go for a run with me. You stay here and protect the house from crickets and mice."

The cat looked so pitiful that he stroked her from head to tail a few more times. When he locked the door and tucked the key into his sock, she turned around and ran back to the kitchen.

"You didn't want to go anyway," he chuckled. "You just wanted to make me feel bad for leaving you alone."

He did a couple of stretches and then took off in a slow, easy jog toward the city park. He would have rather been FaceTiming with Amelia on the phone than out running, but he did love the smell of the wet earth and the cool evening air after a good rain. That all brought back visions of Amelia at the two recent funerals, and at the festival. It's a wonder they had both lived through all those events.

"The one woman I've met that I could maybe fall for, and my mother messed it all up before I was even two years old," he grumbled.

When he reached the park, he was already wet with sweat from the humidity and the exercise, so he didn't even care that the bench was wet. He plopped down, took several long breaths, and closed his eyes. It was hard to believe that not long before, the whole park was covered with food vendors, rides, and carnival games, and that he and Amelia had had a beer together. If only they could . . .

His train of thought was interrupted when he heard the slap of a runner's feet on the wet road not far from where he was sitting. He opened his eyes and a lollipop made of green persimmons couldn't have wiped the smile from his face.

"Ask and you shall receive," he muttered.

"Hey." Amelia sat down on the bench beside him. "So, you jog, too?"

"Yep, I do." He smiled at her. "You always run to the park and back?"

"Yep." She pulled her earbuds out and let them hang.

"What were you listening to?" Nick asked.

"Miranda's 'Storms Never Last,' some Joan Baez because my granny loves her, and 'Hard Rain Don't Last.' Seems like my random setting was stuck on songs about storms," she told him.

Nick was amazed that they liked the same music. "Guess great minds think alike, and also enjoy the same music. You like Creedence?" If talking about music kept her beside him for a while longer, then he could think of all kinds of bands to discuss.

"I was listening to 'Bad Moon Rising' when I sat down," she answered. "And you?"

"I'm an eclectic listener, too." He grinned. "I've got my playlist on random, too, and tonight it gave me some George Strait, some Billie Eilish, and the last one was by Maren Morris."

"I like all of those," Amelia said. "Do you always run the same route?" This just might be the answer to that prayer that Bridget was talking about. No one could fault them if they just happened to run into each other at the park when they stopped to rest at the halfway point of their evening run.

"Pretty much," he admitted. "If I leave at the right time, I can get home right at dusk."

"Me too. If I don't, I can stop by Aunt Liddy's, and she'll drive me out to my apartment." There was chemistry between them. She could feel it, and his eyes said that he could feel it, too. But there wasn't anything either of them could do about it.

"Have you heard from Harry?" she asked and then wished she could take it back. She didn't really want to talk about Harry Davis. She wanted to hear Nick's slow Texas drawl telling her about himself.

"Yep, he's rented a condo right on Laguna Beach in the Florida Panhandle and is loving every minute of his time. He says that every day that passes, he is surer that he's going to retire for good," Nick answered. "He says that he might never leave that area and has spotted a house he's going to look at. It opens up onto the beach, and he is planning on looking at it next week. He's invited me down there for a long weekend this summer. Want to go with me?"

"We would both be excommunicated from our families if we did that." She took a long drink.

Oh, but it is tempting, isn't it? the voice in her head said.

"A nice thought, though, isn't it?" he asked.

"Yep." She took another drink. "I'd better get back to it or Aunt Liddy will have to take me home for sure. Maybe I'll see you again some evening?"

"Anytime, and Vera says to tell you hello." Nick got to his feet and disappeared out into the semidarkness.

She gave him a few minutes and then started on her run again. She planned to stop at Aunt Liddy's, but when she got to the snow cone stand right across the street from Nick's house, she could see that Liddy's car was gone and there were no lights on in the house.

"Just my luck that Aunt Liddy lives kitty-corner to Nick. I couldn't get away with spending time at his house if I wanted to," she muttered as she leaned against the wall of the snow cone stand. She put her hands on her knees and took several long breaths, hoping to kick the insane idea out of her mind about going over there and knocking on his back door—but it didn't work.

"That would be crazy. My hair is sticking to my sweaty face, and I look like crap," she muttered. "But Aunt Liddy isn't home, and it's dark."

He's already seen you like this, the voice in her head reminded her.

As if she couldn't control her feet and they had a mind of their own, she found herself jogging across the street. She was panting when she knocked on the back door but had caught her breath when Nick opened the door.

"Amelia?" His face registered shock. "Come in. Is everything all right?"

"I'm fine, and we both know I shouldn't be here, so tell me to go home," she said.

"Can't do it," he said as he slowly shook his head. "I'm too glad to see you to do that, and quite frankly, darlin', I don't give a damn about what my mother thinks."

"I came to see Vera," she said.

"Well, she is receiving guests this evening." Nick grinned as he stepped back and motioned her inside. "She's retiring at this very moment somewhere in the house. I'll have to call her out of one of her hidey-holes, so it could take a little while."

The old wooden screen door reminded Amelia of the one at her Granny Dee's place out on the small island. She had the urge to slam it after she'd stepped inside the wide foyer but closed it carefully instead.

"One of my earliest memories is getting in trouble for slamming that door," Nick said. "I would slide down the banister, hit the floor at a run, and go out that door like lightning was licking my butt."

"I can remember doing about the same thing at my Granny Dee's house. Mama yelled at us girls for that more than anything else when we visited my grandmother."

"Can I get you a glass of sweet tea, some lemonade, or a beer?" Nick asked.

"Lemonade would be wonderful." She glanced around the foyer and into the living room off to her left. "What a beautiful home. So cozy and comfortable."

"I could give you a tour when you have something to drink," Nick said. "We can start with the kitchen. Just follow me."

Be careful what you wish for. You might get it. No, that's not right. You got it! the niggling voice in Amelia's head said. *I wish my family could see beyond his kinfolk and give him a chance.*

The foyer had a marble-topped credenza against one wall and four ladder-back chairs lined up on the other side where the staircase went up to the second floor. He led the way to a doorway on the left that opened up into a huge country kitchen with an old yellow-topped chrome table and matching chairs.

"My Granny Dee has a table and chairs just like this," Amelia said.

"Do you like it or hate it?" Nick asked as he poured lemonade over ice in two glasses. "Have a seat. I'm sure Vera will come out of wherever she's hiding when she hears voices."

"Absolutely love the table and chairs," she answered. "I should've called before I just dropped in, but I was still out for a jog and thought about Vera and . . ."

Nick's grin lit up the whole room. "And me?"

"Yes, and you"—Amelia pulled out a chair and sat down—"but I still should have called first. It would have been awkward if you had guests. I look a fright, and if your mother had been here . . ." She paused. "That would not have been good."

"But she's not, and honey, you are beautiful in my eyes," Nick said.

"Friends don't call friends honey," she said.

"Amelia Juliet Taylor, you know better than that," Nick said in a mock scolding voice. "In the South even our worst enemies are called honey—maybe in a sarcastic tone, but still honey. And you are not my enemy."

"Not even if our families are at war?" she asked.

"Not even," Nick said.

Vera came out of the living room, rubbed around Amelia's legs, then jumped up onto her lap.

"Aren't you a beautiful lady," Amelia crooned in a high-pitched voice. Vera flopped over on her back and lay in Amelia's arms like a baby. "If I could have a pet in my apartment, I would steal her from you."

Nick brought the lemonade to the table, set the glasses down, and then took a chair across from Amelia. "I'll share her with you anytime you want to drop by."

Amelia cradled the big calico cat in one arm, picked up the lemonade with the other, and took a sip. "This is homemade, isn't it?"

"Yep, made from my Granny Monroe's special recipe," Nick said.

"It sure hits the spot after you've been jogging for more than a mile." Amelia felt both at home and like she was on a major guilt trip at the same time. "And petting Vera is better than therapy." She tried to concentrate on the cat, but the guilty feeling throbbed like a headache.

"Have you ever been to a therapist?" Nick asked.

"Yep." She remembered the months of therapy it took for her to find her self-confidence again. She never wanted to go through that again, and yet if she didn't get up and walk out of this house, she might have to—for the sheer guilt alone. "How about you?"

Nick shook his head. "Nope, but looking back over my life, I probably should have been seeing one for the past twenty years anyway. When things got crazy in my world, I usually called Uncle Harry, and he would talk to me for hours. Or if things got really bad, I would drive up here and spend the weekend with him."

"Therapy doesn't necessarily mean a paid person with a notebook and a long leather couch," Amelia told him. "With me, it was someone like that. I was in an abusive relationship with a guy I met in college and it lasted for several years. Not physical, but mental, and Mama thought it would be best if I had some therapy."

"Did it help?" Nick asked.

"Oh, yeah. If it hadn't, I wouldn't have had the courage to knock on your door like I did," she answered. "My self-esteem was nil, nada, zilch, but after months of talking to the therapist, I was much better."

He swallowed a couple of gulps of cold liquid and went on. "After an hour of visiting with Uncle Harry, I was much better, too. If I'd known then what I know now, I might have run away from home when I was ten years old and come to Bonnet to live with him."

"Good thing neither of us knew what was going to happen in the future, isn't it?" Amelia said. "But, as they say, hindsight is twenty-twenty. If I'd realized that Elliott would try to control every facet of my life, I would have never dated him in the first place, much less got serious about him.

"I can see the questions in your eyes," she said. "His name was Elliott Schermerhorn Winthrop the Third. He was a trust-fund baby with more money than Midas, and I was supposed to feel honored that he picked me to date. Of course, it took years for him to 'break me in'"—she put air quotes around the last three words—"as he called it. When I realized that I'd been cut off from all my friends and family, I rebelled, and that narcissist broke up with me very publicly on social media. That was two years ago, and I haven't dated much since. Trust issues and the family worrying about me are probably most of the reasons why, because I feel like I'm over Elliott."

"I'm surprised your dad didn't shoot that sorry bastard," Nick said. "I can't imagine treating a woman like that. But Elliott and my mother could share DNA."

Vera hopped down out of Amelia's lap and headed off toward the living room with her tail held high like she was the queen of the house.

Amelia watched her go and then turned back to Nick. "Matilda does seem to have her fair share of self-love."

"Oh, honey, she's got enough of that to go around to dozens and dozens of folks." Nick smiled. "Still want a tour of the house?"

"Yes, please," Amelia answered. "I've always loved these old two-story places. They have so much history. My granny lives in an old house out on an island in the bayou. I've spent hours with her on the screened-in back porch, drinking homemade lemonade that tasted a lot like this. The adults get her special brew that I'm sure has liquor of some kind in it." Amelia pushed her chair back, stood up, and then set the chair back where it belonged.

"Then follow me." Nick would have rather sat with her in the kitchen until the break of dawn and talked to her about anything and everything, but he also wanted to see how she would react to the faded wallpaper that had angered his mother so much. He led her into the living room first. "As you can see, this is where I watch a lot of reruns of *Law & Order* and *Criminal Minds*."

"I'm so sorry if I interrupted your television shows," she said.

"Vera and I will turn off the television for a visit with you anytime," he drawled. "What do you think of the living room?"

"Like I said before, it's cozy, and peaceful. Feels like that old screen door is closed to the world and even to time." She seemed to take everything in at once. "I like a fireplace in the wintertime, and the hardwood floors are to die for. In southern Louisiana, not many houses have fireplaces. It seldom gets cold enough to warrant building a blaze, but I've always thought I'd love to lay in front of one on a cold winter night. What I like best is the high ceilings and the wainscoting. If these walls could talk, I wonder what stories they could tell us."

Thinking about how spoiled his mother had been when she had lived in the house, and the arguments and pouting sessions that had gone on there, Nick was glad the walls were forevermore mute. Then he remembered the stories that he'd heard in hushed tones about his grandparents and sure didn't want to know the details of their lives. Could all that be washed away if someday he found someone like Amelia—or maybe even Amelia—and raised a happy family in the place?

"Across the hall"—he motioned with his hand—"is the formal dining room, the office, and the master bedroom. Uncle Harry sprung for a closet and a bathroom in the bedroom when he did a little remodeling after my grandparents passed away."

He showed her the office first. "The real estate business started right here, and the furniture is still the same as it was back during Prohibition. Matter of fact, there's a secret cabinet behind this door where Great-Granddad stored his bootleg whiskey." He touched a button under the massive oak desk and part of the paneled wall opened up to reveal a well-stocked liquor cabinet.

"That's amazing," Amelia said. "Is one of those bottles filled with some of the original bootleg 'shine he bought? Both of my granddads made it down south, but they didn't sell it."

"Just one jar." Nick touched a full mason jar on the top shelf. "Uncle Harry said he kept it for good luck. It's probably not even worth drinking, but here it is. It was probably clear when it was put in here, but it's turned kind of amber now. Uncle Harry told me his father told him it was called apple pie moonshine, so that could be the reason it's not clear, though. I've tasted apple pie 'shine a few times, but I've often wondered if the flavor of this one would be better, the same, or horrible."

"Don't open it," she said. "We both need all the good luck we can find."

"Amen to that," Nick agreed.

With his hand on her lower back, he guided her to the formal dining room. When he flipped the light switch and the chandelier above the table for ten lit up the room, she gasped. "Oh, Nick, this is gorgeous. The vintage wallpaper has faded just enough to give the whole room a soft look. The lace cloth and curtains seem to say, 'Come on in and sit down for a good family meal and visit.' Is that your great-granny's china in the cabinet?"

"I guess so." Seeing things through her eyes made him realize just how much his Uncle Harry had done for him. That she thought the house was beautiful made him even more proud of his inheritance.

"This place should be on the historical registry of homes," Amelia whispered as she ran a finger over the glass front of the china cabinet.

"It's not quite a hundred years old," Nick said, "but I'm glad you like it. I know from what Uncle Harry told me and what Mother has said that it wasn't always a peaceful place. But it has been to me."

"I can understand that. Just being shown through the house, I can feel its warmth wrapping itself around me like a fuzzy blanket on a cold winter night," she sighed.

"Now the second floor," Nick said, still unable to believe that Amelia was actually right there with him. Sparks, vibes, electricity, chemistry—whatever it was called—flowed through her T-shirt and into his hand when he placed it on her lower back again and together they walked up the wide staircase to the second floor.

"Oh. My. Goodness!" She gasped. "This hallway is like a den. I can imagine sitting in one of those wingback chairs and reading a book with my feet propped up on an ottoman."

"Anytime you want to grab a book from the bookcases in the living room, or bring your own, you are welcome to however much time you want to spend in this hallway," Nick said. "I'm sure the walls would love to tell a story someday of how a gorgeous woman came to visit and admired the house so much that the young man who lived here gave her permission to visit anytime she wanted."

"Go on," she said. "I'm liking this fairy tale."

"I've told you my part," he said. "It's your turn to tell another part of the story."

"Well, the young man and the lady who liked to read became very good friends in spite of the opposition of their families," she said. "Now your turn."

"Tune in to the same channel and at the same time next week when the beautiful lady comes back to visit the cat again." He showed her through the four huge bedrooms and the bathroom at the end of the hallway.

"Is that clawfoot tub bigger than normal?" she asked.

"Yes, it is," Nick nodded. "Great-Granddad was six feet, five inches tall and Great-Grandma was just under six feet, so he had that thing made special for her. If the lady in our story gets tired of reading, she can always have a long soak in it."

"That thing is big enough to be called a swimming pool, or at the very least a hot tub, and I thank you for the offer," Amelia said. "Now that the tour is over, I should be going on home."

"Let me drive you," he said. "You're wearing dark clothes and—"

"Yes, and thank you," Amelia said. "I was going to jog across the street and ask Aunt Liddy, but she's not home. Though if you're afraid we'll get grounded . . ."

"If we do, it'll be worth every minute." He took her hand in his and led her back downstairs. "Jeep or truck?"

"You're the driver," she answered.

Just that much made Nick appreciate her even more. "Truck it is, then. We'll save the Jeep for when we go back-road traveling in the country."

"Oh, we're going to do that someday?" she asked as he grabbed a set of keys from a rack beside the door.

"If you're willing to face the consequences of your Aunt Liddy's wrath, you just name the time, and I will pick you up." He was careful not to let Vera out when he and Amelia left the house.

"Okay"—she drew out the word—"but maybe we shouldn't go public with our friendship for a little while."

"I agree, but that doesn't mean you wouldn't want to look at a piece of property some Sunday afternoon." He opened the truck door for her.

"A woman *does* get tired of paying rent," she said in mock seriousness, "and I would like to have a cat, so looking for a place of my own might be a smart move."

Five minutes later he was parked in front of her apartment building. "Which one is yours? I'll walk you to your door."

"It's the first one on the ground floor to your right, and since this is not a date, you don't have to walk me to the door," she said.

"Then I suppose a good-night kiss is out of the question?" he teased.

"You suppose wrong." She leaned across the console, cupped his face in her hands, and kissed him—long and with enough heat that he would need a cold shower when he got back to his house.

Chapter Twelve

Nick knew his mother well enough to know all her moods, and when she marched into the real estate office that Friday morning, it didn't take a degree in advanced psychology to know that she was on the verge of a full-blown hissy fit. She tossed her purse on the desk and swept an arm across the top of the desk, sending papers flying all over the floor.

"Who pissed in your oatmeal?" Nick wasn't in any mood for his mother's temper that morning.

One of her forefingers with a bright red nail shot up just inches from his nose. "Don't you even start on me. I thought I'd come in here and find a nice lady sitting behind the desk. Have you even bothered looking at the list of people I gave you as prospective office managers? Today is supposed to be my last day, but you can't run this whole office alone." She ignored the papers and sat down behind the desk. "Who's going to answer the phone when you're out showing property, or do the filing, or make appointments?"

Nick picked up all the strewn papers and stacked them on the top of the filing cabinet. "I've pretty much been running it all by myself. You're seldom ever here, and it doesn't look like you've been doing much in the way of filing when you are here. Most of the time, you're out with your new posse, anyway."

"And that's where I'm going today, too," she shot back at him. "Tina and I are talking to an electrician and a plumber this morning about my new bed-and-breakfast, and then we're going to lunch with Kayla and Gladys. I just stopped by to tell you that I'll only be here for an hour."

"Think you might take care of that pile of filing while you are here?" Nick asked.

"I hate to file," Matilda answered. "Whoever you hire can do that for you, and besides, these days everything is on computers."

"Uncle Harry always kept a hard copy of everything, too," Nick told her. "If the computers crash or the internet is down, we can go right on with business."

Matilda pulled a compact out of her purse, checked her face, and reapplied bright red lipstick that matched the shirt she was wearing. "You don't have to do things the way Harry did. He was old and set in his ways. He's left now, and this office—for that matter, the whole town—is stuck in the past and needs to move forward. I'm making it my mission to see that it does just that. I'm starting with the Grey Manor and moving forward from there. People will soon begin to see that I'm right and look up to me."

Nick shrugged and began to file the papers himself. "I've got a lady coming in on Monday for an interview. I reckon I can run it single-handedly until then. Don't worry about me or this office."

"I'll answer the phone for you for an hour, and I'll be back this afternoon for a couple of hours. Don't you want me to sit in on your interviews?" Matilda asked. "You need a woman who has class and style in the front office so that when folks come in, they will see this is a serious business."

"I need a woman like Wanda," Nick said. "What she looks like isn't any big deal. She just needs to be able to do the job."

Matilda lowered her chin and looked up at Nick through fake eye-lashes. "And that's the very reason this business is going to fail. And I'm going to stand on the sidelines and laugh when it does."

Nick glanced over at her and then went back to filing. "I'll bet you a hundred bucks that your grandiose vision of an English-themed B and B goes under long before my business."

"I don't even know you." Matilda sighed.

That attitude and the long dramatic sighs had quit working on Nick years ago. He had heard her say that same comment about not knowing him more times than he could count on his fingers and toes.

Wait for it! Wait for it! It's on the way, the voice in his head said.

"I don't know why you treat me like this," Matilda said in her lay-a-guilt-trip-on-thick tone. "I gave you and your father all my best years so you would have a good, stable home. I gave you everything you needed, and now you act like I'm carrying the plague."

And there it is. This time it was his uncle's voice in his head.

"I'm calling bullshit on that, Mother. I had nothing to do with why you stayed with Dad. You liked the money and the status he gave you," Nick told her. "Filing all done. I'm going to my office."

He could almost hear his mother's body humming with pent-up anger. "You are so ungrateful . . ." The phone rang, and she stopped in the middle of what would have been a tirade and answered it in a sweet voice. "Hello, Gladys."

Nick crossed over to his office and closed the door. He took his phone from his hip pocket and sent a text to Amelia: I could use one of your kisses right now.

He got one back immediately: That might have been a mistake.

He smiled and typed: I don't think so.

He laid the phone on his desk and opened his computer. Through the window into the outer office, he could see his mother smiling and nodding, and then everything changed in an instant. The chill from the stone-cold face she turned toward him flowed across the room and made him shiver. He was accustomed to her guilt trips, her pouting, and other expressions, but this was a brand-new one. She put her phone in her purse and marched toward his office without taking her eyes off him.

She slung the door open without knocking, popped her hands on her hips, and demanded, "Who is she?"

"Who is who?" Nick asked. There was no way in heaven, earth, or hell he was telling his mother about Amelia. She could and would ruin whatever chance he had.

"Who is the woman you've been seeing on the sly? You're making me look awful with your sneaking around like a teenager, so who is she?" Matilda growled. "Gladys says that she lives out in the apartment complex south of town and that's where Liddy's niece lives, so tell me right now."

"I'm busted." Nick shrugged. He had to think fast, and the only name that popped into his head—the one that would rile his mother into forgetting about any woman he was interested in—was Liddy Latham. "You've caught me." He let out a long whoosh of air. "I've been giving Liddy Latham a lift out to the apartment complex to see Amelia. I didn't consider it a date, but I did buy her a snow cone a couple of nights ago." He paused and frowned. "But I didn't get a good-night kiss from her, so I don't think it was a real date."

"Good God!" Matilda sunk down into one of the wingback chairs on the other side of his desk. "That's even worse than dating Amelia. Why would you disgrace me by striking up a friendship with those women?"

"April Fools." Nick chuckled.

If looks could kill, the daggers shooting out of Matilda's eyes would have dropped him dead right there.

"That's not funny, and if you are seeing Amelia"—Matilda raised her voice a notch—"I will disown you and rewrite my will to leave my bed-and-breakfast and all my money to a charity, and you won't see a dime of it. I mean it."

"In the words of the infamous Rhett Butler, 'I really don't give a damn,' or something like that," Nick told her. "I will see whomever I want to, Mother."

Matilda lowered her finger. "I demand that you tell me why you've been going out to that complex where Amelia lives every night this week."

"That complex has about fifty apartments, Mother. Amelia isn't the only single woman who lives out there, but"—he leaned forward and lowered his voice—"I have been driving out there and just sitting in my truck, trying to catch a peek of her taking out the trash or maybe sitting at her table grading papers if she's got the drapes open. I figured one of your new posse would call you and rat me out, and it makes for a great April Fools' joke."

Matilda got up and started out of the room. "I'm tired of your crap. I'm leaving early. Tina is meeting me at the stone house so we can have a long look at the place and make some notes about remodeling."

"I heard that that place is haunted and that everyone in town is surprised that it sold so fast. Amos wasn't the first one to die in the house. Maybe if you bill it as the only haunted bed-and-breakfast in the area, it will bring in more guests. You could hire Gladys to record moaning sounds, and maybe rattle some chains up in the attic when you have rooms booked." Nick wanted to get her totally away from even thinking about Amelia.

"That house is not haunted, and I won't have you spreading rumors that it is." Matilda left the door to the office open, picked up her purse, and disappeared into the kitchen area.

When he heard the back door close and the click of the lock, Nick made a note to ask for her set of keys when she returned. If she didn't hand them over, he would have the locks changed. There was no way he wanted her coming and going at will, peeking into his business as well as his personal life. He had dodged a large-caliber bullet that morning. He was ready to face off with his mother anytime, but he and Amelia had agreed to keep their friendship on the down-low for a few more weeks.

Amelia had never been so glad to see a week come to an end. With spring in full bloom everywhere, the kids were getting more restless by the day. The last quarter of the school year was always the toughest, but this year seemed exceptionally crazy. She slipped her laptop into her tote bag, locked her classroom door, and was halfway down the hall when Daniel caught up to her.

"Savannah and I are having a game night at her place tomorrow night, and we need one more player. You interested?" he asked.

"Sorry," she answered. "Already got plans."

Daniel opened the door for her. "Savannah says you've got a glow that only comes about when a woman is pregnant or when she's in the first days of a new relationship. Are you pregnant?"

"Not only no, but hell no!" Amelia gasped.

"Then who is he, and why haven't you told me?" Daniel asked. "Keeping things from your best friend isn't right. I had to get dramatic."

Amelia headed across the parking lot toward her car. "Maybe I'm glowing because it's Friday, or"—she lowered her voice as she opened the car door and put her tote bag over on the passenger's seat, then turned back and wiggled her eyebrows at him—"because I'm having an affair with our principal."

"You're not getting me to bite on that." Daniel laughed. "It's April Fools' Day."

"Well, rats!" Amelia said with a giggle. "I haven't been able to pull one over on anyone all day."

"It's Nick Monroe, isn't it?" Daniel said. "That's the only guy in town that you wouldn't tell me about. Let me and Savannah help y'all out."

"How would you do that?" Amelia was relieved just to tell someone about Nick.

"It's like this." Daniel lowered his voice and scanned the parking lot to be sure no one could hear him. "Remember how we've been looking at a couple of houses that Nick has listed this past couple of weeks? We want to have one ready to move into after our trip to Las Vegas the weekend after school is out."

Amelia slid in behind the wheel but left the door open. "Keep talking."

"We could invite Nick to our game night," Daniel said with an impish grin. "There's only one other couple coming right now, and they're our friends from Bowie, so they don't know the situation."

"You'd do that for me?" Amelia asked.

"Of course," Daniel said. "Truth is, the other couple are Savannah's friends, not mine. The woman was her college roommate the last year she was at the university, and her husband is one of those rich dudes who inherited an oil business. He's also one of those bragging types, and she's almost as uppity as he is. I could use a little backup for the evening."

"Well, since you put it that way," Amelia said with a smile, "you could invite me and Nick, and if we both show up"—she grinned—"it's not either of our faults, now is it?"

"Seven o'clock. We'll have finger foods, beer, and wine," Daniel said. "And thanks. That other couple is no April Fools' joke, I have to warn you."

"Then I'll bring my charming smile and brag you up in front of them," Amelia told him.

"I'll count on it." Daniel closed the door for her and headed on across the lot toward the elementary school.

Amelia started the engine and put the car in reverse, but before she could take her foot off the brake, her phone rang. Thinking it was probably Nick, she answered without even looking at the caller ID. "I'm on my way home. Are you about ready to call it a week?"

"Nope, I've got to go to the city council meeting tonight at the courthouse," Liddy said.

Amelia was so glad that she hadn't said anything revealing that she couldn't think of another thing to say.

After a couple of seconds, her aunt asked, "Are you still there? Did we lose connection? I swear, sometimes these cell phones are about as useless as tits on a boar hog."

"I'm here," Amelia said. "I was just about to back out of the parking lot here at the school."

"Good," Liddy said. "I caught you in plenty of time. I made a pan of brownies today from your recipe. Come on by and we'll have a piece and sit out on the screened back porch and have a visit."

"I'll be there in less than five minutes," Amelia said.

"Front door is open. I'll get the sweet tea ready and meet you on the porch," Liddy said. "Haven't got to see you all week, so this will be a treat."

You are stepping in quicksand. Granny Dee's voice was back in her head. She made a mental note to be sure and drop in a few times the next week so her aunt wouldn't get suspicious.

Amelia nodded in agreement but silently argued that it wasn't fair to her or Nick that their folks had an ongoing feud. She eased through a couple of stop signs and glanced over at Nick's house as she passed by before she parked in Liddy's driveway. She got out of the car and took the porch steps two at a time.

"I'm here, Aunt Liddy," she yelled as she went through the living room and kitchen and out to the screened porch.

"I just grabbed a package of peanut butter crackers for lunch, so this sure sounds good." Amelia eased down into one of the two rocking chairs. "What's been going on all week? Any new gossip?"

"Oh, yes, ma'am." Liddy poured two glasses of tea from a pitcher that was sitting on the table between the chairs. "I already cut the brownies into squares, so you can help yourself. If I'd known you didn't have more than crackers, I would have made a pot of soup for you." She sat down in the second chair. "I figured you'd want sweet tea, so I poured us each a glass."

Amelia picked up a brownie and took a bite, then took a sip of tea. "Tea that you buy in a store just can't touch what you make. But then, that's no surprise. No one can make a lemon pie like yours, either. I love your pies, but this chocolate hits the spot right now. It's been a day at school. The kids are always a handful the last nine weeks, but this year they seem even worse. Or maybe it's me, and they're just feeding off my desire for the year to be over."

I'm talking too much. Aunt Liddy will know that I'm nervous, Amelia thought as she finished her brownie and picked up a second one. *Eat. Don't talk. Let her say something.*

"I remember back when I worked at the school. Spring seems to make the kids want to be outside, not inside doing lessons. The lemon pie is because of my secret ingredient," Liddy told her. "It's not much, but it gives the pie just a little kick and brings out the lemon flavor more."

Amelia nodded in agreement. "Who would have ever thought a little limoncello would make it so much better? When are you going to give me the recipe so I know how much to put in?"

"It's in my will, and the recipes, written by hand by my mama, are in the bank safe deposit box," Liddy answered. "I've left the recipes to your mama. You might inherit them from her."

"Whoever put you on to making them this way?" Amelia asked.

"My mama, and before her, it was her mother," Liddy said. "I'm told that my great-grandmother used a little vodka in her pies, but once Granny discovered limoncello, we've used it ever since."

"Why have you kept it such a big secret?" Amelia asked.

"Because we take them to church, and all those folks who think Jesus only drank grape juice would be offended at a pie with liquor in it," Liddy explained.

"As long as they stay in the family, that's all that matters. Your pies are a tradition for family dinners. Do you have any idea how many you've made and taken?" Amelia asked.

"Nope. I don't keep count. David, in the Bible, got into trouble for numbering the people. I wouldn't want it said that I numbered my pies. I have to be extra good as it is, because I refuse to forgive and forget where Matilda is concerned. Speaking of her, did you know that Nick Monroe has a girlfriend, and she lives out in your apartment complex?"

Amelia had to swallow fast and then gulp down tea to keep from choking. "Well, dang it, Aunt Liddy. I thought I had a chance at dating him after the way he was flirting with me at those two funerals."

"Girl, don't you tease me like that," Liddy said. "I know that it's April Fools' Day, but that's not funny. Do you think he is seeing Savannah on the sly? Poor old Daniel would be devastated if that's happening, but I don't think he's seeing her."

"Why?" Amelia could almost feel the color leaving her face as she finished off her tea. "I'm going to the bathroom. Be right back."

She was on her feet and headed through the door before Liddy could say anything else. She leaned her head on the bathroom door when she'd closed it behind her. After she had taken in several long breaths, she pasted a smile on her face, flushed the potty in case Aunt Liddy could hear, and washed her hands.

"What were we talking about?" she asked as she entered the porch and sat back down.

"Nick dating someone in your apartment complex," Liddy answered.

Well, there goes the hope that she would go on to another subject. I'd rather she ranted about Matilda, Amelia thought.

"Now that I think about it, I don't think he's seeing Savannah. Daniel spends every waking minute with her. I'm surprised that they don't just move in together," Liddy said.

"Aunt Liddy!" Amelia gasped. "I never thought I'd hear you say that."

"The way that society looks at things has changed over the years." Liddy raised a shoulder in half a shrug. "Seems smart to me for a couple to live together for a while before they get married. The only way you ever know a person is to live with them. That would save a lot of heartache. If my Richie had lived with Matilda, he would have figured her out, and he might be alive today. If you hadn't lived with Elliott that summer, you would have never figured out that he was evil."

"Amen to that," Amelia agreed.

"Did I ever tell you about the time my mama caught me smoking?" She didn't wait for an answer but went on. "She gave me a whole pack of cigarettes and sent me to the back porch. I couldn't come in the house until they were all gone. I was green and throwing up my toenails by the time that pack was finished. All I have to do is smell one of those things and I get sick even now, sixty years later."

"What's that got to do with Elliott?" Amelia asked.

"By living with him, it was like smoking a whole pack of cigarettes in one day. You got to see him in action twenty-four seven, as you kids say today. I prayed that you were smart enough to see through him, and you finally did," Liddy said. "You know Daniel and Savannah. Please tell me that she's not about to break that sweet heart of his."

"She is not," Amelia answered, trying to think of a way to distract Liddy from talking about Daniel or Nick. "There's lots of single women out in the complex—Olivia O'Hara, for one."

"I hadn't thought about her." Liddy frowned. "She's such a mousy little thing, but I'd rather see him dating her than messing up Daniel's life. Poor Olivia. Matilda will eat her alive. I bet that's the reason he's dating her on the sly. Once he introduces her to his mother, she'll run like a jackrabbit with a hungry coyote on its tail. Give me just a minute here." She picked up her phone, typed in a message, then laid it back down on the table. "I had to tell Ruth Ann about Olivia. We've both been worried that you were dating him."

"But, Aunt Liddy, I *am* dating him," Amelia said. "Olivia and I've been sharing him. I think I might be ahead of her since he says she's better in bed, but I'm a better cook. We all know the way to a man's heart is through his stomach. You got any advice for me when it comes to the bedroom?"

"Don't tease me about this, Amelia Juliet." Liddy shook her finger at Amelia. "I might be open minded when it comes to a couple living together, but what goes on in the bedroom stays in the bedroom, and I don't discuss those things with anyone."

"Oh, come on, Aunt Liddy," Amelia whispered. "It's just me and you out here on this porch. Did you and Uncle Marvin have any good sex secrets that I could use to get a leg up?" She giggled. "That's poor wording, isn't it?"

"Amelia Juliet!" Liddy raised her voice a notch. "Don't you tease me about such things."

"You just second named me twice, so you *are* serious," Amelia said. "I've never known you to judge a person by another's half bushel."

Liddy finished off the rest of her tea before she answered. "I'm not either of those things. I'm protecting you from a life of misery. Nick might be a decent guy, but his ancestral background is against him. His Grandpa Floyd was a philanderer, and so was his grandmother, Linda June. Nick's mama followed in her parents' footsteps, and his daddy traded in Matilda for a different woman. I got to admit, knowing Matilda like I do, I wouldn't hold that against Gregory."

Liddy changed the subject. "Now, on to the next couple of things I wanted to talk to you about. Can you help us with the church Easter egg hunt and the potluck?"

"No, ma'am," Amelia answered. "We have Friday off school and the following Monday since we didn't have to use our snow days. I'm getting out of Bonnet and away from all this stress for the long weekend. Want to go with me?"

Liddy seemed to be thinking about joining her, but she finally shook her head. "I would love to, but I'd better stay here and help with the Easter doings at the church. Where are you going, anyway?"

"Galveston, or South Padre, or I might even fly to Destin, Florida, for a couple of days. I need to get away and de-stress, and I love to be near the ocean," Amelia said.

"You sound like Harry. I'll pass this time, and honey, you do realize that you're going to the Gulf, not to the ocean," Liddy said with half a laugh.

At last, we're on a different subject, Amelia thought.

"If the water is salty, then it's the ocean," Amelia argued. "You said you had a couple of things to ask me. Is there anything else?"

"Second was to tell you, not ask you," Liddy answered. "You remember Donna Sue that works down at the Bluebonnet Café?"

"Yes, I do," Amelia answered.

"Her granny died this morning, and the funeral is Monday. They were hoping she would hang on until Mother's Day, when she would be a hundred years old, but she didn't make it. I was just sure they'd plan a late-in-the-day service, but they've decided on graveside at eleven o'clock, so you won't be able to help us." Liddy sighed. "I was going to ask if you'd make brownies and send them with me to the funeral dinner."

"Of course," Amelia said. "I can't be there, but I can send food."

"Thank you." Liddy nodded. "I'm proud of you for stepping up to help when you can at the funeral dinners. It means a lot to me."

Amelia reached across the space separating them and patted her aunt on the arm. "You are so welcome. When school is out for the summer, I can help more." She wondered just how proud Aunt Liddy would be of her if she knew that she had been seeing Nick on the sly. She couldn't help but wonder if her aunt already knew that she'd been talking to Nick and if she was giving Amelia enough rope to hang herself.

"Oh, there was one more thing," Liddy said. "Ethel is planning a little get-together tomorrow night at her house. Your folks are going, but Bridget and Clovis have duty at the hospital. We're all going to play dominoes, and she's invited Thomas Mason, that sweet guy who works at the bank. We always thought he would wind up with Olivia. They are so much alike, but I guess she likes the bad boy type. Why don't you come join us?"

Amelia could see right through that little ruse. If her mother and aunt could set her up with some other guy, then Nick would be out of the picture. "I'll have to take a rain check. Daniel and Savannah are having a get-together at her place, and I promised I would come over there." She went on to tell Liddy about the uppity couple. "My favorite Aunt Liddy taught me to never go empty handed, so should I take brownies, or maybe my sugar cookies? Or I could do a bottle of wine, or a lemon chess pie?"

Liddy smiled. "Brownies or cookies. Anyone can buy a bottle of wine. Baked goods say so much more, but you don't get to make lemon pies until I'm dead."

"Then I won't ever make them, because I refuse to let God take you from us." Amelia stood up. "You reckon I could take two or three of those brownies home with me for a midnight snack tonight?"

"Of course. I've had plenty, so just take the rest of them. Paper plates are in the pantry, or you could put them in a baggie. They're on the shelf beside the plates." Liddy stood up at the same time Amelia did and followed her into the kitchen. "The wind is picking up. You keep a watch on the Weather Channel. The weatherman says we're in for a storm later tonight, but he doesn't always get it right. If you hear the tornado siren blow, you get on up here and go to the cellar with me."

"I love the rain. It always makes me think of the way it sounds on the tin roof at Granny Dee's house in Louisiana," Amelia said.

"It was raining and storming the night Richie was killed," Liddy whispered. "I'll never forget the smell of wet dirt when the policemen came to my door."

"We'll hope he's wrong." Amelia flashed on a mental picture of her and Nick, sitting on the park bench right after the rain and how she'd loved the scent of the earth and the fresh, clean smell in the air.

Liddy helped her get the remainder of the brownies in a bag and gave her a hug. "I'm so glad you aren't always dieting and trying to get skinny."

Amelia shook her head. "The way I like to cook and eat, I'd put on weight like crazy if I didn't jog several evenings a week. Thanks for the visit and the brownies. This is laundry night, and I like to get there before the after-five crowd comes in so I don't have to wait for machines."

"I've told you a million times to bring your laundry here. It costs money to wash at that laundry, and besides all that, you never know how clean those washers are," Liddy fussed as she followed Amelia to the door.

"I appreciate that, and I love you." Amelia gave her another hug. "But if I can claim three washing machines, I can get it all done in an hour."

"You kids today!" Liddy continued to fume. "Always in a hurry with everything. Got to have faster computers, faster phones, get the laundry done faster."

"But you love me anyway," Amelia said. "Aunt Liddy, you've got chocolate smeared all over your shirt."

Liddy immediately looked down.

"April Fools." Amelia giggled.

Liddy air-slapped Amelia on the arm. "You got me, after all. Go on home before I figure out a way to fool you."

"See you Sunday morning," Amelia said. "I'll pick you up at ten thirty for church."

"I'll be ready," Liddy told her.

Amelia glanced over at Nick's house as she left and wished that she could go over there. Was she downright crazy to be secretly befriending him—or for kissing him, for that matter?

When she got back to her apartment, she called him. She was just about to hang up after five rings when he answered.

"Sorry about that. My phone was in my bedroom, and I was just getting out of the shower when I heard it ringing," he said breathlessly. "Are you coming over?"

"Not tonight," she said, "but we need to talk."

"Huh-oh," Nick sighed. "I don't like the sound of that."

"Do you feel like what we have is a flash in the pan that will burn out in a few weeks?" she asked.

"No, ma'am, I do not, but I would like to be able to take you to dinner right out in public or maybe to a movie or sit beside you in church."

"Would you mind waiting until after Easter to do that?" she asked. "Just to give us a little more time to figure out exactly where we are. This is so complicated."

"Not one bit," he said.

Amelia felt like a weight flew off her shoulders. "I like you, Nick. I really do, but I just want to give this a little time before we . . ." She paused.

"Have to battle our families?" he chuckled.

"Yes." Relief continued to cascade through her.

"I agree with you. We need to figure out exactly where we are before we go public, but that doesn't make it any easier," he said. "Easter it is, then? For both of us? And Amelia, I like you a lot, too."

Liddy, Ruth Ann, and Paul walked into the conference room at city hall together that evening to find it completely full and folks lining the walls. Liddy was sure glad that as members of several committees she and Ruth Ann always had seats at the long table. As usual, the Doughnut House provided several dozen pastries for the event, and the big two-gallon coffeepot was ready when Don Hollis, the president of the city council, tapped on the end of the long table with his gavel.

Liddy sat down beside her brother and glanced around the room. No Matilda, so that was a good sign.

She'll make a grand entrance, the voice in Liddy's head said.

Liddy figured that was probably true but took a little comfort in the fact that she and Paul were sitting and Matilda would have to stand.

"It's good to see so many folks out tonight. Did you all come to play a joke on me since it's April Fools' Day or are you here to talk about getting the potholes in your street fixed?" Don asked.

"Why, Don, there ain't a single pothole in Mulberry Street where I live," one old fellow piped up from the back of the room, "and if you believe that, then you are the April Fool."

Everyone in the room chuckled at the joke—even Don. "We haven't had a turnout like this since I've been on the council, and I'm glad to see so many of you taking an interest in our town. First thing on the agenda is choosing a replacement for Harry Davis. This person will serve until the November election and can throw their hat in the ring at that time if they're of a mind to do so. Since I'm the president, I will take nominations into consideration and then make my decision by the next meeting."

"I heard that Paul Taylor isn't running again," someone yelled from the back of the room. "Does that mean there'll be two places to fill?"

Paul stood up from his place at the table where the five members had reserved seats. "I don't know where you heard that. I have every intention of running again, and I would like to nominate my daughter, Dr. Bridget Doucet, to serve in Harry's place until the election. We need to encourage our young folks to step up and help with community affairs," Paul said.

"I figured you'd nominate Clovis," Liddy whispered when Paul took a seat.

"I thought about it," Paul said.

Before he could go on, Tina was on her feet with her hand in the air like a grade school child. "I would like to nominate Matilda Monroe to fill Harry's place. Whether she is chosen today or not, she will be running for her brother's position come election time. She's bringing new ideas to town, and she's bought Amos's house with intentions of turning it into a bed-and-breakfast. She would be an excellent person to have on the council and would work well with the rest of the elected members."

Liddy jerked her head around to see Matilda and the rest of her posse standing just inside the door. Too bad there was too big of a crowd for her to strut in like a queen. Maybe it would be good for her to run for the council and lose. Liddy looked forward to seeing the number of votes posted in the local newspaper, and she hoped that Matilda only got four or five.

"Any more nominations?" Don asked.

No one said a word until Gladys spoke up. "Why can't you just make the decision tonight?"

"Because I want to be fair, and I never do anything without studying the issue," Don said. "Now, we'll go on to the idea of the city financing benches to be scattered up and down the three blocks of Main Street. They'd be a good addition to our town's beautification program, plus give our older folks places to sit during the parades."

"I guess they just came to see the circus," Ruth Ann whispered to Liddy when folks began to file out of the room in droves.

"How many benches are we thinking about?" Liddy asked.

"Three per block on each side of the street, so eighteen," Don answered.

"I will donate the money for twenty-five benches," Matilda said in a loud voice from the other end of the table, where she had sat down the minute someone had vacated the chair.

"That's very generous of you," Don said, "but I'd have to wait until we find out about the zoning issue before we could accept it anyway, Matilda. It would be inappropriate for you to donate anything, especially with advertising on it. That could be misconstrued as a bribe. I don't do anything that can get me thrown in jail."

"Just putting my money where my heart is, and that's right here in Bonnet, Texas, where I plan to make my home and run my bed-and-breakfast," Matilda said.

"We'll figure out what kind of bench we want and have an invoice ready at the next meeting if it's not a conflict," Don said.

"That sounds fine, and now, if you will excuse me, I need to get back to work. My landscaper is coming this evening—I want my place to be one of those places that everyone shows off to their friends and relatives. I would like for you to put a little plaque on the back of each bench saying that it was donated by Matilda Monroe, owner of the Grey Manor bed-and-breakfast. That's Grey, G-R-E-Y."

"Matilda, have you thought about the fact that Amos's house is located in a residential area, and it's not zoned for commercial use?" Don asked.

"Praise the Lord," Liddy muttered under her breath.

"Amen." Ruth Ann reached over and touched her on the arm.

Matilda's face went ashen. "Well, then you can just zone it commercial tonight."

"Yeah, right, as if Don is a magician," Liddy whispered.

"Some businesswoman she is if she hadn't even thought about zoning laws," Ruth Ann said out the side of her mouth.

"No, I can't," Don said. "Rezoning is a lengthy process. You will need to demonstrate how this change would improve the area and benefit your local community. Using examples could also help your case, such as showing properties that are similar to yours that have been rezoned to commercial and served as a benefit to the town. I would suggest that you have a lawyer draw up papers to present to the city council. Then, since that property is in the middle of several blocks of residential homes, the whole town might have to vote on the issue. The neighbors might not want a business of any kind around them, so they would have the right to voice their opinion at a council meeting."

One man from the back of the room raised his voice. "I can tell you right now, I will be voting a big fat no on that issue. I live about a block from Amos's place, and I damn sure don't want businesses around me. If we vote that commercial, then we'll have a doughnut shop or one of those CBD shops right next door to us."

The rest of the folks in the room applauded.

"Just another instance of the 'good old boy network.'" Matilda turned and focused on Liddy. "Don't think you've won."

"Hey." Liddy threw up both palms in a defensive gesture. "I never wanted to buy that old house anyway, so I didn't win anything."

Matilda stood up and shook her finger at Don. "You can forget about my offer to donate benches. I don't know why I even try," she fumed as she whipped around and headed toward the door with her little posse following behind her.

"Well," Liddy said from the chair at the other end of the table. "Looks like it's just us regulars left here. What else do we need to talk about, Don?"

"That pretty much closes it out," Don said. "We might as well have another doughnut and refill our coffee cups. But one more thing, Paul.

Have you heard back from that grant for the new benches and the lights to put up on Main Street?"

"Yes, and by the next meeting we should have a formal reply, but off the record, it has been approved," Paul answered.

"I'm glad you aren't leaving us," Don said. "For the past twenty years, you have written grant after grant for this town and done it all without a bit of recognition."

"I don't help out for praise. I do it out of civic duty," Paul said.

"I think Bridget would make a wonderful councilwoman," Don said. "I was thinking of asking Nick Monroe to step into Harry's place, but Bridget would sure be a good member."

"Or Daniel Patterson," Liddy suggested. "He and Amelia have agreed to sit on the festival committee, and I heard through the grapevine that he is looking to buy a house. That means he and Savannah are planning to stay around these parts."

"That's three excellent candidates," Don said. "Bridget, Daniel, or Nick."

"Anyone would be better than Matilda," Liddy said. "She's stirred up trouble since she was just a kid. In my opinion, a zebra might paint itself snow white and stick a glittered-up horn on its head, but it won't ever be a unicorn."

"Amen!" Ruth Ann agreed.

"I like the idea of Bridget or Daniel better than Matilda filling Harry's spot. I'd even support Nick over her," Paul said. "Harry always had the community at heart, and I'd hope that Nick would be the same."

"I'll keep that in mind," Don said.

Chapter Thirteen

Amelia hated to give up the last bottle of homemade muscadine wine that her Granny Dee had sent home with her after their last visit, but it went *so* well with her brownies, and it was, after all, for Daniel.

There was no way Savannah's friend, Miss Uppity Britches, could look down on a rare bottle of bayou wine. "I hope she loves it and tries to go looking for something like it in the liquor stores," Amelia said as she slipped the bottle into her purse and picked up the pan of brownies. "I also hope she tries to find a bakery that makes brownies like mine. Aunt Liddy's secret might be a little limoncello in her pies, but mine is a little chocolate vodka. And"—she locked her apartment door behind her with a chuckle—"I've got to get a cat so I can talk to someone other than myself."

She walked across the breezeway to the apartment facing the back and rang the doorbell. Daniel slung the door open. "Thank God, you're here," he whispered.

His expression reminded her of a little boy who had been sent to the principal's office, or maybe a mouse cornered by a big, mean tomcat.

"That bad, huh?" She handed him the wine. He stepped to the side so she could walk in. "It's already chilled and ready to pour. My Granny Dee's special wine. She makes it every year from the muscadine grapes that grow wild on her little island."

"Thank you," Daniel said and then lowered his voice to a whisper again. "Nick just got here five minutes ago, but *they* arrived half an hour early."

"I'm here now, and I'll protect you." Amelia scanned the room and found Nick sitting on the love seat. He slid a sly wink her way, and she sent one back.

"Hey, everyone," Daniel called out. "We're all here. Amelia's brought her granny's special Louisiana wine and brownies."

Amelia set her platter of brownies on the coffee table with the other finger foods. "Granny Dee's wine goes very well with desserts. I'm Amelia Taylor. Daniel and I teach together at the high school here in Bonnet."

"Amelia, you already know Nick," Savannah said, "and this is Misty and Benjamin Cordell."

"Pleased to meet you," Benjamin said.

Since he seemed to intimidate Daniel, Amelia had thought he would be tall, dark, and handsome, but not so. He looked to be about the same height as Daniel and wore glasses so thick they made his brown eyes look even bigger than normal. The overhead light bounced off his bald head, and his belly hung out over his belt. But, she mused, that was an expensive shirt he wore, and those loafers probably cost as much as Amelia made in a month.

"Likewise." Misty covered a yawn with her hand.

Amelia wondered how Savannah, with her sweet attitude, got mixed up with a woman like Misty. But she wouldn't worry about that now, not when Nick was patting the cushion beside him. "Isn't the drive from Dallas to Bonnet nice once you leave the hustle and bustle of the city?" Amelia sat down on the love seat beside Nick as a surge of warmth and attraction swept over her.

"I thought it was boring. Nothing but trees and miles and miles of those bluebonnets. I don't understand why everyone thinks they're so wonderful," Misty said. "They're just so common."

"She thinks anything short of a Dallas nightclub is boring," Benjamin said, "but then I like that scene, too, so I shouldn't complain."

Amelia couldn't resist pushing her a little. "When I was in college, we hit the bars some on weekends, but not anymore. Too many other things take up my time."

"Oh, yeah." Misty looked like she'd rather be anywhere else in the world than sitting in Savannah's living room. "Like what?"

"Like family, friends, my job," Amelia answered. She shifted to address the room. "You can dive right into those brownies anytime you want."

Daniel hopped up from the sofa where he had settled in beside Savannah. "I'll bring some glasses and Amelia's wine." He returned in a minute with six stemless wine glasses and the bottle. "How many shall I pour?"

"I'll have some." Benjamin had already helped himself to a brownie and taken a bite. "These are amazing. Do you make them from scratch?"

"Yes, I do." Amelia nodded. "It's an old family recipe passed down from my Granny Dee. She loves to cook, make wine, and putter about in her vegetable garden."

"They are really good," Savannah agreed with Benjamin.

Misty finally picked up a brownie and took a small bite. "Very good, but I wouldn't dare have a whole piece. I have to watch fat grams and calories like a hawk or I'd go over a hundred and twenty pounds."

"Wine?" Daniel glanced over at her.

"Of course," Misty said. "This is kind of like a wine and chocolate tasting. Remember the one we attended when we took our last cruise?"

"That chocolate or wine wasn't as good as either of these," Benjamin declared. "Can we buy something like this on the market, Amanda?"

"Amelia," Nick corrected him.

"Sorry about that," Benjamin said. "I'm not good with names, but I never forget a good chocolate or wine. This is the best muscadine I've ever put in my mouth."

"No, you can't buy either one on the market," Amelia answered. "And that's the last bottle I'll have until the muscadine grapes get ripe again down in southern Louisiana. We usually help Granny harvest them in late August or September, but I'll miss getting in on that fun since school will have already started by then."

"Fun?" Misty's tone was heavy with sarcasm.

"I loved helping harvest the grapes and make the wine. I have an older sister and we had a tradition of visiting Granny's place during wine-making season. She lives on a little island off the coast of Louisiana. What you are drinking is a five-year vintage, and in my opinion, it's the best year for it. The one that's only aged for a year isn't bad, but it doesn't have the blend of flavors that this one has." Amelia took a sip and let it sit on her tongue for a while before she swallowed it.

Dammit! I should have gone to the liquor store and bought a bottle of something cheap, she swore silently. *It's for Daniel,* she reminded herself, *and it has been a great conversation starter.*

"Are we ready to play Pictionary?" Savannah asked.

"I hate games. You should remember that from college." Misty sighed. "Let's just visit for a little while."

"Um, sure. You're the guests," Savannah said, her tone subdued.

Amelia wanted to kick Misty outside in a mud puddle when she saw how disappointed Savannah was. That woman was well on her way to being another Matilda—maybe it had something to do with names that began with *M*. That anyone could make her friend feel like that aggravated Amelia so much that she forgot she was sitting beside Nick at a party.

"Have you always lived in Dallas?" Nick asked Benjamin.

"Yes, I have," Benjamin said, "but during the summer, we traveled a lot. I've been on all the continents, and someday Misty and I are hoping to move to Italy. But for now, we will be moving from Dallas to Houston within the year. My father is building a new office in that area, and he's putting me in charge of it—my family has been in the oil business for the past three generations."

Misty covered another yawn with her hand. "I'm already shopping for a new home, and we'll get ours listed real soon. We're looking for just the right place for entertaining, but I will be so excited for us to finally move into a bigger house. Your grandmother owns an island, so I'm sure I don't even need to tell you about keeping up an image. But this is just a steppingstone on our journey to Italy."

"My Granny Dee does own her little Louisiana island, but it's nothing fancy." Amelia handed Nick another brownie. "Her house started out as a four-room home and was built on through the years to accommodate her twelve children. Her house looks like a patchwork quilt, with pieces added on as she and my grandfather had more kids. I'm sure she never even thought about an image."

"If I ever own an island, it sure won't have a house like that. It will be something fabulous." Misty yawned again.

That little devil on Amelia's shoulder made her change direction. "Speaking of fabulous, my sister, Bridget, and I have a thrift-shopping day at least twice a year. I can tell you enjoy that, too—there are some amazing finds, like the shoes you are wearing! I have a pair just like them in my closet. Isn't it exciting when we can find them at less than half price?"

Misty's eyes narrowed into slits. "I don't know what you are talking about. I got these at an exclusive little shop in Dallas."

"Oh, really?" Amelia shrugged. "Well, Bridget and I drive up to Oklahoma City or else down to Dallas and hit all the thrift stores that we can find, and the rule is that we can't spend more than a hundred dollars that day. That includes lunch at a little hole-in-the-wall burger joint we like, and our doughnuts and coffee for a midmorning snack." She picked up the plate of brownies and passed them over to Benjamin. "Nick loves these, so y'all better have another one before they're all gone."

"Are you serious about thrift shopping?" Savannah asked, ignoring Misty's shake of her head. "I've always wanted to do that, but my mama would have had a cardiac arrest if I ever did."

"Dead serious." Amelia nodded. "At least half of the clothes in my closet came from thrift stores. Sales start the week after July Fourth, and the week after Christmas, and sometimes the thrift stores put their clothing stock on sale for half price then, too. We should make a thrift-shopping day in this area. Want to join us, Misty?"

"I do not!" Misty gasped. "I wouldn't be caught dead in one of those places, and I never worry about buying my shoes on sale." She laid a hand on her forehead and said, "Savannah, honey, I hate to cut our evening short, but I'm getting a horrible migraine. Benjamin is going to have to take me home so I can get my medicine and lie down until this thing passes."

"I'm so sorry." Daniel stood up. "Would some aspirin help until you can get home and take something stronger?"

"No, thank you." Misty was already on her feet and blowing Savannah a kiss. "Next time we'll have a little dinner party at my house, or maybe we'll wait until we have our new home. That way I can show it off to you."

"That would be wonderful." Savannah got to her feet and walked them outside.

When they were gone, she closed the door and slid down the back side. "I owe you big time, Amelia."

"Yes, we do." Daniel moved off the sofa, plopped down beside his fiancée, and took her hand in his. "Do we really have to visit them in their new place, darlin'?"

"Hell no!" Savannah said. "They just reminded me of how much I don't like uppity people. They probably won't ever invite us anyway."

"You could invite me to go with you to visit her. There's lots of good thrift stores in Houston and in Dallas, too. I've been to some in both cities." Amelia giggled.

"Were you serious about that?" Savannah asked. "I really thought you were just joking."

"I've got champagne tastes on a beer budget, so thrift stores are my shopping centers," Amelia told her. "Teachers don't get paid enough to buy brand names. My sister found her dream wedding dress in a little shop called Twice as Nice in Dallas."

"I would marry you for your brownies, but I have to see if I can marry you twice over. You wouldn't break a man's bank account with that kind of shopping." Nick leaned over and kissed her on the cheek.

"No, but I don't accept proposals until at least the tenth date," Amelia teased.

"Y'all are too cute," Daniel said as he popped a small cookie into his mouth.

Savannah kicked off her shoes, scooted over to the coffee table, and picked up two more brownies. "Pour me another glass of that amazing wine. I don't know why I let Misty stress me out like this, or why I even thought I needed to invite her to my apartment. I guess it's because, six months ago, she invited me to be in her wedding. I was reluctant, but she had been my roommate during our junior year at college, and I didn't feel like I could turn her down. Besides, she made it seem like such an honor to just be a bridesmaid, and Mama was so excited for me to get out in society." She stopped and took a breath. "I knew she would turn up her nose at this place and I would be nervous through the whole evening. I eat too much when I'm stressed out, but I don't give a damn tonight."

Daniel got up from his place on the floor, sat down beside Savannah, and draped an arm around her shoulders. "It's all right now, darlin'. You planned a great evening with snacks and games. It's not your fault that she was ungrateful. I think what really rattled her was all the talk of thrift stores. She was afraid that just talking about them would put stains on her shoes."

"How were y'all ever roommates?" Nick asked. "Were you in the same sorority?"

Savannah grimaced. "My mother insisted I be in the same sorority that she was in when she was at the university. I hated it, but it is what it is. But don't let Misty fool you. She was in college to snag a rich husband, and she did."

"How about you, Nick?" Daniel asked. "Were you in a fraternity?"

"Oh, hell no!" Nick laughed. "I refused to be in one because Mother wanted me to be. My dad went to college for an education, not to party, and he wasn't in a fraternity. I followed in his footsteps."

Savannah smiled up at Daniel. "That's why we're eloping to Las Vegas. We won't have to deal with family on either side, or friends like her that my mother would insist on inviting. Holy crap on a cracker!" She slapped a hand over her mouth. "Mother would make me ask Misty to be in my wedding since I was in hers. Oh, hell no! I'm not about to change my mind about Vegas."

"Thank goodness," Daniel sighed.

"This wine is beginning to do its job. The stress is leaving my body," Savannah said. "Amelia, thank you for bringing it, and, Nick, thank you for coming, and . . ." She covered a yawn with the back of her hand.

Nick slipped an arm around Amelia's shoulders and drew her closer to his side. "Thank you for inviting me. It's nice to be able to see Amelia without it being a problem."

"You are both welcome, and my apartment is open to you anytime you need a hideaway," Savannah told him.

"You're a good friend, darlin'." Daniel refilled her glass. "How did you put up with that woman for a whole year?"

"I stayed in the library a lot," Savannah admitted. "Then she moved into an apartment of her own our senior year, and I had the room to myself for the last year. I doubt that she'll even call me again after tonight."

Two conflicting emotions washed over Amelia. The first one was a warm, fuzzy feeling because she was sitting close to Nick in the company of friends. The second was a twinge of sadness.

"I'm so sorry. I had no idea that talking about thrift stores would give her a headache," Amelia apologized, with a silent apology for the half-truth.

Savannah gulped down the rest of the wine in her glass and reached for another brownie. "Honey, she didn't have a headache. That was just an excuse so that she could get out of this boring evening. I've seen her play that migraine card too many times to count."

Nick shared the last of the wine between his glass and Amelia's. "I wonder how much one of those migraine cards costs. Can you buy them at Walmart without a prescription? Or do you need something from a doctor like you have to have to get a medical marijuana card?"

"Do you need one?" Amelia teased.

"No, but I believe my mother has one in her purse along with all her dozens of credit cards. I've seen her play it often. I'm wondering if you only get so many plays on a card before you have to get another one."

Savannah giggled and then said, "Or, if you forget to get it punched, do you get a migraine for real?"

"Do they come in different colors?" Amelia asked. "You know, like pink for girls, blue for guys."

"Why is pink only for girls?" Nick asked. "My favorite shirt is pink. Granted it's that color because I washed it with red socks, but it's still my favorite."

"Maybe," Daniel said, "you get them by degrees. The first one is blue, and it's free, but it only has one punch on it. But the next one is pink and costs twenty bucks."

Savannah reached for a napkin and set her glass on the coffee table. "You have to give back each one as you use it up or they don't give you the next one. By the time you get to a red one, it has ten punches on it and you have to pay a hundred bucks for it."

"I believe my mother's is red, and it's quite possible she's on her third or fourth one since I was a little kid," Nick said.

"I bet that Misty is on her second red one. She used up her first one that color while we were still in college," Savannah said. "I'm having that last brownie if no one wants it."

Amelia passed the platter over to her. "Do you think we could get a dessert card instead of a migraine card? It will stipulate that if you own one, the sweets you eat would have no fat grams or calories."

"Or carbs." Savannah nodded. "I want one of those instead of a migraine card. They could sell them at any fast-food restaurant, and you could buy them at the drive-through window."

"Kind of like scratch-off lottery cards that you can get at convenience store windows?" Daniel asked. "Sounds like we all should begin patenting our ideas. We might make more money with them than we do teaching or selling houses."

"Hey, that reminds me," Savannah said between bites. "Tomorrow afternoon we're going to look at two houses that Nick has listed. Amelia, you should come with us. We're going to grab a burger after church and then tour. We've been approved for a loan, and we'd like to be ready to move into our new place when we get home from Las Vegas."

"That's great, and I'd love to go with you," Amelia said, "but shouldn't that be something just you and Daniel do together?"

"Both houses are within our price range, and I've made a list of pros and cons on each one. Daniel loves me so much that he's going to tell me to pick whichever one I like best," Savannah said.

"You got that right, darlin'." Daniel finished off the last of his wine and kissed her on the forehead.

Amelia wanted to go. She really did, but that would mean having lunch with Nick right out in public, and that caused conflicting thoughts for sure. Savannah was her friend. Daniel was her best friend outside of her family. Nick was well on the way to being her boyfriend, and she wanted to spend time with him. But then there was Aunt Liddy to consider, right along with her sister, mother, and father—and Clovis would definitely have something to say about it, too.

Nick brought her hand to his lips and kissed each knuckle. "Do you think that your aunt and my mother will start brewing up poison if we have a burger together? Daniel and Savannah would be our chaperones, and it is for business."

"Probably, but I'm willing to chance it if you are." Amelia could almost feel the heat of disapproval bearing right down on top of her.

Chapter Fourteen

"oday, we're going to Bridget's house for Sunday lunch," Liddy reminded Amelia after church services.

Nick sent a sly wink her way when it was time to step out into the center aisle and then hung back to let her and the rest of her family go on ahead. She wanted so badly to tell everyone right then and there that they had been talking regularly on the phone and at the park on the nights when they jogged, but they'd agreed to wait until after Easter to take the lid off that bucket of snakes—no, it was more like a fifty-five-gallon drum of earsplitting screaming from her aunt and his mother.

"I'm having lunch with Daniel and Savannah today and then going with them to look at a couple of houses," Amelia said.

Bridget took her by the arm and pulled her in between two pews. "I heard that you and Nick were both at Savannah's apartment last night. Aunt Liddy knows, and she is *not* happy. You are playing with fire, girl, and you know what happens when you do that, don't you?"

"You get hot," Amelia answered, "and sometimes you get burned."

"That's right." Her sister released her arm. "There are millions of boyfriends out there who *won't* drive Aunt Liddy insane. This is serious stuff, Amelia Juliet."

"I know how serious it is, believe me," Amelia said.

"Hey." Savannah stopped at the end of the pew. "You want to ride with me and Daniel? Our appointment to see the first place is one o'clock. We don't want to be late, and if we hurry, we won't have to wait on our lunch."

"Are we done?" Amelia asked Bridget.

"Not really, but go on," Bridget answered.

Amelia wrapped her sister up in her arms and hugged her tightly. "Don't worry about me."

"Can't help it," Bridget sighed. "You haven't got a good track record when it comes to men."

"I'm trying to better it," Amelia told her.

"Not much if you are going to parties with you-know-who," Bridget whispered.

"Voldemort? We'll talk later," Amelia teased.

Bridget giggled. "In this family, that you-know-who is almost as bad a villain as Voldemort."

"If you say so." Amelia gave her another quick hug and stepped out in the aisle with Savannah. Once they were a few steps ahead of the family, Amelia said in a low voice, "Thank you. We're more than even."

"Not really," said Savannah. "I'm so excited that you are going with us. Neither Daniel nor I know jack squat about buying a house."

"Neither do I," Amelia admitted. "I was too young to even remember when my folks built the house they're in now, and my grandmother has lived in the same place all her married life. She had to have some remodeling done after the last hurricane, but a stick of dynamite couldn't get her out of her place. I'm not sure she's even been to the mainland in years, and . . ." She sighed. "I talk too much when I'm nervous, so please bear with me."

"You know I bake and eat when I'm nervous." Savannah led the way out into the bright sunlight. "So, I understand that your Aunt Liddy knows about last night."

"Oh, yeah, she does. My sister said that she's not one bit happy about it, so I figure she's waiting for the right moment to fuss at me," Amelia answered. "And she'll really be hot under the collar when she hears that Nick will be there today since he's the only Realtor in town. I'll be so glad when Easter comes and goes so we can figure out if we want to suffer the wrath of both sets of family enough to bring this out in the open."

"Why are you waiting that long?" Daniel walked up behind them and took Savannah's hand in his.

"To be sure. This is one big step," Amelia answered as she got into the back seat of Daniel's car.

Daniel slid in behind the wheel. "Y'all should go away together and spend some time getting everything straight in your minds before you go public."

"Like that's going to happen." Amelia managed a smile, but in her mind, she visualized the two of them on a beach somewhere—any-where—where family did not matter.

The drive from the church on one end of town to the Dairy Queen on the other end took all of three minutes since both traffic lights were green. But they had not beat the after-church rush, because the café was filling up fast by the time they arrived.

"Thank God Nick slipped out the side door and claimed a table for us." Daniel waved at him as they entered the café. "Tell me what you ladies want, and I'll put the order in."

Thank God it's a table and not a booth, Amelia thought. Although she would have loved to sit right next to him, it wouldn't be such a good idea with a café full of folks who knew her aunt and his mother.

"Half a dozen tacos and a chocolate malt," Savannah said.

"Same here." Amelia nodded.

"Why don't y'all go on and hold down the table so Nick can come put in his order, too," Daniel suggested.

"Be glad to," Savannah agreed. "We sure don't want to lose our spot and have to sit on the floor to eat."

From halfway across the room, Amelia locked eyes with Nick, and suddenly, there was no one in the café but the two of them. It didn't matter that the buzz of gossip was thick or that folks were digging around in their purses and pockets for cell phones. By nightfall, his mother might be ready to burn her at the stake or stone her to death, but that didn't matter. She was going to have to make up her mind soon whether to listen to her heart or to her family.

"Today's lunch is on me." Nick stood up as Amelia and Savannah reached the table. "Since you are looking at my listings, it's the least I can do. I just hope you and Daniel fall in love with one of them."

"Thank you," Savannah said. "We like both of them, so it might be tough to make a decision."

"Miz Taylor, it's good to see you," Nick said.

"Nice to see you, too." Amelia hated all this secrecy.

"I invited her to come along with us to give me some help on deciding which house I like best," Savannah told him, her tone pitched louder. "I needed a woman's opinion. But right now, you'd better get on up to the counter and put in your part of the order."

"I believe we have a lot of disappointed people in this café," Savannah whispered. "And I also think that Nick chose this table so everyone could see us and wouldn't jump to the conclusion we are hiding."

"Plus, it puts us each on a side so that no one is sitting beside someone else in a booth," Amelia said. "Tell me more about these two houses we're seeing today. I'm so nervous right now, I'm about to jump out of my skin, as Granny Dee used to say."

"I know exactly how you're feeling. I was so nervous to take Daniel home to meet my folks that I got physically sick. Our family backgrounds were just too different—my parents' house is a virtual mansion compared to where he was raised," Savannah said.

"Then bring on the Pepto." Amelia fiddled with her silverware. "I keep asking myself if any man on the face of the earth is worth this."

"Then let's talk houses and get your mind off all these people around us." Savannah patted her hand. "One is an older home on an acre of ground. It's two stories and has three bedrooms upstairs and one on the ground floor. The other is a brand-new brick home and has a small fenced yard. I don't want to tell you too much because I want you to get the feel for them when you first walk in."

"Fair enough," Amelia said.

"What's fair?" Nick asked as he and Daniel sat down in the last two chairs.

"That I don't know much about these places we're going to look at," Amelia answered. "That way, I can truly see which one I like best, but the decision should be which one you two are most happy with. I'm just along to offer a woman's opinion on what color curtains or towels to buy for either place."

"If you were buying a house today"—Nick flashed a smile toward her—"what would you be looking for?"

"Well, that's kind of a moot point," Amelia said, "because I'm not in the market to buy right now."

"But if you were?" Nick pressed.

"I'd be looking for something that has character," Amelia said. "New places or fancy houses don't appeal to me. I like my Aunt Liddy's place with all its nooks and crannies and its screened-in back porch. And I want cats, as in more than one, and a bayou nearby where I can fish or go shrimping. You got a listing like that?" Amelia rambled on.

"Well, Miz Taylor," Nick said in a true Texas drawl, "I don't have anything like that on the market right now, but if I ever get a listing with those particulars, I will give you a call. I know I can find a creek, if not a bayou, and there's no problem finding cats, but shrimp fishing in the middle of this particular part of the state of Texas might be tough."

A server brought their food out on a tray and set it in the middle of the table. "Let me know if I can get you anything else."

"Thank you," they all said and reached for their individual orders. Amelia's hand brushed against Nick's. The sparks that flitted around the whole café were so hot that Amelia was surprised the smoke alarms didn't go off. She was about to congratulate herself on not having a visible reaction when her phone rang. Normally, she would have ignored the call, but it was from her Aunt Liddy, and she had no doubt that if she didn't take it, the woman might come storming right down to the Dairy Queen.

"I should take this," she said. "Excuse me for just a minute." She pushed back her chair and stepped outside. She took a deep breath and let it out slowly, then answered on the fifth ring.

"Hello, Aunt Liddy," she said.

"What are you doing at the Dairy Queen with Nick Monroe?" Her aunt's tone was shorter and colder than she'd ever heard it.

"Daniel and Savannah are going to look at houses, remember?" Amelia answered. "How many Realtors do *you* know in Bonnet?"

"Just Nick, but that doesn't mean you have to have lunch with him right out in public," Liddy said. "I've gotten four calls already, and one of them said that Nick paid for dinner. That tells me it's a date."

"It tells *me* that he's trying to pave the way for Daniel and Savannah to make a decision about buying a house from him today," Amelia said. "I bet he does this for most of his clients. It's a marketing ploy, I'm sure."

"I don't like it," Liddy said.

Before Amelia could answer, Nick pushed the glass door open, winked at her, and answered his phone. Evidently, Matilda had gotten news of the lunch, too.

"Am I supposed to be rude and tell my friends if they are buying a place through Nick, I won't go with them?" Amelia asked.

"Of course not," Liddy said, "but I don't like you talking to him, not even in a business sense. Just get on back to your dinner before it gets cold. I hear you're having tacos, and they get soggy if they sit too long."

"Is there anything your gossip vine doesn't tell you?" Amelia asked with a giggle. "I could leave them and come have lunch with you if it's bothering you this much. Should I leave my tacos or bring them with me? And when I get there, can me and you and Mama and maybe Bridget talk about different sex positions? I think I might be a step or two ahead of Olivia right now, but I could use all the help I could get from you wise women."

"Absolutely not," Liddy declared.

"Then can I go on back in the café and eat?" Amelia asked.

"Of course you can," Liddy said. "Leaving now would cause an even worse scene. But remember this: when it comes to you and Nick, the people in town are watching you closer than God does, and they report everything to me so fast that it would make the angels' heads swim. Folks even have bets going as to whether Matilda will eventually take over this whole town and turn my own funeral dinner all vegan."

"Are you serious?" Amelia asked.

"Yes, I'm serious. I've got a hundred dollars riding on myself. But enough about that. You call me tonight and tell me what house Daniel and Savannah decided on."

"Yes, ma'am," Amelia said. "Are you keeping track of me to see if we really are looking at houses or if Nick and I are checking into the nearest motel?"

"Just remember how many eyes are on you," Liddy said and then the phone went dark.

Nick could have sworn that the temperature outside the Dairy Queen rose by at least twenty degrees as he listened to his mother rant for a full minute about Amelia sitting at the table with him.

"What do you expect me to do, Mother?" He finally got a word in edgewise. "Should I lose a good sale on property because I refuse to have Sunday dinner with a friend of my prospective clients? That would be horrible for business."

"You were with her last night and now today," Matilda said.

"So, you've already built up your own little network of spies?" Nick asked.

"No, but I've built up a network of friends who keep an eye on you. You're sitting at a table right out in the middle of the Dairy Queen, and you paid for dinner. You're having a double-meat cheeseburger and onion rings," Matilda answered.

"Well, Mother"—he dragged the last word out into several syllables—"that should tell you that I don't plan on kissing Amelia today."

"Oh, hush," Matilda growled.

"I can do that with no problem," Nick said. "Goodbye, Mother."

"Don't you hang up on me. You have a lot of explaining to do," Matilda said. "You're inventing reasons to be with that woman. There are dozens of women in this town you can date. Why do you have to fixate on that one?"

"I like it better when you tell me to hush," he said. "But right now, I really am going to end this call—my burger is getting cold. Your posse can keep you informed of what's happening. And, Mother, I'm past thirty years old. Whoever I fixate on is my own damn business and none of yours. Goodbye, Mama."

"Don't you call me that. It sounds so white trash." She hung up on him.

Nick chuckled and went back to the table, sat down, and glanced over at Amelia. "Was that your aunt?"

"Yep. Was that your mother?" Amelia asked.

"Good grief," Savannah whispered. "We barely even got our food. How many spies do they have in here?"

"Seems that both parties *do* have spies, and they even have a bet going as to who's going to serve the other's funeral dinner," Amelia answered.

"So, it's a fight to the death." Daniel laughed.

"Looks that way," Amelia said.

Nick's knee touched Amelia's under the table, and he felt the chemistry just like he had every time he was with her. No, that wasn't right—the electricity was even there when they were just talking on the phone or when he thought about her, which was nearly all the time.

What happened to that guy who was going to never have a real relationship because of his mother and the past history in our family? Uncle Harry was in his head and chuckling after every word.

Amelia Taylor happened to him, Nick answered.

Chapter Fifteen

Amelia and I are going to sit on that bench and let you two go in and walk through the house together," Nick said when they reached the first house. "That way neither of us will influence your first thoughts and ideas about the place. Come get us when you're done looking it over, and then I'll come in and give you the usual pitch as to how much storage space there is and how big the closets are."

"Do you always do business this way, or are you just wanting time alone with Amelia?" Daniel teased.

"This is my method," Nick answered. "It would be bad business if I pressured you into buying something that you hated later on. I'd never get a referral that way. Plus, it *will* be nice to have a few minutes with Amelia where no eyes are staring at us."

"Not so." Amelia sat down on the pretty park bench under a big shade tree in the front yard. "Aunt Liddy says that the people in this town have more eyes on us than God."

"And maybe the devil, too." Nick chuckled and handed Daniel the key. "Take your time and give it a good going over, and then we'll drive about two miles out of town to the next one."

Daniel and Savannah disappeared into the house, and Nick sat down close enough to Amelia that their shoulders, hips, and thighs were touching. He draped his arm around her shoulders and said, "Do you think we can make it until Easter without having the whole town explode?"

Nick's phone rang, but he ignored it. Five seconds later it rang again.

"You better get that or it's going to keep ringing," she said.

"Only my mother calls until she gets ahold of me, and I don't want to talk to her," he said, but he took the phone from his shirt pocket. "Nope, this time it's Uncle Harry. I'll have to call him back. He's out there on his own, and he might be in trouble." Nick scrolled down until he found Harry's name and then called the number.

"Hello, did I catch you at a bad time?" Harry asked.

"Of course not. Are you okay?" Nick asked.

"Finer than frog hair split five ways." Harry laughed at his own joke. "I bought that house. It's a little bigger than I need, but I like it, and I love it here. I was sitting on the beach last night and the water lapping up seemed to be saying that it wanted me to stay in Florida, so I just took that as a sign that I should stay right here. I just signed the papers ten minutes ago, and I had to tell you about it."

"What if you don't like it in six months?" Nick asked.

"I'm a real estate agent," Harry said with another laugh. "I can sell it and move on. What I called for is to ask you to fly down here over your Easter break and see it. It's available for me to move into now, so I'll be in and settled when you get here."

"I'm happy for you, Uncle Harry." Nick glanced over at Amelia. "I really am. I can hear happiness in your voice, and I'd love to come see you. But can I bring a friend?"

"Sure, but only if it's Liddy Latham's niece." Harry chuckled. "I'll vote for anything that Matilda is fighting against."

"Think y'all will ever bury the hatchet?" Nick asked.

"It's not a hatchet, son. It's a heavy-duty power saw," Harry said. "I can't wait for you to see this place. You may want to leave Bonnet and put in a real estate place here in Panama City Beach."

"I doubt that, but it'll sure be good to get out of all this tension in Bonnet for a few days," Nick said. "Soon as I figure out the flight schedule I'll get back with you, but in the meantime, you could send me some photos of your new place."

"Oh, no!" Harry's tone sounded pretty definite. "You'll just have to wait and see. Bye now."

Nick shoved the phone back into his pocket and turned to focus on Amelia. "Uncle Harry was serious about retiring. He bought a house in Florida, and he's invited me to come stay with him over Easter weekend. How many days do you have off for Easter?"

"Friday and Monday," she answered.

"Want to go spend a long weekend on the beach?" Nick asked. "Uncle Harry said I could bring a friend."

"Can I think about it?" she asked. "Going away for a weekend together is a big step."

"Of course," Nick answered. "It might be good for us to get away from all this stress and tension around us and see exactly what this is between us, don't you think?"

"What about when we come back home to the reality of having to admit to our families that we like each other?" she asked.

"Do you really believe that reality hasn't set in already? Both of us had to leave the table and answer calls not an hour ago."

"You've got a point there," she said.

"Hey," Daniel called out from the doorway into the house. "We're ready for the sales pitch now."

Nick stood and offered his hand to Amelia to help her. She put her hand in his, but when she was on her feet, he didn't let go. "If anyone is watching, let them report that back to my mother and your aunt. I didn't hear a word of what the preacher said this morning."

"Yep. Same here." She kept holding his hand as they walked across the yard and into the house.

"Any comments before I give you the two-dollar sales pitch?" Nick asked.

"This place is practical and beautiful. We love the open-space living area and the walk-in closets," Daniel said.

"But . . . ," Savannah sighed.

"If there's a *but*, then you have doubts." Nick smiled.

"But it feels kind of cold, and I don't mean the temperature. There's no personality, and I don't feel love surrounding me," Savannah told him. "Daniel says we can fill it with our own love and memories. Yet right now, it just feels sterile to me, like something I'd run away from rather than something I couldn't wait to come home to at the end of the day."

Amelia knew exactly what Savannah meant. She felt the love of generations in the old frame house when she went out to the island to see her Granny Dee. New homes were beautiful with all their fanciness, but they didn't have the feel of a house like Nick's.

"We could go see the second one and then come back for the official Realtor's tour of this one," Nick suggested.

"I'd like that very much." Savannah nodded. "Amelia, would you do a quick walk-through with me one more time? Then would you ride with me and let the guys go in Nick's vehicle?"

"Be glad to." Amelia followed Savannah through the house.

Nick locked up when they had finished and walked Amelia out to Savannah's car. He opened the door for her and said, "We're doing good. No phone calls yet."

"Shhh . . . ," she whispered. "You'll jinx it for sure."

He just chuckled as he closed the door and then went to his Jeep.

"He's a keeper," Savannah said. "How you two are keeping this under wraps when you are so clearly in love is beyond what I could possibly do. And now truthfully, how did you like that house?"

"Wait. How did *you* like it?" Amelia asked. "I don't have to live there."

"It reminded me of the guesthouse out back of my folks' place. We had an indoor pool, a tennis court, and riding stables, and the guesthouse was kind of like what we just looked at. I can't explain it better, but . . ." She paused.

Amelia gasped. What world did she just peek into? "I knew you came from a wealthy family, but now I understand why you and Daniel are eloping to Vegas."

"Yep, the wedding would be a nightmare." Savannah turned her car around in the cul-de-sac and followed Nick out of town.

"But you are worried about what your folks will say when they come to visit, right?" Amelia asked. "You don't want them to look down their noses at your home, or worse yet, to make remarks about how they could have bought you something nicer if you hadn't been so stubborn."

"Yep, you nailed that. I'm an only child. Daddy and Mama both almost had heart attacks when I told them I wanted to teach school. I love little kids, and I hate the idea of sitting in an office all day. Yet they wanted me to get an MBA and then come home and work at the firm with them. They keep reminding me that, someday, I'll inherit the business and the estate, and I need to learn how to run it."

"That's in the future." Amelia reached across the console and patted her on the shoulder. "Today you just have to think about buying a house. Are you and Daniel planning on having kids? That will determine how big of a house and what kind you want to buy, too."

"At least four," Savannah answered. "I don't want to raise a child on its own—I always wanted a sister or a brother."

That reminded Amelia of what Nick had said about being an only child. From there her thoughts went to Harry and Matilda. Either of them might have been better off if they'd been only children.

"So, when you get married, do you intend to have children?" Savannah asked.

"I want kids, and Lord knows that my parents and Aunt Liddy sure want grandkids, but I'm like you. I'd want at least two, maybe three."

Savannah drove down Main Street and followed Nick out east of town. When they had gone past the new high school on the right-hand side of the street, Amelia blurted out, "Nick asked me to go to Florida to visit his Uncle Harry with him over Easter weekend."

"What did you say?" Savannah asked. "You've only known each other a few weeks, but I think it's a great idea."

"Really?" Amelia asked. "Have we really known each other long enough to do that? How long did you know Daniel before y'all went away for a weekend?"

"Six months, but that was different," Savannah told her.

"How so?"

"We were dating. My folks knew we were dating, even though they didn't like it. We didn't have a Matilda or an Aunt Liddy in our lives, and we could be public with what we were doing. Y'all could use some time at this point to figure out if you're friends, if this is a relationship, or what else it might be. Then if and when you tell the families, you'll have some solid ground to stand on for the battle you'll face," Savannah answered.

Nick turned right and followed a lane up to a two-story white-frame house sitting on a little rise. Bluebonnets, with a splash from Indian paintbrush and yellow daisies, filled the area on both sides of the lane, and a huge weeping willow tree graced the front lawn. A steady breeze had kicked up, so when Savannah parked the car and they got out, Amelia could hear the squeak of the porch swing as it swayed back and forth.

"A big wraparound porch," Savannah whispered. "This is even prettier than the picture made it seem. I'm already in love."

"What do you think?" Daniel wrapped his arms around Savannah from behind and pulled her to his chest. "Tell me before we even go inside."

"I always thought I'd have to live in a house like I grew up in. It's beautiful, but I want our home to be full of fun and laughter, and I don't want a single thing in it that I have to put away when the kids are growing up. If it's not useful, then we don't need it. Let's go inside and see how this one feels. It's sure nicer than what the picture in Nick's brochure showed."

Nick handed off another set of keys to Daniel and led Amelia up to the porch swing. "If we were buying a house, would it be one with a park bench in the yard or a swing on a porch like this?" he asked.

"Neither one," she answered. "The only house I've seen in Bonnet that I would buy isn't for sale. It's an old heirloom house that's been passed down from generation to generation and is right across from my aunt's place."

Nick pulled her down beside him on the swing. "I know that old place, but it doesn't have water surrounding it."

"But it's got a cat, and that means a lot." Amelia smiled.

"Well, God bless Vera." Nick grinned.

Daniel tapped on the window and motioned for them to come inside.

"That was fast," Nick said. "Want to bet which one they like best?"

"I don't bet very often. I'm way too tight with my money." Amelia stopped the swing with a foot and stood up. "I knew when we drove up the lane that this would be Savannah's favorite, and Daniel will go along with anything that makes her happy."

Amelia sucked air when she walked into the house. She wondered for a moment if someone had hauled Nick's house from town to the country and plopped it down in a field of bluebonnets and wildflowers. The general layout was the same—a foyer that ran from the front door to the back, living room and kitchen on the left side, and a dining room and office on the other.

"Did you have time to really look at the whole house?" Nick asked.

"No, we just got into the foyer and Savannah was in love with it," Daniel answered. "We're ready for you to show us the rest of it officially."

"The cabinets could use some updating." Nick led the way into a big country kitchen. "According to the papers I have, they were put in about thirty years ago, but they have been taken care of, so they're still in good shape. There isn't a dishwasher, and the floor tile is serviceable, but most folks nowadays like the new wood-look laminate planks. The utility room is right through here, and the seller is willing to leave all the appliances. The washer and dryer are a year old. The upright freezer is quite a bit older but still works. This side door leads out into the fenced backyard," he said as he threw the door open.

"I wouldn't change a thing in this house. It's got personality, and there's warmth in every room. It says, 'Come on in and prop your feet up,' and"—Savannah leaned back to peek inside a utility room cabinet—"it says, 'This is a place to raise a family.' Speaking of that, I want a swing in that big old tree." She pointed out the back door. "One of those baby swings at first and then a regular one when the kids are older."

"Are you dropping a hint?" Daniel teased.

"No, but you already know that I don't want to wait until I'm thirty to start a family," Savannah answered.

"How about you? Do you want to wait until you're thirty?" Nick whispered for Amelia's ears only.

"I'm twenty-eight right now. I imagine I will be over thirty before I get started," she answered.

"This is it, isn't it?" Daniel asked Savannah.

"I want to see the upstairs before I make up my mind for sure, and this should be *our* decision, not just mine." She laced her fingers with his and led him to the staircase.

Nick followed them. "You might want to stop and see the living room on the way. It has a stone fireplace that works, with bookcases on either side."

Savannah peeked into the room and smiled. "And lovely wainscoting that matches the banister up the stairs, and I love this ivy wallpaper. How long do you figure it's been hanging?"

"Wouldn't know about that," Nick said. "The folks I showed the house to last week said it would be the first thing to come down."

"Oh, no!" Amelia and Savannah said at the same time.

"I want a dog," Daniel said out of the blue.

"Hey, we haven't even talked about pets." Savannah's eyebrows shot up.

"Okay, then," Daniel said. "Let's talk about them. Do you want dogs or cats, or both, or maybe a goat or a couple of alpacas to keep this big yard mowed for us?"

Savannah cocked her head to one side. "One dog would get lonely when we're at work. After we go to Vegas, we'll go to the pound and get a couple. One for you and one for me," Savannah said. "I don't want those little yappy things, either. I want big yard dogs. I could never have pets at home because Mother wouldn't allow it, but I always loved big dogs."

"Labs or huskies sound good to me," Daniel said as he pulled her toward the stairs. "Three bedrooms. One for us, one for the girls, and one for the boys."

"And when we get old, we'll move our bedroom down into the office," she said.

"You're planning on living in this house that long?" Daniel asked.

"Honey, I would never leave the memories we'll make here," she told him. "We can sit on that front porch and swing our grandbabies when they come along."

"And tell them stories about how their daddy or mama used to make forts or playhouses under the branches of the willow trees," Daniel said as they went up the stairs.

"Looks like they've made their decision. Shall we go back out to the swing while they make their memories?" Nick asked.

"I'd like that, but first, I've made *my* decision," Amelia said. "I would love to go with you to Florida for Easter weekend."

Nick drew her into his arms for a quick hug. "I'm sure that Uncle Harry isn't brewing up any poison, so we'll be safe down there."

"We may have to hire tasters when we get home, though."

"To date you, darlin', I'd hire a dozen and they could work around the clock," Nick promised.

Chapter Sixteen

Nick opened up the real estate office on Monday morning, put on a pot of coffee, turned on the lights, and unlocked the front door. Today, he was interviewing Thomas Mason for the office manager's job, and Nick sure hoped he would be the perfect fit so that he wouldn't have to go through the process a dozen times.

He hadn't even had time to pour a cup of coffee when the man entered the office—a short guy with a mop of curly black hair, brown eyes, and maybe thirty pounds more than he should have. "I'm Thomas Mason." He stuck out his right hand and shook with Nick and then handed him a folder.

"Nice to meet you, Thomas. Thanks for being so prompt." Nick took the folder from his hand. "You take your coffee black or with cream and sugar?"

"Black, but I'll get it for both of us," he said. "I've been in here lots of times, so I know where things are. Wanda was my mama's cousin, and we used to stop by here to visit with her when I was a little boy. I loved Wanda"—his eyes misted over, but he didn't shed tears—"and she was so nice to me. For Christmas last year I gave her that little sign up there that says 'Sometimes you win. Sometimes you learn.' She told me exactly that when I interviewed for a job over in Gainesville right out of high school and didn't get it." He talked as he poured two cups of coffee and carried them to the office.

Nick sat down behind Wanda's desk and motioned for Thomas to have a seat in one of the two chairs on the other side of the desk. "Thank you for bringing me coffee, but you don't have to do that."

"No problem." He glanced around at the office. "I'm glad you left things the way they are and didn't take down all her plaques. It keeps a comfortable look in the place."

"I thought so, too." Nick remembered having to rehang every one of those small signs. "What makes you want to change jobs from the bank to here?"

"I'd have my own office, and just one boss," he answered, "and I wouldn't be working with . . ." He paused.

"With what or who?" Nick asked.

"I shouldn't say this, but working with that many women who are always talking about their problems and gossiping behind each other's backs gets tiresome. It'd be nice to have a male colleague for once," Thomas answered.

Nick liked the man. He was honest, and he liked the office just the way it was. "You wouldn't know anyone looking for a job as a real estate agent, would you?"

"Yes, I do," he said, "but I don't know if you would want to hire someone I'm dating and very serious about. I also work with her at the bank. She's been studying for her real estate license and plans to take the test the first of June."

Nick felt like he'd just fallen into a fresh pile of cow manure and came up smelling like roses. He had heard his Uncle Harry use that expression too many times to count, and the memory put a smile on his face. "Think she would come in and talk to me sometime soon? I'm looking for an assistant agent."

"Is noon soon enough?" Thomas asked.

"That would be great," Nick said. "When can you start to work?"

"I can give the bank a week's notice and be ready to start next Monday," he said. "Are you saying I've got the job?"

"If you want it, it's yours," Nick said. "I think you and I can work very well together."

"Thank you!" Thomas said. "I'm so excited for this opportunity, but I figured you'd want a lady to work the front office."

"Looks like to me"—Nick tapped the résumé on his desk—"that you are really overqualified for this job, and I'm lucky to have you."

The door flew open, and Matilda came in like the wind right before a tornado.

"Mother, meet my new office manager," Nick said. "This is Thomas Mason, and he'll be joining me next Monday."

"Pleased to meet you, ma'am," Thomas said with a big smile.

Matilda looked at him like he was a common kitchen ant that needed to be squashed. "You are unhired. You can leave now, and don't ever call me ma'am. That's what you call an old person."

"Sorry about that," Thomas apologized and then looked over at Nick.

"Please don't leave, Thomas. I'll get this straightened out," Nick said. "Mother, in my office, please."

Matilda's high heels seemed to beat out pure anger as she stomped from one office to the other.

Nick followed her and eased the door shut. "Have a seat."

"I don't want to sit down," she said. "I want you to go out there and tell that man to get the hell out of my office."

"This is my business, Mother, and I've hired Thomas. He's actually overqualified to do the job. His résumé is outstanding. Besides all that, you can't unhire anyone. He's going to fit right in here, like Wanda did."

"But I've told Kayla that you would hire *her* and pay double what she makes at the chamber of commerce. That man can go down there and apply for her job. I won't allow you to make a fool out of me, Nick," Matilda fumed. "Besides, I've told you about a million times that you need a classy woman in the front office."

"You better give Kayla a call and tell her that the position has been filled," Nick said. "If she's about to quit her job, you might want to make that call right now. And another thing, Mother, I don't want someone from your posse in here keeping watch on my every move and telling you how much money I make or don't make or, worse yet, who I'm dating. Thomas will keep all things that happen in this office confidential. That's all I've got to say to you." Nick opened the door and nodded toward Thomas. "Everything is just fine. I'm looking forward to seeing you next Monday at nine o'clock. We'll talk about lunch and break schedules when you get here."

"Yes, sir." He nodded. "Should I still tell Olivia to come in at noon?"

"Of course," Nick said. "Mother will be gone by then."

"Thank you once again." Thomas headed out the door.

"The thanks goes to you. I think we'll make fine partners in this business," Nick called after him as he left. When the door had closed, he turned to Matilda and said, "That was rude, uncalled for, and embarrassing."

"He's a man, for God's sake, and he looks like he dresses out of thrift stores, and that wrinkled shirt he was wearing didn't cost a dime more than ten dollars." Matilda crossed the room and sank down in the chair Thomas had vacated. She took her phone out of her thousand-dollar designer purse and dialed a number. "Darlin', I'm so sorry to have to tell you this." Her voice went from sarcastic to sugary sweet. "Nick had already hired someone. Of course, he's sick about it, because he knows you would have been perfect for the job."

Nick shook his head at the blatant lie.

"Yes, it was Thomas, and, darling, we all know that he won't work out in a stressful job like this. Everyone knows an office needs a female secretary. I'm sure that Nick will be calling you as soon as this Thomas person shows him that he's not the one for the job. See you at lunch. My treat today." She slipped the phone back into her purse and glared at Nick. "You almost ruined a friendship."

"You lied," Nick said.

"No, I didn't. Within two weeks, you *will* be sick about hiring a man to run the office, and you *will* find out that Kayla is perfect for the job, and you *will* wind up hiring her," Matilda disagreed.

"Don't hold your breath," Nick growled. "You never have looked good in blue."

"Oh, hush," Matilda fumed. "I came in here to help you get some office help, but I also came to tell you that we need to put Amos's house on the market. I've backed out of the deal to buy it since it's too much trouble to get it zoned commercial."

"Did you lose your friend Tina when you did? Or did you figure out that the people in this town would not want to zone that part of town commercial and would vote against your plan?" Nick asked.

"You always have to be a spoilsport about everything," Matilda growled.

"Will you lose Kayla's friendship when I don't hire her? If that happens, you'll be getting kind of thin on friends. Uncle Harry isn't coming back to Bonnet. He bought a house in Florida."

Matilda gave him another go-to-hell look and said, "I'm glad Harry isn't coming back. I don't like him. Never did and never will. Tina will bring you all the particulars. Since I brought the property to you, do I get a small commission?"

"No, ma'am, you do not," Nick said. "Tell me, how much escrow did you have to eat?"

"I didn't put up a dime, so I didn't lose any money," she answered through clenched teeth. "The bed-and-breakfast I'm staying in is going on the market, and I like it better anyway. This town has closed ranks against me, but I might have a chance over in Muenster. I do have some German DNA, you know, and those people over there are a hell of a lot friendlier than they are here in Bonnet."

Nick's mood lifted a little. Unless she backed out of this deal, too, she wouldn't be in Bonnet all the time. "When is this deal in Muenster going down?" he asked.

"The owner and I sat down to have breakfast together this morning, and she told me she was listing it this week. I asked her if she'd be willing to cut out the middleman and sell it outright to me. We struck up a deal, and I agreed to keep the staff that helps run the place," Matilda answered.

Nick chuckled and then grew serious. "That's why you were so hellbent on me hiring Kayla, isn't it? You promised her a job at your bed-and-breakfast, and you had to renege on it. You're lucky that she'll even go to lunch with you, and it *should* be your treat after a stunt like that."

Matilda stood up and flipped her hair back in a dramatic gesture. "Some days I wish I'd never had a child. All you do is argue with me. I've got to go see Don Hollis at the courthouse and tell him that I'm not interested in running for city council. I've already withdrawn my membership in the chamber of commerce and plan to join the one in Muenster."

"What about funeral dinners? Are you going to give Liddy Latham some relief on that?" Nick asked.

"Not in a million years. I plan to keep coming to church over here with our family's people—like Barbara. When there's a funeral dinner, I will be right there offering my services to plan and produce meals that are also healthy. I will see that woman and her lemon pies six feet under, and that's a promise."

"What about that property of hers you are so hell-bent on having?" Nick asked.

"Oh, honey, if there's a loophole the size of the eye of a needle, my lawyer will find it, and they'll have no choice but to sell it to me," Matilda sneered.

"And what if Liddy's husband was right and there's no oil under the ground?" Nick asked.

"I've got plans to make an eighteen-hole golf course out there, and maybe eventually a country club. Tina would so love to have a club closer than Nocona," Matilda answered. "Until my dying day, I will be fighting for that land just to get back at Liddy."

"Mother, do you even know how much money that would take?" Nick asked.

"I might have to get investors, but Tina will come in handy for that. I'm leaving now. I'm done answering questions." Matilda stiffened her back and marched out of the building.

"Baby steps," Nick muttered as he got up from his chair and headed to the kitchenette to pour himself another cup of coffee. He sent Amelia a text: **Office Manager hired. Interviewing another agent at noon.**

She sent one right back: **Great!**

"I'm Olivia O'Hara." A short lady with light brown hair that she wore in a ponytail at the nape of her neck introduced herself at five minutes past noon. "I brought my résumé and all the classes that I've taken toward my real estate license and a copy of the application to take my test. I've been a loan officer at the bank for five years, so I could be a help in mortgage assessments if you hire me. I also have my appraisal license."

Nick motioned for her to have a seat and opened the folder she'd handed to him. "Well, you are certainly qualified. Why are you wanting to make a change from banking?"

"Because of your Uncle Harry," Olivia said. "I was one of those nobody kids in town. I wouldn't be where I am today if it hadn't been for Harry Davis. He gave me a job helping Wanda after school."

"I thought you looked familiar," Nick said with a smile. "I met you several years ago when I came to visit Uncle Harry."

"That's right. I was about eighteen that year." Olivia nodded. "With what Harry paid me and what my mama made as a waitress, we were able to keep food on the table for me and my little brother. Then Harry paid for me to go to a junior college and get an associate degree in business, and he got me the job at the bank. He used to tell me that if Jack ever retired, he would hire me, and he pushed me to study for my real estate license."

"Why would he do all that for you?" Nick wondered if Harry had a child or two that he had never claimed.

"I'm not sure. I used to wish it was because he was my legal father, but that was just a dream. I look exactly like my daddy's mother. He was a truck driver that got killed when my brother was just a baby," she said. "But Harry was good to us, and we weren't the only ones that he helped out without anyone knowing about it. When I went to college, Mama got cancer and died six months later. Harry stepped up and pulled some strings to get my brother into the Air Force Academy. He's now in the service and doing very well. I owe Harry, and it's been my lifelong dream to have a position here. That may be too much information, but it's the truth, and I wanted you to know, whether you hire me or not."

"Thank you for that." Nick flipped through the papers in his hands. "When can you start to work? You can work as my assistant until you pass your test, and then you can be a full-fledged salesperson who gets a share of the commissions."

"Next Monday. I need to give the bank a week's notice," Olivia said.

"Let me show you your office, and then we'll go down to the Dairy Queen and grab a burger to celebrate," Nick said.

"You mean I get my own office?" Olivia asked. "I just figured I would work out of this one with Thomas."

"Nope, your spot is right behind mine." Nick pushed back his chair, got up, and led the way. He flipped on the light. "Things are pretty much like Jack left them. You might want to make some changes. I'll get some business cards with your name on them ordered this week."

He picked up the ones Jack had used and started to toss them into the trash, but he just couldn't do it.

"This is amazing," Olivia said. "Thank you so much, Mr. Monroe."

"Just Nick. We're all three going to be working like partners," Nick said. "Don't you want to talk about what I can pay you?"

"You saw my pay stubs in the file. If it's comparable to that, I have no complaints," Olivia answered.

"I can't double it, but I can give you half as much again as you are making and a commission on each sale you make after you pass your test, plus I'll put you on our insurance plan. How does that sound?" Nick asked.

Olivia stuck out her hand. "That's beyond fair, and more than I expected. With that kind of raise, Thomas and I might be able to set a date for our wedding."

"Then congratulations." Nick grinned and shook on the deal. "I'll look to see you next Monday morning, but right now, we've got time for a quick lunch. Would you mind calling Thomas, too? We can all celebrate together. I need to talk to him about a few more things anyway. My mother burst into the office—and by the way, don't let her intimidate you when she pops in and out—and things were such a mess when she left, I didn't get a chance to even talk to him about salary, benefits, or bonuses."

"I'll text him right now. He told me that he would have taken the job even if he had to take a cut in pay. I probably shouldn't tell you that, but it's the truth," Olivia said as they walked out into the bright sunshine and headed down the street to the Dairy Queen.

When they walked into the café, Thomas waved from a booth. Nick and Olivia headed that way, and when they were close, Thomas slid out of the seat.

"I got the job." Olivia wrapped her arms around him and hugged him tightly.

"So did I!" He hugged her back.

Nick was more than a little jealous and hoped that someday he could hug Amelia when he had good news to share.

"I'm buying lunch to celebrate finding teammates," Nick said. "What are you having? I'll go order."

"The burger basket for me, mustard and no onions, and a root beer," Olivia answered, "and thank you."

Thomas followed Nick to the counter. "Same for me, and I'll go with you to help carry the drinks back to the booth."

"Then we'll just make it three orders of the same thing," Nick said, "and after Easter when we're all settled in better, I'd like to invite you both over to my house. We can have our first company barbecue."

Three huge trees shaded his backyard. He figured it would be a perfect place to set up an outdoor kitchen with a barbecue. His first memory was playing with his toys in that yard while his Uncle Harry sat in an old metal lawn chair and talked to him. The paint was all gone from that chair these days, but Nick decided he would have it redone and buy some more patio furniture. He intended to do some casual entertaining maybe with this couple, Daniel and Savannah—and hopefully Amelia, too.

"That sounds great," Thomas said.

Nick had to stand in line for a couple of minutes, so he sent a text to Amelia: Just hired Thomas Mason as my office manager and Olivia O'Hara as my assistant.

Seconds after he hit the send button, his phone rang. When he saw that Amelia was calling, he quickly answered on the first ring.

"Congratulations!" she said. "Now you've got a staff. Are they going to be ready to start work before we leave at Easter? That's not far away, and we'll be gone that Monday afterwards."

"They are starting work next Monday morning, so they'll be there a whole week before we go. Everything is working out great, and thanks for agreeing to go with me," Nick said. "I wish Daniel and Savannah needed to look at another house or two tonight."

"Me too," she said, "but we probably shouldn't push our luck that far. Aunt Liddy wants me to take her grocery shopping in Gainesville this evening. I think maybe she's got plans to keep me too busy to think about you."

"Is that going to work?" Nick moved up in the line to the second place.

"I doubt it," Amelia said. "Thursday evening I will be going with her to a cookbook-making group at the church. I won't be jogging that evening. Tell Vera that I miss her, and maybe things will be better after Easter."

"She will miss you. I probably won't be jogging tonight, either. I've got a late showing of a house, but I'm looking forward to Easter weekend so much, darlin'," he said and then ended the call.

He stepped up to the counter and ordered. As soon as he finished, his phone rang again. His mother had an uncanny ability to know when he was talking to Amelia, so he almost didn't answer it. Then he saw his dad's picture pop up on the screen, and he stopped at the condiment counter to talk while he picked up packets of ketchup.

"Hey, Dad, what's going on?" Nick said.

"Not much," Gregory answered. "Just wanted to hear your voice and check on you. What's going on with the bluebonnet battle?"

"That's funny, but then it isn't. Tempers are still flaring, and the tension is as thick as a fog," Nick told him. "Uncle Harry invited us to Florida over Easter, and A agreed to go with me."

Gregory chuckled. "You do know you'll have to pay the fiddler when you get home, don't you?"

"Oh, yeah," Nick answered. "This one is special, Dad. She's made me rethink my vow about being a bachelor like Uncle Harry."

"I can hear it in your voice, but take my advice, Son. Don't rush into anything. It can ruin your life. Get to know everything about her, maybe even live together a year before you pop the important question," Gregory suggested.

"I promise I will," Nick said. "Got to go. Our food is ready. I'm celebrating with a couple that I hired today—an office manager and an assistant who is about to take her real estate test."

"That's great, Son. Call me when you have more time. Betsy sends her love," Gregory said and then the screen went dark.

Nick picked up the tray with the food on it and took it back to the booth where Thomas and Olivia waited.

Chapter Seventeen

Liddy and Ruth Ann already had customers waiting that Tuesday morning when they opened the hospital gift shop. A solid hour of one person or group after another came in to buy flowers or presents for women with new babies or patients who were recovering from illnesses or surgery.

Finally, in the middle of the morning, business came to a standstill, and Liddy propped a hip on the stool behind the counter. "Amelia is seeing Nick on the sly. I know it even if she won't admit it."

"I think so, too." Ruth Ann sighed. "Paul and I talked about it last night. We agreed that fussing at her is only going to make her dig her heels in deeper. Bridget tried to visit with her about it, but she wouldn't listen to anything her sister had to say."

"So, you think we ought to do the old 'if you can't lick 'em, join 'em' thing and hope to hell that she wakes up?" Liddy asked.

"Maybe if we join them, it might even give Matilda a heart attack," Ruth Ann said.

"I'm not sure I can do that." Liddy sighed. "I don't care if that man has wings hiding under his shirt and a halo that he takes off every morning when he starts to work, I can't bear the thought of Amelia having Matilda for a mother-in-law."

"But just think how much fun it would be to see steam coming out her ears," Ruth Ann said. "And after the last disaster with Elliott,

I'm hoping she's learned a few things. Why couldn't she be more like Bridget? She dated a few guys, had a couple of relationships where she didn't bring the guy home to meet us, and then she brought Clovis home. We loved him from day one."

"We all liked Elliott the first couple of years, too," Liddy said, "and look how that turned out. If we're right, I hope she understands what she's getting into even dating Nick. Matilda can be a real bitch."

"Not can be," Ruth Ann said. "*Is* a real bitch."

Liddy shook her head slowly from side to side. "Think of the future. I'd have to be at the wedding with that woman. You know she'd want her vegan food at the reception, and Amelia told me once that she didn't want a wedding cake. She wants me to get one of those pie stackers and make my lemon pies to go on it. She said we could put the bride and groom figures in the meringue on the top pie, and it would look like they were in the clouds."

Ruth Ann sat down on the second stool. "What a cute idea."

"Matilda would throw a hissy fit at that, and Amelia would change her mind to keep peace." Liddy dug a bill from the pocket of her jeans, bought two candy bars, and handed one to Ruth Ann.

"That's where you are wrong." Ruth Ann tore the paper away from the candy bar and took a bite.

Liddy unwrapped her candy but didn't bite into it. "Her keeping the peace is why she hasn't told us. She doesn't ever want to upset the family after what we went through getting her out of that horrible depression. That's why she stayed in that miserable relationship as long as she did. She kept thinking Elliott would change, and that his mental abuse was her fault. Matilda will get under her skin, and no matter how much Nick cares about her, eventually that woman will tear them apart."

"Give Amelia more credit than that," Ruth Ann said between bites. "Remember she's got Irish and Cajun blood in her veins. I don't think Matilda will even get a hit if she's pitching, much less get a run to first base. Did you hear what happened when Nick hired Thomas and Olivia? I saw Ethel in the grocery store this morning and she told me." Ruth Ann went on to tell her what had happened the day before when Matilda tried to unhire Thomas. "I don't think Nick would let his mother say a word against Amelia—if we're right."

"Nooo!" Liddy almost choked on a bite of candy.

"Yep." Ruth Ann plugged some change into the pop machine and bought two cans of Dr Pepper. "I didn't know that Olivia was even working on her license, but I guess all she has left to do is take the test. I was hoping we could match Thomas up with Amelia, but rumor has it that he is going to marry Olivia before long."

"Win some, lose some," Liddy said, "or in the case of Amelia and Nick, it's lose some, lose some." She was so hoping that she could fix Amelia up with Thomas. He seemed like such a good, kind man, but evidently Olivia had beat her niece's time with the guy.

"Maybe they'll decide they don't even like each other." Ruth Ann handed a can of soda pop to Liddy. "It could just be a flash-in-the-pan type thing. Once they own up to dating, and everyone knows, the glamour might be all over for them."

"I hope so," Liddy said. "I sincerely hope so."

"Paul is meeting us at the fish place for lunch today after we get done here," Ruth Ann said. "Maybe he's got some new ideas about all this since he's slept on it."

"Sounds good. Listen . . ." Liddy cocked her head to one side. "There's the music. There's been another baby born. Folks will be swarming in here to buy stuff in the next few minutes. Just thinking about hearing that sweet music play if Amelia has a baby with Nick gives me hives."

By Thursday evening, when it was time to attend the cookbook meeting at the church, Liddy was still worrying more than she had since she found out Richie was seeing Matilda on the sly. She had been the president of the previous committee that had put together a cookbook for the church to sell, and it was time to have another fundraiser for the church's missionary account. The last one had been so profitable that Liddy was already thinking of making a motion to print up twice as many books for the first order.

With Matilda's decision not to buy Amos's house and turn it into a B and B, and to bow out of the race for the council as well as take her name off the chamber of commerce roster, Liddy figured it was pretty clear sailing, as Marvin used to say. Matilda might poke her nose and her tofu shrimp into the funeral dinners, but for the most part she would be stirring up dust over in Muenster instead of Bonnet.

Liddy was the first one to arrive at the fellowship hall, so she set up one long eight-foot table to hold the desserts and made a big pot of coffee. Since Ethel had offered to bring a couple of gallons of sweet tea, she didn't bother with making that. She set her pie on the end of the table and then got busy setting up chairs in two rows.

"Thank you, Jesus, for that zoning law," she whispered as she finished with the chairs and made sure the microphone attached to the lectern was working.

She put the previous cookbook with its faded cover and several smudged pages on the lectern so she could show it to the folks who would be voting on how many books they needed to order.

Liddy had made up her mind to confront Amelia after the meeting that evening—come hell, high water, or elephants walking down Main Street in Bonnet, Texas. She was sick and tired of worrying about it, and tonight was the night she intended to get it all off her mind.

Ruth Ann arrived next and brought in a pan of cinnamon rolls. "I love it when we decide to have a dessert bar instead of a potluck," she said as she took the pan to the back of the room. "I only ate half a sandwich for supper since I intend to eat enough to put myself into a sugar stupor by the time the evening is over."

"Me too, and I am having it out with Amelia tonight, so I can use all the energy I can get," Liddy declared.

Ruth Ann shook her head. "Give it another week or so, maybe until after Easter. I'm hoping that wherever she goes over the holiday makes her come to her senses."

"All right," Liddy agreed. "But when she comes back from her little vacation, I'm not going to let her sidestep."

"I agree, and we'll all be right there with you," Ruth Ann said. "Paul and I are ready to get this settled, one way or the other, too."

Ethel came through the back door with two gallons of tea in her hands. "This isn't bought tea. I just save my milk jugs and wash them out good to use for transporting tea. I'll get it poured up into pitchers so it looks a little nicer. There's a storm brewing out there. Wind is getting up."

"I heard we were under a tornado watch," Ruth Ann said. "Might keep some folks at home."

"We can only hope that Matilda is afraid of storms." Ethel chuckled.

Ruth Ann made a sign of the cross with her forefingers. "Don't even say her name. We're hoping she finds a church to go to over in Muenster, and eventually keeps all her vegan ideas over there."

Liddy heard the door open and turned to see Amelia and Savannah coming into the room. She breathed a sigh of relief and scolded herself for even thinking that Matilda would be interested in helping with a cookbook.

"That wind just about blew me away before I could get in here," Amelia said. "I had to hang on to my brownies with all my might. Think the storm will hit before we finish the meeting?"

"It's not supposed to be here until about midnight. We should all be home and snuggled down in our beds by then, but if we're not, we'll have plenty of desserts to keep us happy right here," Ethel answered.

Liddy hoped the storm wasn't an omen of things to come but, if it was, that it didn't have anything to do with Matilda. "I'm glad you and Savannah could make it tonight, and is that Olivia coming in the door now?"

"I brought them with me," Amelia answered. "They both love to cook and are interested in helping with this project, Aunt Liddy. Is that all right?"

Liddy reached into her bag and brought out a stack of papers. "Of course it's all right. We can use all the help we can get. I'm glad to see that you're stepping up to help us old women out with this. You girls can start by putting one of these on each chair."

"We'll do that"—Amelia took the flyers from her aunt's hands and handed off a stack to her two friends—"but, Aunt Liddy, you will never be old, so don't be giving me that line."

"Do we need to rustle up some pencils or pens?" Olivia asked.

"No, the flyers are for them to take home," Ruth Ann answered. "We'll meet again after Easter to collect all the recipes, and I'd like to welcome all three of you. It's so good to see fresh new faces, and when we get the recipes, you girls can help us sort them and get them ready to send to the publisher. We'll have a night at my house to do that."

"Yes, ma'am." Olivia nodded. "That sounds like fun."

Liddy gave the girls time to get the papers distributed, and then when the room was full of women and the table was full of all kinds of sweets, she raised her voice. "If everyone will have a seat, we'll begin this meeting and get our business over with so that we can dig into those desserts." She waited for them to get seated and went on. "You will notice that the paper you are holding says that your recipes must be emailed to Ruth Ann by the end of next week. Be sure that your directions are clear and understandable. One recipe per email please, and put the name of it in the subject line so we know what category to file it in. As much as most of us cook by taste, Ruth Ann does the proofreading of our cookbook and she wants real measurements. Today's younger cooks don't know what a smidgen or a pinch is."

Several of the women nodded, and a few giggled. Before Liddy could say anything else, the back door swung open. Matilda, Gladys, Delores, Tina, and Kayla all waltzed in.

"Well, dammit!" Liddy said under her breath.

She was reminded of homecoming candidates riding on parade floats. If Matilda began to do the royal wave, Liddy would not be responsible for what happened next. Matilda carried a fruit salad to the table, and the other four set their dishes down beside her bowl. Then Matilda led the procession back across the room to sit down in the front row of seats right in front of Liddy.

So much for thinking that I would be free and clear of that woman since the sale of Amos's house didn't work out, Liddy thought, but she had bigger fish to fry later that evening. Matilda was not going to get under her skin—not tonight.

"For you latecomers"—Liddy looked down on the five women—"we were just getting started. The flyer you are holding tells you how to submit your recipes. No fancy fonts or little graphics. Just the recipes. One to an email. We will schedule a meeting for the Thursday after Easter, and hopefully we will see a copy of the book at that time. Everyone can look over their submissions and make any changes before it actually goes to press. You'll see the categories on the paper. It spans appetizers to casseroles, so y'all be thinking about what you want to contribute."

Matilda stood up, took a step forward so that she was right beside Liddy, and leaned over to speak into the microphone. "As you all know, I'm a vegan. I don't cook, but I do have a fabulous lady who does that at the bed-and-breakfast I'm buying over in Muenster. I want to propose that we have a special vegan section for each category so that we can offer possible recipes to all the people who want to eat healthy. Each section, whether it be meats or desserts, should have an equal number of vegan recipes."

Amelia came forward from the back of the room and took her place on the other side of her aunt. "I believe this idea bears discussion, and a vote. Who all here thinks we should include an equal section for vegan recipes in each category? Before you vote, remember that the appetizer part of the book now covers ten pages, and if we are fair, the new book will have twenty pages devoted to that. Then the cakes take up about thirty-five pages and the pies another thirty. In order to make a book twice the size of this one, the publishing cost would be phenomenal, and the thing would weigh a ton."

Savannah stood up and said, "I love to cook, and I actually bought one of the last copies of this book when I came to Bonnet. I've used it a lot, but I wouldn't buy a book that cost more than thirty dollars. The whole idea of producing this book is to donate the profits from it to the missionary fund, so you might think about that, too. If we have no sales, there won't be anything to donate to our missionaries."

Olivia raised her hand and stood up from the back row. "I don't know a lot about publishing, but I'm guessing it costs by the page. I have no problem with what anyone eats or when they eat it, but there's no way I would spend that much money on a gift for a friend who wasn't interested in kale or tofu. And I've bought at least twenty cookbooks of different kinds over the last few years to give away at Christmas and birthdays."

Tina popped up like a windup toy and raised her voice. "You are all a bunch of prejudiced people. We came here to offer our help, and you're shooting us down like we are nothing."

Gladys was next on her feet. "This has nothing to do with the size or the cost of a cookbook. It's y'all taking sides with Liddy because of this feud. Matilda is just trying to help the whole town, and Liddy can't let go of the past."

Ruth Ann stood up and in a calm voice said, "I disagree. I think these three young women have presented a valid argument, but to be fair, we could include one or two vegan recipes in each section if this group of women wants to submit them. The same way we always have a few vegetarian ones."

"But not a portion equal to all the rest of our categories," Ethel said from the middle of the room. "Savannah and Olivia have made good points about the cost of each book, and how big that would make the whole thing."

"I agree with Ethel," another lady said. "Like Olivia, I buy a lot of the cookbooks to give as gifts. The folks I give them to wouldn't ever even look at the vegan recipes, and if the book costs twice what it does now, I couldn't afford to buy it."

Matilda edged Liddy away from the microphone and leaned forward to speak into it in a saccharine-sweet voice. "All this disagreement has nothing to do with cookbooks, does it, ladies?"

"That's what we're here for," Liddy answered, "and I, for one, think it has everything to do with cookbooks and our donations to the missionary fund."

One lady in the back of the room said, "Liddy is right. Let's vote."

"Everyone that wants to include an equal number of vegan recipes in each section, raise your hand," Amelia said.

Five hands went up.

"Everyone that wants to add no more than two to four vegan recipes in each section, raise your hand," she said.

Half a dozen hands went up.

"Now, everyone that wants to exclude those recipes and keep the cost of the book down to a reasonable cost, raise your hand," she said.

Most of the women raised their hands.

"Miz Matilda, ma'am, we appreciate your offer." Amelia turned to face her. "But as you can see, the vote is to leave things as they are. I suggest that you and your friends put together a vegan cookbook of your own, have it published, and sell it right here at the church and donate all the profits to the missionary fund."

Matilda lowered her chin and glared at Amelia. She opened her mouth to say something, then clamped it shut. She knotted her hands into fists, and with all those rings on her fingers, Liddy was afraid if Matilda hit Amelia that she herself wouldn't be able to control the anger building up inside her.

"All right, that concludes our business," Ruth Ann said. "Now, let's all go enjoy some desserts. I'm headed right for that pecan pie back there, and yes, there is one of Liddy's lemon meringue pies on the table, too." She brushed against Matilda's shoulder as she started across the room.

"Don't touch me," Matilda growled.

Amelia stepped right up into Matilda's space. "What is the matter with you? Don't you realize that folks come to Bonnet because they love this place the way it is? We don't want change. We want to live in peace with our neighbors and enjoy small-town life."

Matilda put her hands on Amelia's shoulders and gave her a push. "This Podunk town needs some class. Not that you or your kind would know anything about that."

Liddy left the lectern and slapped Matilda's hands away from her niece. "Don't you ever touch Amelia again."

"I won't if she stays away from my son, but, Liddy, I don't care if you are old, I will punch your lights out if you touch me again," Matilda hissed.

Amelia stepped between them. "Your beef is with me tonight. I've been taught to respect my elders, but if you lay hands on me again, I will go against my teaching and when I'm done kicking your smart ass, you will need plastic surgery. Not the fun kind, either. If you threaten my Aunt Liddy again, you will deal with me, not her. Now, get out of my way. I've got a hunger on for a whole plate full of sugary desserts."

"I told you to stay away from my son," Matilda said.

"He'd be happier if you stayed away from him, I'm sure," Amelia said and then marched over to the table where the other women were already filling their plates.

Matilda whipped around to focus on Liddy. "You will not run me out of my church."

"*Your* church?" Liddy chuckled.

Matilda raised a hand, and for a moment, Liddy thought she might have to yell for Amelia to come make good on her promise about the plastic surgery, but the woman finally dropped that hand to her side.

Delores took a couple of steps forward and said, "Matilda, darlin', let's go get some of your delicious fruit salad," and then she lowered her voice. "You are making a scene that will turn all these people into enemies."

"Go to hell," Matilda told her. "I'll do what I want when I want."

"You're just angry right now." Delores took her by the arm and led her back a couple of steps. "I think making our own cookbook would be a wonderful idea, but we shouldn't sell it through the church or give the proceeds to the missionary fund. We should sell it at your bed-and-breakfast and donate the money to the library in Muenster."

Amelia had returned with a plate holding a slice of pecan pie, a square of her brownies, and a piece of lemon pound cake that Olivia had brought. "I thought you'd like this, Aunt Liddy, and Miz Matilda, ma'am, I'd be glad to get you a plate if you want me to. You're looking a little spindly."

"I can handle my own plate, and I won't gain ten pounds when I eat it. I don't know why I worry. Nick would never go for a chubby girl like you." She whipped around and her four friends followed her to a table like little puppies chasing after a soup bone.

"Are you all right?" Amelia asked Liddy.

"I'm just fine, and thank you," Liddy answered. "And don't let that woman get under your skin. You are not chubby."

Liddy could have easily strangled Matilda and enjoyed watching her turn blue for that last comment. Amelia had just begun to be comfortable in her skin after having to keep a diary of what she ate so Elliott wouldn't think she was too fat.

"That woman just came here to rattle you. She knew she didn't have a leg to stand on when it came to doubling the size of our cookbook. Are you going to put the secret to your lemon pie recipes in there this time?" Amelia asked.

"Hell no!" Liddy said and then bowed her head. "Forgive me, Lord, for cussin' in the church."

Amelia giggled. "I don't think He's going to zap you dead over one word that's even in the Bible. He didn't hit me with a lightning bolt for threatening to rearrange Matilda's face. I'm going to get myself a plate now. I'll bring you a cup of coffee when I come back."

"Thanks, darlin' girl." Liddy sat down on the second row of seats. No way was she going to sit in the chair where Matilda had been just a few minutes before. Some of that ugly attitude might have gotten stuck on the chair.

Ruth Ann came over with plates piled high and sat down beside her. "I'm not real worried about Matilda running roughshod over my daughter anymore."

"You got that right," Liddy agreed with a smile. "If Nick and Amelia do start dating right out in public, Matilda won't have a chance."

"I told you she had spunk," Ruth Ann said.

"Comes from the Taylor side of the family," Liddy said, and her grin grew even bigger.

Chapter Eighteen

Are you nervous?" Nick asked as he and Amelia found their seats on the plane that Thursday evening. Nick was a grown man, and yet he had a few butterflies flitting around in his stomach, too. What if after the long weekend Amelia decided he wasn't worth the battle?

"Not about flying," she answered as she ducked her head and sat down by the window. "Maybe a little bit."

Before Nick could say anything else, the captain's voice filled the cabin of the airplane telling the passengers that a brochure with the safety precautions was located in the pocket of the seat right in front of them, that they would be in the air soon, and they would be landing in Pensacola right on time.

"At least we get to sit together, and no one is going to call home and tattle on us," Nick said, hoping that this was just the beginning of a long, beautiful relationship—in spite of his mother, her family, and the horrible feud.

"That's the pro," Amelia agreed.

"What's the con?" Nick asked.

"I like you, Nick—a lot," Amelia said, "but what if in these next three days we figure out that the attraction we feel isn't there when we don't have to worry about the feud?"

"I like you, too." He took her hand in his. "We should be honest with each other, and honey, I've got to admit, I'm afraid that you will decide that I'm just not worth the war we'll have to fight to be together."

"I can stand up for myself, and go to war for my family, but hurting someone's feelings that I care about is a different matter," she admitted.

"I heard about the cookbook meeting." He remembered his mother ranting for a good fifteen minutes about the way her ideas had been voted out.

"Sorry about that." She blushed.

"Don't be." Nick squeezed her hand. "She will push and push and push until you push back. If you hadn't stood up to her, it would have been twice as hard next time."

"My temper gets away from me sometimes," she told him.

"So does mine, but as long as we can keep an open communication between us, maybe we won't get mad at each other," he suggested.

"And what happens when we have our first big argument?" Amelia asked.

"Then if we're far enough into this relationship, we'll have really good makeup sex," Nick teased. "Did I tell you already that I had decided to be a bachelor for the rest of my life, like Uncle Harry? I tried introducing a couple of girlfriends to my mother and she had them running away in tears."

"When I run, it's jogging for my health," Amelia said.

"Which is why I think maybe what we have just might work out," he said as the plane rose up into the air.

Nick's phone rang when they were almost to the baggage claim. He took it out of the hip pocket of his jeans and said, "Hello, Uncle Harry, where are you?"

"I'm in the parking garage. Call me when you are outside, and I'll circle around and pick you up," he answered.

"Will do," he said. "We shouldn't be long. We're just now getting to the baggage area."

Nick picked their two suitcases from the conveyor belt and called his uncle back. "We should be waiting on the bench by the time you get here. We've got our luggage and we're ready to walk out."

"I'll be there soon as I can," Harry said.

Nick ended the call, rolled his small suitcase to the automatic doors, and stood to the side to let Amelia go first. "I can almost smell the salt air all the way up here. Ever been to this part of Florida?" He so wanted her to enjoy the weekend. She deserved it and needed it after the past few weeks of constant conflict with his mother.

"Yep, and I love the white sand," she said as she headed for the nearest bench.

"Think you'd want to live here?" Nick asked.

"No, Bonnet is my home," she said. "This is a wonderful place to visit, but I wouldn't ever want to leave Texas. How about you?"

"Me either," Nick said.

Nick waved at the familiar truck when it came to a stop in front of the bench. But when Harry got out and hurried around the front to help load their suitcases, Nick could hardly believe his eyes. Harry was dressed in khaki shorts, flip-flops, and a Hawaiian print shirt.

"Look at you, going all local," Nick said.

When the luggage was loaded, Harry stopped and gave Nick a quick hug. "I told you I love this place. No more dress slacks and ties for me. Crawl in and let's get this buggy rolling."

They got into the back seat, and Nick reached across the console and took Amelia's hand in his. "Thank you so much for inviting us down here. It's been a trial to even spend time with each other in Bonnet."

"Yes," Amelia said. "We are grateful to have a weekend where we don't have to worry, and thank you for letting me tag along with Nick."

"Happy to," Harry said as he glanced in the rearview mirror. "You look so much like your mama, it's not even real. If I'd been ten years younger, I would have given Paul a run for his money when he brought Ruth Ann home to meet Liddy and his parents."

"Thanks for that. I've always thought my mama was a lovely person," Amelia said.

"Now, tell me all about the war in Bonnet. No, wait until we get home and have a cold beer in our hands, because I want to see your faces when you tell me," Harry said. "But, Nick, you can tell me about the real estate business, and then, Amelia, I want to hear about your job. We don't need to talk about depressing things right here at the first."

"Uncle Harry, have you had anyone to talk to since you've been down here?" Nick asked.

"No. Is it that obvious?" Harry asked.

"Little bit," Nick said.

"I've missed being out and around people I know, but giving that up is worth being at peace for the first time in my life." Harry pulled out away from the airport and headed east. "Now that I'm here in Florida for good, I'm checking into volunteer work and even the senior citizens group."

"Good grief, Harry!" Amelia said from the back seat. "You're not old enough to be a member of the senior citizens."

"Thank you, darlin' girl." Harry glanced up in the rearview mirror and smiled at her. "But I'm looking sixty-five right in the eyeball. This group gives us old people a nice discount on food and a lot of other things down here."

In Nick's eyes his Uncle Harry would always be forty years old, even if that wasn't the truth. His first memories were of Harry playing with him in the backyard and carrying him on his shoulders as they went from the real estate agency to the Dairy Queen for an ice cream cone. Then later Harry would take him along if he was showing a ranch to a prospective buyer, and Nick had caddied many golf games for Harry and his cronies when he was in his early teens. Try as he may, he couldn't think of any really good memories with his mother. Not surprising.

"Have you played any golf?" Nick asked.

"Yep, and they've invited me to join the club," Harry answered. "Were you afraid I'd come down here and do nothing but get fat and die?"

"That's probably what I would do," Nick laughed.

"I don't believe you," Harry said. "When you retire, I hope that you have kids and grandkids to keep you busy, whether you are chasing them around in your yard or here in the sand. Just wait till you see my house. I hope you like it."

"I'm sure I will," Nick said.

"Good, because I had it put in both our names. The lawyer suggested that I do it that way so that it will automatically be yours when I die. That way you'll have a vacation home," Harry told him. "We're almost there. We can't watch the sunset over the water tonight, but we can see the sunrise in the morning."

"That's an omen," Nick whispered to Amelia. "Starting out with a sunrise."

"Figuring out a beginning for whatever this is between us?" Amelia asked.

Nick laced his fingers with hers and gave them a gentle squeeze. "See, we even see things the same."

"They're together in Florida," Liddy said over supper that night. "Olivia said that Nick was going to Florida to see Harry, and Amelia was all secretive about where she was going."

"She called me half an hour ago to let me know her plane landed safely," Bridget said as she dumped plastic eggs from a bag out onto the table. "I asked her what the weather was like in Galveston, and she said she had changed her mind and had flown to Pensacola, Florida."

"Isn't Harry over near Panama City?" Ruth Ann asked.

"Yes, but that's more than two hours from Pensacola," Bridget answered.

Liddy brought out a huge bowl of miniature candy bars and set them in the middle of the table. "Did she say where she's staying or what her plans are?"

"She said she had a place right on the beach and that tomorrow she's going to lay on the sand and de-stress," Bridget answered as she popped open an egg and put a candy bar inside it.

"If she was with Nick, she wouldn't be de-stressing," Ruth Ann assured the other two women. "She would be worried and feeling guilty about not telling us the truth."

Liddy sat down at the table and started filling eggs. "She did tell the truth. I'm sure of it, but she didn't tell us who might be on the beach with her, did she? And she didn't say the beach was in Pensacola or if it might be over in Panama City."

Bridget shook her head. "At least if she's with Nick, he'll protect her from all the Elliotts hitting on her."

"Whose side are you on?" Liddy asked.

"Right now, I just want to be able to talk about anything and everything with my sister again. I'm tired of all this feud crap," Bridget said. "In the past year, we've gotten to where we tell each other everything, and I can feel that she's holding back on me now, like she did with Elliott."

Liddy slipped half a dozen eggs into the tote bag at the end of the table. "Exactly."

"Only this time, I think Amelia is holding on to secrets because she wants to, not because of Elliott controlling her," Bridget said.

"Remember back when we used to spend hours coloring and decorating eggs?" Ruth Ann asked. "Nowadays, parents wouldn't let their kids eat eggs that had been colored two days before Easter."

"It's probably why we are so strong and healthy. We didn't have all those preservatives in our food," Bridget said.

"Why are we changing the subject?" Liddy asked.

"I thought we'd beaten the dead horse into a pulp," Bridget answered. "Aunt Liddy, Mama, are you going to be all right if Amelia comes home and tells you that she and Nick are together?"

Liddy took a deep breath and let it out slowly. "I've made my peace with it, and besides, Matilda will never support such a thing, so I'll be the good person who gets to see the grandbabies anytime I want. If it gets serious and they get married, they'll live across the street from me, not from Matilda. I'll get to rock the babies"—Liddy grinned—"and Matilda won't."

"If she does, she will be worried about them messing up her outfit," Ruth Ann chuckled. "Can't you just see her if a baby did some projectile vomiting on her pretty white pantsuit? And while we're on the subject of babies, are you going to sit back and let your sister give us the first grandbaby, Bridget?"

"One never knows what the future might hold," Bridget answered.

Chapter Nineteen

Amelia inhaled deeply, taking in the salty smell of the water, and listened to the waves as they slapped against all that white sand before her. The sun was taking its lazy time about coming up out there in the east, but that didn't matter. She had all morning to simply sit there with Harry on one side of her and Nick on the other. She poured a second cup of coffee from the pot sitting on the table in front of them.

"I wonder if heaven is like this," she said.

"That's exactly what I thought the first morning I sat out here on the deck and watched the sunrise," Harry said. "It was like a sign telling me that this was the first day of the rest of my life, and I didn't have to worry about anything except whether to have a plain maple doughnut or one with sprinkles."

"What did you worry about before?" Nick asked.

"When Matilda left Bonnet to go to college, I heaved a sigh of relief. She had been a thorn in my side since the day she was born." Harry reached for a second pastry. "I think I'll have a maple one this time. Next to milkshakes and ice cream, doughnuts are my favorite food. I hope I never get to be a diabetic. I'm not sure I could leave those things alone."

Nick refilled his coffee cup. "Why were you so relieved when my mom left?"

"Dad had a religious mother, Granny Davis, who would have disowned him if he'd made Mother get an abortion. That might not sound like an answer to your question, but you have to understand why Mother even had Matilda in the first place. If it hadn't been for the fact that my grandmother might have thrown her out of the house—and believe me, in those days she still ruled the roost in that place—Mother probably would have opted not to have the baby. But birthing her did not mean she had to bond with her. So Matilda had everything materially that she could want, but very little love from my parents." Harry bit into his doughnut.

"Do you guys want to talk about this alone?" Amelia asked. "I could go for an early-morning run on the beach."

"Nope," Harry said. "From now on I intend to be transparent, as they say these days. Besides, if you and Nick are ever going to live through what Matilda will throw at you, it's best you understand the past.

"Mother hated having to live with her mother-in-law. And rightly so, because Granny thought Daddy could have done better," Harry explained.

"Why?" Nick asked.

Amelia could still be living with her folks and saving a lot of money that she paid out in rent, but she wanted to be independent. However, if she'd stayed in her folks' house, Elliott would have had trouble manipulating her the way he had.

Matilda thinks Nick can do better, Amelia thought.

Don't go there. Ruth Ann's voice popped into her head. *Don't think about Elliott or Matilda. They're both poison.*

I am strong, Mama. Trust me. She wondered if she had sent a message to her mother through telepathy.

"Why, indeed," Harry sighed. "Mother was a wild child. She was a lot like Matilda. She slept around, drank a lot, and pretty much had a horrible reputation."

"How did you find out all this?" Amelia asked.

"My grandmother kept a journal. No one went into Granny Davis's room, not ever. When she died, Daddy closed the door and told me that room was off limits. I was sixteen that year and didn't care about a bedroom, even though I did miss my grandmother. While Mother worked, Granny took care of me. She would've probably taken care of Matilda, but she died not long after my sister was born. Granny and I had a good relationship. If Matilda had had that in her life, she might have been a better person." Harry stopped to eat a few more bites of his doughnut.

"I love my Granny Dee and my Aunt Liddy, who is like a grandmother to me," Amelia said. "Aunt Liddy kept me while Mama taught at the school, so I kind of know how you feel."

"And we think we know everyone in the whole town of Bonnet, right?" Harry asked.

"Until now I thought I did, but now I'm wondering if everyone hasn't got a closet full of secrets," Amelia answered.

"Believe me, they do," Harry told her. "Some of them hidden so deep in the dark corners that even the rumors and gossip haven't sorted them out."

Harry took a sip of his coffee and went on. "I've got fond memories of your Aunt Liddy bringing you to town with her, Amelia. She told me once that keeping you and your sister was her salvation. If it hadn't been for you girls, she might have lost it, or maybe just gone ahead and shot my sister. Truth is, I wanted to shoot her myself when Liddy's son died."

Nick frowned and cocked his head to one side. "I don't remember a room that was off limits. Where was Granny Davis's room?"

"Do you remember that big gold chair up in the hallway?" Harry asked.

Nick nodded. "I took a few naps in that chair."

"It sat right in front of the door to keep anyone from ever going inside, but when my mother died, I braved the fear and went into

Granny's bedroom," Harry said. "I fought through the cobwebs and dust, and when I was cleaning the room completely out, I found the journal. I got quite the education."

"How long did Granny Davis live after Matilda was born?" Amelia asked.

"About a month," Harry answered. "Mother said that she got rid of one burden just in time to get another one."

"That's so sad." Amelia couldn't imagine feeling that way about a child—especially one of her own if she ever became a mother.

"And that's enough of the story for today. It's depressing, and you're down here to have a good time. You kids should go take a long walk on the beach. Go east so you can appreciate every bit of the sunrise," Harry suggested.

"Why don't you come along with us?" Amelia asked.

"Y'all need some time alone to get things all worked out so you can face the battles ahead of you. You don't need a chaperone or a third wheel. If I'm not here when you get back, there's a key under that sleeping cat over there. I bought it because it reminds me of Vera. I can talk to it like I did Vera, but I don't have to buy kitty litter or cat food." Harry stood up and shooed them away with a motion of his hands. "Get on down there and enjoy the beach. You've got three days to figure out what should take three months. Make the time count."

Amelia wondered if maybe Harry got left out when it came to caring, too, if he could transfer his love for Vera to a ceramic cat.

Nick pushed up out of his chair and held out a hand toward Amelia. She let him help her to her feet and didn't try to pull her hand away when he kept it in his. Then he clamped his free hand on Harry's shoulder and said, "Thank you. I remember a wise person telling me once that to understand the future you had to know the past. I'm glad you are opening that door."

"You're welcome, son." Harry smiled.

Nick led Amelia down the long flight of stairs to the beach and kicked off his sandals at the bottom of the steps. "The sand is still cool, but it will warm up when the sun shines down on it. What did you think of that story?"

Amelia removed her flip-flops and set them on the third step going up. "It makes me wonder if there's skeletons like that in my family history. Somehow, I can't believe there are. We've always been so open about everything." She suppressed a giggle.

"What's funny?" Nick slowed his stride to keep in pace with her.

"I said we'd been open about everything, but that wasn't really true," she answered.

"What have you kept secret?" Nick asked.

"What goes on in the bedroom stays in the bedroom, and Aunt Liddy can get riled up pretty quick if I ask her about any of that," Amelia answered.

"Then she hasn't read *Fifty Shades of Grey*?" A wide grin covered Nick's face.

"If she did, it's probably hiding somewhere in the darkest reaches of her closet, and since her house is still standing, I doubt that it's anywhere in her house," Amelia answered.

"Why wouldn't her house still be standing?" Nick asked.

"Because after the first chapter, Aunt Liddy's face would be so hot with a blush that it would set the whole house on fire," Amelia told him. "Let's sit down and put our feet in the water."

Nick plopped down, stuck his toes in the water, and tugged on Amelia's hand. "Come on in, the water is warm."

Amelia sat down close enough to Nick that when she stretched out her legs, her left foot bumped against his. The chemistry was there for sure, but if they were going to face the battles with both Matilda and her whole family, she wanted more than an attraction. She turned to look at Nick and found him staring at her with a dreamy look in his eyes. Then his hands were cupping her cheeks so gently that they reminded her of soft butterflies. She moistened her lips, and he slowly brought his mouth to hers in a kiss that was both sweet and hot at the same time.

"I've wanted to do that all morning," he whispered in her ear when the kiss ended. "I want more than friendship, Amelia Juliet. I want a relationship. I want to tell everyone—hell, I want to stand on the top of the roof of my house and yell that you are my girlfriend."

"I'm a little afraid of heights, so I don't want to crawl up on the top of your two-story house, but I want the same thing, and right now, I don't even care if God has eyes everywhere." She brought his lips to hers for another kiss.

On Saturday morning, Nick awoke before Harry and Amelia, so he slipped out of the house, made a run to a place that made crepes, and brought back enough for breakfast. He put on a pot of coffee and headed out to the deck to watch the sunrise and think about Amelia. So far, the trip had just solidified the feelings he had for her. Holding her hand, kissing her good night at her bedroom door, rushing out to get fancy crepes for her, and waiting impatiently for her to wake again was proving that he wanted to be with her—that this was not a flash in the pan.

"I'm following my nose." Harry poked his head out the open sliding glass door. "Do I smell bacon?"

"You do." Nick grinned. "But I didn't cook it. I bought each of us a breakfast crepe and then a dessert one. I hope you still like strawberries."

"Oh, yes, I do," Harry told him. "I'll bring out the coffee. Is Amelia still sleeping? Bless that woman's heart. She's had to deal with a lot this past while."

"Yes, she is, and yes, she has," Nick said. "I might be falling in love with her."

"Might be? Boy, that's written all over your face every time you look at her." Harry went inside and brought three mugs of coffee out to the deck. "I found a sleepyhead in the kitchen and brought her out here. Do you know this woman?" he teased.

"Good morning. Did I miss the sunrise?" Amelia yawned and accepted the mug Harry held out to her.

"No, darlin', you didn't." Nick stood up and kissed her on the forehead.

"Oh, look at the sunrise. The reflection is so beautiful in the water."

"Girl, you are welcome to come see the sunrises and sunsets with me anytime you want." Harry sat down in one of the three chairs. "I'll always have a chair for you and one for Nick."

"Thank you." Amelia sipped her coffee. "Nick and I might be down here so often that you get sick of us."

"Not going to happen," Harry said. "You just said Nick and you. I thought when we were at Margaritaville last night for supper that you kids seemed like a couple. So, you're going home to face the dragons and come out in the open with your relationship?"

"Yep, we are." Nick then picked up Amelia's hand and kissed the knuckles one by one.

Harry reached for a bacon, egg, and cheese crepe. "Nick got his romantic streak from me."

"Then I owe you a big thank-you and a hug." Amelia picked up a strawberry-and-cream-cheese crepe.

"I'll save that hug for later today," Harry told her.

"You promised to tell me more about Mother," Nick said.

"Okay, then," Harry said. "So, I was fifteen and here's a new baby in the house. Daddy is still mourning his mother, and my mother didn't want one child, much less another when she was closing in on forty. She wouldn't have a thing to do with Matilda and stayed away from the house as much as she could. Daddy hired a housekeeper and babysitter to take care of Matilda, and she was around until I went to college.

Then there was a whole list of women who came and went. Matilda was a handful and had temper fits that no one could control if she didn't get her way. At four, she ran the house, and at six, when she went to school, things got even worse. She had screaming fits if she didn't get to sit where she wanted. She threw things in the lunchroom and fought with the other little kids on the playground. Finally, the principal gave my folks an ultimatum—get control of their child or she wouldn't be attending public school. She should have had therapy, but folks didn't do much of that back then," Harry said. "When I came home and started my real estate business, she hated me, didn't want me living in the house, and threatened to run away if Daddy didn't make me leave."

"I always figured she got all her controlling and narcissistic behavior after she was a teenager," Nick said. "Did Granny and Gramps get her under control?"

"Not the right way," Harry said. "They gave her things to be nice. Something every week that she was a good girl, like a fancy bracelet or a new dress. Then when she was sixteen, she got a car and threw a hissy fit because it was used and not brand new. When I told her that I had to work and save for my first car, she threw a plate of food at me."

"Holy crap! What if a child of mine gets her genes?" Nick had begun to worry.

"It wasn't genetic, son," Harry said. "It was environmental. I think she knew from the day she was born that she wasn't wanted. I tried to help her, but nothing worked. When she went to college, we were all happy, and yet felt guilty at the same time. Things settled down at home, and I hoped that she would find herself while she was there, or maybe something that she could throw herself into that would make her think about someone other than herself."

Amelia was beginning to feel sorry for Matilda. There was probably no way she could ever change her now, but to have lived life with no joy in giving to others and receiving no joy in return—that had to be pitied.

"She told me about wanting a new house, but your parents wouldn't give her one," Nick said.

Harry shook his head slowly. "That was when she was sixteen, too. I'd found a little garage apartment about a block from the folks' house and moved into it by then. I couldn't help Matilda, and Daddy thought it might help her if I wasn't living there all the time."

"I'm sorry you had to go through all that," Nick said.

"It's over now, thank God." Harry sighed. "Everyone in town knows that my dad was a womanizer, and that Mother had her affairs, too. Matilda found out about that and tried to blackmail them both into building a new house. That might have been the first thing she didn't get—well, and that I lived there in the house with them for years before I finally got my own place."

Amelia decided right then and there that when she had kids, she was staying home with them until they went to school. She could take a few years from teaching and surround her children with love. Matilda was nothing more than the product of her upbringing. Sure, she could have overcome it when she had a child of her own, but she might have been too far gone by then.

Harry picked up a strawberry-and-cream-cheese crepe, ate a couple of bites, and washed it down with coffee. "So, she got smart in college, but not in education. She latched on to Gregory and sweet-talked him into falling in love with her, or at least the woman he thought she was. Then she came home and demanded that the folks give her a huge, fancy wedding. They couldn't begin to afford what she wanted, so she came to me and said I owed her a wedding since I was her brother. At that point, I didn't have that kind of money, either, so I refused. She went back to college after Christmas and talked Gregory into eloping with her. The rest you pretty well know," Harry said.

"I feel sorry for her," Amelia said.

Nick shook his head. "I don't. She could have changed at any time. There are lots of kids who grow up in worse circumstances and don't act like that. But I do understand now why she treated me the way she did when I was a little kid. I'm sure grateful that Dad gave me one parental role model, and that you stepped in to help him, Uncle Harry."

"You are welcome to what I could do," Harry said. "And, Amelia, I feel sorry for her, too, but on the other hand, I'm damn glad to be away from her. She's my sister, and God says I got to love her, but He doesn't say I have to like her. Now, look at that. The sun is finally throwing some color out over the water. It's time for you two to have a morning walk or run or make-out session on the beach."

"Harry!" Amelia blushed.

"I kind of like that latter suggestion better," Nick teased.

"You better take advantage of where you are," Harry told them. "When you go home, things might not be so pleasant."

"Amen to that." Nick winked at Amelia.

"I should make a run to the bathroom before we go. Just be a minute." Amelia stopped to give Harry a hug and then rushed inside the house.

"I'm in love with Amelia," Nick said. "I don't want to rush into anything, but I plan on marrying her someday."

"Is this my self-proclaimed 'I want to be like Uncle Harry' nephew talking to me?" Harry asked.

"When Wanda and Jack died on the same day, and you decided to retire at the same time, it made me realize that time isn't guaranteed to any of us, and that when opportunity knocks, we should open the door, not chase after it when it's a mile down the road. That bit of wisdom comes from you. I think I knew I was going to fall in love with Amelia when I went to get dessert at the funeral dinner and saw her across the table from me. I thought that love at first sight crap was just that, crap, but I believe in it now."

"But remember, you got to fight for anything worth having," Harry told him.

Amelia opened the door, came out onto the porch, and kicked off her flip-flops. "Might as well take them off up here as at the bottom of the steps."

"You are so right." Nick removed his sandals and set them by hers. "Look, darlin', even our shoes are a couple."

"Like I said," Uncle Harry chuckled, "he gets that romantic streak from me."

"Run, walk, or make out?" Amelia asked when they were on the beach.

"Maybe some of each." Nick smiled. "I've got this big, big favor to ask, and you can say no."

"Sounds serious." Amelia was terrified that Nick might drop down on one knee and propose to her right there on the beach. It was a romantic place, but she wasn't ready for that—maybe later, but not now. She wanted a normal relationship—the dating, arguing, makeup sex, the whole nine yards—to prove to herself that he was "the one" for her.

"It kind of is. My dad called last night after you turned in for the night. He wanted to know if we could change our plans just a little and fly out tomorrow night instead of Monday morning. He'll send the company plane to pick us up at Dallas and then return us on Monday afternoon so we can drive back home to Bonnet from there since my truck is—"

"Yes," Amelia said before he could finish the sentence. "I would love to meet your dad."

"And Betsy, my stepmother?"

"Of course, but how does Uncle Harry feel about that?" she asked.

"He says it's fine with him but that we owe him a whole week this summer to make up for it," Nick answered.

"Sounds like a good trade to me, but company plane?" Amelia asked.

"It's not a jet." Nick stopped to brush a kiss across her lips. "But it'll get us from Dallas to Sweetwater in just a little over thirty minutes, and Dad says that supper will be waiting for us. I've also got a confession to make, and I need to do it before we go to my dad's."

He paused so long that she was afraid he was going to tell her that he was dying with some rare disease.

She had fallen for a controlling man, and then really fell hard for a dying one. That and the fact that Nick looked so damned serious that it had to be something really big.

"Is it cancer?" she whispered.

"No! Why would you think that?" he asked.

"It's the way my luck would run," she told him.

"As far as I know, I'm healthy. My confession is that I'm pretty rich," he said. "I'm one of those trust-fund guys like Elliott. I didn't want to tell you because I thought you'd turn your back on me. I'm not Midas rich, and I don't flaunt it, but . . ."

Amelia's arms snaked up around his neck. "Money or no money doesn't matter to me. Happiness does. I kind of got the gist of your wealth from what Matilda has spread around town about taking her rich husband to the cleaners."

He pulled her even closer to him and tipped her chin up. "You are amazing," he whispered and then his lips were on hers.

She was panting when she finally took a step back. "We better not keep our eyes closed much longer or we'll miss the rest of the sunrise, and we only get to see one more."

"Kissing you is worth it." He grabbed her hand and began to jog down the beach with her right beside him. "And, darlin', we can come back here anytime we want and see a sunrise every single morning. When we're old, we can bring the grandkids and watch them play on the beach."

"Oh, so now there's grandkids?" she asked as she kept pace with him.

"Someday, if we're lucky," he answered.

Chapter Twenty

The sunset was marred by dark clouds that Sunday evening when Harry drove them back to the airport. Harry had the radio tuned to a country station and pointed to it when Darryl Worley started singing "Hard Rain Don't Last."

"Listen to those lyrics," he said. "Remember them when you get back to Bonnet and you tell everyone that you are a couple. The hard rain will fall on you, but it won't last if you stand your ground. Nick, you be sure to call me when it's all done."

"That song and several others were playing on my MP3 player the first night Nick and I met at the park. We'd both been jogging, and later I was brazen enough to go to his house," Amelia said.

"But she said she had come to see Vera," Nick told Harry.

"Then thank God for Vera." Harry nodded. "If you need to move and get away from it all, just let me know and I'll rent you a condo until we can find a house for you on the beach."

"Hopefully, it won't get that bad." Amelia crossed her fingers. She would never want to leave the support and love of her family. She turned to focus on Nick and, as usual, found him staring at her. "What? Is my mascara running, or do I have barbecue on my face?"

"No, I'm trying to memorize your face," he whispered. "Do you think our folks' reaction to the news will cause us to have our first argument?"

"There won't be a fight or an argument. They love me too much for that," Amelia said and hoped that she was right. Harry had been so sweet and kind to her that she had felt welcome in his home. She wanted her family to take Nick in like Harry had done her—for himself, not to please her.

"Ever been to Sweetwater?" Nick asked as they checked their baggage at the airport.

"No," she whimpered.

"What's wrong, Amelia? Are you all right?" he asked.

"No, I'm not, and yes, I want to meet your father, but I hated hugging Harry goodbye. He seems so lonely, and there's so many miles between us, and . . ." She laid her head on his shoulder and let the tears flow. "I'm sorry, Nick. I hate goodbyes. I cry every time we have to leave my Granny Dee's house in Louisiana."

"Shhh . . ." He wrapped her up in his arms and held her. "It's okay. I don't like them, either."

"Then why aren't you sad?" she asked.

"Because I have you to hold," he whispered.

"He's right," she sobbed harder. "You do have a romantic side, and it probably came from him since . . . well . . . ," she stammered.

"Matilda is my mother," he finished the sentence for her, "and she doesn't have one, but my dad does, and you'll be meeting him in just a little while." Nick took a step back, pulled a white hankie from his pocket, and dried her eyes. "I'm happier than I've ever been, Amelia, and I'll work hard to fit in with your family."

"Just be you and they can't help but like you." She smiled through the tears. "I know you will." She took the hankie from his hand and dried her tears. "I'm sorry I got mascara on it," she said as she handed it back.

"No problem. I may not even wash it but keep it so I'll have your tears forever." He kissed her on the forehead.

Amelia was right on the edge of saying, "I love you, Nick Monroe," but those words shouldn't be said when she'd been crying.

"I've never seen a sunset from the sky," Amelia said when they were in the second plane, this time a small four-seater flying out of Dallas. "The colors are breathtaking."

"I love seeing a pretty sunset from the sky, too," the pilot said. "I'm Lanny, and I assume you are Amelia?"

"I'm sorry," Nick said, "I should have made introductions."

"No problem," Lanny said. "We were all busy trying to get things loaded up, and you did give me a hug."

"Thank you, Lanny," Nick said, "and, Amelia, as pretty as the sight is, it's not as beautiful as you are this evening."

Amelia had chosen to go casual that day—white capris, a light blue blouse that matched her eyes, and white sandals. She'd tamed her curly hair with a straightener and let it flow down past her shoulders.

"Thank you," she said, "but should I have dressed up more?"

Dammit! she swore to herself. *I shouldn't question any decision I make. That's insecurity coming out in me.* A memory of Elliott telling her what to wear, how to fix her hair, and even supervising what she bought—whether it was groceries or clothing—flashed through her mind.

Don't go there. Nick is not Elliott. He will let you make your own decisions.

"Darlin', you would look good in a gunnysack tied up in the middle with twine." He took her hand in his. "Introducing you to my dad means so much to me. Thank you for agreeing to adjust our weekend."

Amelia vowed that she would work harder to never compare Elliott and Nick again. That wasn't fair to Nick, and it brought nothing but pain and anger to her. Elliott had stolen her independence. Nick liked her just the way she was. "Look at those streaks of pink and orange, blue and purple. It's like something an artist would do." She angled her phone on the window and took a picture.

Nick held his phone up and took a picture of her with the last light of the day flowing through the plane window. "I bet my picture is prettier than yours."

She leaned over and kissed him on the cheek.

"Fasten those seat belts," the pilot said. "We'll be on the ground in about five minutes."

"Thanks for doing this on your weekend, Lanny," Nick said as he snapped his seat belt into place.

"No problem," the older gray-haired guy said. "I'm just glad Gregory got the plane in the divorce. I wouldn't have still been flying if he hadn't."

"How long have you been flying for Dad?" Nick asked. "I don't think I know."

"Since a year before he was born. That's when your grandpa bought his first plane. My dad worked for him as a driver, and he paid for lessons for me to get my license. I had just done a stint in the army— Vietnam. Your grandpa saw that I needed something in my life and saved me. I've flown or driven him and your dad for too many years to count."

"Think you'll ever retire?" Nick asked.

"When they sing that final song over me and put me six feet down," Lanny answered as he set the little plane on the ground. "Welcome to the Monroe Estate, Miz Amelia."

Amelia jerked her head around to look Nick in the eye. "Monroe Estate? I thought we were flying into an airport. Wealthy is one thing. This is quite another altogether!"

"Well, of course we are. This little airstrip is on the back side of the Monroe Estate," Lanny cut in.

"Dad keeps two planes here, Amelia," Nick said with an embarrassed grin. "Lanny, are you driving us to the house, or is Dad waiting for us?"

"I'm taking you. They're busy getting things ready for you kids," Lanny answered.

"You didn't tell me you were a descendant of Midas," Amelia whispered.

"I was afraid you'd think I was like Elliott and not give me a chance, and besides, I'm not a rich man, darlin'. I'm just a real estate agent who has money, and I would give all the dollars that're mine or will be mine away to be able to date you right out in public. There's some things that money can't buy." Nick took her hand in his.

When they were out of the plane, Lanny led the way over to a black SUV and held the back door open for them. Then he rounded the front and slid in behind the wheel. "I heard you went to see Harry in Florida. Was it nice and warm when you were there?"

"It was wonderful," Amelia answered. "The weather was warm, but not really hot like in the summertime."

"Sand was cool under our feet in the mornings, but it warmed up when the sun came up," Nick added.

"Betsy loves to go there for a weekend when they can get away. They have amazing crepes that we all just love." Lanny turned into a tree-lined lane and then stopped in a circle drive in front of a large house.

The double doors leading into the house flew open and a man and woman stepped out. The man had his arm around the woman's waist, and both were dressed in jeans, flip-flops, and T-shirts. His was untucked and hers was mostly covered with a bright-red bibbed apron printed with "Will Cook for Shoes" on the front.

Gregory was tall, blond, and looked like an older version of Nick. Betsy barely came to his shoulder, and her gray hair was cut in a bob right below her jawbone. She had curves and a bright smile that lit up her light blue eyes.

"We've been looking for you for half an hour," Gregory called out.

"Are you hungry?" Betsy shook free of Gregory's embrace and met them in the middle of the driveway. "We don't need introductions, Amelia. We've heard so much about you that we feel like we already know you. I'm a hugger." She wrapped her arms around Amelia, gave her a fierce hug, and whispered, "We're so glad Nick found you."

"Thank you," she whispered, "and it's wonderful to meet you, Miz Betsy."

"Just Betsy will do just fine," she said as she stepped back. "I've got a little light snack laid out for you kids. I know that you're probably worn out, but we promise not to keep you up too late. Your quarters have been cleaned and are ready for you, Nick. We're just so danged excited to see you." She tiptoed and gave Nick a hug. "Now you can go hug your dad. He's so excited that you're here."

Amelia didn't realize that Nick had let go of her hand until she and Betsy were on the porch, but suddenly it didn't matter anymore. These folks had already accepted her—just on what Nick had told them. She sent up a quick prayer that her family would be even half that good about Nick.

"Follow me to the kitchen," Betsy said as she led the way across a huge foyer. "Greg and I eat in here most of the time. I love to cook, so we let the cook retire, but we kept the staff that cleans the house. I also like to garden, so the landscaping crew lets me piddle around in the flower beds. I picked a bouquet to put on the table."

"She talks too much when she's nervous." Greg chuckled. "That's one of the things I love so much about her. Welcome to our home, Amelia. Please treat it as your own, and if you need anything you can't find, let us know."

"Thank you," she said.

"Betsy has taught me to be a hugger, too." He took a couple of steps forward and wrapped Amelia up in his arms. "Nick really has told us a lot about you. I'm so sorry that you kids are having to face the problems of the past. Stand strong and don't let anything ruin your future."

Nick crossed the room and laced his fingers with Amelia's.

"We're as common as salt in that saltshaker right there," Betsy said, "so we want you to feel comfortable in our home."

With a homey greeting like that, Amelia already felt at home.

"Thank you." Amelia smiled.

"Nick, I'd like your opinion on a property investment," Gregory said when they had visited for an hour around the kitchen table. "Are you too tired to spare a few minutes to look it over in my den? I hate to drag him away from you, Amelia, but I really need help."

"Go on," she said with a smile that reassured Nick. "I'm fine right here with Betsy. We'll get this kitchen cleaned up and have a girls' visit."

Nick rounded the small table for four and kissed Amelia on the forehead, then whispered, "I won't be gone long."

Gregory led the way through the living room and into his office. He shut the door and sat down in one of the chairs facing his oversize desk instead of taking the one behind it. "I don't really have any investment properties for you to look at. I wanted to talk to you about Amelia, Son."

"What about her?" Nick's worry meter suddenly went sky high.

"You've only known her a month, and you met her right after your Uncle Harry left. You've never been interested in a long-term relationship before now." Gregory picked up a pen from his desk and toyed with it. "I'm afraid I see too much of myself and your mother in this situation. I'd vowed that I would be a bachelor, and then I met Matilda. We were engaged within a month and eloped because that's what she wanted."

"We've circled the bush about a permanent relationship, Dad. But we just decided this weekend to take it from friendship to the place where I can say she's my girlfriend. We haven't gotten serious enough that she's ready for a diamond ring just yet," Nick answered.

"You know what's at stake financially," Gregory said. "Don't do what I did, Son. Have the good sense to insist on a prenup."

"That's something for us to talk about later if our relationship goes that far," Nick said. "Dad, why didn't you have one? Didn't Grandpa advise you . . ."

Gregory held up a palm. "Yes, he did, and yes, my father had a prenup when he married your grandmother. It never came into play because my mother passed away first, but she was the one who insisted that they have one. I thought that Matilda loved me like Mama loved Dad, but I was wrong. She's a master at deception, as you well know. I like what I've seen in Amelia this evening. I really do, but there are those problems with your mother and Liddy Latham, and the fact that you are a wealthy man with what your grandfather left you, and now what you've inherited from your Uncle Harry. Be smart. That's my advice," Gregory said.

"I promise I will," Nick assured him, "and thanks, Dad. One question, though—did Betsy sign a prenup?"

Gregory pushed up out of his chair and clamped a hand on his son's shoulder. "*She* insisted that we have one, just like my mother had. She doesn't need or want a dime of my money. She's wealthy beyond measure in her own right. Probably even more than I am, but like she said, we're both as common as salt in that saltshaker right there."

"That surprises me." Nick laid a hand on his father's. "But I kind of like a little salt on my food."

"Don't we all." Gregory smiled and started toward the door. "I'm happy, Son. I want the same thing for you, and I'm glad to hear that you aren't rushing into things. My advice is that you two live together for a while just to be sure you know one another."

Nick got to his feet and followed his father. "I would love to ask her to move in with me—maybe at the end of summer when the lease is up on her apartment."

"That's a wonderful idea. You never know someone until you live with them awhile," Gregory said as they left the room. "Your mother is going to have a hissy fit, and I wouldn't be surprised if Liddy didn't have her own version of one, too. You will keep me posted, won't you?"

"Will do," Nick agreed.

Amelia couldn't believe her eyes when she and Nick climbed the stairs and circled around the balcony to what he called the west wing of the house. All kinds of little nooks and crannies offered comfortable chairs and places to sit and read, or just to think about things.

"There's a guest room right across the hall from my quarters," Nick explained as they made their way down a short hallway, "or you can stay with me if you want to."

"For real? Would that be taking your folks' . . ." She was struck speechless when he opened the door into a room that was bigger than her whole apartment.

"I'm past thirty, darlin'," Nick said, "and Dad has known for years that I've been with women. But I have never brought another woman to this house. I did introduce Mother to a couple and learned right fast that was a mistake."

They walked into the enormous room. "Welcome to my quarters. It started out as a nursery, and the bedroom through those glass doors was for my nanny. When I got older, this was my toy room, and the nanny was let go. The housekeeper took care of me most of the time. Then when I was a teenager, it became a living room. I lived in this place until I went to college and rented my own apartment." He swiped at his brow. "I guess talking too much when you are nervous is contagious."

"I want to stay with you," she said.

"I can sleep on the sofa if you're not comfortable," he offered.

"Oh, no!" She walked right into his space and wrapped her arms around his waist, laid her cheek against his chest, and said, "I want to spend a whole night with you in my arms, and, darlin', if we ever get so far as to commit to a permanent relationship that involves the M-word, you better draw up a prenup. I wouldn't ever want people to say I married you for your money. I love you because you are who you are, not because of how much money you have in the bank. And, honey, if and when we have kids, you'd better understand that there will be none of that nanny business, or housekeepers, either."

"Like I said before"—Nick kissed each of her eyelids—"you are amazing."

Then he scooped her up into his arms, closed the door with his heel, and carried her to the bedroom.

Chapter Twenty-One

Liddy was restless all day on Monday, so she made a lemon chess pie and then made a lemon meringue. That done, she roamed through the house where she'd lived since she and Marvin got married all those years ago. *So many memories,* she thought as she stopped by the buffet in the dining room and stared at an array of pictures. She picked up the one of her and Marvin on their wedding day and ran a forefinger over her late husband's face.

"Am I doing the right thing by accepting Nick as Amelia's boyfriend?" she whispered.

Are you doing it to make Matilda mad or because you've figured out that he might not be like his mother and will be good to Amelia? Marvin's voice was so clear in her head that she looked over her shoulder to see if he was there.

"Probably a little of both," Liddy muttered, "but mostly because I don't want to alienate Amelia. I love her."

She set that picture back down and picked up one of Richie with his father on the day he graduated from the university. For a brief few weeks Richie had been happy, and then Matilda came back to Bonnet for a visit, and nothing was the same.

"It's Matilda's son, Nick," she said, "and your cousin Amelia. I'm trying, Son, I'm really trying, but it's not easy. Every time I look at Nick, I remember that last day and the argument we had."

There was nothing from Richie.

The phone startled her so badly when it rang that she carried Richie's picture with her as she hustled to the living room and grabbed it from the coffee table.

"Hello," she said.

"Did I catch you at a bad time?" Ruth Ann asked.

Liddy had no trouble recognizing Ruth Ann's deep southern accent. "No, I was rushing from the dining room to the living room. I haven't learned to attach a cell phone to my hip like all these kids do these days."

"Ain't that the truth." Ruth Ann chuckled. "I'm restless today. Start something, but don't finish it. I hope Bridget and Clovis aren't feeling the same way. I can leave a book on the end table because I can't focus on it, but if they leave a person in the ER in critical condition, it could be disastrous."

"I hear you. Why don't you come on over here and we'll sit on the porch. We'll be restless, but we'll be together."

"Be there in five minutes. I just have to put my shoes on and grab my purse," Ruth Ann said.

She was there in less time than that and didn't even knock on the door. "Hey, are you on the porch already? I brought a pan of lemon squares I made this morning."

"I'm in the kitchen. The coffee is ready. I guess lemon has been on our minds," Liddy said.

"Oh, my!" Ruth Ann said. "Those pies look wonderful. Let's save them to have when the kids get here. They think they're surprising us, but we're onto them, aren't we?" She carried her plate of lemon squares to the screened porch and set them on the table between the two chairs.

Liddy followed her with two mugs of coffee in her hands. "Does it seem strange to call them 'the kids'? That sounds like we're accepting Nick like we did Clovis, and I'm still struggling."

"Me too." Ruth Ann sat down in a rocking chair and took a mug from Liddy. "But I've decided to trust God. I've prayed that a good man would come into her life, and maybe God has answered my prayers in His way."

Liddy remembered that she hadn't gotten so much as a feeling from Richie. "I guess I got my answer."

"What's that?" Ruth Ann asked.

"I was just . . ." Liddy went on to tell her about talking to Marvin's and Richie's pictures. "I'm not losing my mind, I promise."

"I hear voices in my head all the time. Mostly from my mother, and I'm grateful for them," Ruth Ann told her.

"Thank you," Liddy said as she scrolled down to find Amelia's number, then called her. "They should be on the way from Dallas by now. I'll put it on speaker so we can both talk. I can't wait another minute to hear her voice."

"Hello, Aunt Liddy," Amelia answered.

"Your mama is with me, and we're having lemon squares on my back porch. Want me to save you one?" Liddy asked.

"Hi, Mama, and yes, please, on the lemon squares. You know that anything lemon is my favorite. Did you make me a pie, too, Aunt Liddy?" she asked.

"You'll have to wait and see," Liddy answered. "Where are you and what does that fancy-schmancy GPS thing you use on your phone tell you about when you'll be home?"

"In about an hour," Amelia answered.

"That's perfect. Bridget and Clovis are coming over to see you, too. Clovis asked for a pitcher of my famous lemonade and we'll have coffee made. Does Nick want coffee or something cold?"

"Why would you ask that?" Amelia asked.

"Because I told you that God has eyes everywhere, and you can't fool me or your mama," Liddy said. "Your car hasn't left the apartment complex all weekend. You could lie to me and say that Daniel or

Savannah took you to the airport, but so far, you haven't started telling us lies. You've beat around the bush and avoided any questions, but you haven't told an out-and-out lie."

"Is it safe? Is there poison in the pie?" Amelia asked.

"Why would you ask that?" Liddy glanced over at the pie on the counter.

"Romeo and Juliet?" Amelia answered with a question.

"You're a real Juliet, but I can't see Matilda naming her son Romeo," Liddy said.

"Think about the story," Amelia said.

"Oh! Now I see what you mean," Liddy said. "There's no poison, and we'll talk about whether you are safe or not when you get here. I promise Nick will leave here alive, if that's any help."

"Are y'all really mad at me?" Amelia sounded genuinely worried.

Liddy closed her eyes for a brief second and reminded herself that losing Amelia like she had Richie would be far more painful than seeing her with Nick.

"I was," Liddy answered, "but one does not choose who they fall in love with. Marvin was not my mama's choice."

"Just promise me you won't rush into anything," Ruth Ann chimed in.

"I promise," Amelia said, "and we just wanted to be sure this was going to work out before we caused y'all any undue worry."

Liddy leaned her head over to the side, and sure enough, she could hear road noise in the background. "Am I on speaker, you rotten girl?"

Liddy was both annoyed and glad at the same time. A little aggravated because she wanted what she and Ruth Ann said to be private, and glad that Amelia wasn't letting anyone run her life like Elliott had done.

"Yes, you are," Amelia answered with a laugh.

"Nick, I don't bake lemon pies for just anyone," she told him.

"I remember your lemon pie very well, Miz Liddy, and I thank you for doing that for us, and for inviting me to your house. Can I pick up a bottle of wine?" he asked.

"No. Just bring my niece home safe." Liddy picked up a tissue and dabbed at her eyes. "I'll see y'all within the hour." She ended the call.

"Don't you dare let them see you shed a tear," Ruth Ann scolded as she handed Liddy another tissue. "If Matilda finds out that you were upset instead of happy for them, she'll gloat. It could be a sweet thing for both of those kids, and not a mess at all. Just keep in mind that promise she made about not rushing into anything."

Liddy nodded.

"And think of it like this," Ruth Ann continued. "If they do get married on down the line, she'll be living right across the street from you. You know my girls love you more than if you were just an aunt. And when they do get around to having babies, they'll probably call you Nana Liddy. But I will fight you for Mee-Maw. That's what I called my grandmother."

"Fair enough. I like Nana Liddy just fine." Liddy finally managed a smile.

Nick's hands began to sweat and stick to the truck's steering wheel. "We've got to tell Mother. She's got spies all over town. If she finds out that we were both at your aunt's house, she's going to go up in flames."

"Reckon we could make a few dollars selling tickets to that show?" Amelia teased.

"Maybe so, but since she is my mother, for better or worse—most of the time the latter—I'm going to give her a call," Nick said.

Amelia laid her hand on his shoulder. "Don't tell her over the phone. She deserves to hear it from you, face-to-face. Think she might be in town, like at Tina's or Delores's house?"

Nick took a deep breath, picked up his phone from the console, and called her. He was about ready to give up when she picked up on the fifth ring.

"It's too late to wish me a happy Easter or send flowers. I always made sure you had a lovely Easter basket, even after your father married that witch. Did you spend Easter Sunday with them?" she asked.

"Happy Easter, Mother, and we both know that you had your secretary take care of sending me something on Easter, so don't give me that line. I'll try to do better on Mother's Day," he said.

"See that you do," she said.

"Are you in Bonnet?" he asked.

"Why?" She snapped the one word out.

"I'd like to talk to you. Could you meet me at the Dairy Queen in maybe"—he checked the clock on the dash of his truck—"ten minutes?"

"Is this something about your father? Has he finally woken up and realized he made a mistake?" Matilda's laugh was edgy, almost brittle sounding.

Nick wondered why his mother would immediately think of his father. Was there a bit of love down deep in her heart for him after all? Or was she hoping for revenge?

Revenge, the voice in his head answered his question.

"I believe he did, but not with Betsy," Nick answered. "It's not about Dad. Can you meet me for a cup of coffee or a glass of unsweet tea?"

"Tina and I should be finished going over how I'm going to redecorate my quarters in the bed-and-breakfast. I'm closing on the sale this week, and Tina has introduced me to her decorator out of Dallas," Matilda said. "I don't suppose you'd be interested in seeing my new designs."

"No, ma'am," Nick said. "Remember, I'm the country hick who likes the way Wanda decorated her office."

"Don't remind me."

A vision of his mother shivering from head to toe came to his mind. "See you in ten, then?" he asked.

"I'll be there," she said.

"Want to drop me at Aunt Liddy's first?" Amelia asked.

"Not just no, but hell no!" Nick shook his head. "I need you beside me, just like I hope you need me beside you when we meet your family. Matter of fact, we might need a sleepover in my house when this is over, to comfort each other through the night."

"You are so right," Amelia said, "but I'm sure not looking forward to being beside you when you tell Matilda."

"Right back at you, but at least we get lemon pie at Liddy's, and she's already sounded fairly resigned to the idea of us." Nick drove into town and parked in the Dairy Queen lot.

"You told her ten minutes. We've got five to spare," Amelia said.

"I need time to get in there, share a hot fudge sundae with you to fortify myself, and get ready for her anger." Nick slung open the door and got out, jogged around the truck, and helped Amelia out. "I'm kind of hoping that one of her spies sees us going into the café together and tattles. That way, I won't have to say much when she gets here. She'll be so mad that she'll storm in and out in under five minutes. Your family evidently has had time to process the news."

They were at the counter ordering a sundae to share when Matilda breezed through the side door and slid into a booth.

"Order me an unsweet tea," she called out.

"She's early," Amelia whispered, "and she hasn't threatened to shoot me yet."

"Your back is to her," Nick said. "She doesn't even recognize you, since she can't see your beautiful face."

Amelia hip-bumped him. "You're romantic even in the face of death."

"Like Romeo and Juliet, we'll go down together," he teased. "You can bet that Mother will make a dramatic exit since she didn't make an entrance. She's famous for making one or the other, sometimes both."

The teenager behind the counter made their ice cream, set it on a tray along with a cup of coffee and a glass of tea, collected the money, and made change. "If y'all need anything else, just holler at me. It's a slow night."

"Thanks." Nick smiled and handed him a bill. "Keep the change."

"Hey, thank you, sir." The kid broke out into a grin.

His mother's eyes widened when she realized that Amelia was with him, and he could have sworn he could see steam shooting out her ears when they slid into the booth across from her.

"What in the hell is this? I've told you repeatedly I will not tolerate you seeing this woman," she growled.

"Hello to you, too, Mother," Nick said. "How was your weekend? We had a lovely time in Florida with Uncle Harry, and then we spent a little time with Dad and Betsy." He handed Amelia a plastic spoon. "You can have the first bite, darlin'."

"Good God! You're sharing food?" Matilda's whisper went right along with the look in her eyes—so toxic that a hazmat team wouldn't have come near her.

"We are sharing everything, Mother, and we are about to go have a piece of lemon pie with Liddy Latham," Nick told her as he dipped into the sundae and filled his mouth with ice cream.

"You are doing what?" Each word got a little louder than the last one.

"Having lemon pie and meeting Amelia's whole family as her boyfriend. Liddy might not like me any better than you like Amelia, but she's willing to make us one of her famous lemon chess pies and give us a chance."

"I will never, ever give this woman"—Matilda sneered at Amelia—"a chance with you. If you get yourself tied up with her and her family, you *will* leave her at home when you come see me." Matilda stood up and made her grand exit, head held high and back ramrod straight.

"Mother," Nick called out.

Matilda turned at the door to glare at him.

"If Amelia isn't welcome in your home, then neither am I," he said.

"Your choice," Matilda growled at him and marched out of the café.

"That went well." Nick smiled at Amelia.

"You think so?" Amelia asked. "Nick, I wouldn't feel right coming between you and your—"

He brushed a kiss across her lips. "Darlin', Mother called that shot. You didn't. It's really her choice, not mine at all. I love you, and isn't there a place in the Good Book that talks about leaving everyone behind and cleaving to the one you love?"

"But . . . ," she started again.

He silenced her with another kiss. "I can do this all day, and enjoy every minute of it." He grinned.

"You win," she whispered.

"Now that we've got that one over with, we've got about ten minutes before we need to be at your aunt's place for pie, so eat fast," Nick said.

"I'm so, so sorry. I was hoping that she would . . ." Amelia looked like she might cry.

Nick put an arm around her and pulled her close. "Honey, I learned long ago not to think I could change Mother. She is who she is, and not even God could change her. I'm not even sure the devil himself could make her any different than she is. I've accepted it. Don't be sorry. We did what was right. Whether she accepts us or not is up to her."

"But she's your mama." Amelia sighed. "Did you just say that you love me?"

"Yes, I did, and as far as my mother is concerned, she's not my mama. She's my *mother*. There's a difference. You have a mama. I have a *mother*," Nick said. "Now, let's go see your family, and then go across the street to my house and relax for the rest of the evening. We'll have had dessert, so let's have a pizza delivered for supper."

"Sounds great to me," Amelia agreed.

"They've been at the Dairy Queen and Matilda stormed out," Ruth Ann told Liddy when she hung up the phone. "I just got a call from Ethel, who happened to get a hankerin' for an ice cream cone and got there right before Matilda arrived. She heard it all, and it wasn't pretty."

"I'm not surprised," Liddy said. "Have they left there yet?"

"Yep, and I hear them pulling up in the driveway. Take a deep breath everyone," Ruth Ann said. "Remember, this could be the answer to my prayer, and if it's not, Amelia is a strong, independent woman now. She's learned her lesson, and we are going to support her."

"Hello!" Amelia's voice seemed to echo from the living room to the kitchen.

"Come on in. We're in the kitchen," Liddy yelled back. "I've got pie and coffee out here."

Lemon pie—it's been comfort food, and now it's a peace offering. Matilda, you are a fool to have never learned how to make a lemon pie, Liddy thought as she cut the chess pie into wedges.

Nick and Amelia came into the house, and Nick hung back a few steps. Amelia went straight to Liddy and wrapped her arms around her aunt in a hug.

"Thank you for making a pie for us," she said. "I'd like to introduce you to Nick officially. This is my sister, Bridget, and her husband, Clovis; my dad, Paul; and my mama, Ruth Ann; and of course you met Aunt Liddy at the funerals several weeks ago. Everybody, this is Nick, and we are dating."

"We've all got something to say, but I'm going first," Liddy said. "I've made lemon pies for funeral dinners, to take to new mothers when they had a baby, to your Uncle Harry on his birthday more than once, and always for Marvin's birthday. This is the first time I ever made one for a peace offering. I was wrong to judge you by your mother, Nick, or to judge any of your other relatives."

"My turn," Bridget said. "Amelia, you didn't have such a good track record in choosing a companion before, so that gave me a bit of worry. But I was wrong not to trust your judgment. I'm here to support the two of you with whatever the future holds."

"You'll have to make some hard decisions later on about who will be at your house for events and who won't, because I will not be around your mother, Nick. I might go to hell for unforgiveness, but if I do, then I'll endure it without a single whine," Ruth Ann said.

"Treat my daughter right, or you will have me to answer to," Paul said. "We aren't going to hold you responsible for your mother's actions. That wouldn't be right, but we will hold you accountable for your own choices."

Nick glanced over at Clovis.

"All I got to say is an echo of what Paul just said. Amelia is like a baby sister to me, and I'll protect her and stand by her," Clovis said. "Do you have anything to say, or should I show you to the door?"

"Just thank you, and I will be here as long as y'all will have me. I adore Amelia, and I will always put her first in my life," Nick said.

"All right, then. There isn't a bit of use in whipping a dead horse, so let's have some pie and y'all tell me all about your weekend," Liddy said as she put pieces of pie on dessert plates and handed one each to Amelia and Nick. "How's Harry? Did he really buy a house and make retirement permanent?"

"He did, and he loves company," Nick said. "I bet he would love to show you around the area if you ever want to visit, and, Paul, he's always looking for someone to play a round of golf."

"That sold me," Clovis said. "When are we going, Bridget?"

"We've got a week's vacation in June. Is that soon enough?" Bridget answered.

"I see where you get your amazing attitude," Nick told Amelia.

"I'll take that as a compliment," Liddy said.

"It's not meant as one," Nick said. "It's meant as the truth."

"You sound a lot like your Uncle Harry," Liddy told him as she sat down in the last rocking chair. "And that's not a compliment, either. It's the truth!"

"Thank you." Nick smiled.

There was something enduring and honest about his eyes and his smile—something he had to have inherited from his father—that made Liddy decide she was going to like the man. But she wasn't going to tell Amelia that night. Not when her niece hadn't confided in her about dating Nick the past month.

Chapter Twenty-Two

"I can't believe you are really going to do this without backup," Ruth Ann said that Thursday morning. "Please let me go with you. What if Matilda brings a gun?"

Liddy patted the side pocket of her purse. "I've got a concealed carry license, and Oakley is right here."

Ruth Ann crossed her arms over her chest. "I still think you should have told Amelia what you are doing, and I can't believe you named that little .22 after Annie Oakley. She wouldn't have been caught dead with a little bitty gun like that. At least let me send my hunting rifle with you."

"I can't very well carry something like that in my purse," Liddy told her. "If y'all hear gunshots, then you can bring your rifle into the church."

"What I can't believe is that you're meeting her in the church and not at the police station." Ruth Ann picked up her purse and started for the door. "We've got five minutes to get there, and I'll be waiting in my SUV with the windows rolled down so I can hear."

"Thank you," Liddy said. "If I don't live through this, you are to make a lemon pie for my funeral dinner."

Ruth Ann shivered. "Don't talk like that. If you don't live, then Matilda doesn't, either. If they convict me, I just hope they let me out of prison to go to your funeral."

Liddy locked her front door and got in the passenger seat of Ruth Ann's vehicle. "*I* chose the church for this meeting, not Matilda. She wanted to meet at either the Dairy Queen or the Bluebonnet Café. I refused to give her a public place to show off. Hopefully, we'll walk out of the church alive and with no bullet holes in either of us. I'd hate for her to start shooting and hit one of those pretty stained-glass windows."

"What about you?" Ruth Ann asked as she started the engine and backed out of the drive. "How long has it been since you fired Oakley?"

"Twenty-eight years. Richie and I went out to the shooting range the week before he died," Liddy answered. "Marvin hid it from me after Richie's funeral, and I just found it last week in a shoebox that held my mama's sewing things. Seemed like an omen to me."

"Good Lord!" Ruth Ann gasped. "It's probably covered with rust and full of spiders."

"Nope," Liddy disagreed. "I cleaned her all up, and she's ready to go. There's six shots. If I can't hit something as shiny as Matilda will be, then I don't deserve to carry her in my purse. Where, by the way, she feels more at home than stuck in the attic."

"What were you doing in the attic?" Ruth Ann asked.

"I needed to go through the memory box where I have Richie's things," Liddy answered. "Just looking at them made me know that I'm doing the right thing today."

Ruth Ann sighed as she pulled into the church parking lot. "Looks like she's already here, and there's Tina and Gladys in the front seat of Tina's Caddy. Please change your mind and let me go in with you."

"Pull up right beside them," Liddy said. "If you park very far away, they'll think I'm intimidated, which I am not."

Ruth Ann did exactly what Liddy asked, leaving just enough room for Liddy to get out of the passenger seat. As she got out of the vehicle, she smiled and waved at the women in the Caddy.

"You hurt one hair on her head and you'll answer to me," Tina called out.

Liddy stopped for a moment, took a deep breath, and opened the door, leaving the dark clouds threatening a storm behind.

"Seems like an omen for sure," she muttered and bowed her head. "Lord, if it's my day to go, let me go down fighting and take Matilda with me. If it's not my day to go, let me leave this church with my dignity. Don't let her make me so angry that I lose that."

"Good morning, Liddy." The preacher came up the center aisle. "Matilda is already here and sitting on the second pew on the left side of the church." He held out a velvet bag that was passed through the congregation for offerings on Sunday morning. "If you have a firearm or poison or any harmful thing, it all goes in here, and I will give it back to you when the meeting is finished."

"Are Matilda's things in there?" Liddy asked.

"No, hers are in a separate bag," the preacher answered.

"That's good. I don't want Oakley, here"—she patted the side of her purse—"anywhere near her things. My purse won't fit in there, but here, you can have it until this is over. There's a gun, a fingernail file, a pink pocketknife, and a flask of whiskey in there. I promise there's no poison in it, and I only use the whiskey for medicinal purposes. In today's world, you don't want me coughing all over the congregation." Liddy handed her purse over to him.

"Fair enough," the preacher chuckled. "I'll be sitting right outside the doors until the meeting is over."

"That's good. I'll try to keep things at least semi-peaceful in here if you'll do the same for what's out there," Liddy told him.

She's on the left. The right side is mine. That's an omen, too, Liddy told herself as she walked down the aisle and sat down in the pew across from Matilda.

The woman wore what seemed to be her signature material and color—white silk with lots of gold jewelry. Liddy was reminded of that scripture that talked about a wolf in sheep's clothing. On the outside, Matilda looked so innocent, but Liddy could see a raving wolf in the woman's eyes.

"You want to go first?" Liddy asked.

"You called this damn meeting, not me," Matilda growled.

Liddy rolled her eyes toward the vaulted ceiling. "Lord, if you are going to send lightning down the dark clouds gathering up there in the sky, please make sure your aim is good. It wasn't me that cussed in church. Amen."

"You are a crazy old woman," Matilda sneered. "You want to know why I even went after Richie when we were both seniors in high school? Because he was a virgin, and I hadn't bedded one of those. He was a feather in my hat. And when I had that fling with him just before he died, that was payback to you for the way you treated me back in high school when I broke up with him. You were hateful to me. If you would have sold that land out west of town to my daddy, then we would have been as rich as the Taylors are, and believe me when I say, I'm going to drill on that land if it's the last thing I ever do."

Liddy glared at her, leaned forward and braced her elbows on the pew in front of her, put her hands together in a prayerful gesture, and said, "Lord, even as you asked Satan to get behind you when the devil was tempting you, I would ask for the same thing. The preacher has my gun, Oakley, in his possession, but I do believe that I could strangle this woman with my bare hands. Please help me keep my hands to myself and forgive me if I was the cause of my son's death. But Lord, I really think that Matilda is just making excuses to cover her own sins. You decide, and I'll abide by your decision. Amen."

"Dammit, Liddy!" Matilda raised her voice. "When I came back to Bonnet, Richie and I'd been talking on the phone for weeks already. I knew our affair would hurt you. I wanted to punish you, and it went even better than I ever hoped. I took your son from you and got away with it. Now, why don't you just sell me that land? I'm going to have it, Liddy, one way or the other."

Liddy closed her eyes and took a deep breath. "Lord help me to give Nick a loving and good family. And give Matilda some peace. She's never getting my land, so help her to accept that. Amen."

"If you don't stop that damn praying, I'm walking right out of here," Matilda growled.

Liddy dropped her hands, sat up straight, and turned so that her eyes bored into Matilda's. "I'm not here to rehash the past, to listen to you bad-mouth my son, or to offer forgiveness. I'm here to see what your intentions are where Amelia is concerned. That's the only thing I want to talk about, so if you're going to keep on this rant you've started, I will keep praying, because it's helping me."

"Why did you want to meet in church, anyway?" Matilda glared at her.

"Because I know *you*, Matilda," Liddy answered. "If we met in a public place, you would do what you always do—make a big scene, do a lot of threatening and yelling, and nothing would be settled. Besides, I figure God is on my side in here. I visit this house regularly, and He and I have long talks a couple of times a day. I'm not perfect, but I'm trying to do the right thing."

"God is just the figment of preachers' imaginations, something to scare people into being good, and to siphon money out of their pockets," Matilda said.

"Then why do you even go to church and play the piano?" Liddy asked.

"To get people on my side when I want something," she answered. "Come to think of it, this is a perfect place for us to meet. No one can hear a thing we're saying."

Liddy pointed up. "I beg to differ. God just heard every word you said, but back to my concerns. I want to know what your intentions are toward my niece. Are you going to be civil at events like weddings, birthdays, family gatherings? I do have a warning. I'll keep it short, so you won't forget it in all your narcissistic ways. Do not hurt her."

"I'm *not* self-centered," Matilda argued. "I just had the best interests of this town in mind, but since all of you want to live in stagnant water, I've taken my business to Muenster." She lowered her chin and set her mouth in a firm line. "Except for the funeral dinners. I will fight you over those, not because I give a damn about whether they serve comfort food or vegan, but because I hate you, and I want to put you in your place. I might even reconsider and let you have the dinners if you will sell me that land." She took a deep breath. "Now, describe 'hurt her.'"

"It's the old thing about sticks and stones and words. Do you remember that little ditty?" Liddy asked.

"I do, but what's that got to do with us?" Matilda asked.

"I can't stop you talking about her, or spreading gossip, but the minute you lay a hand on her and hurt her physically—well, before they take me to prison—I will make sure someone brings a lemon pie to *your* funeral dinner. Are we clear?" Liddy's tone left no room for doubt about her meaning. "She loves Nick, and he loves her. I expect there will be a marriage in the future. You can do whatever you want on holidays and at social events, but I will not invite you to be a part of my plans, and I will not come to yours."

"Thank God," Matilda said.

"Don't thank a higher being that you think is just a figment of someone's imagination," Liddy scolded. "I have accepted Nick into our family. I'm going to be a part of their lives. You can do whatever you want."

"Are we done?" Matilda asked.

"Unless you've got something more to say." Liddy stood up.

"Just one more thing. I will never accept any relative of yours, and if my son is idiot enough to marry your niece, I don't really want to be a part of their lives. If he continues to see Amelia, he has seen the last of me." Matilda stood up and started down the aisle.

"I will pray that someday you wake up and realize what you have missed," Liddy called out. "You are going to be a lonely old woman, Matilda."

"I don't want or need your prayers, Liddy Latham," Matilda shouted as she left the sanctuary.

Liddy sat back down and bowed her head. "Thank you, Lord, for answering my prayers. No blood was shed, and if Matilda stays true to her word, she will keep away from Amelia. Help her to someday see the error in her ways and change into a loving mother and grandmother, and if she can't do that, then just give her to the devil. She doesn't believe in you anyway. Amen."

"Amen!" Ruth Ann slid in beside her and wrapped her arms around her.

"She came out in a huff, snatched her things from the preacher, and got in the car with Tina and Gladys. She didn't even look my way," Ruth Ann said.

"She says that she wants nothing to do with the kids if they should ever get married," Liddy told her.

"Well, that's a prayer answered," Ruth Ann assured her. "If she can't be nice, then it's best if she just stays away."

"Amen!" Liddy agreed.

"Paul wants us to meet him at the Bluebonnet Café and have their Thursday special for lunch. He's been hungry for turkey and dressing for days," Ruth Ann suggested.

Liddy stood up with a nod. "She told me that I'm the reason Richie is dead, and she was glad that things went the way they did. She says that everything she did was because she hates me."

"Good God!" Ruth Ann sighed. "You don't believe her, do you? She's just laying blame for her own sins on you."

"I hope so," Liddy said. "She also says she'll stay out of our business here, except for the funeral dinners. She hates me and intends to put me in my place."

"Hmmph!" Ruth Ann snorted. "Let her try. As my mama used to say, 'That ain't damn likely,' and pardon me, Lord, for saying that word in church." Ruth Ann got to her feet and led the way outside, where the sun was peeking through the dark clouds.

Epilogue

Eighteen months later

Amelia's hair was in rollers, and she was wearing a pair of shorts and one of Nick's T-shirts. Her suitcases were packed with too many clothing changes, but Nick refused to tell her where they were going. She hoped that they were going back to the beach in Florida, but she wouldn't be disappointed in any place that Nick chose.

"Lord, have mercy!" Bridget fussed at her. "You're not ready yet? We're supposed to be at the courthouse in thirty minutes."

"Where's Taylor?" Amelia asked. "I wanted to love on him just a little bit before we leave. I won't see him for two whole weeks."

"He's six months old," Bridget laughed. "He won't be walking or singing the ABC song when you get back. Now let's get you ready."

"I just have to fix my hair and put on my dress," Amelia told her. "I can do that in fifteen minutes. My bags are packed. If you'd tell me where Nick is taking me, I probably wouldn't need half as much as I have packed."

"I'm sworn to secrecy," Bridget said. "Don't you worry about anything but getting to the courthouse before the judge leaves. He only works until noon on Fridays, and y'all have to get to the airport in time to make your flight."

"So, we're flying?" Amelia asked.

"You might be, and you might not be. I might have said that to throw you off the track." Bridget grinned. "Shoo! Get out of here and go get dressed. Harry just texted me that he's already at the courthouse. I think he's tickled that y'all asked him to house-sit for you and take care of Vera. Gregory and Betsy are outside the courthouse now, waiting on you two to get there, and Aunt Liddy, Mama, and Daddy just left going that way. Clovis is already there with Taylor."

"Matilda?" Amelia asked as she pulled the rollers from her hair. "Have you heard anything about her?"

"She and Tina are in Dallas at some kind of bed-and-breakfast owners' conference," Bridget answered. "She won't be there. She made her choice to cut her son out of her life. We can't help that, but we can love him enough so that he doesn't miss the relationship that could have been if she'd been different. Some things don't have a happy ever after ending, darlin' sister."

"But Nick and I can, right?" Amelia asked.

"If you work at it as hard as you have this past year and a half, you sure can." Bridget took Amelia's dress off the hanger and held it out to her.

"So, everyone is there except the bride and groom?" Amelia asked.

"If you're thinking of running, I could use a vacation. We can get in my car and be out of town before anyone misses us," Bridget teased.

"You know very well that you wouldn't think of leaving that precious baby of yours behind for an hour, much less two weeks," Amelia told her as she slipped into her dress. "Is Nick ready?"

"He's pacing the floor in the living room right now," Bridget answered.

Nick parked the truck in front of the courthouse, patted his pocket to be sure that he had the rings, and then leaned over and kissed Amelia. "You are the most beautiful bride I've ever laid eyes on."

"You clean up right well yourself." She grinned. "Where are we going after we say our vows?"

"I love you, darlin', but you're not going to trick me into telling you that. It's a surprise. I believe everyone is getting out of their vehicles, so it's time. No second thoughts? No regrets?"

"Not a single one, and I love you, too, Nick, and I plan to tell you that every morning when I wake up and every night before I shut my eyes to go to sleep," Amelia said.

"We're all here except for Mother, and . . ." He shrugged. "That's her choice. Maybe someday she'll wake up."

"There's always hope," Amelia said. "Now, let's go get married."

"I'm ready." Nick got out of his truck, rounded the back end, and opened the door for Amelia. Together they walked up the sidewalk and into the courthouse.

Amelia had chosen a simple white sundress and added a pale blue sash for something new and blue. The old was a pearl necklace that her Aunt Liddy had given her the night before at the family dinner at Paul and Ruth Ann's house—a gift that had been passed down from mother to daughter for generations in her family. Aunt Liddy told her that since she didn't have a daughter or daughter-in-law, Amelia would have to take up the slack, and to pass it to her own daughter when the time came. Something borrowed was pearl earrings that Bridget had loaned her.

They were met at the door by the court clerk, who handed Amelia a bouquet of yellow roses tied with a blue ribbon. "From your groom," she said, "and the ceremony has been moved to the courtroom. Don't worry, he won't make you swear to tell the truth, the whole truth, and nothing but the truth." The woman laughed.

"Thank you for the bouquet." Amelia smiled up at Nick.

He started to kiss her, but Uncle Harry stepped between them. "Save that for later. Follow me. I know the way to the courtroom. The judge and I are old golfing buddies. We're planning to get a game in this afternoon."

"I'm so glad you're here," Nick said, "and thank you again for taking care of Vera for us."

"I'm glad to do that for you. It will give me time to play some golf with some old buddies and fill in at the real estate office if Thomas or Olivia needs me."

Harry opened the door into the courtroom and stood to one side. "Y'all go on in. I love you both and wish all the best for you."

The judge stood in front of the bench where he usually sat. Today, he wasn't wearing his black robe but a pair of khaki pants and a blue polo shirt. "Come right on up here, and let's get this done," he said. "Harry and I've got a caddy waiting for us, and I understand you kids have a plane to catch."

"Yes, sir." Nick looped Amelia's arm in his, and they walked down the aisle.

The ceremony took about ten minutes, and then Nick was told he could kiss the bride. He bent her backward in true Hollywood fashion.

The judge chuckled and said, "If that kiss is any indication, this marriage should last fifty years or more. Harry and I are leaving."

Amelia said, "Hey, Aunt Liddy!"

When her aunt looked up, she tossed her bouquet right into her hands.

"I'll preserve this for you, but, honey, I won't ever be getting married again. I had the perfect husband, so why take a chance I'd get something less another time around?" Liddy laughed.

"Thank you all for making this a special day for us, but I'm told that Nick and I have a plane to catch," Amelia said.

"Yes, we do." Nick scooped Amelia up in his arms and carried her out of the courthouse amid applause and catcalls.

When they were inside the truck, Amelia cupped his face in her hands and asked, "Can you tell me now where we are going?"

"We'll be spending tonight at a hotel in Dallas," he said, "and then tomorrow morning we'll fly to Belize. Dad has a vacation home down there that we'll be staying in. It's right on the beach, so you don't have to wear shoes for the whole honeymoon unless you want to go out and shop in the nearby village. Our honeymoon is a gift from my dad and Betsy."

"Are you serious?" Amelia gasped. "I was thinking maybe we'd stay in Harry's house in Florida."

"Are you disappointed?" Nick asked.

"Nothing you could ever do would disappoint me." Amelia brought his lips to hers for a long kiss. "I love you so much!"

"I hope you always feel that way about me." Nick grinned. "And, darlin', I love you more than words could ever say."

Author's Note

*I*n the past so many of my awesome readers have asked for the recipes I mention in my books. With that in mind, I consulted Aunt Liddy, and she said that since we had become such good friends during the writing of this story, I could include her two recipes in the book. I hope you enjoy them, and you might want to buy limoncello in a big bottle—just so the neighbors won't see you going into the liquor store so often.

Aunt Liddy's Lemon Chess Pie

- 1 pie crust (Aunt Liddy buys one already made and then slips it into a pretty pie dish)
- 5 large eggs
- 1½ cups granulated sugar
- 1 tablespoon lemon zest (about 1 lemon)
- 2 tablespoons fresh lemon juice
- 1 tablespoon limoncello
- 1 tablespoon yellow cornmeal
- 1 tablespoon all-purpose flour
- ½ cup salted butter, melted and cooled slightly

Prick the bottom of the pie crust with a fork. Freeze for 20 minutes.

Preheat oven to 450°F.

Whisk eggs, sugar, lemon zest, lemon juice, limoncello, cornmeal, and flour together in a large bowl. Whisk in butter and set bowl aside. Bake the crust for 8 minutes. Remove and lower oven temperature to 325°F. Give the filling a quick whisk and then pour it into the hot pie crust. Bake for 35–40 minutes, until the surface is light brown and the center jiggles just slightly when shaken. Cool for 4 hours before serving.

Aunt Liddy's Lemon Meringue Pie

- 1 pie crust, baked (Aunt Liddy buys hers already made, but shhh . . . don't tell anyone)
- 1 cup granulated sugar
- 2 tablespoons all-purpose flour
- 3 tablespoons cornstarch
- ¼ teaspoon salt
- 1 cup water
- 2 lemons, zested and juiced
- ½ cup limoncello
- 2 tablespoons salted butter
- 5 egg yolks, beaten
- 5 egg whites
- 6 tablespoons sugar

Preheat oven to 350°F.

To make lemon filling: In a medium saucepan, whisk together sugar, flour, cornstarch, and salt. Stir in water, zest and juice from the lemons, and limoncello. Cook over medium heat, stirring frequently, until the mixture comes to a boil. Stir in butter. Place egg yolks in a small bowl and gradually whisk in ½ cup of the hot mixture, then whisk the egg yolks back into the remaining filling mixture. Bring to a boil and continue to cook while stirring constantly until it thickens. Remove from heat and pour into baked pie crust.

To make meringue: In a large glass or metal bowl, whip room-temperature egg whites until foamy. Add 1 tablespoon of sugar at a time and continue to whip until stiff peaks form. Spread meringue over the pie, sealing edges. Bake for 10 minutes or until the meringue is golden brown.

Dear Readers,

I don't always have the opportunity to write a book in the same season as when it is published, but this time I did. And we had spring in Oklahoma this year, which is another oddity. Usually, we go from freezing to scalding-hot weather in a couple of days. Maybe the weather is trying to make up for the year that we've had with the covid issues. (I refuse to capitalize the name of that virus in hopes that I will offend it, and it will disappear forever and never come back.) Whatever the reasoning, we are glad to have nice cool spring weather and see our Arbuckle Mountains turn yellow with an abundance of coreopsis blooms.

As always, there are so many people to thank for helping me take a rough idea and turn it into the book you hold in your hands. Some of those have gone on past this lifetime, but they remain in my heart and give me the courage to keep writing—a few of those are my grandmothers, my mama, and my sister. A saying about life goes: *You don't meet people by accident. There's always a reason—a lesson or a blessing!* Many of the people I have met have taught me valuable lessons, and many others have brought blessings into my life.

Today, I'd like to thank those who came bearing blessings. To my editor, Alison Dasho—thank you for continuing to believe in me. To my publisher, Montlake—thank you for everything from covers to promotion to all the behind-the-scenes folks who work hard to make this the best book possible. To my agent, Erin Niumata—I couldn't ask for a better friend and agent. To my agency, Folio Literary Management—thank you for taking care of everything for me. To all my readers—y'all are awesome, and I appreciate every one of you. To my family—I love every one of you. And of course, as always, to Mr. B—you've always been my biggest blessing.

I hope you enjoyed reading about Aunt Liddy and the war between her and Matilda Monroe in Bonnet, Texas, and that the characters stay with you long after the last page.

Hugs to you all,
Carolyn Brown

About the Author

*C*arolyn Brown is a *New York Times, USA Today, Washington Post, Wall Street Journal,* and *Publishers Weekly* best-selling author and RITA finalist with more than 125 published books. They include romantic women's fiction and historical, contemporary, and cowboys-and-country-music mass-market paperbacks. She and her husband live in the small town of Davis, Oklahoma, where everyone knows everyone else, knows what they are doing and when, and reads the local newspaper on Wednesday to see who got caught. They have three grown children and enough grandchildren and great-grandchildren to keep them young. For more information, visit www.carolynbrownbooks.com.